ALLEN COUNTY PUBLIC LIBRARY

3

D0357286

The

THE SCARLET EMPRESS

"*The Scarlet Empress* offers the cost of freedom and the continuing sacrifices required of those who value liberty."
—*Booklist* (boxed, starred review)

"Susan Grant [has] written a terrific romantic thriller....
I can't wait to see what she does next!"
—*New York Times* bestselling
author Mary Jo Putney

"Pulse pounding, heart stopping, and spectacular....
I think it is safe to say I totally and unequivocally,
100% recommend this book!"
—*Paranormal Romance Reviews*

THE LEGEND OF BANZAI MAGUIRE

"With its cliffhanger conclusion, awe-inspiring characters
and droll humor, this book is a strong launch
for a very promising series."
—*Publishers Weekly*

"Award-winning author Grant strikes gold with an amazing
new heroine.... This fish out of water tale is exhilarating
and has fabulous potential for future adventures."
—*Romantic Times BOOKclub*
(4 ½ stars, Top Pick!)

THE STAR PRINCESS

"Witty dialog [sic], well-developed characters, and
insightful explorations of cultural and class differences and
political intricacies abound in this funny, sexy story."
—*Library Journal*

JUL 2 9 2006

"[A] spirited love story.... Readers who like their romances sprinkled with sci-fi elements will embrace this book, as will those who prefer exotic protagonists and offbeat settings."
—*Publishers Weekly*

"The talented Susan Grant has penned another keeper that will have her audience anxiously awaiting their next ride to her fabulous world."
—*A Romance Review*

CONTACT

"Drawing on her experience as a commercial airline pilot, Grant brings a masterful realism to this otherworldly romance. Readers...will relish this emotionally charged aviation romance."
—*Publishers Weekly*

"Frankly, if there is any justice left in this post 9-11 world, this book should be the one to take the author out of semi-cult status straight into the Brockmann leagues."
—*All About Romance*

"Depth and passion [are] fast becoming Susan Grant's trademark."
—*WordWeaving.com*

THE STAR PRINCE

"Four and a half stars and a Top Pick! Hang on to your armrests—Susan Grant is about to take readers on an exotic exhilarating adventure."
—*Romantic Times BOOKclub*

"A strong take-charge kind of hero, an intelligent, feisty heroine, strange new worlds, adventure, and an eclectic cast of characters...I was sorry to see the story end."
—*The Best Reviews*

THE STAR KING

"Adventure, wit, and engaging characters that will keep you reading until the last page. Fly high with *The Star King!*"
—Author Catherine Asaro

"Masterful...! If you're looking for some excitement and adventure, [this book] will provide it—in spades."
—*All About Romance*

"Five stars!...absolutely fabulous."
—*Scribes World*

ONCE A PIRATE

"Fans of high-seas adventures will enjoy Grant's debut time-travel romance. Grant's background as a U.S. Air Force pilot brings authenticity to her heroine."
—*Publishers Weekly*

"Five Hearts! *Once a Pirate* is the best romance I have read this year. Susan Grant has a bright future ahead of her, and I hope she can write fast."
—*The Romance Reader*

"Pure entertainment... Sit back and enjoy this one—it's lots of fun!"
—*All About Romance*

JUL 2 3 2008

Also by Susan Grant

The Scarlet Empress
The Legend of Banzai Maguire
The Star Princess
Contact
The Star Prince
The Star King
Once a Pirate

And coming soon from Susan Grant and HQN Books

My Favorite Earthling

SUSAN GRANT

Your Planet, OR MINE?

HQN™

If you purchased this book without a cover you should be aware that this book is stolen property. It was reported as "unsold and destroyed" to the publisher, and neither the author nor the publisher has received any payment for this "stripped book."

ISBN-13: 978-0-373-77106-6
ISBN-10: 0-373-77106-1

YOUR PLANET OR MINE?

Copyright © 2006 by Susan Grant

All rights reserved. Except for use in any review, the reproduction or utilization of this work in whole or in part in any form by any electronic, mechanical or other means, now known or hereafter invented, including xerography, photocopying and recording, or in any information storage or retrieval system, is forbidden without the written permission of the publisher, Harlequin Enterprises Limited, 225 Duncan Mill Road, Don Mills, Ontario M3B 3K9, Canada.

All characters in this book have no existence outside the imagination of the author and have no relation whatsoever to anyone bearing the same name or names. They are not even distantly inspired by any individual known or unknown to the author, and all incidents are pure invention.

This edition published by arrangement with Harlequin Books S.A.

® and TM are trademarks of the publisher. Trademarks indicated with ® are registered in the United States Patent and Trademark Office, the Canadian Trade Marks Office and in other countries.

www.HQNBooks.com

Printed in U.S.A.

Dear Reader,

I admit it: I'm a sucker for fairy tales. Give me a "princess" and a "prince" with the odds stacked against them and a happily-ever-after and my nose is stuck in that book until the last page is turned. It's probably why my eighth novel, *Your Planet or Mine?*, is at its core a fairy tale in the tradition of *Cinderella* and *Pinocchio*. It's about having a huge heart even when life isn't so kind. It's about starting life behind the power curve but never giving up on your dreams. And it's about magic.

Jana is a speech-impaired little girl who believes in magic and grows up to save the world, and Cavin is the precocious boy who as a man turns his back on a hard-won career to rescue an entire planet, all in the name of a magical phenomenon called love.

If you've read my books before, you know you're going to get a fun and sexy adventure that's just "a little bit different" from the rest. If you're new to my stories, I do hope you'll enjoy my special blend of romantic comedy sprinkled with the fantastic, because I sure love writing it.

Susan Grant

For Courtney and Connor Gunning,
the two best kids in the whole world.

ACKNOWLEDGMENTS

Many wonderful, generous people helped me in the writing of this book. Thank you to California State Senator Jeff Denham, Allison Brennan and Dan Brennan—for their expert help in writing about California's state capitol and what it's like to work there (any errors are my own); Carolyn Curtice and Barb Smith for their patient read-throughs of this book in manuscript form; Pamela White, aka Pamela Clare, for invaluable advice from a real journalist; Connor Gunning for his unequaled knowledge of Halo-2 weaponry and warfare; literary agent Ethan Ellenberg for his untiring support; Tracy Farrell, one terrific editor, for being so excited about the story; and the real Sadie for, well, just being Sadie.

No dogs, big or small, were harmed in the making of this book.

Your Planet,
OR MINE?

3 1833 05031 1528

PROLOGUE

NINE-YEAR-OLD JANA JASPER squirmed in bed, bursting with excitement, when her parents came to her bedroom to say goodbye before leaving to catch a red-eye flight from Sacramento to Washington, DC. She had a big secret.

"Listen to Grandpa," her mother said, kissing Jana once on each cheek and the lips as she issued orders in her Russian accent. "Do as he says."

Jana nodded. *Mom,* she yearned to shout, *there's a boy stuck in our tree! Right here, outside my window.*

"Grandpa can't chase after the three of you like he used to."

And he glows in the dark. Blue and green. Just like the light sticks we got on the Fourth of July.

Her mom cradled Jana's face in soft hands that smelled like roses. "I already spoke to your brother and sister, but I did not tell them this, my little dreamer. Don't become so lost in your imagination that you forget to have fun. Promise me."

Lost? But she never felt lost when she played pretend. Not like she did in real life sometimes. Jana nodded anyway. Was the boy still in the oak tree? She was dying to know. But she didn't dare steal a look after she'd just made the promise about dreaming.

Jana took a peek anyway. She couldn't help it. The boy was there, snagged between the shoulder blades by a branch below her window but above the bottom floor. How did that happen? Maybe he flew into the tree and got stuck. Kicking and swinging his arms, he fought like a bug caught in a spiderweb. It wasn't his body that glowed, or his clothes, but something that covered him from head to toe like a wet suit made from a soap bubble. You could see right through it to his strange clothes.

Why would anyone wear a dark shirt with long sleeves in August? And those pants, too tight and tucked into weird lumpy shoes with rubbery soles that looked a little like Grandpa's fly-fishing boots. She didn't know what to think about his hair. The brown color was the only thing normal about it. Not only was his hair longer than hers, some pieces were tied in skinny braids. But it didn't look like girl's hair at all. It was wild and exotic. And so was he.

Like Peter Pan, she thought. Her own magical boy!

"There's no such thing as magic," her first grade teacher had said after seeing a picture Jana had drawn of a fairy godmother giving her a box with a big bow that said Gift of Gab, so she'd be able to talk up a storm like the other kids. "Jana, magic is how people explain what they don't understand." Jana remembered feeling sorry for Miss Richards.

It didn't matter anyway because soon after that, Jana left to be homeschooled. Dad and Mom said they took her out because she was unusually bright and needed special attention, but Jana knew the main reason was because she didn't talk. She *could* talk; it was just that the words got all jumbled up before she had a chance to get them out. Or she'd think too hard about what she wanted to say and when she was finally ready the chance to speak had passed.

"Janushka!" Mom clapped her hands together to get her attention. "Already you have escaped. Off in your imaginary world."

Jana made a smile that said, "Sorry."

Mom pulled her close to press a kiss to her forehead. "Maybe you will take me with you sometime. We will run together in your dreams. What do you think of that?"

Jana giggled.

From where he stood leaning against the bedroom door, her dad shook his head at them and grinned. He was dressed in a black business suit, a white shirt and a colorful tie. Love made his eyes bright, but there was worry there, too. Jana saw it. She wanted to be like other kids, so she could make her dad feel better. "Do you know what the reporter told me today after the interview, Jana? He couldn't believe there was a Jasper who didn't love to talk."

Jana blushed hotly.

"Ah, munchkin." Her father walked to the bed and pulled her into his arms. As a rule, Dad kept his children out of the spotlight, but because the campaign was about to start, more people wanted interviews with the entire family. Jana dreaded it. When she was little, her silence could be explained away as shyness; but not anymore. Today, she'd ached with embarrassment at not being able to do anything else but smile or shake her head to answer questions the man had so patiently asked her. But her father's hug told her all was forgiven.

Everyone looked up to him. He'd been a state senator for longer than she could remember, and before she was born, a state assemblyman. Now he was running for U.S. Congress, just like Grandpa did before he became the governor of California and served two terms.

Because of the campaign, Dad and Mom would be gone for two weeks. Jana, her older sister, Evie, and their big brother, Jared, would be with Grandpa on the family ranch that journalists called a "compound" and Jana called home. When people mentioned *Jasper*, they said words like *political dynasty* and *California's first family* in the next breath. Dad would remind Jana, Evie and Jared, "We're public servants first and foremost. Our duty to others comes before our own interests and ambition. There is no greater calling than to serve your fellow men and women. Never forget that, children. Never forget you're a Jasper."

Jana never forgot. Ever. She took her role as a Jasper seriously, tried to live up to the family name. *If only I could sound like a Jasper.*

If she wished hard enough, would it happen?

Maybe if she could borrow some of that glowing boy's magic.

The instant her parents left the room, Jana sprang to her knees and reached for the latch that unhinged the screen covering the window. The boy's magic was strong, but not strong enough to get him loose. *Mortal girl to the rescue,* she thought, and pulled off the screen.

"Jana, don't you worry about the newsman teasing you for you being so quiet. That young man saw only what was on the outside when everyone knows it's what's on the inside that counts."

Jana gasped. She spun around with the screen in her hands. Her grandfather stood in the doorway of her bedroom. She managed a smile, but her heart thumped in time with the ticktock of the old clock in the hallway that President Roosevelt gave Grandpa's father a long, long time ago, before even Dad was born. Would he know what she was up to? Would he guess her plan to climb the tree?

Grandpa lifted a thick silver brow. "I thought your father fixed that screen." With a grunt of exasperation he took it from her and placed it on the floor. "This old place is falling apart."

Leaves made swishing noises outside. Grandpa squinted at the sliver of night sandwiched by her curtains. "Now what do you think that is? An owl? Or squirrels with insomnia?"

It's a boy. A magical glowing boy!

"You'd better sleep with the window closed." He reached over her bed and slammed the window shut. Jana couldn't hear the boy's struggles anymore.

She grabbed her grandfather by the sleeve and tried to get him to look outside. *He's stuck. Look, Grandpa.*

"Is something out there?" He took a quick glance outside, but the boy was below eye level, glowing so softly that unless you looked in the exact spot, you would miss him. "What do you see?"

Pointing, Jana tried to tell him, but the more excited she got, the more the words jammed up in her throat. *Magic,* she mouthed.

"You and your imagination. We should all have the ability to look at ordinary things and see magic."

She burrowed into his arms for a hug. He felt big and soft and warm. She loved him so much it hurt.

"Ah, Jana. You have so much heart. More than all of us Jaspers combined." He moved her back to see her. "Heart is what will take you to the top. It's what this country needs. Heart and the smarts to go with it. You're going to go far, Jana Jasper. Mind this old man's words. Don't let anyone tell you different." His blue eyes glowed. "The highest office of this country is not beyond your abilities. A Jasper in the White House. Now, that sounds mighty appealing. I'll be sure to take my vitamins so I can be around long enough to see your inauguration." He tucked her in bed and gave her a scratchy kiss on the cheek. "President Jana Jasper. All hail the chief."

Jana's face turned hot at the same time her throat got thick. She hated the thought of disappointing him. *One day, Grandpa, I'll make you proud. I'll make all of you proud I was born into this family.* How, she didn't know yet, but she'd figure it out.

At the door he stopped to say, "As for that magic, if a woman named Mary Poppins shows up, tell her where to find me. I think it's going to be a long two weeks for Grandpa. Good night, punkin."

She smiled sweetly.

The second the door closed, she yanked open the curtains and threw open the window. The trapped magical boy dangled in the same place. He'd stopped kicking, though. Maybe he was getting tired. "Peter," she whispered dreamily. After she saved him, he'd be loyal to her forever, like a genie released from a lamp. Maybe he'd grant her three wishes, even, out of gratitude.

She threw one bare foot over the sill. The rough tiles of the roof were still warm from the day's hot sun.

She pulled her other leg through the window and stood in her nightgown, balanced on the curved area of the roof below her bedroom window. From there, she eyed the nearest oak tree branch she'd need to shimmy down to reach Peter and unhook him. Could she make it? No problem, she thought. She'd climbed more trees than she could count.

She made the leap and ran along the center of the branch like it was the balance beam at gymnastics camp. As it narrowed, she dropped to her butt and scooted forward. Her legs dangled, knocking loose bark and leaves. In the corner of her eye, she caught movement. Peter had twisted around and was looking up at her.

No, not looking, *staring,* working his way up from her toes and chipped, glitter nail polish to her skinny suntanned legs sticking out of her pink nightgown until he reached her face and stopped. As if he had any reason to stare. *He* was the one dressed in weird clothes. And *he* was the one hanging from a tree like a human-size inchworm. But he had a friendly face and the kind of mouth that looked as if it smiled a lot, only it wasn't smiling now. It was wide-open in shock.

Haven't you ever been rescued by a girl before? A mortal girl?

Jana inched forward until she'd reached the limb directly above his and went down on her stomach to slide the last little bit. She took a swipe at him, but missed. The limb creaked.

One…more…inch… Grunting, she stretched out her arm and hooked her fingers in the boy's glow-bubble outfit.

It didn't feel hot, or even slippery. It was smooth and cool, like rubber. *Hold still, I got you.* The boy seemed to understand she wanted to help. She squeezed the glow-skin to get a better grip on his shirt. It would take a good, hard lift to unhook him. But she couldn't budge him. No wonder he hadn't been able to get free. His body weight was keeping him hooked. What if he was still stuck here in the morning when Jared woke up? Jana gave one hard yank. *Crack!*

The branch splintered and went down. Like a tick on a dog's tail, she held on. The branch smacked into the one that had snagged Peter and knocked him loose.

At the last second there was a whoosh of wind that seemed to slow his fall, and he landed on his feet. He made eye contact with her and dipped his head once, probably to thank her for unhooking him.

Jana grinned and waved, maybe a little too hard. Her branch made a grinding sound and flipped over. She yelped and hung on. Somehow, she was still attached to the limb when the spinning stopped.

She opened one eye. Then the other. The good news was that she was still alive. The bad news was that she now hung upside down like a possum. If not for her fear of hitting the ground headfirst, she would have been wild with embarrassment about her panties showing.

The magical boy waited below, looking worried for her, but the branch was broken; she couldn't climb back the way she came. Her only choice was to fall. She let go with her legs and hung by her hands. It was a long way down to the ground. *Bend your knees when you hit.* That's what Jared would say.

Jana let go. For a frightening second, wind shrieked past her ears. She hit the ground and rolled onto her side. That wasn't so bad. She climbed to her feet, shaking off leaves like a dog shook off water. With a big grin, she spun in a pirouette and curtsied. But the boy was jogging backward so fast that he stumbled. Looking even more upset, he jumped up off the grass and escaped into the shadows.

A gust of wind blew through the garden, whipping Jana's hair around her face. A row of plastic daisy pinwheels spun, clicking and clacking, and near the barn, a gate creaked open and slammed shut.

"Squeee!" From her pen near the barn, Jana's frightened potbellied pig squealed above the commotion. Before Jana could reach the pen to soothe her, Minnie had pushed the gate open and escaped.

The prissy little pig scurried down the path leading away from the garden. *Minnie!* Jana thrust her feet into pink rubber flip-flops lying on the patio and raced after her pig.

No blue-green glow. Peter was nowhere to be seen. Was he afraid of her? He'd sure run away fast.

Her flip-flops scraped on the gravel as she hurried along the dirt path behind the barn to a place where Minnie liked to forage. *Min,* she thought urgently. *Minnie, come back!*

Then, something rustled in the dark. Tingles raced up her arms. The air felt strange. Tickly. *Someone's watching you.* Jana's tingles turned to goose bumps, and suddenly she wished she were back in bed.

A crackling noise came from the shadows. Whatever it was, it was coming closer.

"Squeee!" A round, little shadow darted out of the thigh-high weeds—and ran straight to Peter, who stepped onto the path and grabbed Minnie before she escaped.

The glowing boy was holding her pig! Fascination and wonder froze Jana in place as Peter walked toward her. She met his gaze and sucked in a silent breath. The air felt electric. *Magic.* All the hair on her body stood on end.

"Squee," he said and offered her Minnie.

She took the pig and hugged her close. *Thank you,* she mouthed. Peter's smile filled her stomach with squirmy butterflies.

A twig snapped from somewhere in the bushes. They jumped apart and took off running—Peter into the fields, and Jana toward the house. The magic boy! She'd met him! She skipped all the way back to the yard to put Minnie away. After making sure the gate was latched and locked, she ran to the back door, punched in the secret code for the keypad that disarmed the security system, and ran upstairs to bed.

"Peter," she whispered in a dreamy voice. Resting her chin on her hands, she curled up by the windowsill. He'd be back; yes, he would. Peter would come before morning and transport her to Neverland—she was sure of it. But the next thing she knew, she was waking bathed in sunshine in exactly the same place as before.

CAVIN BURST THROUGH the hatch and into the familiar surroundings of his ship that floated above the forest floor. The vessel was invisible to anyone without the proper technology, something no one on this primitive world had. Excitement pulsed through him as he stood in the decontamination shower to wash off his soiled biobubble. He'd been to a hundred unexplored alien worlds traveling from planet to planet with his scientist father, but never one like this. Never one with anyone like *her*. The incredible alien girl!

Cavin leaped out of the shower, his heart bursting with folk songs…which died in his throat as soon as he saw the worry in his father's eyes.

"Your vital signs are elevated, Cavin." The man frowned from where he sat at a worktable littered with samples he'd collected since they'd landed. "Pulse high. Body temperature in the caution zone. What have you been doing out there, son?"

"I, ah—"

"You didn't go too far from the ship, did you? There is a humanoid settlement in the area, and you mustn't go near it."

Cavin took a seat at the table. Crocks of hot food sat next to research gear and data files. It was a man's ship. No frills. No softness. Sometimes he wondered if his father had purposely eradicated all signs of femininity after Cavin's mother died.

Hungrily, Cavin ladled soup into a bowl and dug in.

"Cavin?"

His father studied him with a concerned look on his face. It felt strange to have the man's full attention. It so rarely happened. "Yes, sir?"

"Did you approach the settlement at close range?"

"I got caught in a tree," Cavin answered without exactly answering. He turned around and showed where the branch had snagged him. In an instant his father was scanning him, taking more readings.

"Was there a rupture?"

Cavin shook his head. Though there might have been if he'd tried to rip himself free of the tree. If *she* hadn't gotten to him first. But it had been worth it, the entire embarrassing fiasco. He had finally got to meet her after watching her for days and developing a curiosity that resulted in him swooping in too low and getting stuck when he'd tried to get a closer peek at her dwelling.

"You're lucky it was only a tree that caught you, son. If you'd been captured by the locals, it would have put this entire mission in jeopardy—and maybe cost you your life."

"I'm sorry, sir." He didn't want to put his father at risk. He'd be more careful next time.

His father pulled another biosphere off the shelf filled with many similar spheres of scurrying creatures and went back to work.

The trapped animals were terrified, Cavin realized. Just as he'd been, caught in the tree. "Why did we come here, Father?" he blurted out. "To this planet out of all the others?" He'd never paid much mind to the samples they took, or his father's job as a whole, but then he'd never visited a world that mattered. The girl had made this world matter.

"The same reason as always. To determine if this planet can be classified as fit for habitation."

"One look around could tell anyone that."

"For Coalition habitation, son."

Cavin put down his utensil. A minute ago his stomach had been growling; now he'd lost his appetite. "So, if the Coalition likes the data you send them, this place goes on the invasion list."

"It goes on the *acquisition* list."

"What's the difference?"

His father gave him a funny look as he injected a white gas into the biosphere that held a long-eared mammal with a jumping nose. It sagged onto its side, as if asleep. Bio-stasis solved the problem of feeding the samples during the long voyage. "If a planet is deemed to be of use, the population will be removed to another location and replaced with Coalition citizens. By definition, it's acquiring, not invading."

"But the people here are humans like us. Don't they have a say?"

"The galaxy is littered with humans, Cavin. Seeded with our DNA so long ago no one really knows why or how. But not all humans are part of the Coalition, and the Coalition is who we serve."

Cavin frowned at his bowl of soup. "It just seems wrong to take this world without asking."

"Tell it to the Coalition," his father said irritably, knowing full well that Cavin wouldn't dare do it. No one in their right mind would, unless you wanted to disappear and never be heard from again. Then he sighed. "I'm a scientist, not a government man. I collect data and pass it on. I do my job, and they do theirs."

"But when is it going to happen? When's the Coalition going to come here?" He needed to know. This time, it mattered.

"Even if the planet is determined to be of use, it could be years, son. Many, many years. Maybe not even in your lifetime."

Ah, gods. For the girl's sake, Cavin hoped not.

AT BREAKFAST, Jana's grandfather carried the *Sacramento Sun* and a cup of coffee to the table. "When I went outside to get the paper, the alarm was off."

Jana's face burned. She'd forgotten all about resetting it when she came inside last night.

"I distinctly remember turning it on before I went to bed. But this morning, it was off." He opened the paper with a loud snap, eyeing Evie, Jared and Jana in turn. "How do you suppose that happened?"

Jana turned her gaze to her cereal to avoid her grandfather's eyes.

"You weren't sneaking out to meet a girl, were you, Jared?"

"I wish," her brother muttered.

"Hmm. And you, Evie? Is there a boy?"

"No!" She sounded indignant.

Jana sneaked a peek at Grandpa. He lifted a brow at her. "I know it wasn't you, Jana."

She sank down in her seat. Evie and Jared watched her with sudden interest.

"Jana?"

By now, her chin was level with the edge of the table. *Minnie,* she mouthed bashfully to her sister.

As always, Evie filled in the blanks. "Minnie got out again and Jana had to go find her."

"Good thing you found her," Grandpa said. "Because we've got some unwelcome wildlife coming around. Something damaged the oak tree last night. Broke a couple of branches. I'd say it looks like a bear's work if I thought they came this far down from the hills."

It wasn't a bear. It was Peter! Jana giggled. All eyes went to her again.

Jared winced. "What's wrong with her?"

"Nothing's wrong with her," Evie said. "But she's definitely acting different."

Because today I am *different.* Jana sighed.

As Grandpa worriedly read the ingredients on the side of the cereal box as if it would somehow explain her behavior, Jana tossed her bowl into the dishwasher and pirouetted into her parent's bedroom.

Brightly painted Russian matryoshka dolls decorated her mother's night table. Each doll held smaller, identical dolls nestled one inside the other. Jana gathered up the egg-shaped matryoshkas and carried them to her room. With reverence, she spread them out on her comforter. Every one held a love note from Dad, which was, as he always said, the only way a brand-new assemblyman visiting Moscow as part of an official California agricultural delegation had stood a chance at winning the attention of a beautiful Russian ballerina. Every couple of days over the course of a few weeks, he'd send Mom another doll with a new letter tucked inside. "My marrying your mother was a long shot," he'd say, wearing a funny little smile as he pushed his glasses up his nose. "But I did. Never be afraid of going for it, even when someone tells you your chances of succeeding are one in a million."

Jana was going for it, too. Tonight. Despite one-in-a-million odds, she'd find Peter again.

IT SEEMED TO TAKE forever for the house to grow silent, but as soon as it did, Jana sneaked out the back door. She crawled onto the patio glider with a blanket to wait for

Peter. The rising moon was huge and full. Everything was still, hushed, waiting for something to happen.

There's magic in the air tonight. She wasn't sure what she sensed but it was out there all the same.

Evie would have told her that love was in the air. After catching Jana watching *Peter Pan* for the third— no, *fourth* time, she'd forced her to sit down for a "talk." Jana did her best to explain Peter, only to have Evie declare her to be in love. "But now's not the time to get emotional, Jana," she'd said. "He owes you three wishes. Okay, so he rescued your pig, but you *saved him.* It's the same as letting a genie out of the bottle. Three wishes, Jana. Don't forget…"

Don't forget… Jana smiled and hugged the blanket closer.

"…SQUEE."

Jana opened her eyes. Her chin was resting on her chest. She was curled up in a blanket on the glider. Why was she outside? And why was Minnie whispering? Heart pounding she stared confused into the darkness.

"Squee?"

It wasn't Minnie. It was a voice—a boy's voice.

Peter! In an instant, she was fully awake. He waved to her from behind an oak tree as he glanced around nervously. His suit glowed softly around him, but she could see him clearly, from his braids to his boots. When he met her eyes, his expression lightened. "Squee," he said, as if it were the only thing he was able to pronounce.

Her heart swelled up. Peter battled with words, too.

He took a few steps backward and motioned for her to follow. On his left wrist was a thick, black cuff.

She'd noticed the bracelet the night before but not the lights blinking on it. When he pressed something on the cuff, leaves scattered in a whirlwind. The breeze whipped Jana's hair around her head. The wind whistled, louder and louder, as it had last night in the garden, then Peter's feet lifted off the ground.

Jana's heart pounded with awe and delight. He could fly!

He didn't go very high, and after a few seconds, he came back down, but it was magic, real magic.

Jana clapped her hands. Peter grinned. In another whoosh of wind, he rose up again, bouncing on his rubbery boots when he landed.

She ran to him, but he lifted off before she could reach him. Stretching out her arms, she tried to catch him, but he floated away. Laughing, she came up on her toes like her mother had taught her, pirouetting through the shimmering grasses as the wind shook the trees.

My turn, my turn. She ran to him when he landed, her arms wide open. With a questioning look, he pointed skyward. Jana nodded like crazy. *Yes, yes. I want to fly.*

He grabbed her around the waist and tried to take off with her. He managed to get into the air for a couple of seconds, but her feet dragged and never left the ground. The commotion woke a family of quail. Jana laughed at the sight of the birds fluttering into the air in the light of the full moon. *Let's chase them.* Peter lifted her again and they crashed, laughing as they hit the ground.

But that didn't stop them. They tried again, and again, each time too heavy to fly. Only after they were completely exhausted, did they stop to rest.

Jana gasped to catch her breath, holding her palm to a stitch in her side as she followed Peter to the end of a dock jutting out on a small pond on the property. They fell to their stomachs, chins held in their hands, to watch the moon reflected on the water. Peter stuck out his arm, palm up, to blow a gentle wind from his wrist cuff, just enough to shatter the moonlight into a million little pieces.

Jana clapped. Peter's face glowed in the light from his bubble-skin. A funny, soft, happy feeling she'd never experienced before filled her. For once she didn't feel the pressure to speak, to struggle to explain what she felt. *This was the best night of my life*.

Then Evie's voice echoed in her mind: "Don't forget." Jana showed Peter three fingers. *Three wishes*.

He shook his head in confusion.

She dipped her finger in the water and drew a wet number three on the dock. Peter stared at the number as if he didn't know how to read. He studied the fingers she showed him, then also using pond water, drew a symbol. She shook her head. Was it another language?

"Jana!" a man's voice bellowed.

Grandpa.

Peter shot to his feet. His panicked eyes begged her to understand something but she didn't know what. He had to go; that much was obvious. Why was he so frightened of being seen by Grandpa? It made her wish for words—not from her for once, but from him.

Reluctantly, she left Peter by the pond. A moment later, a gust of wind told her he'd escaped.

"Jana! Where are you?"

The harsh beam of a flashlight arced back and forth.

Anxiety made wiggles in her stomach as Jana ran to meet her grandfather. "You scared me, girl. Scared me good. What are you doing out here this time of night? You're covered in leaves and burs." He reached out, snatched her by the wrist and pulled her back to the house.

At the back patio door, Grandpa crouched down. He grunted, knees creaking. "Why did you leave the house? Talk to me, Jana. Find the words."

Peter—he came and we played. He's magic. Oh, Grandpa, when I'm with him, it feels like I can do anything.

Anything but talk, she realized, the words knotting up in her throat. Without his glasses, Grandpa had trouble reading her lips in the dark, but she kept trying. The more she wanted to explain, the less she was able to do it until she finally gave up. Tears of frustration pressed behind her eyes.

A leaf dangled from her bangs as she bowed her head. Despite his angry expression, Grandpa removed it tenderly. "Jana, your imagination is a wonderful thing, but sometimes you have to stop to consider the consequences of your actions. I didn't know you were out playing. I thought you were missing. And that maybe someone had hurt you."

Jana tasted a bitter rush of guilt. She wasn't used to being the one who misbehaved, and she wasn't sure she liked it, either.

Grandpa took her hand and brought her back to her bedroom. He turned on the light and picked up one of the colored-pencil drawings on her desk. "Who's this? Is he a friend of yours?"

Yes! She nodded with enthusiasm.

His expression hardened. He thrust a pad and pencil at her. "Tell me who this boy is, who his parents are, and how you know him."

Jana took the pencil and paper and scribbled: *Peter is magic!!!*

Grandpa read what she wrote with no small amount of relief. "Ah, an imaginary friend." Then he gave the drawings a closer look, this time with a different kind of worry. Jana knew about the different looks of worry; at one time or another, she'd seen them all directed at her. Then he sighed and put the papers down. "As much as I love your imagination, it's my responsibility to keep you safe—and inside—at night. I won't tell on you, but in return, I want your promise. No more going out in the middle of the night."

And not see Peter?

He nodded.

The ache to disobey her grandfather was strong, but the desire not to disappoint him was stronger. She might not sound like the rest of the Jaspers, but she could do a lot better in acting like one. It about killed her, but she nodded.

"Good girl." He didn't leave her room until he was satisfied she was tucked in under the covers. "Stay." He shook his finger at her in a warning, to which she gave an obedient nod. Then he was gone, back to bed.

"CAVIN, YOUR BIOSIGNS are even more elevated than last night," his father observed as Cavin burst, gasping, out of the decon shower. There was the near miss with the girl's elder, but Cavin didn't dare reveal how close he'd come to discovery.

"You didn't get stuck in another tree, did you?"

Cavin shook his head. He bent over, hands on his knees, to catch his breath. "No, sir. Just exploring, sir."

"I'm glad you have the energy, because I'm going to put it to use. The tie-downs in the cargo bay are loose. Tighten them for me. Then help me get these biospheres labeled and loaded. We're soon to be on our way."

Cavin's mouth went dry. "We're leaving?" *Not yet, Father. I've only just gotten to know her. She's...she's wonderful. I can't stop smiling when I'm with her. I can't stop looking at her.*

"Tomorrow night."

"But—"

"I need your help getting ready. There's more left to do than I thought. I've fallen behind."

Would he have the chance to see the girl one more time? He had to. No matter what his father said.

As he climbed down to the cargo bay, Cavin wished for a way that the alien girl could be loaded on board, too. Then just as quickly as the thought had come into his head, shame obliterated it. He didn't want to own her. He didn't want to control her. He wanted her to be with him only if he made her as happy as she made him.

IT WASN'T QUITE DARK when Jana heard the whisper of wind outside her bedroom window the next night. She moved aside the edge of the curtain and peeked outside. Peter stood at the base of the tree, glowing softly. His entire face seemed to melt in an expression of relief and happiness when he saw her. He beckoned to her urgently. *Come down.*

I can't.

Please.

Jana shook her head.

Shoving fingers through his hair, Peter paced in front of the oak tree. He seemed different. Sadder—and also as if he were in a hurry.

Something was wrong. He needed her, but she'd promised she wouldn't leave the house. Jana had never felt so empty in all her life. Was being good supposed to feel this bad?

Grandpa said she had heart, but all she knew was that her heart was hurting right now. Hurting for Peter. She cast a longing look out the window, but Peter was gone. She uttered a squeak of dismay.

No! She wasn't going to let him leave thinking she didn't care. With her knuckles pressed to her mouth and her heart kicking her ribs, Jana walked out into the hallway and pretended not to see the portraits of dead and alive Jaspers watching her defiance with disapproval. Just this once, she told them. *Just this once.*

Down the flight of stairs, out into the backyard, then she broke into a run. With none of the grace of her ballet-dancer mother, she got the toe of her flip-flop caught in a rut of sunbaked mud and went down hard on one knee.

It stung like a thousand bumblebee stings, but she picked herself up and limped back into a run. It hurt but she didn't care. When she reached the tree, Peter was gone.

A flare of panic took her breath, but she fought to

calm down. Where did he go? Would he have gone to the pond? She turned in that direction and ran.

By the time she reached him where he sat on the dock, staring out at nothing, she was breathless with fear and pain. When he heard her footsteps, he turned around.

"Squee…" The soft and special way he smiled took her by surprise with a strange cartwheeling, heart-flipping feeling. But when he saw the blood dribbling down her shin, his expression changed. He stormed toward her and took her by the hand, pulling her into a stand of oaks where the only light was that from his glow.

Peter touched his wrist cuff. On it, tiny lights began to flash. Jana's mouth fell open as sparkles appeared at the crown of Peter's head. The sparkles looked like fairy dust as they formed a ring around his head like a halo. But then they fell, taking his glowing outer skin with them in a shimmering wave of light until the glow-bubble hung low around his waist.

Jana gasped. Underneath the bubble-skin he was a real boy, as human as she was, as human as any of Jared's friends.

No, she thought. Jared's friends were *sub*human.

Peter dropped to his knees and brought his finger to her throbbing knee. Jana jerked her leg away. Her skin was raw; it would hurt.

Peter gave his head a single shake. His confidence reassured her. Holding her breath, she let him touch his fingertip—real, warm skin—to her wound.

Tiny, crawly little shocks pricked her knee and shin. It felt like the time she'd stepped on a frayed plugged-in cord that had gotten wet next to the pool. The tingles spread up her leg. Static electricity snapped. Her scalp tingled. Jana let out a delighted, surprised laugh—her hair was floating!

Then the tingling stopped. It took a few seconds to realize the pain in her knee had gone away, too. She dropped a shocked stare to her leg. Where the scrape had been, the skin was now smooth and pink. Except for the small patch of missing suntan and the streaks of blood on her shin, it was like she'd never hurt herself.

It was the proof he was magic. *The proof!*

Peter stood. He pointed to his chest then with both hands he made a sweeping motion at the sky.

Questioningly, she pointed to the sky full of stars.

He nodded. *Yes. There.* The sadness on his face was sharp. He was leaving and wasn't coming back.

Her eyes ached. *Be brave, Jana. Don't cry.*

He touched his fingertip to her mouth, so lightly, like he'd done to her scraped knee, his gaze deep and dark. Then he held up three fingers.

Her hopes rising, she held up three fingers, too. *Three—the three wishes!*

Then Peter reached for his wrist cuff. Sparkles danced around the edge of the sagging bubble-skin as the glow rose slowly. In a hurry, he walked away.

But Jana bolted after him. She had to see him one last time before the bubble sealed him completely. She wasn't sure what she was going to do when she caught up to him, but Peter took care of that.

His hand slid behind her head and he pressed a warm, firm kiss to her lips. Then just as quickly he let go and threw the glowing bubble-skin over his head as he hurried away.

Wow, Jana thought, standing there, her heart racing. *Wow.*

A wave of emotion surged up inside her. All at once she was scared, mad, sad, happy—she couldn't explain the boiling feelings inside her, only that she couldn't hold it all in. It came bursting out of her in a rush of words: "I'll never forget you, Peter! I never will!"

His pace slowed for a second. He'd heard her. But it was as if he were afraid to turn around, because if he did, he wouldn't be able to leave. A heartbeat later, he lifted off the ground with a gust of wind and vanished.

She brought a shaking hand to her throat. What had just happened? *You spoke.* "I spoke," she murmured, feeling the vibration of her vocal cords under her fingertips. "I spoke," she said, louder this time. "I spoke!" She threw back her head and laughed out loud. Peter had fixed her. He'd fixed her on the inside like he had the outside. Jana whooped and pirouetted, arms flung out wide.

"Jana? Was that you yelling?" In pajamas, her sister approached.

"Listen, Evie. *Listen.* I can talk."

Evie shrieked and grabbed her in a fierce hug. Squealing and dancing, they spun around, arms around each other. "You got the three wishes, Jana. You got them."

"Two out of three." Jana gasped.

Evie grabbed her by the shoulders to stop the spinning. "What do you mean two out of three? What were the other two?"

"Two was—" Jana blushed "—a first kiss. I kissed Peter!"

Evie pressed her hand over Jana's mouth. "Now that you're talking, you're going to need to learn to control what comes out." She lifted her hand. "It wasn't a French kiss, was it?"

"What's a French kiss?"

"Did he put his tongue in your mouth?"

"Ugh. No!"

"Good. You're only nine." With dread Evie asked, "What was number three?"

"It hasn't happened yet," Jana said in a dreamy voice. "Peter is going to marry me."

Evie made the loudest snort. "You can't wish that."

"Why not?" Jana felt herself deflate.

"Granting you the three wishes set him free. If he marries you, he's not set free. It's like making your third wish that you want three more wishes. That's not allowed, either."

"But—"

"Jana. You can't marry the genie, okay? It goes against the rules of magic."

Never be afraid of going for it, even when someone tells you your chances of succeeding are one in a million. "I'm going to marry him." Jana skipped ahead of her sister, headed home.

"You won't feel this way once you fall in love for real," Evie shouted after her.

Jana laughed and kept skipping. She didn't have time to argue, not now. She had plans to make, a future to look forward to, and she was going to create it from the ground up. No more being the troublemaker Jasper, the one everyone worried about. No more trips to Dr. Wong, the child psychologist, to see why she couldn't speak. All she'd ever wanted was to be normal, to be like everyone else. Now that she had the chance, she wasn't going to blow it.

CHAPTER ONE

FROM THAT DAY FORWARD, Jana talked. And talked. With eloquent abandon. She talked her way through the rest of her school years, through four years at Stanford and a Rhodes scholarship to Cambridge University in England. By the time she was twenty-nine, she'd talked her way through a landslide election that ended with her taking office as the youngest state senator in California history.

As the first female Jasper to hold public office, much was said about her gift of gab and how it helped forge a real connection with her constituents. To her dismay, even more was said about her social life.

"You go through men like I go through chocolate," Evie told Jana after the breakup of her most recent relationship. This time, it had been an actual engagement. It was the third time Jana had gone that far with any of the men she'd dated and she'd hoped the third time would be a charm, but as soon as the marriage plans began in earnest, she'd gotten cold feet. Now at thirty-two Jana was back to being California's Most Eligible Bachelorette, a title she wore as comfortably and as enthusiastically as a purple tutu. Lately, even her family had gotten in on the matchmaking pressure.

Everyone except for Grandpa, wheelchair-bound in his nineties but with a mind as sharp as ever.

Clutching a mug of coffee, Jana sat across the dining table from him as she did every Tuesday morning. Foggy daylight filtered through the French doors in the breakfast room. Bagels and cream cheese were set out on antique china that had been in the family since the 1800s.

"Jana, your personal life and your political future are intertwined." Grandpa crossed two thick fingers and shook them at her. She supposed he thought she needed a visual. "You're going to have to commit to someone soon, or risk being seen as a person who can't commit to anything at all."

Sixty years between them, but to this day, they remained the closest of friends. He'd certainly been the best political mentor around, but nothing beat getting a second opinion on men from one who'd been around for almost a century. "I don't sleep around," she said. "I date around."

"To the public, to your rivals, it's the same thing."

"My social life is nowhere near as exciting as everyone thinks."

"And there you have it, girl. It's what people think that counts, not what you actually do—or not do. What you have to work on now is changing the perception that you're a playgirl who won't, or can't, settle down. Marriage will do that for you. Use your stubbornness, punkin. That relentless drive. Focus on the kind of life partner you want and go for it. Don't consider anyone who doesn't fit your specifications, and you won't be left with doubts. Choose wisely."

She drained her coffee and gazed at the grinds left

on the bottom of the cup. They formed a little heart. Oh, for goodness sake. She shook the cup, scattering the grinds. There, now they more closely resembled her love life: no direction, no substance. "I want magic, Grandpa. That's what I'm looking for and can't find. A man with the kind of magic you can taste in the very first kiss."

Surprised, her grandfather sat back in his wheelchair.

"I want to feel like I did when I kissed my imaginary friend Peter when I was a little girl," she blurted out, feeling her face warm.

"You kissed him?" Gripping the armrests of his wheelchair, he leaned forward. "You never told me that."

"He was imaginary, remember?"

"Yes, but…" he blustered.

"Besides, I was nine. Kissing any male who wasn't a family member would have been too mortifying to admit. But I tell you, Grandpa, imaginary or not, he spoiled me for anyone else."

"Good thing you didn't tell me this then. I'd have gone after that boy with my shotgun."

Jana laughed. "I can picture you raging all around the ranch, firing at nothing, trying to catch something that wasn't there."

"Is it any different from what you're doing right now with your love life? Trying to catch something that's not there?"

Was that what she was doing? Was that why it never worked out? Deflated, Jana sagged back in her chair. Sometimes, her grandfather's insight sliced right to the heart.

His blue eyes softened with love. "Don't settle,

punkin, but don't pine for what never existed in the first place, either."

"I won't settle. I promise you." *How can you say that when every man you've ever dated has been a compromise?*

She'd never stopped searching for the magic she felt with Peter, looking for it in every male she'd kissed since, comparing each and every one of them to an imaginary figure from her childhood. How sad was that? Jana pouted at the coffee grounds strewn across the bottom of her cup.

"You're all heart, my girl, but now it's time to leave your heart out of it and give this manhunt some serious thought. Picking the right man will increase your odds of winning the White House."

"That's years away." Nothing could convince him she wouldn't be the president someday.

"No time like the present to prepare for the future."

Jana checked the time. "Speaking of which, I've got to go. I'm supposed to be at the fish farm by nine."

Vaguely unsettled by the conversation, she picked up her attaché bag and hooked the strap over her shoulder, smoothing a hand over the skirt of her butter-yellow suit. "Well, keep your eyes open for me," she said with forced cheer, "because I trust your taste more than Mom's."

Mom liked Alex Neiman, a cute restaurateur who co-owned the trendy new vodka and caviar bar Ice with cousin Viktor. Alex was making a concerted play to win Jana over, wooing her, wooing the family, but she still had to be convinced Alex wasn't interested *because* of her family and their celebrity.

Or maybe she was just tired of men. The search for The One had certainly been futile. She wasn't ready to give up, but then she wasn't motivated to keep searching, either. Maybe a little vacation from the dating game would do her some good.

She came around the table and bent down to kiss her grandfather's cheek before leaving him to his newspaper and coffee in the sprawling old ranch house that had framed their childhoods, generations apart.

AN HOUR LATER, Jana felt more like prey than a politician as she stood on a narrow footbridge over seething tanks of already-huge, teenage sturgeon waiting to speak. A fish burst out of the water. Its white mouth wide-open in anticipation, it aimed for her feet. Jana sidestepped away and it dropped back into the pool. Ice-cold water sliced across her shins.

She'd been on the bridge with her communications director, Steve, and the owners of the fish farm for all of five minutes, and she was the only one who was wet. Rivulets of water ran down her calves and into her shoes. Obviously canvas open-toed heels with raffia bows were the wrong fashion choice. Who knew coral-colored toenails would be a siren's call for five thousand hormone-driven fish?

"I was told they can't see very well," she said out of the corner of her mouth to her communications director as they watched the circling shadows. "They find their food by sense of smell. Yet, look at them. They want us."

"They want *you*," Steve whispered back. "You're the only one getting wet."

Jana wiggled her toes. "Think it's the nail polish?"

A sturgeon leaped out of the water. The impact of its ugly whiskery head bouncing off the bottom of the bridge made a rubbery thunk. Water sliced across Jana's skirt and hose. *I'm on your side, little fishies. Your side.* Protecting California's wildlife had been a priority since she'd taken office. A thankless job, if the sturgeon had anything to say about it.

The report she'd read before coming here had informed her that this particular species could reach fifteen hundred pounds and live a hundred years or more. Jana thanked her lucky stars that at three feet or so, these fish weren't much more than hatchlings—*female* hatchlings. Still, she didn't like the way they clustered at the edge of their tank, blowing rubber-lipped kisses at her. She whispered in Steve's ear. "I'm afraid if I refuse their advances, they'll settle for eating me alive."

"Sort of like Brace Bowie," he murmured back.

Jana swore under her breath. No, *exactly* like Brace Bowie, developer, businessman and ex-fiancé number three. The breakup was complicated by the fact Brace had sunk a lot of money into cousin Viktor's caviar bar. She had a feeling he wanted to pull out of the investment, but felt awkward leaving Alex and Viktor hanging. Coincidentally, a week later, Brace was called in for questioning regarding the bust-up of a black market sturgeon fishing ring. A suspect arraigned on poaching charges had pointed a finger at him. He'd come out clean, but the negative publicity had hurt his business.

Jana'd had nothing to do with the investigation, but neither she nor anyone else could convince Brace, and he'd come back slinging mud at a flashy press conference accusing her of pouring millions of taxpayer dollars into building her own empire, with an army of Department of Fish and Game "enforcer-commandos" to "strong-arm" her policies. He was going make sure she lost her senate seat in the November election. For ten nightmarish weeks until the city made him take them down, he'd displayed huge signs on several of his project sites downtown calling her legislative motives into question with slogans like: Spend-Happy Jasper Wastes YOUR Tax Dollars! Vote Her Out This Fall!

"Whatever happened to taking it like a man?" she muttered to Steve. "Then again, maybe if he'd been more of a man, I might still be with him." Add Brace to her long list of bad choices. That man-vacation was sounding better by the minute.

The owner of the fish farm walked up to the microphone to begin the festivities. "Ladies and Gentlemen, let's give a warm welcome to Senator Jana Jasper, who will lead us in our ceremonies today."

To the sound of polite applause, Jana stepped up to the podium. "It's opening day at Good Egg Sea Farm and that's truly a reason to celebrate. Caspian Sea beluga sturgeon hover on the brink of extinction, wiped out by habitat degradation, commercial fishing and a black market run by the Russian Mafia. But with a little freshwater and aquaculture expertise, we've turned this small section of our state's Central Valley into the caviar-farming capital of the world!"

She waited for the cheers to quiet down before continuing. "Welcome to California's new gold rush! Black gold. And we're not talking crude. We're talking *gourmet!*" To more applause, she waved her hand in a sweeping motion at the huge circular tanks around her. "As Chair of *your* Natural Resources committee, I promise to champion legal enterprises like this one cease-lessly. Together we can stop the drain that illegal activities like poaching take on our wildlife budget—" A flip of a tail from an oversexed teenage sturgeon shot a spray of water that caught her across the jaw.

She continued, despite her cold-blooded hecklers. Using a tissue that Steve handed her to wipe off the drips. "Aqua-farms like Good Egg discourage poaching, smuggling and illegal importation. This keeps hard-won budget money where it belongs—funding crucial programs that help to protect California's environment. Congratulations, Good Egg. Not only are you good for California's taste buds, you are good for California's future!"

As the crowd applauded heartily, one of the aqua-farm owners handed her a pair of scissors. To cheers and whistles, Jana cut through a bright purple ribbon draped across the footbridge.

As the crowd applauded, a reporter and a photographer entered the farm. They didn't look familiar. Other than Good Egg's staff, their families, representatives from Fish and Game, the only other observer was a reporter cloaked in a Moscow-style trench coat and hat representing a small newspaper serving the area's Russian community. What an outfit. He looked more like a spy on undercover assignment rather than a bored part-time journalist hunting up news for a slow day. No one from the *Sacramento Sun* had bothered to show up, despite Steve's press release. Apparently, the opening of a sturgeon farm wasn't big news except to the local immigrant community.

Steve narrowed his eyes, signaling that he didn't recognize the newcomers, either. She hoped it wasn't one of the tabloids. When the Kennedys were being low-key, out of boredom the gossip rags came looking for Jaspers, who as a rule weren't nearly as interesting. But now that she was newly single, maybe they'd wanted fodder for some lurid rumors: *Sex-starved senator participates in sturgeon orgy.*

Or, better yet: *"A woman without a man is like a sturgeon without a bicycle," claims perennially spouseless State Senator Jana Jasper.*

A splash from the holding tank hit her across the chest. Jana inhaled on a gasp as a stream of cold water found its way down her cleavage. She glared at the prehistoric-looking fish ogling her from the churning water. *No one says you can't be turned into sushi— right here, right now.*

The unfamiliar reporter smirked and whispered to the photographer. Jana's instincts, always good, prick-led. What were they up to?

She stepped away from the microphone. Welcome sunshine pushed through shreds of lingering fog and warmed the March morning. Under a fluttering banner was a buffet line from the heavens: bowls of hard-boiled eggs, the whites separate from the yolks, minced onion, lemon slices, sour cream and toast to go with a rainbow of different caviars from inexpen-sive but tasty bright-orange salmon eggs to the much more expensive rich and nutty, creamy-tasting stur-geon roe. Jana inhaled the aroma, her mouth watering. She'd inherited her mother's taste in fine Russian cuisine, and caviar was a favorite. It tasted best with iced vodka, but when Good Egg's sales and marketing director offered her a flute of champagne to go with the feast, she was grateful. Every job had its perks. She took a sip.

A few flashes from the Russian newspaper's camera, then, "A question, Senator!"

She turned around. The reporter she suspected was from a tabloid waved at her. "Jeff Golden, *Los Angeles Times*," the man called out.

He was from the *Times?* Her hopes zinged up then plummeted. The *Times* was a major paper, though out of the area. It would be great publicity for her pet cause, or would it? With her luck, the guy was a Hollywood columnist suffering a slow week.

"Yes, Jeff," Jana said pleasantly. Maybe he wouldn't ask the usual questions: Will you ever settle down? Who are you seeing now?

I'm taking a man-vacation, actually.

The reporter returned her smile. He seemed friendly enough. "With today's allegations against your father, U.S. Senator Jasper, and your brother, Jared Jasper, for the misuse of campaign funds, do you feel your own activities will be called into question next?"

Allegations? What allegations? The roar in Jana's head almost drowned out the mumbling, the startled looks in people's eyes, the cameras flashing. "Repeat your question, please."

"Is the so-called spotless, eighty-five-year-old Jasper record in the political arena finally over? Or will this investigation expose what has always been there?"

Freeze your emotions. Appear calm. All her life she'd been trained to be in the public eye; her reaction to the unexpected question was almost instinctive. "I thank you for your interest, Mr. Golden. I have no comment at this time."

She surrendered the podium to Steve. "Cancel lunch with the lumber lobbyists," she told him in a private voice. Her heartbeat was all over the place but you couldn't tell from looking at her.

"Done. Don't worry about anything this afternoon. I'll cover it or reschedule it."

Today would have seen her up and down and in and out to appointments, committee hearings, meetings and back at the office. She answered with a curt nod. Having someone like Steve on the staff was invaluable. He and Nona, her chief of staff, could empty her day as fast as they could fill it.

Steve turned back to the reporter and smoothly changed the subject to one on which he and Jana were informed, while the circle of people standing around Jana widened, leaving her alone.

In politics, when you were on top, you were there in the company of friends. When you hit bottom, you were on your own.

Normal face. Keep smiling, and remain pleasant.

Turning away, she whipped her cell phone out of her purse. Before she had a chance to hit her father's private number, the phone rang. Mom, the caller ID read. Jana turned away and walked off the footbridge where too many curious ears were perked. "Mom, what's going on? I heard—"

"Come home, Janushka. Right away." The phone went dead.

Only to light up immediately. Jared. Her brother.

"Jana, drop what you're doing and meet me at the ranch. I'm on my way."

"For the love of God, Jared, tell me—"

He hung up.

"—what the heck is going on," she finished lamely. She stood there, staring at the phone in her hand. Dad's integrity was beyond question. Jared was as full of himself as ever, the consummate ladies' man and hotshot pilot, but as a National Guard officer and business owner he was as honest as they came. He, like Dad, had never come within smelling distance of scandal. An unblemished public record was a source of Jasper pride. Now this. It was time to get back to the ranch and find out exactly what was going on.

CHAPTER TWO

JANA'S MOTHER and grandfather waited for her in the cozy, wood-paneled library. The room smelled as it always did in the cool months—of wood smoke and orange oil. The crackling fire added an atmosphere of tranquility that was completely false; all it took was one step into the room for the tension to hit Jana like a brick wall.

Grandpa sat in his wheelchair with shoulders hunched. *He looks ancient,* Jana thought. Her mother's beautiful face was chalk-white. She was dressed elegantly in a white silk shirt, lots of gold chains and slim tan pants, but strands of blond hair slipped from her chignon: a telltale sign of trouble in a woman whose appearance was always immaculate.

Jana's hands were cold as she pulled the heavy wooden doors closed behind her. "Okay, what happened?"

"The Coalition for Higher Ethics came forward with figures that bring into question your father's campaign funds," her mother said.

"The CHE?" Jana made a dismissive snort. "They're a political action group—from the *other side*. They're lying."

"Of course they're goddamn lying," Grandpa growled. "But that never matters, does it? Guilty until proven innocent in the court of public opinion."

"When's Dad coming home?"

"I don't know," Mom said with a tired sigh. "He may have to stay behind over Easter in Washington to take care of this."

Easter recess began at the end of the week. Dad never "stayed behind" during Easter recess or any extended break for the House. As in the Sacramento Capitol, the last couple of weeks before any recess were always packed with things screaming to be finished before the congressmen returned home, but when it was time to go, Dad was home for the holidays. All the Jaspers shared a deep attachment to the family and the ranch, and rarely did they spend the holidays anywhere else.

"Hey..." Tall and rumpled-looking in an open-collared button-down shirt and khaki pants, Jared strode through the double doors, shoving them closed behind him. In one smooth move, he slouched his athletic body in a leather recliner and steepled his hands in front of his nose—a sure sign of Jared's unhappiness.

He was a Jasper, there was no getting around that, but he was so undercover about it that few people realized he was one of *the* Jaspers. Remaining above suspicion was almost an obsession with him; he'd never wanted favoritism or to influence decisions that could affect his business. Jana had happily taken up the slack for her siblings, whose interests lay outside the family predilection for politics. "Jared, how the heck did you get mixed up in this?"

Grandpa shot her a sharp look.

Don't talk like a Girl Scout, he always told her, *or no one but the teacher's union and local church leaders will hear a thing you say.* "Okay, Jared, tell me what the *hell* you're doing in the middle of this shit?"

The curse words felt strange on her tongue, but Grandpa nodded, satisfied.

"They say the campaign contributions are from Delta Development," Jared said through his fingers.

Double D was a real estate development consulting firm specializing in securing public and private funding for projects across the entire central valley of California. It was easy to see the potential ugliness in the charge that Jared's business was secretly securing the support of a congressman who could influence legislation to benefit Double D's clients. A congressman who happened to be his father. "Come on," she groaned. "They have to know you wouldn't be that stupid."

"They say I contributed under a fictitious name. Donation laundering to hide the source."

Jana sat heavily in the chair opposite him. "Hell."

"Call it what it is, girl!" Grandpa yelled. He'd gone red, white and blue: white hair, his eyes vivid blue, his face red. It meant he was truly enraged, something that didn't happen very often. "No need to candy coat it. It's bullshit, plain and simple."

"Your pressure," Mom warned him.

He waved her away.

Jana pushed out of the chair and paced in front of the fireplace. "Let's take this step-by-step. The charges are blatantly false—that, we know. So, we've either got an overzealous action group looking for publicity, or it's a direct attack, someone who wants us to look bad."

"Like that loose cannon, Brace Bowie?" Jared asked. "Mr. Billboard."

"He was out to bring me down, not the family," she pointed out.

"We're a single entity to most people. The worse you look, the better he looks."

"And after you were so nice to him," Mom said. Her mother was as protective now as she was two-and-a-half decades ago when Jana was teased in school about not talking.

"I think it's too early to point fingers," Jana said. "Especially at Brace. We haven't heard anything from him since the city made him take down those signs. This isn't his style. Nasty billboards are his thing, not charges that could lead to prison, if Dad had been guilty."

Grandpa growled, "It doesn't matter who's behind it. Don't you see? Even after the kitchen is clean, this is going to stick around like the smell of rotten eggs. If this sways the election this fall...if Jana doesn't win..." Gripping the handles of the wheelchair, he hung his head.

Poor Grandpa. All his hopes and dreams were pinned on her.

Jana went to him. Kneeling, she rested her hand on his leg. "It's a long time between now and November, plenty of time to throw open all the windows and air out this stink. Now, tell me, you've been in this game a long time—tell me what to do to help get this kitchen smelling sweet again."

He grabbed her upper arm. "Stay clean. You say

you're the Girl Scout of politics? Be her, then. Nothing less than virgin snow in everything you do and say until this is over. You hear me, girl?"

The feelings that coursed through her now brought her back to her childhood when she didn't want to be the troublemaker, when she was the Jasper everyone worried about. When all she'd wanted was to be *normal*.

Grandpa wagged a finger at her. "No making headlines for anything but the bills you pass."

"I'll stay in, I swear. No dating. I'll be a nun." It fit nicely with her plan to take a break from dating, anyway.

"A nun?" Jared made an amused sound in his throat. "Don't you think that's a little above the call of duty? Don't set these kinds of examples of extreme celibacy or Mom's going to expect me to do the same."

"I'd never expect that from you, Jared," Mom said dryly.

As Jared gaped at his mother, who despite her angst had cracked a small smile, Jana assured her grandfather, "Just call me Miss Snow, Virgin Snow. I'll stay under the radar. I'll keep my nose clean."

And she would. The last thing she needed was more trouble, especially man trouble, if she was going to keep public opinion on the Jasper side—and the Jaspers out of jail.

AFTER DINNER, Jana left for her high-rise apartment downtown. She always had her room to use at the ranch, and she often did, but her cell phone was filled with text messages and voice mail, and she had a pile of paperwork to go through before the next day, not to mention preparing for an appearance with the first lady that included breakfast with a Brownie troop and judging their Save The Environment poster contest. Jana looked forward to a busy night. It would keep her mind from chewing on things she couldn't help or change.

Her grip on the steering wheel remained finger-throbbing tight as she motored past Evie's neighborhood on the way from the ranch to the highway. Roseville: a paragon of suburbia. The thought of taking refuge for the night in her sister's noisy, loving home almost made Jana swoon, but Evie wasn't home. The lucky girl was in Disneyland on vacation with her kids, John and Ellen. She'd picked a great time to be gone. But then Evie had always had a killer sense of timing.

Jana rolled into the parking lot of the Safeway supermarket in Evie's neighborhood. "Ice cream," she murmured. "Must have ice cream." Yes, Ben & Jerry's Phish Food…chocolate ice cream with gooey marshmallow, a caramel swirl and fudge fish. Not only would it give her the chocolate fix she needed to get through this, she'd be able to wreak symbolic vengeance on the sturgeon, one little chocolate fishie at a time.

She sat there, the motor running, her hands seemed glued to the steering wheel.

She thought of her normally lighthearted brother's battle-weary face, how wan her mother had looked, and Grandpa's rage when he should have been happily tending spring peas in the garden. They were good people. The best. They didn't deserve what was happening. A weird sobbing breath came out of her. She bit her lower lip. *No meltdowns, Jana.* No, they'd beat this thing. All it would take was an accounting of the books. No crime had been was committed. By next week it will have blown over.

Her part in all this was simple: keep a low profile, stay under the radar and stay out of trouble. Be *normal.* Now, how hard could that be? *Chin up.*

Jana killed the engine. She opened the car door and let the cool night air rush in. Fog would form before long, but for now the moon was visible. Big and creamy yellow-white, it peeked over the roof of the supermarket. How long had it been since she'd gazed at the moon. *Too long,* she thought with a strange, poignant longing. The conversation she had with her grandfather about looking for magic had brought back memories of another time. Another Jana.

A long-ago summer evening when everything seemed possible.

There's magic in the air tonight.

A soft laugh escaped her. If only there *were* magic in the air. She could use some to speed along the investigation into her father's campaign finances.

Pulling her suit jacket around her, Jana took off across the parking lot. The March evening had turned damp and chilly. It was a night to be wearing jeans and a cashmere sweater, not a wrinkled, water-stained butter-yellow suit and low-cut silk print blouse that had seemed so appropriate for a sunny morning's appearance at a fish farm.

Jana aimed for the frozen food aisle. Number five. She knew it by heart, having made this stop routinely.

A towering, military action figure stood stock-still in front of a display of Easter candy. Clad in dark green and black body armor and a helmet with a gold-toned visor, the figure looked like a character out of her nephew John's futuristic Halo2 Xbox game. And it was at least seven-feet tall in thick-soled Buzz Lightyear boots. She was no marketing guru, but why on earth put something like that next to the chocolate bunnies, plastic grass and Peeps?

The soldier must have cost big bucks to make, though. She admired the wealth of detail put into the construction as she sidestepped around the figure. A slight movement of his head made her jump back.

"Omigosh, you're real!" Her hand went to her heart. "I thought you were a giant action figure." In a way, he was. The boots added six or more inches, but even without them, he'd be above average in height. The armor hugged his body and emphasized broad shoulders, narrow hips and strong legs. *Nice,* she thought. But he was blocking the path to heaven, aka aisle five and ice cream. "Excuse me." She stepped around him.

"I've come a long way to find you," he said. His voice was deep, mellowed by a slight accent she didn't recognize.

She smiled. "Let me guess—from a galaxy far, far away?"

"No, this one."

She laughed and tried again to squeeze past him.

"Jana. Wait."

She stopped in her tracks, lifting her gaze seven long stories to where his face would be if his visor wasn't hiding it. "Do I know you?"

He raised his visor. Short brown hair framed a handsome, hard-featured face: cut cheekbones, a strong nose and a classic cleft chin that needed a shave. His mouth was the only friendly thing on his face. Actually, he had a great mouth. It was easy to imagine his lips curving into a smile, something he clearly was not willing to do while stuck with display duty in Safeway on a Tuesday night. For a guy decked out in such an outrageous outfit, he appeared awfully serious.

She turned to go for the third time.

"Jana."

She sighed.

"Do you not remember me?"

She turned around. "No. Sorry."

"I had hoped you would…but it has been a very long time."

She watched his lips form the words. Something about that mouth, his face, did tug at her memory. Had she seen him before? Where? A fund-raiser? If he was an actor, maybe it was at the B Street Theater downtown.

He watched her puzzle out how they knew each other, and seemed pleased by it somehow. "Do you remember now, Jana?" His eyes were intense, piercing green. It made her heart skip a few beats in response. She'd heard the expression wearing your heart on your sleeve many times, but this man wore his heart in his eyes.

No! She'd made a promise to her grandfather. It meant no flirting with strange men dressed like alien commandos in supermarkets. No flirting with men period. She needed to be good. To stay out of trouble. "No, I don't remember you. I'm really sorry. Usually I'm good with faces, but I'm tired tonight. I've had a heck of—no, a *helluva* day. Nice seeing you again, though."

With a cheery wave, she left as quickly as she could and aimed for aisle five. Dinners…snacks…bingo! She paced in front of the ice-cream freezer, looking for her target. But reflected in the glass doors, she saw something loom over her, looking at her as if *she* were the target.

Startled, she spun around. It was the Halo2 guy, looking so adorably abandoned and earnest that she nearly lunged at that delicious mouth of his with the intent of kissing it into a smile. The fantasy was so sudden, so vivid and overpowering, that she likened it to the sturgeon at the fish farm and how they'd reacted to her toenail polish. There was only one way to prove she was higher on the evolutionary ladder than they were, and that was by ignoring her primitive sexual impulses.

"Hi, again." She grabbed a container of Phish Food. "Bye," she said and let the door fall closed.

Heels clicking on the linoleum, she left the man far behind. Probably she should pick up some milk while she was here. At home, she was all out. She snagged a bunch of ripe bananas on her way past a display and headed for dairy. Her arms were filling up with impulse purchases. She always did this. Soon she'd need a cart.

She turned up aisle nine. At the end stood the man in interstellar body armor. About-face. She spun on her heel and chose the next aisle over. It had been a horrible day. The last thing she needed was to be stalked by a store model, even one this arrestingly handsome. Or was it arrestingly familiar? Arrestingly something. Whatever it was, it was exactly what she didn't need right now.

But halfway to the milk, the muscled Halo2 hunk caught up to her. She didn't care how arresting he was;

if he kept this up he was going to get himself arrested. "Listen, I'm in a hurry. I—"

"Jana."

The way he said her name reverberated to her toes. Her coral-painted toes. The ones the sturgeon liked. The ones that put her into heat over strange armored men in supermarkets. *Note to self: never wear coral nail polish again—not out in public, anyway.*

"We met as children," he said.

"We did?" She searched her memory and came up with nothing.

His body armor creaked as he took another step closer. "I never forgot you. It was why I had to come back for you."

He sounded so genuine, too. Too bad it was all an act. But when she looked into his eyes, really looked deep and hard, her heart gave a little hitch. *Magic.*

No! No magic! Anything but that. She gave her head a hard shake. "Sorry, I have to—"

"Jana, you must listen. Earth is under threat from space. There is time to prepare, but no time to waste. You must take me to your leader."

"Very convincing, but I have to get going. I have to work tomorrow. Early. An appearance with my *leader's* wife leads the day, as a matter of fact." And Jana would bet Mary Ann Schwarzkopf was at home relaxing, not being chased through a grocery store by a guy dressed in interstellar body armor.

"Please, your world is scheduled for acquisition. I came here to inform you of this news at great risk. A risk I have gladly taken for you, Jana." Emotion seethed in his eyes. "Come, we must talk—but not here."

The more he said, the crazier he sounded—and looked—and she was getting a little scared. Forget the milk. She'd drink her coffee black for breakfast.

She made a beeline for the front of the store and the safety of the checkout line.

"What's the Halo2 promotion for?" she asked the cashier as she swiped her ATM card through the reader.

The woman shrugged as she bagged the items. "They don't tell me anything."

Jana was about to say that the man was a bit of a stalker, and a little too into the role-playing for his own good, but she'd hate to see him get in trouble if this was something he needed to do for the money.

Jana worked hard, maybe to the sacrifice of what was commonly known as a life, but she worked out of a passion to serve, not for the money. Fortune had been kind to the Jaspers, and because of that, she felt she owed something back to society. Her circumstances were fortunate, yes, yet she never forgot that others didn't have it as easy as she did.

Maybe she was making too big of a deal out of this. Stress had probably magnified the situation. He was a guy in costume, someone she'd met and didn't remember, and he wanted to flirt. That's all. On any other night, she'd have probably flirted back.

Jana grabbed the groceries and walked out into the night air. Fog had covered more of the sky. The visibility would go down soon. She wanted to get home before it did. Fog in the winter was part of living in Sacramento, but she wasn't any good driving in it. She picked up her pace. Out in the open space bordering the parking lot, an owl hooted. Where suburbia met the wild. People paid good money to live here and hear owls and coyotes along with lawn mowers and leaf blowers. She paid good money to live in the city, too, but all she heard were police sirens and car alarms.

Heavy footfalls crunched behind her. Body armor rustled. The action figure had followed her outside.

Darn it. No—*damn it.*

She threw a nervous glance around the parking lot. *Be calm. Be aware of your surroundings.* One checker helped a couple load groceries in their trunk, but they were several rows away across the lot. If she screamed, they'd hear her. Probably.

She rummaged through her purse for her mini canister of pepper spray disguised as a key chain as she calculated how hard it would be to swing the bag of groceries and knock him out. Pretty hard, seeing that her bag was filled with bananas and a melting container of Ben & Jerry's Phish Food that she was dying to eat and couldn't because of this crazed hunk in the Halo2 body armor who wouldn't leave her alone.

"Jana…wait."

She wanted to scream. To scream at the top of her lungs until all the frustration had emptied out of her and she was left a quivering but satisfyingly empty blob on the ground.

However, lacking the freedom to scream herself into a coma, all the emotion of the day threatened to explode as she turned on him. Only with a monumental effort did she keep her temper under control. "Look, I've had a very, very bad day. You have no idea how bad. Please don't follow me anymore. I'm not interested in flying saucers and spacemen and alien invasions…"

She let her voice trail off as a couple walked past and gave them both a strange look. Jana wanted to sink into the pavement and disappear. Wasn't she supposed to be keeping a low profile? It was really hard when a guy who was almost seven feet tall in his platform combat boots kept following you around ranting about alien invasions.

She backed up. "I'm going now, and you're going to stay here." She opened her cell phone. "Or I'll call 911." Her thumb hovered threateningly over the 9.

He lifted his arms to the sides, entreating her, palms up. "Please. Squee…it's me."

Jana's breath caught in her throat, and her eyes widened. What did he say?

Squee. She hadn't heard that word since…since she was nine years old. Only one person had said that word, ever. Only one.

"Now you remember, Jana. Finally." His voice sounded huskier, almost tender. "I can see it in your eyes."

He stood there, watching her reaction, an armor-clad hulk with a short military haircut, a square chin and vulnerable eyes—vulnerable *green* eyes.

Peter. Her wild, exotic, magical boy. *I wished for you to come back. I wished.*

No magic. "No!" She blinked out of the trance. "You're not him."

There were a few heartbeats of silence. Then he said, "Yes, I am."

CHAPTER THREE

JANA'S HEAD SPUN as if she'd been drinking. She might as well have been, with this grown man standing in front of her in the parking lot of Safeway insisting that he was her childhood imaginary friend, reincarnated. Or re-in-*something.* She narrowed her eyes and, using a mental version of the age progression used in the photos on the backs of milk cartons, tried to imagine Peter—and came up with a man who looked frighteningly close to this one.

"You're imaginary." She backed up, shaking her head. "You're not real."

His voice deepened another notch. "Is it not a good thing that I am in fact real?"

Jana stuttered at the sexy glint in his eyes. For a brief, sharp instant of panic, she was brought back to the days when she couldn't get out the words. "Are you really Peter?"

"Peter?"

No, of course he wouldn't know that name. She'd given it to him. But she'd ask some questions only Peter would know. "Where were you when I first saw you?"

He stepped forward. She stepped back. "Is this a test?" he asked.

"Of course it's a test. Answer the question, or we're done. Where did I first see you?"

"I was hanging from a branch in a tree outside your dwelling. You freed me."

Another wave of dizziness came over her. She looked in his eyes, hoping one last time to see a stranger. She didn't. She saw Peter. Adulthood had gifted him with a great mouth, just the way she liked them: wide with a friendly tilt at each end, with lips thin enough to be masculine, and luscious enough for long, deep, curl-your-toes kisses. That was, if he knew how to use that mouth. *Don't go there, Jana, not now.*

He stepped forward, and again she stepped back. "If you're an alien, where did you put your spaceship?"

"At the site of my original landing at your habitat."

"You mean at the ranch? You left your spaceship *at the ranch?*" It was the very last thing her family needed now. In her mind, the headlines roared: Jaspers Summon Aliens For Secret Meetings. Public Trust Erodes Further.

"Yes. I hid it using invisibility technology. Just as my science vessel was hidden many circuits ago— many *years* ago, rather—when I first visited your world with my father. But I landed under attack. My pursuer found my ship and nearly vaporized it. But I got him back. I don't think he'll be flying his ship any time soon, either."

"You're stranded here?" *Don't yell, Jana. Use your quiet voice.*

"Until I can figure out another way home, yes."

Suddenly, the world exploded into blinding white light.

The man-who-would-be-Peter grabbed her, pushing her out of the way as something whizzed by her jaw with a breathy shriek.

The next thing she knew, she was lying on the asphalt with Peter's heavy body crushing her. "Assassin," he hissed in her ear.

His hot breath made her shiver. "Get off—"

He pressed his glove over her mouth. "He'll hear you. And then he'll kill you."

Kill? Assassin? The odor of hot metal and burning rubber seeped into her rattled mind. Her vision cleared. Silvery dots littered the ground like mercury. But it wasn't mercury; the drops were cooling off too fast, solidifying. It was molten metal.

She followed the trail of silver to the door of the car next to her—a late-model SUV. The front looked normal, the rear looked normal, but a jagged, smoking line ran from top to bottom down the center. Something popped. Then, with a horrible creaking, cracking sound, the two halves of the car collapsed outward and smashed to the pavement.

Real terror, sharp and cold, shot through her. The car had been sliced clean through. What kind of weapon cut through a car like a hot knife through butter?

Another burst of light ripped apart the pavement, only inches from where they hid. Chunks of gooey asphalt flew into the air. The bitter smell burned her nose and eyes. Halo2, aka Peter, twisted around and returned fire. People screamed from somewhere farther away in the parking lot.

Jana shook from fear—of getting hurt or killed, definitely; but running a close second was the fear of seeing the headlines in the newspaper in the morning: Jasper Taken Hostage—Was It Staged To Deflect Public Scrutiny From The Ongoing Investigation? She moaned. There were times when the best publicity was no publicity, and this was one of them.

Halo2 hauled her off her feet. "Keep your head down!"

He dragged her with him down the row of cars. Somehow she held on to her shopping bag and purse. His gloved hand pushed on the back of her head every time she tried to take a look around. Another flash of light, and the air snapped with static. He threw open a car door and shoved her behind the wheel. "Get in!" he ordered.

"This isn't my car—"

"In!"

"I don't have keys!" she screamed back at him.

He thrust out his left arm. Around his wrist was a very expensive-looking piece of tech, fitted to his arm like a gauntlet. Riddled with tiny lights, it was labeled with letters in a language she didn't recognize. He aimed the thing at the ignition and the car started.

Holy crap, she thought. *How did he do that?*

He fell into the passenger seat and pulled the gold visor over his face. "Drive."

"This is stealing."

"Drive!"

Another burst of light arced terrifyingly close. She jammed her foot on the accelerator and they were off. With a squeal of tires, they roared out of the Safeway parking lot.

"Who's shooting at us?" she demanded.

"A REEF. He's a bioengineered, computer-enhanced

soldier developed to be an assassin from birth. Part man, part robot."

Like the Terminator. Jana's mind whirled in disbelief. She was behind the wheel of a stolen vehicle, fleeing a robotic killer with an alien. This was *not* the way to keep a low profile.

She kept one hand on the steering wheel and moved her other to the door handle as she calculated the speed and weighed it against how much it would hurt if she jumped out now. She'd run back to her car, head home. A few bandages and a good night's sleep later and she'd be ready for her breakfast with the first lady and the Brownie troop.

"Both hands on the wheel! We're in line of sight and he's got a plasma rifle. One mistake and we're powdered DNA!"

Jana grimaced. "You don't have to yell!"

He softened his tone a little. "My name is Cavin, by the way. Cavin of Far Star. I never told you that."

"Apparently there are a lot of things you never told me." He looked too human to be believable as an alien, but here they were in the midst of a firefight with a robot-assassin who could slice cars in half, and not only was Peter's—uh, Cavin's—clothing nothing she'd ever seen outside one of her nephew's video games, with a flick of his wrist, he was able to start and steal whatever vehicle he wanted.

"Ah!" Jana flinched at the screech of brakes and a blaring horn. She'd run a red light. She, who'd gotten only one ticket her entire life—and that was for going two minutes overtime at a parking meter.

"This way." Cavin jerked the wheel to the right and

pointed her down a side street lined with neat rows of upscale homes. They were less than three blocks from Evie's house. She could walk there. She could borrow Evie's Honda and still make it home before midnight. She let up on the accelerator.

"Faster." He turned the rearview mirror to better see it. "He's got us in his sights."

A man walking his dog stared at them as they flew by. "We're going to hit someone!" She took her foot off the accelerator.

Cavin slid his leg over as if to cram his heavy boot on the gas. His foot hovered menacingly. "Either you do it, or I do it."

Jana shoved his leg away. "I'll do it." At least she'd be able to maintain some sense of control. But the SUV sputtered and slowed. A chime dragged her attention to the dash. The low fuel light was on. Hooray! It was the best luck she'd had all day. "It's out of gas."

"Out," Cavin said.

"Yes. Completely out." She laughed maniacally. God bless busy parents who pushed filling up to the last minute.

"No, *out*." He leaned over her lap and shoved open the door. "He's coming. We've got to get out now and run."

"Where?" She turned around. The street was dark and empty. "I don't see him."

Cavin thrust the wrist gauntlet at her. A tiny map showed a red X. It slid with menace toward a white square. "Tell me we're not the square," she said.

"I wish I could." He pushed her, and she stumbled into the street. She grabbed for her purse and the bag of groceries. The smell of bananas was strong, telling her that they'd gotten crushed. But she didn't dare leave the groceries behind and turn them into evidence that could link her to this fiasco. "What about fingerprints? Mine are in the database and—"

"I wiped the car clean. No trace of DNA is left."

God bless technology. Cavin grabbed her by the hand and pulled her down the center of the street. By now, all the dogs on the block were barking. A few porch lights were on that weren't on before. Where could she run and hide where no one would see her? A ski mask would have come in handy. In the future, she'd have to remember to keep one in her purse.

The heel of her left pump broke off. "Piece of shit." Oh, Grandpa would have been proud of the deterioration in her language. She hopped along and threw off the other shoe. It clanged against a mailbox. In about two seconds, her panty hose were trashed. Pebbles pierced her heels. "Ow, ow." She dropped the bananas, thought about backtracking to retrieve them and nixed the idea. She still had the shopping bag and the all-important receipt with her identity attached. Space invaders or not, she didn't want to be linked to this mayhem in any shape, any form.

She was still within walking distance of Evie's house. The plan to commandeer the Honda would still work. She'd be home by midnight. "I have a plan," she gasped.

"What's that?"

"You go on ahead. Run where you need to. Lose the assassin, and I'll hide." She tried to wriggle her hand from Cavin's strong grip.

"No, Jana." Cavin grabbed her wrists and pulled her close. Shadows fell across his face, illuminating the urgency there. His expression was masculine, take-charge. He was adorable, but there was nothing "pretty-boy" about him. With a swell of longing, she realized he was everything she'd been looking for in a man, and couldn't find.

Miss Snow...Miss Virgin Snow. She squeezed her eyes shut, the visual equivalent of holding her hands over her ears and singing, "Lah lah lah."

"I didn't know about the assassin, Jana. I'm sorry for that. I thought whoever had pursued me had died in the crash, and never did I assume it was a REEF. Mistakes, all. But if you take off alone, there's no guarantee the REEF will follow me and not you. At least with me you have a chance. Trust me, Squee." Again, the pet name made her heart twist. "Like the night you let me take you into the air. We flew."

"We crashed. Together we were too heavy."

He looked to the sky and shook his head. "Gods, all these years I remember the flying. She remembers the crashing. What about afterward when we watched the moon rise over the water? We didn't know a word of each other's language, but it didn't matter. We didn't feel the need for speech. Do you remember that?"

"Yes," she said in a smaller voice.

Apparently satisfied by her answer, Cavin tugged her along again, but this time at a reasonable jog. She half limped, half ran to keep up with him. Gasping to catch her breath, she shoved damp strands of hair off her forehead. All of it had spilled out of the chignon she'd anchored with two cloisonné picks, and who knew where those had gone. Her suit was stained and smelled like bananas, and her panty hose hung in shreds. "What are you?" she asked. "The truth."

"I'm a man."

"Yes, I got that part." Loud and clear, too. "*Who* are you, besides an alien?"

"I'm a soldier in the Coalition Space Force. I enlisted too young to become a pilot and then when I was finally old enough, I realized I liked what I was doing more. A ground fighter—a 'grunt' as it is known here on Earth. Staying alive, keeping my friends alive…I wasn't looking for glory."

His hair was cropped short now, a military cut, but still as shiny as she'd remembered. She wondered what they'd said to him at training camp when he'd showed up with his long braided locks. "What's the Coalition? Your planet?"

"No, the Coalition controls thousands of worlds. Including Earth."

Jana bristled. "Earth still controls Earth."

"Not for long." Cavin aimed his wrist gauntlet at a brand-new silver Lexus sedan parked in a driveway. "The Coalition parliament and the queen have approved your world for acquisition."

"They what?"

Bip, bip went the sound of a car alarm being disarmed. Lights came on inside the Lexus.

"Hey, what are you doing? Cavin, no—"

"Get in."

She folded her arms over her ruined suit. "Make me."

He scooped her up into his arms and dropped her into the driver's seat, leaning over her to buckle her seat belt. His mouth and those mesmerizing lips were very close to hers. "Drive, or die at the hands of the most feared assassin in the galaxy."

"You argue very convincingly," she said, a little breathless.

"This isn't an argument." His voice was thick, telling her he felt the heat between them, too. "It's an order."

"Hey!" Someone shouted from an upstairs window. "Get out of my car!"

Jana's stomach dropped. The man aimed his cell phone at her to take a picture. She ducked down before he could get a clear shot. Drive away or run? Quickly she weighed the risk of having to explain her role in all this versus the still-viable chance of getting through this at the end, alive and undiscovered. "Get in, Cavin."

He landed in the passenger seat. The car started as the doors slammed, encasing them in leather-soft, luxury-car silence. Cavin had no leg room. His knees were crammed against the dash, halfway to the ceiling.

"He took a picture of you," she said frantically.

"He thinks he did. My armor's AI saw the camera and blurred the return image. The suit is capable of enhanced invisibility, as well. How do you think I followed you to the market without being seen?"

"I haven't had time to think about it. It's been a little busy. But now that you bring it up, how did you get from the ranch to the store—fly?"

"Only to the nearest road. I hitchhiked on a series of cars and then a truck. Hung on for the ride."

"Omigod."

"They never knew I was aboard."

"Unlike me," she muttered. She left streaks of rubber on the driveway as she backed up, tires spinning. The car careened down the block, leaving a trail of bedroom and porch lights coming on behind them.

CHAPTER FOUR

THE SAFEWAY BAG SLID across the backseat of the Lexus and thumped into the door. The smell of chocolate mixed with that of factory-new leather. So much for eating the Phish Food. "Where's the assassin?"

Cavin checked his gauntlet. "Gods, he's—" A ball of lightning ripped past her window. The air smelled as if it was on fire.

Jana screamed. "What the hell was that?"

"Plasma mortars."

"Rifles? Grenades? The guy's a traveling arsenal."

"Accelerate!"

The urgency in his voice was enough motivation to obey without argument. If Jana slid any lower in the driver's seat, she wouldn't be able to see over the dashboard. "How did he sneak up on us like that?"

"My wrist gauntlet shows the pursuit. Unfortunately, it also helps the assassin hone in on us. I can switch it on long enough to take a peek then I have to turn it off. Until just now, it was off."

Great, just great. All that advanced technology and he couldn't use it. "Why's this guy after you? Because you came here?"

"Someone hired him. Someone driven by arrogance, and ignorance, and fear."

Okay. He did not sound happy. There was more going on here than she knew. But nothing she had time to worry about now. Her plate was full enough keeping the car moving at top speed without killing any innocents.

"My visit to Earth has nothing to do with the REEF's attempts to kill me, but it does complicate things."

Jana rolled her eyes. "Ya think?"

She raced through the surface streets and merged onto the highway, headed west. She didn't know where she was going, only that she wanted to get there fast.

The fog was thickening. Cars traveled slowly. She wanted to drive even slower than they were, but she remembered the threat of Cavin's boot over the accelerator. Jana drove as fast as she could stand it until the visibility became so poor that she could see no more than a couple of car lengths ahead. She lifted her bare foot off the gas pedal.

"Don't slow down," Cavin ordered.

"I can't see."

"I can."

"How can you see?"

He tapped on his visor, which he'd pulled over his eyes. "With this I can see for miles ahead. Fog, darkness, no problem."

"No problem," she muttered, imitating him. "How do you speak English so well if you're an alien?"

"A universal translator brain implant."

"You have something lodged in your head?"

"Yes. I have several bioengineered, enhanced features throughout my body. All soldiers do."

"Enhancements, huh." Jana's mind went wild with possibilities as she ran her gaze from his head down to his big...thick...hard...platform boots. Then she forced her attention back to the road. "But how did you get access to the language?" She was a self-avowed intellectual geek; she loved asking questions to satisfy her curiosity. But now she asked as much to cling to sanity as to learn. Lose her anchor to reality, and she feared she'd dissolve into a useless, trembling puddle. "Do you know other languages, too?"

"Not *know*. Ability to access is a better description. Most of Earth's dialects are available via my translator. Not all, because unfortunately, we were limited to those dialects we could harvest from the communications signals leaving the planet. Your TV, music and radio radiate out into space—think of a pebble dropped in a still pond. The Coalition captured the ripples."

Again, intellectual fascination battled with a primal fear of something far more powerful than anything on Earth. "Say something in your language."

He spoke a few words that reminded her of her mother's Russian. It was a blessedly normal-sounding language, devoid of weird buzzing noises and the insect-like clicking sounds one would expect from an alien language, if one actually spent the time to ponder alien languages. She knew she never had. Until Cavin, Jana assumed the concept of aliens visiting Earth was the invention of really bored people with low-quality cameras living in remote parts of New Mexico and Nevada.

"It is the official language of the Coalition," he said. "The queen's tongue."

It seemed very Buck Rogers to actually have a queen of the galaxy. "What's she like?"

"Queen Keira? I saw her only once, at a distance

during her coronation. She was very young. She's a grown woman now, and said to be quite beautiful, but somehow she's resisted taking a consort. She almost killed a man who tried to take her by force."

You go, girl. "Almost killed? Why didn't she finish the job?"

"Once she had sliced off his male parts with her plasma sword, I suppose she felt that killing him at that point would have been considered an act of mercy. He lives on as a palace eunuch as a reminder for those suitors who would attempt to force themselves on the queen."

Man trouble. Jana felt a certain kinship with the young queen. She wondered if Brace Bowie could benefit from similar treatment. "What did you say, by the way, when you spoke in your language?"

"Concentrate on your driving."

She made a face at him and focused on the road ahead. Suddenly, the visibility shrank to fifty feet or less. Ahead was a solid, white blanket of fog. A bare minimum of reflector bumps kept her centered in the lane. "I can't see. Help me out here." Her foot came off the gas.

"No! Do not slow. Go...go right. *Right.*"

She swerved into the right lane—and moaned as they narrowly missed a late-model Volkswagen.

"Left!"

She veered left. Another car swept past in the fog. Focus on the reflector lights. Stay between the lines. She saw no more than a few car lengths ahead, and she must be going sixty or seventy, at least. *Concentrate. Stay between the lines.* Jana wanted to barf from nerves. All that held her back was the thought of soiling someone else's car.

"Foot off the fuel pedal slightly," Cavin said. "Now…right turn."

She did as he said.

"Accelerate."

As Cavin calmly issued directions, the Lexus wove in and out of the slower cars, making them look as if they were standing still. By now, they were almost to downtown Sacramento. The fog was even thicker here. She was driving almost completely blind. On the plus side, if she couldn't see anyone then no one could see her. Except the assassin.

To calm herself, she counted backward from ten, found it too complicated and stopped. *Stay under the radar, keep a low profile*. Only hours ago she'd promised her grandfather exactly that. "Snow," she whispered. "Virgin snow."

"Snow?" Cavin peered outside into the fog. "It is forty-six-point-two of your degrees outside. That is too warm for the precipitation to freeze."

Jana decided against an explanation. It was all she could do to concentrate on staying in her lane and pray this nightmare came to an end soon. "Where's the assassin now?"

"He lost us, it seems."

Jana shot him an outraged look. "Why didn't you say so?"

"Because your local law enforcement vehicles have been redoubling their efforts to catch us."

Her heart tumbled. "What?"

"Left—now!" Cavin shouted.

She swerved into the left lane, but not before she almost clipped a police car. By the time she managed a small scream, the police car's flashing lights had disappeared in the fog.

"Cavin, we almost hit a police car!" An image of its two occupants' startled faces burned in her mind.

"Exit here."

"Why?" Jana asked even as she obeyed his order.

"The police have formed a roadblock ahead. They've an array of weapons aimed at us. And they've thrown spikes in the road that will tear apart these tires and cripple the vehicle."

Jana's stomach ached. Her head throbbed, and her throat was dry. "But the police will recognize this car. If the fog clears, we're done." And she'd get to explain it all during the arrest. Yet, even if she could talk her way out of any blame, how could she leave Cavin to take the fall? She couldn't. He was Peter, first of all, and they shared some sort of bizarre bond that was as powerful now as it was decades ago. He looked too human for anyone to believe he was an alien, and the gee-whiz tech he had on him would only get the military involved, the FBI, CIA, DIA, DHS, too, and every other acronym-laden organization in existence. By morning, he'd be on his way to an undisclosed mental facility, where he'd "disappear" and she'd be on her way to the front page of the *Sacramento Sun*. The headline scrolled across the back of her eyes: Can We Trust Them? Jaspers Continue Downhill Slide. She grimaced.

"Here, Jana—stop!"

She fishtailed to a stop at the bottom of the entry ramp.

Several old cars were parked along a gritty street.

Across the road was a bar with no name and a neon sign that said Cocktails. Fog drifted in cottony strands, muting the letters. "That one," he said, pointing to an old Chevy decked out in green and purple iridescent paint.

Jana eyed their new target dispassionately. Her lack of upset over stealing another car was a testament to how shell-shocked she was.

Before abandoning the Lexus, she grabbed her purse and the sticky grocery bag. At the bottom of a puddle of thick melted ice cream and the little chocolate fish she'd never get to eat but no longer had the appetite for, she found the receipt and shoved it in her purse. Now the only evidence left behind would be a squishy Safeway bag and a container of Phish Food.

Cavin took her hand and they ran across the street. The pavement was cold, and her feet were freezing. A flick of his wrist and the Chevy's door locks popped up. Jana slid behind a steering wheel molded to look like a thick, linked chain. The interior smelled like cigarettes. A statue of Mary sat on a square of red velvet on the dash. *Save me.* Jana crossed herself as Cavin started the motor. The Chevy roared to life with a deep rumbling that echoed down the quiet street. In seconds, shouting patrons swarmed out of the bar like angry bees.

All Jana saw was a blur of tattoos and black leather before she jammed her foot to the gas pedal so fast that Cavin had to grab hold of the dash to keep his balance. Up the entry ramp she raced, and onto the highway headed back to where they'd started.

"Left," Cavin directed. As she veered onto the far left lane to go around a slower car, Jana thought of the

Safeway near Evie's house. Her Jeep waited for her there. Her little brown Jeep. The memory spurred a yearning so sharp that she almost burst into tears. But she needed to keep her wits about her. No crying. No falling apart. She was a respected politician, a state senator.

A state senator who had stolen three cars in one night.

Two involuntarily. One eagerly.

Heaven help her.

"No making headlines for anything but the bills you pass."

Jana winced at the promises she'd given her grandfather. If this ended badly, how could she face him tomorrow? Or her father and brother for that matter?

She felt Cavin's gaze on her. "You're thinking," he said.

"About my family. About my father fighting charges that he misreported the funds used to finance an election campaign. A lie, Cavin, a horrible lie. And I'm supposed to be helping by staying out of trouble. How am I doing, huh?"

He acted unhappy at the news. "I've seen your entire record of public accomplishments. You have achieved much. I am not surprised at all."

"How do you know so much about me? My real name, my job?"

"The Coalition has collected data on Earth's leadership. We know the identity of all leaders, and where to find them."

The back of her neck prickled. "Even a state senator? A minor player in the grand scheme of things?"

"From tribal leaders to kings."

Something told Jana the information wasn't being

gathered to put together a guest list for a tea party. The whole thing was starting to sound too much like *War of the Worlds*. Obviously, plans had been a long time in the making.

Maybe as long as *twenty-three* years ago. "You said your father was a scientist, that he brought you to Earth. What was he studying that he had to come all the way here?"

Cavin shifted in the seat. "His job was to investigate the suitability of your world for Coalition use," he said a little awkwardly.

"Use," she sneered. "Call it what it is—an invasion!"

"For what it's worth, that's the same thing I told my father."

"How could you keep it from me? We played, we laughed together, and all the time you knew your people planned to invade Earth. Why did you let me believe you were magic?"

"Because I didn't know a word of your language, Jana, and you didn't know a word of mine. Why do you think I called you Squee?"

The soft and special way he said the word gave her a heart sensation she hadn't felt since she was nine. "Where was your mother? Why didn't she come?"

"She was dead."

"Oh." Jana slid lower in the seat. "I'm sorry."

"I don't remember her. My father felt her absence more than I ever did. He buried himself in his work to compensate for her loss. I grew up independent, perhaps a little wild. I hated being cooped up so much on the long voyages that when we finally arrived at the next planet I'd stay outside as much as the conditions would allow. Then we came to one world populated by humans, and I saw an alien girl. She fascinated me."

"Why?" she almost whispered.

"Because she was so full of life. She was so silent most of the time, then, when no one was around, she'd laugh. Laugh and dance." He rotated his index finger. "Spinning around on her toes."

Jana remembered that girl, too. She'd been gone a long time. With an unexpected sense of loss, she didn't realize how much she'd missed her.

"I watched you for days while my father worked. One night I decided to fly up to the porthole of your dwelling to see where you went at night. I swooped in too low, tried to fly out of my error and got tangled in the tree."

And the rest was history.

"I called you Peter," she confessed. "After Peter Pan. He was a character in a children's story. A magical boy who flew and never grew old."

"I grew old."

"Not to me. I look at you and I see Peter. I see someone I never forgot."

"Never?" His mouth seemed to want to form a grin that he wouldn't allow. The result was a boyishly charming half smirk. "That didn't seem to be the case in the market, Jana. You ran from me."

"You expected me to remember you on the spot after twenty-three years?"

"Yes."

"And if I'd walked onto your spaceship, no notice, and said I needed to talk to you, you would have remembered me?"

"Yes," he said with conviction.

Jana gave a little huff of disbelief.

"It is true. You grew up to be more beautiful than I could have imagined, but when I look at you, I still see the same girl that took my heart. You were beautiful then, and even more so now as a woman."

A flush of heat burned her cheeks. "Thank you," she whispered. Other men had called her beautiful, but their words hadn't affected her this way.

"Believe me, Jana, when I say I didn't fully understand my father's line of work back then. The mission to your world was the turning point."

"Yet it didn't turn you into a pacifist. You grew up to be a soldier."

"I came to see the reasons behind the Coalition's methods, even if I didn't agree with them all. The Drakken would change your mind, too."

"They're the bad guys, I take it."

"Far worse than anything you have here on Earth."

"I don't know about that. We have some pretty evil characters on this rock."

"Take them and what they do to the *nth* degree, and you have the Drakken."

Jana was glad fog covered the stars tonight, so she couldn't see them. She couldn't help thinking of all the evenings she forgot to look at the stars because she was too busy, rushing here, rushing there. Tonight had changed that forever. Not only was there other life out there, other *human* life, there were battles and governments and decisions being made on a vast scale where Earth was nothing but an insignificant speck. Less than a lowly pawn in a chess game. She'd never look up in the sky and see the stars the same way again. She wasn't sure if she ever wanted to look at the stars again. "Cavin, how is Earth going to keep the Drakken away? We can't even keep the REEF away."

"It's the Coalition I have come to warn you about. The Drakken aren't a threat here."

"The Coalition? But the Coalition are *your* people."

"Yes."

She glanced sideways at him, but he'd blanked his face of emotion. "But doesn't—doesn't that...?"

"Doesn't that make me a traitor? Believing Earth deserves the chance to defend itself? That the loss of use of one planet won't make or break the Coalition? Yes, I suppose it does make me a traitor to have such unconventional views. I don't intend for the Coalition to find out, however. Treason is a capital crime. I'd be executed, and not mercifully, either."

"Cavin..."

"If the REEF doesn't get to me first."

"*Cavin!*" She took a few deep breaths to calm down. He risked his life to save hers, and everyone else on Earth. And now he expected her to be the one to sound the alarm. The sensation of being swept out to sea in advance of an approaching tsunami consumed her. "All we have to do is talk. Mediate a compromise. Explain to the Coalition that we live here, and—"

"They won't care."

"The United Nations will get involved. It's not a lost cause. Sides farther apart have reached agreement through diplomacy. We don't have to go to war."

"Earth can't go to war. You don't know how to fight the Coalition. You'll lose." His voice took on an edge.

"Jana, I'd talk to my government personally if I thought negotiation would do any good."

"No!" Engaging in direct communication with his people would end any question of him being seen as a traitor at home. It would confirm it. They'd know he was here and what he'd done. "You're here to help us help ourselves, not to earn a death sentence. I won't risk you being executed. I won't." She couldn't bear the thought of Cavin being put to death. She'd never be able to live with it. "If we can't fight them off, or talk our way out of this, what does that leave?"

"Bring me to Groom Lake in Nevada. An inert Coalition spacecraft is hidden there. I have a plan. It requires activating the ship to deter the invasion force. Powering up a spacecraft generates a single signal that Coalition sensors can detect. But if I take that signal and multiply it by a hundred, I can make it appear as if Earth possesses its own space fleet."

"You want to find the Roswell saucer and hack into it."

"That's one way to describe it. Unlike modern craft, it has no safeguards. I will hack in to the shipboard computer. I have the codes." He tapped his head. "Memorized."

Her laugh sounded more than a little bit manic. "That's urban legend. A rumor. There's no flying saucer hidden there, or anywhere."

"Correct. It is a scout vessel."

"Oh, a scout vessel, that explains it." She wiped sweat off her forehead. He wanted her to get him inside the most guarded and secret military base there was so he could hot-wire a spacecraft that wasn't supposed to be there. Could it possibly get any worse? "That's Area 51. Dreamland. It's where they test top secret aircraft. You'd need a special clearance to get on base. Top secret, minimum."

"That's why you must take me to your leader. He will bring us there."

"With no proof on your part other than a sincere smile and a few cool gadgets? I don't think so. You look too human."

"I am human. We're all humans. Same DNA, different planets."

"That's not going to help your story. You have to be able to prove you're an extraterrestrial, or people will think you're lying." Or crazy. Jana rubbed her forehead. Cavin would talk, but no one would listen. And she'd be laughed out of the capitol right behind him. Jana played out the scenario in her mind: *"Oh, Governor Schwarzkopf, do you have a minute?"*

"For you, always, Jana," he'd say in his thick accent, holding his cigar high so as not to singe her hair when he pulled her into his usual bear hug.

That's when she'd step back and introduce Cavin. The governor would wonder about the armor. "His name is Cavin, and I know he looks as human as you and me, but he's an alien."

"Illegal?"

"No, extraterrestrial."

The governor would take a puff of his cigar then, and make eye contact with his security officers, just in case.

"He wanted me to bring you here, so he could tell you…well, I think Cavin can explain it all better than I can." That's when she'd wave Cavin forward. "Go on,

*honey, tell him about that spaceship you want to use at
Area 51, you know, to phone home…"*

Jana groaned. She felt a little like Paul Revere,
famed for sounding the early warning that gave the
American colonists the chance to fight off an invasion.
But what if Revere had cried out, "The British are
coming, the British are coming," and they didn't come?
Without a doubt, it would have generated some credibility issues for ol' Paul. The last thing Jana needed was
credibility issues. She couldn't let fear blind her. She
had to think this through. In light of the ethics scandal
with her father, she owed it to her family not to act
rashly.

"This was a long time in the making, Jana, my
coming here. As soon as I learned of the planetary acquisition plans, I left my post without leave and came
here. I couldn't bear it if anything happened to you,
Squee, if I lost track of you."

Emotion thickened his voice, but he quickly cleared
his throat to erase the evidence and became Mr. Tough
Guy again. "If wanting to save you makes me a traitor,
I wear the title without shame."

She bit her lip and forced her eyes to focus on the
foggy road. *Her Peter…her exotic, magical boy…* He'd
jettisoned his future for her. He was willing to die for
her. She'd always dreamed of a hero, and here he was.

"Say something, Jana. Look at me."

"I want to. Trust me, I do." She sucked in another
breath. "But I can't, because the truth is, I'm having a
vulnerable moment here, and until it passes, if I look
at you, if I steal one tiny peek at those eyes of yours,
I'm afraid I'll agree to anything you want, because I

love you, I never stopped, that's why I can't look at you. And now I have to drive—"

"No you don't."

Cavin grabbed the steering wheel at the same time he slid his fingers into her hair at the back of her head to pull her close. Before she could finish uttering, "What the hell are you doing?" he'd sealed his mouth over hers.

A shudder ran through her body, and she forgot all about the highway, and driving, and everything else normally hardwired to the basic instinct for survival.

Magic.

Yes, that's what it was, magic, pure and consuming, what she'd searched for all her life and never found with anyone else. Jana took his face in both hands and kept him pressed to her lips. It was a full-on, open-mouthed kiss, hungry and wet. Her heart pounded a deafening drumbeat in her ears. Not just any kind of drumbeat. The kind they played at primitive exotic ceremonies where you danced and got naked and had sex with people you didn't know.

A horn blared. She and Cavin jumped apart.

"Gods," he said hoarsely and jerked the wheel expertly to the right to avoid hitting the truck they'd veered toward and almost hit.

"I thought you said you'd drive!"

"I was driving! I, ah, got a little distracted at the end. But here, you drive." He let go of the wheel. "And turn left."

She was still so dazed by the kiss, the heart-stopping, head-spinning kiss of utter, unadulterated magic that she didn't react. "You improved a bit since you were a kid."

"So have you. Now, *turn left*, Jana!"

She swerved to the left in the fog. "You don't have to yell."

"If it keeps you alive, I do."

She smelled him—the unique male scent of him; she could feel his body heat burning from across the car. It was terribly distracting. It was all she could do not to pull over and drag Cavin into a ditch and…

"Me, too," he said huskily.

She blushed. "You can mind read?"

"No, but I was hoping my thoughts were the same as yours, based on the look on your face." He reached across the seat to play with a lock of her hair. She felt him rubbing it between his gloved fingers. "You have a very expressive face. And an expressive mouth, or maybe expressive isn't the best word to describe your mouth. I'll need to consult my internal English thesaurus and find something better, like luscious, for instance, or succulent. Better yet, carnal." He pulled her hand to his mouth and brushed his lips over her knuckles, a feather touch that made her tremble. *Magic*.

She tugged her hand away and clamped it around the steering wheel. "No more of that, by the way."

He threw her an are-you-crazy look of male shock. Then abruptly he sat back with a deep sigh. "Ah, Squee, I didn't stop to think you might have a lover, someone important to you. I am sorry." And he sounded it, too. "When I read your background data, I didn't see anything about a mate—a spouse—or a serious male interest."

Great. Not only did people she'd never met know the sordid, depressing details of her social life, aliens she'd never met did, too. "I'm not seeing anyone. No boy-friends. No husbands, past or present."

He made a sound of relief. "But if you were, it wouldn't have changed anything. I would have been disappointed, yes, but I still would have come. I would have saved you, your family."

"My family is under investigation, and I've made them and my career my focus. I can't afford to get involved with anyone right now—even you, Cavin. And if you think that's going to be easy with you hanging around, knowing how I feel about you, you're crazy."

"So, it will be hard to resist me." He sounded more than a little pleased.

"Not as hard as you think. I'm highly motivated."

She could talk the talk, but could she walk the walk?

The fog began to lift some as they sped east. Soon she was able to see without Cavin's directions. Had she survived this unscathed? She was almost afraid to do it, but she let a little of the tension out of her aching shoulders. Just as she did so, the flash of police car lights illuminated the interior of the car. Her luck, it seemed, had finally run out.

CHAPTER FIVE

FLASHING LIGHTS illuminated the dark interior of the car. Earth law wardens, Cavin thought darkly. What more could go wrong? Could he and Jana not, in Earthling terms, catch a break? *"Yenflarg,"* he muttered, forming a fist on the dashboard.

Jana gave him a panicked look. "Please tell me your brain implant's not malfunctioning."

"Lorglor tessmassa," he replied.

At the flash of fear in Jana's eyes, Cavin said quickly, "Kidding, Squee. A bad joke. My translator's fine." She shoved at him. "A badly timed bad joke. I have no idea what a lorglor...whatever I said is, but *yenflarg* is a swearword in my language. Untranslatable, apparently."

"Try." Tight-lipped, she exited the highway, the patrol car in pursuit. "I'm running out of English cusswords."

He drummed his fingers on his knee. *"Yenflarg* is, as best I can describe it, the foul interior walls of a large, muck-eating creature's ass."

Jana made a strangled sound that sounded suspiciously like laughter, but almost immediately, worry turned her pink little mouth into a pout. He immediately thought of kissing that mouth, suckling on those plump lips, and… His body tightened. He made fists and willed the distracting heat to pass. It wasn't the time or place for such carnal thoughts.

Jana stopped the car at the bottom of the entry ramp. "Shut off the motor."

He did. The police car pulled up behind the Chevy and stopped, lights flashing. *"Yenflarg,"* she said with feeling, then: "It's not working, Cavin. This is such a nightmare. Two more exits and we'd have been back to the Safeway. So close and yet so far."

"This will not be a problem."

"How can it not be a problem? Okay, I'm working on excuses and coming up empty here. 'Sorry officer, it was only one gun battle and three carjackings.'" She frowned at Cavin. "Do you think that'll make him more or less likely to overlook the reckless driving?"

Cavin frowned. Charm and persuasion had long been talents of his, and it had always been so with the female sex. But how was he going to get Jana to trust him when at every turn he led her into trouble? Or worse, danger.

She sat rigid in the driver's seat, squeezing the steering wheel. He brushed a finger over her bloodless knuckles. "It will be okay, Jana. Wait and see."

"He's going to know this is a stolen vehicle."

"No, he won't."

You will see. Cavin simply smiled. She'd learn to trust him, yes, she would, one small technology-enhanced act at a time.

The uniformed warden sauntered over to the car. Jana rolled down the window. "Yes, Officer?"

"Good evening, ma'am. License and registration."

He dipped his head and peered inside the car. "Costume party," Jana said, poking a thumb at Cavin, who nodded politely at the officer.

Before she could hand over her identification, Cavin subtly brushed his wrist over the cards. The warden took them and returned to his car.

"What did you do?" she whispered.

"I altered the data. Your identity will now come up as the legal owner of this vehicle."

She smiled. "I like you more and more by the minute."

"Love me, you mean." He'd meant it to come out smug, but instead it sounded tender. Quietly, he added, "For your information, I never stopped loving you, either."

She smoothed her bangs away from her forehead and pondered him with expression of intensity and surprise that took him all the way back to the night he'd kissed her for the first—and what he'd assumed would be the only—time. It had been a very different kind of kiss from the one they'd just shared. It had been his first kiss, innocent and sweet. The expression on her face that night was one he'd selfishly held close through so many years: Her small heart-shaped face pale in the moonlight, her hair parted down the middle, bearing waves on each side from pigtails even after being brushed out.

Our daughter will look like that.

He couldn't imagine anything he desired more than having a child with Jana, except bedding her, yes, definitely that, but that was a more immediate wish as opposed to long-term, but Cavin cleared his mind of all of it. Before he could consider any such blessings from the gods, he had a world to save and a woman's trust to win. Neither would be easy, no matter what their feelings for each other.

He'd never dreamed Jana wouldn't be immediately and thoroughly convinced by him, or that she'd have obligations she'd need to think of first—career and family obligations. In his mind, she'd always recognized him right away. They'd fall into each other's arms and soon after, of course, he'd make love to her. That very night, they'd approach Earth's leadership. The leaders would listen to his plan and act immediately. And when it was over, when the fleet was turned away, Cavin would get his girl.

He'd have to leave for a while, he'd tell her, to honorably resign his posting with the Coalition military. The Coalition would wonder at his decision. He'd never tell them, of course. "I've grown weary of war," was all he'd have to say and it would be enough to seal his fate. Of course, there was the complication of the woman he'd been promised to marry, a woman he'd never even met, but once he gave up his position, he'd no longer fit into her plans. Then he'd find his father, bid him farewell, and return to Jana. She'd agree to be his mate. They'd make a life, make a family. And when the nights were warm in midsummer and the moon was full, he'd let Jana think he was magic all over again. He had it all planned out.

Had, he reminded himself. One day cycle on Jana's infuriating little world had taught him that plans meant little.

He sighed and briefly touched her hair, letting his hand fall. Her unruly blond hair looked soft to the touch. It took all he had not to wrap it in his fingers and pull her to his mouth and kiss her senseless, as he had fifteen minutes ago.

"Cavin, stop looking at me like that."

"Like what?" he asked innocently.

"Like you want to kiss me."

"And what if I did kiss you? Just one more kiss. Would it be so—"

Jana pressed a warm finger against his lips. "Stop."

"Wrong?" he finished in a mumble. Holding himself very still, he watched her react to the feel of his mouth, the prick of his barely surfaced whiskers, the intensity of his stare.

The heat between them crackled.

She let her finger slide to his chin and leaned closer, her eyes closing. "I'm beginning to wonder if resistance is futile," she whispered against his lips.

The warden returned and rapped on the glass. They jumped apart before completing the kiss.

Jana sighed. *"Yenflarg,"* she muttered.

Cavin chuckled. "Such language would make a space-dockworker blush."

"Thank you. I wish my grandfather could hear that."

With a perplexed expression, the warden returned Jana's cards. "Is there a problem, Officer?" she asked him innocently.

"I'd pulled you over for speeding. But my radar says you were driving well under the speed limit."

"We wanted to be careful in the fog," Jana said brightly.

"I wish more folks were doing that tonight."

She nodded with sympathy.

"Say, you're not *the* Jana Jasper are you?"

Jana's laugh sounded high-pitched and false. "People keep saying that. Actually, I think I look more like Drew Barrymore."

"The actress?" He squinted. "Hmm, yeah. But you look more like John Jasper's daughter. My partner didn't think so. 'Senator Jasper's a real fashionable lady, smart and classy,' she said."

As he walked away, Jana said, "Was I just insulted?" She pushed her tangled hair away from her face. Her clothing was soiled, and her bare feet dirty. Only her brightly colored toenails appeared unscathed. Noticing her condition for the first time, Cavin felt the heat of shame. He was supposed to be protecting this woman. "In the heat of battle, I didn't think of what you'd suffered. It was either this, or risk losing you. I hope you can understand."

But Jana had no ear for his apologies. She clapped her hands together. "He didn't think I was me!"

"Unfortunately, our assassin friend will not be so easily fooled. We've outmaneuvered him, for now, but we'll need to take cover."

Reality rushed back into her expression. "You're right. We'll go to my apartment—no, that's not a good idea. My doorman will wonder who you are. And my neighbors are very social, very curious. Look at the way we're dressed; they'll ask questions." Jana tapped her chin. "Must avoid questions."

Then she snapped her fingers. "Evie's house. My sister. No questions there. She's gone for a week, but she wouldn't mind us staying the night. Start the car, Cavin. I'm getting you inside before you make me break any more laws.

"Private as well as public," she added under her breath and, with a screech of tires, roared up the entry ramp to the highway.

CHAPTER SIX

AFTER RETURNING to the Safeway and exchanging the Chevy for her Jeep—where the only evidence of the halved SUV was a charred stain and some broken glass in the parking lot surrounded by yellow crime scene ribbon—Jana sped up Evie's quiet street and into her empty garage before anyone who happened to be up could see the man in body armor sitting in her passenger seat.

She parked and shut off the engine. The garage door rolled down, sealing them off from the street. And then it was quiet. Jana was acutely aware of his presence next to her in the car—his quiet breathing, his body heat, his scent. The memory of that explosive kiss. He, too, sat silently, and she knew he was thinking the same thing. Her. Cavin. Alone together. *Ay yi yi.* What about that man-vacation? Hadn't she sworn off men for a while?

No, you swore off dating.

Same thing, Jana thought. Or did childhood imaginary friends count?

You already kissed him once, almost twice. You're on the downhill slide.

She shook her head. No. She'd made a promise to her family, and she'd stick to it. Cavin was a friend. If he came with benefits, well, she didn't want to know about them.

"Let's go inside," she said and limped to the interior garage door that led into the house.

"I go first." Cavin slid past her, his body in a protective stance. Muffled yipping echoed from the other side. *Yarp. Yarp, yarp.* Cavin tipped his head, his hand going to his weapons belt. "What is that noise?"

"Don't shoot. That's Sadie. Well, sometimes we feel like shooting her, but really, she grows on you." Jana unlocked the house. "After you, sir. You're the one packing heat."

"Heat?" He glanced down at his body.

The man had good instincts, if not perfect translation. "Heat as in a weapon. If REEF is waiting for us, I might fare better if you're the one to say hello first."

He gave her a slightly dismayed, *trust-me-not-to-lead-you-into-danger* look. "The REEF is not here."

"Not yet. But the way my night is going…" At the entry panel, Jana flipped on all the lights until the house was blazing bright. "There, I feel safer now. Even if it's an illusion, I'll take it. My nerves are shot."

But Evie's house was the perfect antidote for stress.

Just for a moment, Jana let herself breathe it all in, the photos everywhere, the houseplants and flowers; the candles in scents like vanilla and pumpkin pie, cinnamon and apple, which, in Evie's absence, replaced the usual sweet aroma of her baking. A pair of old tennis shoes sat by the door leading to the garage. A dust bunny took up space in another corner. On the railing by the stairs, someone had tossed a Stanford sweatshirt. It all cried out that a family lived here, one held together with love.

"When my sister's not here, it's like the house is missing its heart," she said, turning around.

Cavin's green eyes had gone very dark and soft. He'd never looked at her that way before, and especially not as a boy. It was a look she felt all the way from the butterflies in her tummy to her bare feet. "When I am not with you," he said quietly, "it is as if I am missing *my* heart."

If she were a candle, she'd have spontaneously melted into a puddle of wax. And if he weren't wearing platform boots that put his mouth safely out of reach, she'd have spontaneously kissed him, too. "You're not making this any easier. I'm trying to resist you."

He lifted his hands. "I will behave. On the gods, I swear it."

"And on my God, too."

"You have my word."

Yarp, yarp, yarp!

"Sadie, it's me! Where's my little sweet girl?" Jana let go of Cavin and hobbled on her sore feet to the kitchen in search of Evie's dog. Locked behind a baby gate in the kitchen, a little tan dog with a barrel chest jumped up on spindly legs. "There you are!"

A full bowl of water and an empty one for food reassured her that the pet sitter had been by earlier. Twice a day Patti stopped by to take care of the animals and to let Sadie in and out of the kitchen.

Jana spread her arms. "There you are!" The little pooch reminded her of a dog on ice skates, slipping and skidding in her frenzy to greet Jana and simultaneously shred Cavin. Her huge watery brown eyes looked downright mean. Foam dripped from her tiny muzzle. Nails clattered on the maple floor, tapping out a deadly warning to the alien intruder.

Cavin stopped and stared at Sadie, "What is this creature?"

"It's a Chihuahua." Jana lifted up the wriggling dog. "A beautiful little wuhvee-duhvee," she cooed, kissing her. But Sadie would have no part of any soothing ploy. She wanted Cavin with a fanged, descended-from-wolves viciousness that transcended her tiny barrel-chested body. "I'm going to let her down. Is your armor pretty secure?"

Cavin snorted. Jana set the little dog on her paws. In a frenzy of scraping nails and barking, Sadie ran to Cavin, who stood there in his interstellar body armor, regarding Sadie with a hint of amusement curving his mouth as the little dog told him who was boss in the house.

Jana wondered how much exposure he'd had to things like families and homes and pets. Probably very little if he was a career military man for a society actively at war. Judging by the look on his face, he liked the experience. He'd given her so much. She was glad to be able to give him this one small thing, the taste of a home, of family. In his grown-up features, she saw a strong resemblance to the boy Peter: the love of mischief, the ready smile; but there was something new she hadn't noticed in the chaos of the last few hours: a hint of loneliness and longing that made her want to hold him until she'd melted it away.

Or she could just be searching for an excuse to touch the body encased by all that armor.

"There are three cats, too, but they're probably sleeping," she said as Sadie's barking subsided to a steady, high-pitched growl. "They have a bearded dragon, a chinchilla and a parakeet. The last two are locked up in cages. I'd warn you about the two teenagers who live here, but they're away with my sister in Disneyland."

"An amusement park."

"That's right. Good dictionary you've got there." She moved aside the baby gate and stepped into the kitchen. From the counters of speckled brown granite to the rich tiles painted to look like cocoa beans that lined the backsplash to the group of candles in scents like white chocolate, raspberry truffle, and chocolate chip, chocolate was the theme. Unlike Jana, who seemed curiously lacking in domestic abilities, Evie was the most amazing cook. Candy was her specialty. Chocolate, in particular. She'd started selling some of her creations on the side during the holidays. Jana kept urging her to start up her own business, but Evie was still a bit down after the divorce. Maybe in time. She wanted to see Evie happy again. Her sister was her best friend, even after all these years.

Jana used the sink to wash up while Cavin explored, supposedly checking the security of windows and doors, but out of curiosity, too, she knew.

She looked down at her soiled suit, stained blouse, the dribbles of ice cream across her skirt, her shredded panty hose and dirty bare feet and sighed. Now that she wasn't running for her life, the cuts and blisters on the pads of her feet stung. How was she going to wear pumps in the morning? Forget the shoes. How was she going to wake up, period? It had to be nearly 2:00 a.m. and 6:00 was the latest she could wake up to shower and get downtown to her apartment to change and still make breakfast with Mary Ann Schwarzkopf on time.

As she wiped her face, feet and hands clean with

chocolate-scented anti-bacterial soap—only Evie seemed to know where to find these things—Cavin inspected the sliding doors in the breakfast nook. Jana tried not to dwell on why. Evie would kill her if the assassin cut her house in half.

Cavin returned to the kitchen looking tired. "Have a drink," Jana said and offered him a glass of water. His gloved hand shook slightly before his fingers closed around the glass.

He emptied the glass in a few thirsty swallows, then leaned to the left and winced.

"Are you okay, Cavin? You don't look so good."

"I believe now that the adrenaline is fading, I'm feeling the wound under the armor."

"You're *wounded?*" Her heart started racing all over again. "But you can heal yourself, right? Like you did for me that night." Healed her knee and so much more. Gave her the Gift of Gab.

"If I activate the armor for the time and power level the healing would require, the REEF could quite possibly detect it and trace me here. If he does, there will be little I can do to stop him from breaking in and kill—"

"Right. I've got Advil. It's a painkiller. There are Band-Aids upstairs, and gauze pads, Bactine, Ace bandages, whatever you need. Evie's well stocked because of the kids. They're into about a million sports."

She grabbed his elbow and pushed him toward the family room. Sadie followed, ears perked. Hungry for fresh blood, the little beast. "How did you get hurt?"

"It was a rough landing. I hit a tree." He grimaced. "Maybe a few trees."

"You and trees. You really need to stay away from them."

"This time I had an excuse. The REEF was on my tail, trying to shoot me down. I'm not a formally trained pilot, but I do know how to fly a twenty-passenger troop transport vessel. Except, I tried to maneuver it like a fighter. I don't think he expected that." He made a small smile. "I saw his ship go down before I crashed. I thought it was destroyed. Apparently it was not." He winced again.

He flew a spaceship here. A *spaceship*. Cavin looked so normal, so human, that it was easy to forget he came from outer space. He was a space voyager, a galactic traveler who'd seen distant wonders that were the stuff of dreams. The realization left her bouncing between fear and fascination.

"You're alive," she said. "That's what's important." She steered him into the family room, where a newspaper from several days ago still sat on the coffee table next to several little balls of crumpled foil—evidence of devoured chocolate kisses and the addiction Evie bemoaned constantly.

Jana turned a switch and the gas fireplace whooshed to life, bringing instant warmth. "Sit down, Cavin." He sat heavily on the chaise portion of a leather sectional littered with pillows and cozy woolen blankets.

Sadie hopped up on the couch next to him. By now, the growling had subsided to an occasional high-pitched gurgle that the dog probably intended to sound threatening.

"Do you need help getting out of that armor, Cavin?"

Good one, Jana. You've been looking for excuses to get him out of that space suit all night. Behave yourself.

"I have this." He reached for a compartment mounted on the outside of his thigh, withdrew a small tool about the size and shape of a little screwdriver.

Uh-oh. "I hope you're not planning to perform surgery. I give blood regularly, but if I watch it go into the collection bag, I get sick. And then there was the time I passed out after getting a flu shot…"

"It's a tool, not a scalpel. I'll need it to remove the armor. Normally the AI in my suit would open the seams, but it's been malfunctioning since the crash. I'll have to do it manually."

Translated, it meant he was getting undressed. It was all the motivation she needed to keep from passing out.

Cavin pulled off his gloves and used the tool he'd dug out of his pocket to unfasten the armor a little at a time. The outfit had no buttons, zippers or recognizable fasteners. "Jana, I could use your help getting out of these sleeves."

She perked up. *I thought you'd never ask.* She took hold of the sleeve so he could draw out his arm. "Pull," she said, pressing a knee on the couch for leverage. She tossed one casing to the floor and then the other.

His leg casings came off next, then the boots, and finally the torso armor was open. He spread the armor apart like a clamshell and removed it. Jana leaned forward in breathless anticipation. It was like watching the unwrapping of a Christmas present.

Underneath the armor, he wore a black shirt made of soft, plush fabric. Like long underwear, it hugged his chest and broad shoulders. Now that he'd removed his boots, she was able to better guess his height. Maybe six feet one or two. He probably weighed in around two-ten or twenty and not an ounce looked to be anything but lean, hard muscle.

Then she saw the blood.

Wet, dark red, hard to discern against the black shirt. "Cavin…" Jana swallowed hard in an attempt not to be sick. "You're bleeding."

"Seeping, really."

"Seeping, bleeding, leaking, dripping, does it make a difference? It's blood, and it means you're hurt." She ran to the kitchen and returned with towels. "We've been running around all night. Why didn't you say something?"

"And what would that have done other than worry you? We couldn't have stopped and done anything about it." He lifted the T-shirt higher, revealing a flat belly, a fine set of abs, and a bloody bruise slashed through the center by a nasty laceration.

"Ugh," she said, feeling woozy.

"The instrument panel almost gutted me when it shattered."

"Stop." She held up both hands. Then her geeky curiosity rose to the surface. "Why isn't your armor torn?"

"It was at the time of impact. But it sealed over the wound to protect it, as it's supposed to do."

He cleaned the wound using some ointment. Then he squeezed the contents of a different tube over the wound and massaged it in. Her stomach rolled. "You must have incredible pain tolerance."

"Not really. The armor injected enough painkillers to keep it under control."

Not magic, Jana thought, but almost as good.

"But I am sore—" he winced "—on the inside."

"Internal injuries?" she asked weakly.

"My biosigns didn't show evidence of internal bleeding. But that was before I lost the artificial intelligence in my suit." He pulled a handful of something out of his tool kit. Several silver squares sat in his palm, each no bigger than a ladybug. "Little robots. They're mechanical. They don't emit a signal or pulse that the REEF can detect." He spilled them onto his stomach. "Good in a pinch, they're programmed to stitch closed a wound."

The tiny robots crawled over to the laceration, making snail trails in the ointment. Nausea welled up in her throat and she had to avert her eyes. "Won't it hurt?"

"They excrete a painkiller as they go. It's long-lasting, too. The ointment will speed the knitting of my skin. A couple of your Earth days and I'll be healed."

With almost undetectable clicking noises, the little robots set to work stitching closed Cavin's wound. Jana felt the blood roaring in her ears. The next thing she knew, Cavin had pulled her onto the couch next to him. He'd already stretched something that resembled skin over the ugly wound, hiding it. "Did I pass out?" she asked.

"Almost. I see why you chose politics over medicine."

"Most people do at some point."

He laughed. Smiling, Jana let her head fall onto his shoulder. It reminded her of when they'd fallen to the ground exhausted and laughing after attempting to fly in tandem. Twenty-three years had meant nothing; she was as comfortable with him now as she was when she was nine. There were no words to describe his effect on her: a soul-deep contentment, a feeling of having arrived home whenever he took her in his arms. It seemed right somehow, having "Peter" back, as if with his reappearance something in her life had finally fallen into place.

Was she crazy? If sheltering aliens, stealing cars, speeding, evading arrest and lying to law enforcement officers was "falling into place" then surely it was the wrong place!

But she could enjoy being with him, couldn't she? Until she figured out what to do about him. Jana pulled on the hem of his shirt to smooth it over the bandage. "When you healed me that night, the night you left, I thought it was magic."

"I let you think that. I didn't know what else to do."

Their eyes met, and her heart did its usual flip. "It still feels like magic, being with you," she whispered shyly.

His green gaze intensified so swiftly that it felt as though all the air had left the room. "Ah, Squee," he whispered. His fingertip traced her hairline from her cheekbone down to her jaw. "So many nights, I thought of you. When I was still a boy, those thoughts were innocent. But as I grew older, and you grew into a woman in my mind, those thoughts became increasingly carnal."

Carnal…just the way he uttered the word should be illegal.

"In my mind, I've made love to you so many times. Thought of you in my arms, in my bed…" He leaned closer, hesitated, then closed the rest of the distance between them. His thumb brushed across her lips, parting them, but he didn't kiss her. Instead, he slipped his fingers into her hair and pulled her close, pressing his cheek to hers. His skin was hot, his beard sharp. A shudder ran through her and she imagined his entire body pressed against hers, skin to hot skin. "Sometimes you'd be with me on the ship, in my bunk, and sometimes we'd be outside."

His breath rushed past her ear and made her shiver. *Thump, thump, thump* went the drumbeat now centered distractingly in her crotch. "Where outside?" she breathed and felt his lips form a smile.

"Where? Where do I start? Ah…there was a remote assignment once, on a world covered by the thickest of rain forests. The air was steamy, dense. Seductive. It felt painted on you, the air, on your skin. Everywhere it smelled of the plant life, the flowers. It was a long trek on foot to where we had to deploy. We walked all through the night into the day, and the day cycle on that world was very, very long. As the sun rose, I imagined you were there with me, our hair, our clothes, drenched by the rain…"

He touched his lips to her ear. "I'd strip you, kiss the water from your skin, chasing streams of it with my tongue, everywhere it went. Then I'd take you, up against a tree, your legs wrapped around me."

His hot, whispered words seared an image behind her eyes: a steamy jungle; Cavin, his pants down around his knees; her: naked in the warm soaking downpour, pressed against a slippery, wet palm tree, her thighs open, locked around him; he'd feel so hot compared to the rain, thrusting between her legs and bringing her to orgasm.

Jana forgot how to breathe. The drums were pounding now, a wild, primitive beat. "I've never done it against a tree…" Heck, she'd never had sex outside, period. In rooms with windows wide-open, sure, and a few times with a sliding door open to a backyard pool, but that didn't count. The men she'd chosen never would have suggested doing it out in the open or anywhere else she'd want to be with Cavin, which was anywhere and everywhere.

"But it wouldn't matter where I loved you," he whispered hotly, stroking her hair and holding her close. "Inside, outside, it wouldn't make a difference. Only how it felt being inside you, Jana. That's all I've wanted to know. How you'd feel. How you'd respond to me…."

She found his mouth and kissed him. Not soft, not tender—*hungry*. She couldn't help it; she needed to feel him, to feel him now.

It's just a kiss, she thought as he held her face in his hands, his mouth wet and hot, exploring as their breaths came faster, uneven. *Just a kiss*. She lost herself in the sensation, losing herself in him, as if she'd never been able to completely do with anyone else. *Magic*.

What was happening? She wasn't supposed to be doing this!

Jana moved her hands to his shoulders and gave a halfhearted push, but her mouth didn't want to stop.

"Gods," she heard him mutter. "I swore on the gods." He released her and fell back against the cushions.

Jana slumped next to him. They sat there, shoulder to shoulder, dazed and on fire. "You did swear on the gods," she said. "Little good it did."

"You started it."

"Ha. You were the one talking about rain. And trees!"

"Talking, Jana. Talking is different from doing. You kissed me."

"You kissed me back," she pointed out.

"I sure as hell did." She loved the way his speech was growing more and more colloquial. The program in his brain seemed to be improving over time. "But I'm not the one who feels the need to behave. You are. The only reason I am behaving is because I'm trying to respect your wishes and your reasons that I do so. It doesn't mean that I like it."

"Who says I do?"

"How much longer, Jana? How much longer until I can have you?"

The husky, sexy way he said "have you" started up the drumbeat all over again. She wanted him to have her. She wanted him to have her every which way. She wanted him to have her now. She crossed her legs.

All thoughts of interstellar armies and alien invasions went out the window with the dark glint in his eyes. Did he have any idea how sexy he was? Probably. She was sure he'd been with plenty of women over the years, but how did he ever escape getting hitched? "How did you avoid getting married, anyway? Or whatever your culture calls it when you hook up with one woman for life."

He shrugged. "My career kept me on the move and gone from home for six months out of every one of your years, sometimes longer, depending on the deployment. And I wasn't looking for a wife. Maybe, if there had been someone…I might have considered it, but I never found her. I sought the company of women for sex, and vice versa, Sometimes, I'd stay with a lover for more than a few weeks or months, but rarely. If they'd been anything like you, it may have been more, but they weren't."

She thought about the conversation she'd had with her grandfather at breakfast. "If I'd have found someone like you, I would have been married by now."

Cavin leaned toward her. "I'm glad you're single," he whispered hotly in her ear. His breath sent tingles spinning down her spine.

Cavin might be glad she was single, but her family wasn't. Her stomach flip-flopped at the mere thought of mentioning Cavin to them. Grandpa wanted her to make a politically advantageous marriage. And her? She wanted to make it with an alien!

Blissfully asleep, Sadie made a weird whining snore and rolled onto her back. Her legs were sticking straight up. She had the right idea. It was getting close to four. "We'd better get to bed," Jana said.

Cavin stretched. "Where will we sleep?"

"*You* will sleep in the guest room. I'll show you."

Instantly awake, Sadie hopped off the couch and followed them to Evie's extra downstairs bedroom. The walls were painted a creamy chocolate. There were caramel curtains and a whipped-cream-white down comforter dotted with round red pillows. Jana called it the ice-cream sundae room.

With a tender expression, Cavin watched Jana as she readied the bed for him and found the toiletries he'd need. Finally, she leaned against the door frame as he sat down on the edge of the mattress. He scratched a sleepy hand across his chest and looked too delicious for words.

Sadie hopped up on the plush bed and in seconds had passed out again. "You'll have company tonight," Jana said. "Is that okay?"

"It's not who I'd prefer to wrap in my arms all night, but she'll do."

In bed, if his hands are half as hot as his eyes, I might never want to climb out.

"But, you are trying to resist me, so I'll say no more," he said, his tone edged with mischief. "Good night, Jana. Rest well." He settled back on the mattress with a slight wince as he clasped his hands and slid them behind his head.

His words might say "no" but every molecule in Jana's body said "yes." Only the promises she'd made kept her anchored to this side of sanity. Or was that celibacy?

Not to mention her vow to stay under the radar, to keep her nose clean. What had happened with that? Half of her wanted to weep from the frustration of seeing all her good intentions go horribly awry. The other half wanted to beat Cavin to within an inch of his life for his part in making that happen.

"Good night," she said and limped away before she could change her mind about where she wanted to sleep.

She trudged upstairs to Evie's bedroom and without taking off her suit or pulling down the silk, crème brûlée comforter she fell facefirst into the huge downy bed and let it swallow her up.

Peter was back. Her magical, exotic boy, sleeping downstairs in Evie's spare bedroom. Everything she was today was because of him. And now it looked as if everything she'd become would also be because of him. For better or for worse.

THE ASSASSIN MOVED from shadow to protective shadow as he searched for shelter for the night. His damaged invisibility sputtered, causing him to alternate between being visible and not. With or without the assistance of technology, he needed to remain unseen. He was an alien on this world, a stranger. A predator. He would not hesitate to disable any creature that came between him and his objective. And he knew how to do it without calling attention to who or, rather, what, he was.

But now his focus was to get inside for the night.

The street was an urban byway, not residential. The air smelled like fossil fuel and rotting garbage. In the distance, automobiles coursing along elevated roads made muffled roars. It was dark and his sight was obscured by the precipitation that had led to him losing a visual on the man he'd been assigned to track down and kill. A man with views on Coalition policy that apparently had troubled one or more individuals in the highest echelons of government. Reef hadn't been expressly told this, but it was not difficult to infer. It was his job to read what was not written, to see what was not shown, to hear what was not said. The more he knew about his target, the better he could predict his behavior, which made for a more timely and efficient termination.

Far Star was probably a highly capable soldier resistant to cronyism, as well as an independent thinker; unfortunately, in the Coalition military, that was the fastest way to find yourself dead, usually on a battlefield with a plasma hole in the back of your head, or in a transport "accident." But this particular soldier must have been seen as enough of a credible threat by the people who wanted him dead for them to take extra precautions to ensure it was accomplished. And they'd done that by hiring Reef.

But it mattered not, Far Star's personal history. Reef tracked, he found, he killed. It didn't make a difference what sort of life his quarry had led before he ended it. Life itself meant little to Reef. One the other hand, a job well executed meant everything.

But why his target had come here, to this backward, backwoods world, Reef had no idea. It made his task more difficult. Then again, it made the hunt more of a challenge. An easy kill was no fun. And so far this soldier had proved to be anything but easy. Reef was going to enjoy this assignment.

A warehouse loomed ahead. Reef peered through a window. The optical implants on his retinas showed no infrared activity. Using an electromagnetic pulse, he disabled the security system—as well as all the computers, clocks and any machinery stored inside the building. Collateral damage was often necessary to keep him functional by assuring his safety.

Status: secure.

He used his laser knife to open the door and slipped inside. He found a back corner in the dark and hunkered down. It was quiet. He was alone. Different planet, same condition as always, he thought, and tried to keep feelings out of it. A REEF assassin was not programmed to feel lonely. But there was enough human in him to know he was cold and hungry. He turned up the temperature control on his armor, but it didn't respond. It, too, had been damaged in the crash, along with his bioengineered link to his armor. It was the only reason that the soldier, his target, still lived tonight.

Had Reef been in good working order, the soldier would have been dead, and Reef on his way out. Rather, he would have been calling for pickup. His ship was too damaged to fly. But it was what it was. Hundreds of missions and this was his first accident.

His stomach rumbled again. He peered around the dark, hollow building. His retina implant detected a small animal darting across the floor. He lifted his pistol and downed it with a single pulse of energy.

His weapon dangled from his hand as he walked over to the kill. Data scrolled behind his eyes—*Earth species identification: Rat. Weight: 6 oz. Nutritional Feasibility: Edible.*

He picked it up with his gloved hand and dropped it on the cold storage compartment of his suit. If he needed one, he'd have a meal. It was important that he keep up his strength. Tracking a target manually, as he would be doing now, took energy. But for now, as hungry as he was, he'd hold out for tastier sustenance. The human part of him enjoyed the nuances of well-prepared food.

The tinkling of glass echoed from the back of the building. He saw the heat signatures of two humans sneaking around outside. *Humanoid, male. Quantity: 2. Weight: 177, 223.*

Reef dropped into a crouch to stalk them for no other reason than he was cold and they wore warm clothing. According to his enhanced vision, they wore thick upper-body garments with hoods and denim jeans, as they were called here. Reef didn't care for the showy jewelry, but he'd take it and wear it. Any clothes that would serve to camouflage him as a local were valuable, serving in much the same way invisibility did in keeping him out of sight from his target. Especially now that he was operating without the high tech of his armor.

Reef slipped out the back door and stepped in front of the two males. "Give me your clothes."

They stared at him for a moment and broke into laughter. The taller of the two drew a small knife. "How about you give me yours, fucker? Your stash, too."

Reef kicked the pitiful weapon out of the male's hand so fast that it had skittered across the alleyway before the first hint of surprise reached his face.

"Fuck." The shorter male thrust a hand into his coat. Reef's enhanced vision displayed the male's hand closing around a weapon—a gunpowder pistol. Reef fired first.

A plasma burst tore through the man's pocket. A startled yowl interrupted the quiet of the alley. The sizzling pistol dropped to the ground. Before any rounds could explode, Reef blasted it again and melted the pistol.

"My hand, my hand," the male moaned, gripping his wrist above the blistered hand.

Reef aimed. "Give me your clothes."

The other man's breaths exited in rapid puffs of steam. "What are you, that Terminator dude or something?"

Reef accessed his Earth cultural data files. Terminator: *Year created: 1984. Rating: R. Classification: action/sci-fi/thriller. Starring Arnold Schwarzenegger as a human-looking, unstoppable cyborg that feels no pity, no pain, and no fear sent back in time to assassinate the mother of a future revolutionary leader.*

In seconds, Reef had downloaded and viewed the entire movie. "Worse," he replied.

The men snickered nervously.

"Take off your clothes," Reef said in a precise imitation of the movie's villain.

"Shit. He sounds just like him. That robot."

"At least he's not naked."

"Yeah, but check out what he's wearing. Where did you ever see shit like that?"

"PlayStation, man."

"No, man, the *Terminator*. I tell you. Look at him."

The humanoids were too talkative. Reef drew out his spare plasma rifle, spinning both weapons before he aimed them. "Strip. Now."

The two men frantically threw off their clothes.

AFTERWARD, REEF CARRIED the garments back to the warehouse, where he changed and settled in for the night. The clothing was warm. His human body appreciated it. He was cold and his head ached. It wasn't right, feeling so low, physically, mentally. He sensed changes within him, but an in-depth scan showed no neural damage. Perhaps the damage he'd suffered in the crash was worse than he thought.

Rest and stay warm, and he'd heal. Before Reef gave in to sleep, he replayed the day's events in his head. If only he'd been able to ascertain the identity of the female in Far Star's company. But Reef didn't let that small defeat frustrate him. It wouldn't be hard to learn her identity. And if he hadn't yet killed his target, he'd use the female to bring him to his prey. And then it would be: *Hasta la vista, baby*. Reef balanced an arm across his bent knee, leaned his head back against the brick wall and closed his eyes. The robotic assassins from the series of Earth movies had been comically inept, but they did have some good lines.

CHAPTER SEVEN

IT WAS JUST AFTER DAWN when Jana tiptoed down the stairs, dressed in sweats she'd borrowed from Evie's closet. Even a shower hadn't lifted the fuzz left in her brain from getting only two and a half hours of sleep, although it had done wonders for her sore feet. Her hair was soaking wet. She'd style it at the apartment as well as change.

In the kitchen, she scrawled out a note to Cavin then tiptoed toward the door to the garage. Before her hand could touch the door handle, she heard, "Good morning, Jana."

She stopped. Swore. The soiled clothes in her arms stank of old bananas. The sweats were the oldest she could find, and she'd hijacked a pair of her sister's powder-blue Ugg boots to cover up her bare feet. Her wet hair left drips on the lenses of the reading glasses she'd donned to skim through incoming text messages on her cell phone. She looked hideous, she knew, but she hadn't planned on running into anyone, least of all Cavin.

She pasted a bright smile on her face and turned around. "Good morning."

Dressed in black and nearly invisible in the shadows, he leaned against the wall adjacent to the family room. Sadie sat at his feet, casting an equally accusing look at Jana.

"Going somewhere?" he asked.

"My apartment. To change clothes. I have an early coffee meeting with my staff, followed by a breakfast reception, meetings, lunch, hearings and more meetings." *I'm going to dive back into my workaholic life and practice what is known in pop psychology circles as massive denial.* "I'll be back as soon as I can." Jana pushed her glasses up the bridge of her nose. "And don't sneak up on me like that. You startled me. This assassin business has made me a little jumpy."

"You think I am sneaking?" Cavin's smile was deadly. Arms folded, he pushed away from the wall. "I was in the midst of inspecting the security of this dwelling with my assistant, Sadie, when I heard you awaken. Then I see you attempting to exit this dwelling without telling me. Since my unique expertise was what kept you from incarceration last night, I thought I deserved a 'hello' or at minimum, a 'goodbye.' Sadie thinks so. Don't you, little creature?"

Ears perked, Sadie tipped her head to the side. Her luminous brown eyes gleamed with adoration as she awaited his command.

"Look at that, one night with you and she's yours."

"You had the opportunity, but—" he made a spreading motion with his fingers "—you let it slip away."

"Sadie doesn't have to work today. I do. And why aren't you still asleep? I thought you would be. And you should be. You're injured."

"I'll sleep later."

"You didn't sleep at all?" She was beginning to see

a man who was as driven as she was. When something fired his passion, he didn't give up until he'd achieved his goal. Just like her.

"There wasn't enough time to make sleep worth the effort, so I set up a security array."

Her eyes went from his holstered space-gun to the marble-size balls lined up along the threshold of the garage entrance. He carried a few more little balls in his big palm, tossing them like a gangster playing with a handful of coins. "What are those?"

"They're used to form the array. If anyone tries to penetrate the secure area, these will emit a harmless pulse of energy to deter the intruder. Nothing the REEF or anyone else looking for me could detect. Now, back to you," he said and sauntered closer. "And your sneaking. It reminds me of the morning after a romantic tryst, only I was always the one stealing away."

"This has nothing to do with a morning-after. There can't be an after because there wasn't a *before*. Besides, I left you a note," she pointed out guiltily. "I told you where the food is, what to do with the pets, and not to answer the door or the phone. And I wrote down my cell number so you can reach me."

"I don't read your language. Or any Earth language."

"But I thought…"

"The implant is an aural translator only. I'm functionally illiterate."

He reached for her glasses and slipped them off. Her physical reaction to his closeness was immediate. She picked up his scent, warm and male. It was intoxicating, and she felt the echo of the primitive drumbeat of their kisses. *Overcome it. Prove you are a higher life form than the sturgeon.*

With obvious and touching curiosity, he held her glasses up to the light to study them. As tired as she was, and without the glasses to help her see, the details of his face were a little out of focus. The effect softened his features, took away the creases he had from squinting in the sun, smoothed the shadow above his upper lip where he shaved, and erased the tiny scar on his chin. "Primitive eyewear," he commented.

"We do the best we can here on quaint ol' Earth."

He ignored her sarcasm. "Do you use them for magnification?"

"Yes, I'm a little farsighted. I need them for reading. When I'm tired, I depend on them." She opened her hands. "Like now. Give."

"I like how you look in these," he said, studying the glasses.

"So, you're attracted to nerds."

"I'm attracted to you," he said and slipped her glasses back on.

Her skin warmed and her pulse kicked up another few notches, pounding *boom, boom, boom* in a thrumming urgency that begged her to throw off her glasses, shake out her hair and tear off Evie's sweatshirt with seam-popping abandon.

Jana jumped backward and grabbed hold of the garage door handle, clinging to it as if it were the only anchor to the real world outside, where normalcy reigned. Or at least where it had reigned before yesterday. "I'll be late unless I leave now." Like really late, hours-of-mind-blowing-hot-sex-later late.

He held open the door for her as if he were coming along, too. "No, Cavin. You have to stay here. I have to keep you safe."

He reared back in surprise. "To keep *me* safe?"

"From us Earthlings. You make it sound so simple—'Take me to your leader, Jana'—but I was thinking about it in the shower this morning. It's more complicated than you think. You want to get to Area 51 and hack into a spaceship the government denies is there. You want to use said spaceship to transmit false signals to an invading alien fleet that the government also knows nothing about." She pressed two fingers to her temple and prayed her headache didn't turn into a migraine. She'd never had a migraine, but if she were to start, now would be the time.

"We can't be rash and act before we've analyzed all the angles. See, it's never been proven there's life anywhere else but here. Some people think there is, but many more don't. The nonbelievers will probably laugh at you, and the believers will probably want to kill you because they think extraterrestrials are coming to take over, which is exactly what you plan to tell them."

"I'll talk to them. Allay their fears about me."

Her protective instincts flared. He was her Peter, her magical boy. She wouldn't let anyone hurt him. "There's more. You'll be seen as something valuable for your secrets, for the implants you carry in your body. The technology. Whatever country gets you would have a huge strategic advantage over everyone else. Make the wrong people nervous or whet their appetite for knowledge or power, and you could disappear, for good, all for the sake of science and world supremacy."

He looked grim. "Permanent disappearance. This seems to be the theme of my life lately."

"I've been through that once already, losing you, and I didn't like it. I won't let you disappear." Big words, but in reality, could she make that promise? "Let me think of the safest way to do this."

She came up on her toes and pressed a goodbye kiss to his cheek. "Don't talk to the neighbors. Don't answer the door. Pick up the phone only if it's me."

"You worry needlessly. I'm well trained in my conduct with alien species."

"You might be trained, but Evie's neighbors aren't. That's the problem. Stay in, stay low, don't go anywhere."

She cracked open the door. Cold damp air flowed in from the dark garage. Keys jingling, she walked to her car. Had he any idea how hard it was to leave him?

Cavin followed. "Who will watch over you today?"

"Me."

His chin went down so he could look in her eyes. "You."

"Yes. The capitol building is very secure. So is my apartment building. It's brand-new, state of the art. There's a doorman, awesome security, and I live in the thirty-second floor—that's pretty high in Earthling terms. Astronomical, in Sacramento terms. And I was doing just fine until you showed up. I wasn't stealing cars, getting pulled over for speeding, or getting shot at. Of course, I wasn't getting kissed into oblivion, either."

Something fleeting and wonderful flashed in his eyes. Then he frowned. "Don't try to distract me. Rewind, please, to the getting-shot part."

"The REEF."

"He's still out there. REEF assassins never give up. Battlefield legend claims that not even death ends a REEF's desire to kill. Once, as the story goes, there was a REEF whose bloodied and broken human body continued to slither after its target after death, its inner components still whirring as they dragged the mutilated body toward the intended kill."

"Ugh! Gross." Jana wrinkled her nose. "No more war stories, please, or I'll throw up. I get it, okay? This thing, this robot guy, he's persistent. It's the invincibility that I question. He's screwed up too many times for one with a supposedly perfect record."

"He may have suffered a malfunction, perhaps in the crash, but we can't be sure. But unlike me, he can use his nanotech to heal himself and fix his weapons, and it is likely what he's doing now."

She opened the door to the Jeep. Cavin pushed it closed before she could climb in. "Do you want to be around when he breaks his losing streak?" he demanded.

"Chances are if he does find out I'm connected to you, he'll go to my apartment to find me, not here. Evie's divorced, but she kept her married name. How is REEF going to figure that out? I think we're both safer here."

He thought about that. "Perhaps."

"We'll stay another night. Maybe a couple of nights. I'll tell Evie. She won't mind."

Jana opened the car door. Cavin took her arm before she could climb in. "I'll be careful, I promise," she said gently.

The pained look in his face brought her back to the night he had to leave, all those years ago. The air felt just as charged. Then he made a sound in his throat and dropped his hand. "Will every separation we have be this wrenching?"

That's what it was, she thought with a jolt. They couldn't stand being apart.

She fell into his arms. His hug was crushing, broadcasting their reluctance to part. "I never wanted to leave you, not even then," he said. "I wanted to take you away with me and my father as a sample from Earth."

Jana smiled against his chest. "You wanted to abduct me? Now it comes out. Why didn't you? I could have been in the *Enquirer*—on the front page, too."

"I thought it through. I wanted you with me only if I could make you as happy as you made me, not because I forced you. This is no different. Go." He let go and stepped away, placing a palm on his gun. "But come back."

Two decades of life had infused his face with character, but his eyes were still Peter's eyes. "I will," she said. "I'll come back." She pressed a too-quick kiss on his lips and hopped in the Jeep. She wasted no time starting it up and backing out of the garage.

Gritting her teeth, she shoved the Jeep into first gear, catching a glimpse of Cavin in her rearview mirror as she sped away. An achy, swollen feeling filled her chest, and it wasn't because of the stress. It was because of Cavin. Seeing him conjured the same feeling she'd experienced when she saw Evie holding her first baby, or the times she'd find Grandpa gently tending to his vegetables when he didn't know she was watching, or when Mom would purposely say something to fluster Dad, and he'd push his glasses up his nose and give her that goofy, lovesick smile. Being with Cavin was how it felt when she was around her family, only sharpened with a desperate physical attraction.

"You won't feel this way once you fall in love for real," Evie had insisted that night Peter had left and Jana had confessed her wish to marry him.

Jana pondered that as she shifted into Third. She hadn't argued with Evie at the time because her gift was so new, the gift of gab. All she'd ever wanted was to be normal, to be like everyone else. That night gave her the chance, and she'd been determined not to blow it. Boys had been the last thing on her mind, even one as special as Peter. It wasn't until much later that she realized how much his departure had affected her. How much she missed him.

And it wasn't until now that she knew Evie was wrong.

"You won't feel this way once you fall in love for real, Jana." She'd been in love. Three times. Not once had it come close to what it was like with Cavin.

Cavin...

Peter.

Everything you are today was because of him. Everything you'll become will also be because of him. How could any one person have so much influence over her life?

But she'd had just as much influence on his. Now they were finally back together, but for a purpose: uniting to save the world.

Headline! Fairy-tale Romance Has Cosmic Consequences.

Jana jammed the Jeep into Fourth gear as she left the

gates of Evie's street behind. But as fast as she drove, she couldn't shake the now-familiar sensation of being sucked out to sea as it gathered its force and strength. A tidal wave was coming and the best she could hope for was that she'd have time to run to higher ground before it hit.

CHAPTER EIGHT

CAVIN WATCHED JANA go until he lost sight of her vehicle. Why did he let her out of his sight? What was he thinking?

Let her go. The REEF wants you, not her. He couldn't use his personal woes as an excuse to keep Jana prisoner. But he wasn't going to lead her into danger, either. And danger followed him now, claws sunk deep like a deadly parasite. With the presence of the REEF on Earth, the chances of the Coalition learning his whereabouts had become a true concern.

Before, the chances of anyone discovering he'd come to Earth were little to none. Cavin had told no one, written down nothing. He knew how to "disappear" because for years he'd studied how. He had access to classified information few others did, allowing him to do what he wanted, to go where he wanted, and when he wanted. But now a REEF was here, tracking him, bringing the risk of the Coalition discovering his whereabouts. And if they learned he of all people was here, sharing Coalition secrets with Earth, it would bring more than an acquisition force to this backward little world; it would bring the full and deadly force of the Galactic Army.

He paced restlessly in front of the open garage in soft boot inserts that had to serve as footwear in the absence of his armored boots. *You have to let her know who you really are*. He couldn't keep Jana in the dark about him any longer. He should have told her all of it, right away, only at the time, he'd thought it would cause her more worry. His only hope was that the assassin would be as stealthy and efficient as always: discretion was programmed into the killers. REEFs reported back to their benefactors only when a target was eliminated. And Cavin was going to make damn sure this was one assassin who wouldn't complete its mission.

Cavin fisted a hand at his side. Damn the REEF. Damn the bastards who'd hired the assassin. And damn their timing. Gods, why now, when he could least afford complications? Who was behind the decision to terminate him? Who had he frightened so desperately? Neppal? Fair Cirrus? Prime Minister Rissallen? Or, was it the queen? Keira was known for erratic behavior. Perhaps she'd signed his death order.

What did it matter now? He'd come here to save Jana, to save her world. If he had to outrun a REEF assassin while accomplishing that, so be it. He'd outrun worse.

One more thing you didn't plan on, Far Star. Cavin fought the haunting worry of everything he'd planned on spinning out of control. Despite the ever-changing, unpredictable dynamics of this mission, he had to keep command, keep it together. For Jana's sake if nothing else. For his Squee.

She'd so affected him, he could barely think. Her body, warm, soft, pressed close to his. Her scent, the way she tasted, his mind played the sensations over and over to distraction. He set his jaw, hardened his stomach muscles, clenched his fists, as if something so superficially physical could blot out this overpowering desire to make love to her, to taste, touch, feel every inch of her body. But he must never lose his ability to protect her, something he was in danger of doing if they focused too much on each other and not on what was going on around them.

Yet, at times they were as much adversaries as they were potential lovers. Oh, he had no doubt of her feelings for him; he saw it every time he looked in her eyes. But with her family under fire, she viewed him as one more obstacle. He had to change that perception if he was to gain her trust. And to gain her trust, he must learn to adapt to her world, or everything he'd risked his life for, and now her life, would be threatened.

To understand the Earthlings, you must become one of them.

But how? Darkly, Cavin rubbed his knuckles across his chin and thought about what Jana had told him. *They'll be afraid of you.* Jana's comment had caught him off guard. *They don't believe there's life anywhere else but here.*

He peered into the stillness of the overcast morning, taking in every detail of the strange and alien landscape. Similar-looking dwellings lined the street, each with a rectangular patch of grass serving as a separation from the road. Landscaping varied from house to house but not widely. Similarity seemed to be celebrated, or perhaps regulated. Here and there along the street, other vehicles backed out of garages and drove off in the same direction as Jana. A mass migration was underway.

A man motored past and waved. *Jana warned you against interaction with the local inhabitants.* But wouldn't it seem odder if he ignored the overture than if he responded in kind? *My apologies, Jana*, he thought and waved back.

Another car drove down the street, its occupant acknowledging him with a wave. It seemed he was accepted as part of the community simply because he was standing in the open garage. Such a quaint little planet. It hardened his resolve to save it, because when the Coalition was done with it, nothing would be the same.

Cavin turned to go inside. He had much to do.

"Good morning!" A smiling woman crossed the street with two small children and a canine that was far larger than Sadie.

Once more, Cavin weighed acknowledging the overture for communication against the consequences of directly violating Jana's orders. But when uncertainty flickered in the woman's eyes at his silence, he decided it would be wise to respond. "Good morning."

The woman's eyes shone. The little children gawked at him. The dog jerked on its leash and whined when it couldn't flee.

"King, what's with you?" The woman shook her head. "You'd think a German shepherd wouldn't be such a sissy. And he usually isn't. I guess you're just intimidating wearing all that black."

Or more accurately, his bio-implants put out a subtle frequency that bothered the dog. But not Sadie. That creature was an enigma, yet somehow endearing. He could hear her barking from inside the house now, demanding that he return. She thought she owned him, the little beast.

The woman looked him up and down and asked, "We haven't met. Are you a friend of Evie's?"

"Not Evie. I know Jana."

"Ah, one of Jana's friends." She nodded with a knowing smile that gave him the feeling he was only one of many men who considered themselves a "friend" of Jana's.

"We are looking after Evie's house in her absence."

"Patti's not pet sitting?"

Cavin shook his head. Who was Patti?

"Anyway, I'm Cheryl. I live in that house." She pointed across the street to a dwelling similar in hue to Evie's. "I saw you and just wanted to say hi. I'm here all day, so if you need anything, let me know." She waved cheerily, gathered the children, and let the big nervous dog pull her away.

Before he was delayed any further, Cavin made an about-face and strode up the driveway to the house. His wound ached as he walked. The laceration itself didn't pain him, but internally, he was taking longer than he'd expected to heal. The level of nano-meds in his bloodstream had fallen. It meant his implanted computers were not keeping up with his body's demands. And that told him they'd been damaged worse than he thought in the crash. His only hope was that they'd regenerate the damaged areas. But if his bioengineered parts could recharge and regenerate, so could the REEF's.

It made it all the more important to stay one step ahead of the assassin. In order to do that, he needed to finish shoring up the defenses of Jana's sister's dwelling, so if anyone attempted entry, he'd be alerted. With purpose in his step, Cavin returned to the interior. There was much to be done before Jana returned.

NONA AND STEVE GREETED Jana when she arrived in the office. It was her routine to receive a quick briefing every morning from Nona, her chief of staff, while Steve sat in.

Jana hung up her suit jacket in the coat closet and tried to push the bizarre events of the past day out of her mind—and off her face—if only temporarily. "You have a very expressive face," Cavin had told her. She blushed, thinking about what he'd been referring to—sex in a ditch—and hoped none of it was visible to Steve or Nona.

Vicky, the office secretary, hadn't arrived yet, but already her desk was covered with stacked piles of paper and files that looked ready to topple. Jana frowned irritably at the towering stacks. "Look at all those dead trees. People are getting paid better than you are for printing, sorting, stapling, hole-punching, stacking, organizing and distributing mountains of paperwork I could just as easily have called up on the computer. Entire forests were cut down to produce the paper I need to consider policies for conservation and the timber industry. Tell me how this makes sense. Yet, no one in either political party seems interested in staunching the flow of paperwork around here."

She marched into her office, fell into her desk chair and heaved a big sigh.

Nona and Steve peeked in. "You okay?" Nona asked.

"Fine. A little stressed." *A little? Ha.*

Nona nodded with sympathy. "It's understandable."

It sure was. Just yesterday, her father's troubles had seemed like the end of the world. Now, Cavin's news that an invasion was in the works confirmed it.

"Let's get the coffee flowing," said Steve. A carafe of Starbucks waited on the desk along with the usual box of Krispy Kreme doughnuts, Steve's addiction. Nona poured three coffees, each precisely to the same level, adding cream to Jana's, cream and sugar to Steve's, and taking hers black, which fit her personality to a tee.

Nona was short, trim, with a no-nonsense silver bob. She wore absolutely no makeup; she bit her nails to the quick, and had the most stunning turquoise and silver Navajo jewelry Jana had ever seen. Everyone knew Nona was the best chief of staff out there, and she'd still be someone else's if she hadn't made the blunder of having an affair with her previous boss's wife. When the news had come through the grapevine she'd been fired, Jana hired her on the spot. Nona's stumble was Jana's gain.

Jana sipped coffee as Steve briefed. "We've got seven requests for interviews. I expect more as the day goes on. All with regards to the campaign-funds scandal."

"The campaign-funds *lies*," Jana muttered.

"Divert them all, or do you want to take any?"

"What do you say, Nona?"

"Divert them all for now. A low profile is your best defense right now."

A low profile? Jana thought of Cavin and wanted to weep. Her hand shook as she chose a frosted doughnut. "I agree. Steve, write up a benign, general statement and send it out. We'll keep it low-key, act like we've got nothing to hide, and maybe everyone else will take the hint and do the same." She bit into the doughnut. Sweetness exploded in her mouth. "Oh..."

Nona sat down with her coffee, her expression puzzled. "Since when do you eat doughnuts?"

Jana stopped to think. "I guess since now." She tore off another sugary piece and popped it in her mouth. "I don't think I've had a doughnut since...I was nine." When she was the girl she'd forgotten along the way to responsible adulthood, had forgotten until "Peter" came crashing back in her life, looking for her. The doughnut was delicious. Her eyes slid half-closed.

Worry lines dug in between Nona's brows. "It's a witch hunt," she said. "The paper's all over it. Here, it is on the front page." She laid the *Sun* on the desk. Jana, anxious to see what had been written about her father, slid the paper closer.

Car Sliced In Half! Local Police Asking For Help In Hunting Down Suspects In Bizarre Crime.

A piece of doughnut went down the wrong way. Jana choked. Coughing, eyes tearing, she gaped at the newspaper as Nona jumped up to pound her on the back.

Jana dashed away her tears with the heel of her palm and shoved on her reading glasses. Below the headline was a blurry picture—the one the man had taken with his cell phone. All there was to see of Jana was her left leg from the knee down. But the photo had captured Cavin from helmet to platform boots as he bent over to get in the car. His form was more blurred than the rest of the photo, wiped out beyond recognition. Then she remembered what he'd said: the armor was smart; it "saw" the camera and distorted the image.

Three Stolen Cars Recovered. Linked To Crime. And each wiped clean of identifying fingerprints, thank goodness, but what if she'd dropped something out of her purse? Jana sprinted through the article, looking for anything else that could lead the police back to her door:

Male in disguise… Last seen on display inside Safeway… Store spokeswoman denies any knowledge of the display… "We saw him talking to a woman," two witnesses claimed. "She was in her late twenties…"

Only her late twenties? Bless that couple, whoever they were.

"…about five-foot-six or -seven, blond. Looked angry…"

They had no idea how angry.

"…and a little disheveled…"

Jana gnawed nervously on her knuckle. When she went out, anywhere, she was either sharply professional or "dressed down" in designer sportswear. Jewelry, hairstyle, perfect. She always took the time to make sure she was accessorized properly. But not yesterday. No, yesterday was an aberration in every way a day could be. *They won't think it was me!*

"If you get any closer to that newspaper, your nose is going to bounce off that desk," Nona said.

Jana sat up straight and put down the half-eaten doughnut. She'd lost her appetite. "A car cut in half? I can't imagine how it happened."

Nona shrugged. "Aliens?"

Jana pretended to laugh along with Steve.

Nona flipped the paper over. "It gets stranger and stranger. Look. They found a pair of women's shoes on the street where the first stolen car was abandoned."

Jana choked again. Yellow canvas open-toe high heels sporting jaunty raffia bows. Her shoes. She'd forgotten all about them.

"You okay?" Steve asked. "You're not coming down with anything are you?"

Nah, just a psychological collapse. Jana shook her head. "A little vitamin C and I'll be fine." Followed by a bottle of tequila and a nice long coma.

"Pretty shoes, too," Nona commented. "Manolo Blahniks?"

"Yes…" Pouting, Jana gazed at her shoes, her *former* shoes, one intact and one with a broken heel. "A shame to lose those shoes." She blinked. *Act less detached, more sympathetic.* "Tragic that he might have taken a hostage."

"The woman sounded a lot like you. Blond, five-six, about your age…"

"But disheveled," Jana put in quickly. "I'd never go outside looking disheveled. You can't anymore. It's asking for trouble."

"They're questioning two men found naked last night near a warehouse. A man who fits the description of the car slicer, stealer, hostage-taker stole their clothes at gunpoint. Stripped them and left them unconscious in a Dumpster."

Jana froze. It was as if someone dumped ice water on her head, clearing the vestiges of fog in her brain. Someone who fit the description of the armored man? Since it wasn't Cavin, was it the REEF? She skimmed the article, but found nothing helpful.

Jana pulled off her reading glasses as her mood plummeted. The REEF was possibly still out there and, worse, disguised as a local. *Poof* went the massive amount of relief she'd felt at not being linked to last night's crimes.

With every ounce of professionalism that she'd either developed along the way or had bred into her, she dragged her focus back to Nona and Steve. As they briefed the rest of the day's pertinent items, she acted normal. She sounded normal. She felt like a fake.

A FEW MINUTES before nine, Jana waited for an elevator to take her down to the Eureka Room, a dining area under the historic side of the capitol where she and the first lady were hosting the breakfast reception for the Brownie troop. The doors opened and Jana walked into the elevator crammed full with a desk chair and nine other people, assorted staff, lobbyists and legislators, all suit-to-suit and stepping on each other's shiny shoes while Lucky, an overweight woman in her sixties sat in an inconveniently placed, padded chair knitting a sweater.

She greeted Jana with a big smile. "One, sweet pea?"

"No, it's the basement today, Lucky. Thank you."

Jana got the usual amused glances and a couple of raised eyebrows from the others. It was rare Lucky called anyone anything at all, let alone "sweet pea." But since the day Jana had showed up as the youngest senator, Lucky had treated her like a daughter.

As the elevator descended, Jana asked the woman, "How's the family, Lucky?"

She lifted the partially knitted little sweater. "I got a new great-grandkid on the way."

"That's wonderful!" Jana beamed. "Congrat—" Her cell phone vibrated in her hand. "Congratulations," she finished, her eyes going to the caller ID.

The elevator stopped on floor two. As the people shuffled on and off, Jana glanced at the number. It was Evie.

Normal face, normal face. Jana took the call. The doors closed and the elevator started down to the first floor. "Evie, give me a minute, I'm in the elevator—"

"Jana, my pet sitter Patti just called. Told me there's a man at my house who looks like Josh Holloway and says he belongs to you."

"Omigod." Cavin. How could she have forgotten to warn her sister about him? Poor Patti. Jana squeezed her eyes closed, which blocked out the startled and overly curious stares of the other people in the elevator. "Is Patti okay? And who's Josh Holloway?"

"Her sixteen-year-old hormones are rockin', but yeah, she's fine. And you are such a geek, Jana. You don't know anyone. Josh Holloway plays Sawyer on *Lost,* the TV show. But you don't watch TV, do you? Google him."

Right after I finish googling: How to keep your life

from going down the toilet. "Tell Patti I'm sorry I didn't warn her."

"Apparently, your friend was very nice to her. They spoke while he was on the roof."

The roof! Jana almost passed out. "What was he doing on the roof?" she cried. After catching a few looks, she lowered her voice. "Did he say why?"

"He was repairing the security system."

"Oh. Well, see? It's not all bad. At least he's helping around the house."

"Jana, I don't have a security system. I have an alarm, but it's disconnected because of the pets. I tried to call the house just now, but there's some weird busy signal."

Holy Mary Mother of God. Jana wanted to pray, but she didn't know where to start. What was Cavin up to? Why did she ever think he'd behave and remain indoors? The elevator finally reached the basement level and she staggered out, leaving a gaggle of disappointed eavesdroppers behind her.

With a finger stuck in one ear and the cell phone pressed to her other, Jana hurried down the hallway toward the Eureka Room. "Evie, I am so sorry. I stayed in your house last night. I was supposed to call and tell you. This morning, I swear. But it got so crazy—"

"Give it up, girl. The goods. Who's the dude and what's he doing in my house?"

"If I told you, you'd never believe me."

"Try me."

Jana stopped outside the Eureka Room's closed doors and a sign that said Reserved: Private Function. "Remember Peter from when we were kids? The glowing boy? The one who could fly?"

"The one who owed you three wishes but only gave you two?"

"It's him."

At first there was silence on the other end. "He's imaginary, Jana."

"That's what I thought, too."

There was some rustling on the line then Evie's muffled voice telling one of her children, "In a minute. Aunt Jana's not feeling well." Then the rustling stopped. "Aw, sweetie," Evie said. "How are you taking this thing with Dad and Jared? I'm sick over it, but I'm trying not to let it ruin the kids' vacation. Are you okay? Do we need to talk?"

"I am talking, Evie. He came back, and I'm hiding him at your house. Peter, my imaginary friend."

Giggles erupted behind her. Jana turned around slowly. The doors to the Eureka Room were wide-open. At least a dozen little girls with gap-toothed grins were staring up at her as their troop leaders observed her with tentative smiles. Jana blinked away a news headline: State Senator Has Breakdown In Front Of Brownie Troop As Jasper Political Dynasty Continues Tragic Downhill Slide.

"Evie, I'll call you later," she whispered and hung up. Then turned around and flashed a blinding, politician's smile. "Why, hello, girls! Welcome to our State Capitol. I'm Senator Jana Jasper, and I'm honored to meet you." She thrust out her arm and made sure she shook everyone's hand. "We're going to have fun this morning, right?"

"Right," they chorused.

"I can't wait to see the projects you made to call attention to the important issue of saving our environment. But first, how many of you have or have had imaginary friends?"

A few shy hands rose up.

"Is that all?"

A few more hands went up.

The first lady, her security detail, and her personal assistant, Keri, walked up to the group. Mary Ann glanced curiously from the girls and their raised hands to Jana. "We're talking about imaginary friends, Mrs. Schwarzkopf. I had one. Did you?"

"No, but my daughter had one for years." The woman appeared amused by the question.

"Whether you did or didn't have an imaginary friend, it's important to remember just how important imagination is. My grandfather, Governor Jake Jasper, told me that imagination is the ability to look at ordinary things and see magic. We must never stop believing in magic, because without it, we can't dream. And, girls, our dreams are the building blocks for the future. I understand that all of you cared enough about California's future to draw posters in support of protecting our environment. Mrs. Schwarzkopf and I look forward to seeing what you made. Why don't you show us?"

Surrounded by the chatter of excited little voices, Jana placed her hands on the backs of a couple of girls nearest her and ushered them into the room, where they took seats at a table set up for the catered breakfast.

Mary Ann gave Jana a warm smile. She, like Jana, had grown up in a well-known political family. And now, as adults, they found themselves immersed in the game. It gave them a bond that transcended political ideology. "That was a charming way to break the ice," Mary Ann said.

"Thanks. It worked out nicely for something totally off-the-cuff."

"If only I were as good off-the-cuff."

You'd be amazed what a little desperation can do.

Mary Ann left her to address the girls at the podium. The walls in the room were made of bricks restored from the original capitol foundation from the 1800s. Colorful posters decorated one wall and formed a backdrop to the podium. At first glance, the projects were the innocent expressions of young children: bright yellow suns, moons and stars, the Earth, animals, and, in one, people with wings that could fly. Which ones were drawn from imagination, and which were unknowingly real? Did these expressions of childhood in fact a represent something far more serious? As in…the aliens amongst us?

Jana pressed a hand over her mouth, indulged in exactly two seconds of screaming panic then, putting on her "normal" face, she waited for her turn to speak. But no matter what kind of outer shell she presented to the public, one fact didn't change: there was an alien prowling on the roof of her sister's house.

CHAPTER NINE

ANSWER THE PHONE, CAVIN. After a long morning of meetings and appointments, Jana was back in the office. For what seemed like the hundredth time, she'd slipped on her glasses and hit Send on her cell phone. She'd been trying on and off since breakfast and, just like Evie had said, all she heard from the other end was a strange busy signal.

The kind you heard when circuits were dead.

Jana sweated under her pale blue pin-striped suit that matched the sky outside her small window, a sky empty of any hint of an impending alien invasion.

Who was she kidding? *All of Earth* was empty of hints of an invasion. Only *she* knew anything about it. And what was she doing? Keeping it a secret, hoping it would go away. Well, it wasn't going away.

Jana scooted up to her computer and called up Google. She typed in Area 51. *Google him, Jana. You don't know anyone.* She sniffed. "I know a few people, Evie. A few." She backspaced and typed in: Josh Holloway.

The first of a hundred fan sites for the TV star and the show *Lost* popped up. Jana slipped on her glasses and squinted at a photo of Holloway. Okay, he was cute. Cavin had darker, shorter hair and a better mouth, though.

She deleted Holloway and went in search of what she could gather on Area 51. But after a few intent minutes of weeding out the facts from the hype, all she learned was that Area 51 was also known as Groom Lake and was a secret military facility about ninety miles north of Las Vegas. The number referred to a six-by-ten-mile block of land, at the center of which was a large air base the government didn't like to discuss. It didn't add much to what she already knew: the place was a remote testing ground for "black budget" aircraft before they were publicly acknowledged.

There was nothing that stated with any credibility that an alien spacecraft had ever been hidden there. It was a rumor with roots dating back to 1947 when a lieutenant at Roswell Army Air Field issued a press release stating that the army had recovered a crashed flying saucer from the New Mexico desert, sparking a conspiracy theory the Pentagon had never quite been able to kill off. The missing UFO had become urban legend, the inspiration for cheesy movies, some really terrible photos, and one heck of a tourist trade in a place few would otherwise visit.

Jana dug deeper. Maps of the area showed little more than scattered mountain ranges, a dry lake bed, and assorted dirt roads winding across the bleak and parched high desert. The perfect location for a base around which you didn't want people snooping.

She pulled off her glasses. If one were to want to hide a spacecraft, Area 51 would be the place to do it.

Her secretary, Vicky, paged her. "Jana, it's your brother on line one."

"Hey, Jared," she said, picking up.

"Busy?"

"Um, doing research. How are you?"

"So far, so good over here. Are you holding up?"

Jana made a sound in her throat. "I feel like one of those circus performers who balance the spinning plates on sticks."

Jared laughed.

"Each plate's a promise I've made to someone. And all the plates are wobbling." She swiveled her chair and turned her back to the computer.

"Especially the one you made to Grandpa about being a nun."

Jana thought of Cavin and steamy, rain-drenched jungles. "I'm spinning that plate as fast as I can." And how much longer until it crashed?

"That's what you get for trying to do what they tell you. But then you were always the good kid."

That's what you think. "Well, don't be surprised if I turn out to be the biggest troublemaker this family's ever seen," she said glumly.

"I'll believe it when I see it."

"Say, I was wondering if any of your air force buddies were ever stationed at Area 51?"

"No one for years. What do you need?"

Jana spun her desk chair to face the window and gazed fretfully at the sky. "I'm thinking of trying to get an old friend onto the base."

"Who?"

"You never met him. Childhood friend. He's interested in a tour, sort of."

"Is he military?"

"Actually he is."

"What branch?"

"Er…foreign." *Very foreign.*

"Good luck."

"That's what I was afraid of. Anyone in the family? With all our connections, you'd think one of us would know someone who is or was at the base."

"Grandpa knows General Mahoney," Jared said. "He used to be Dreamland's base commander back in the day. He was famous for deflecting the media from what they were really doing out there. He was so good at feeding them bullshit, the guys on the base dubbed him Baloney Mahoney. He's been retired for decades, but I bet he knows people. Ask Grandpa."

Jana had a vague childhood memory of a crusty old officer coming to Thanksgiving dinner at the ranch. Baloney Mahoney. He sounded exactly the kind of ally they needed. But to get to the fact-fibbing general, she'd have to go through her grandfather and, frankly, the thought terrified her. She wouldn't know what to say. "*Why does my friend need to visit Area 51, Grandpa? So he can hack into the spacecraft everyone except conspiracy theory enthusiasts and UFO fanatics say isn't there. Why? It's how he's going to communicate with the alien invasion force that's on their way here. You look pale, Grandpa.*"

Jana pressed her hand to her aching stomach.

"Anyway, kid," Jared drawled, "I called to say I'll see you at lunch."

"No you won't. I've got a working lunch scheduled with the Water Board."

"Viktor said you'd be there."

"Be where?"

"At Ice. Where else? He's trying out a new lunch menu and invited us to come. Normally, my lunches are booked, but now that I'm a pariah, my schedule's wide-open."

"Oh, Jared." She wanted to weep for him, for her father.

"So, I thought, why not? Viktor's family, for God's sake. He invited Mom, too."

A regular family reunion. "Wish I'd known about it. I doubt I could have rescheduled this lunch, though. I'd much rather have eaten with you and Mom. Have some caviar for me," she said longingly before hanging up.

Again, she tried Evie's home number. It was the same rapid beeping noise. That's it. After lunch she was leaving. She'd lie and say she was sick, a first for her, and, all things considered from the past day, it wouldn't be too far from the truth.

But what if she got to her sister's house and Cavin wasn't there? A nightmarish image of men-in-black arriving at Evie's door flashed in her mind: *"We want you to come with us, Mr. Far Star."*

Vicky poked her head through the door. "You've got flowers!"

"Flowers," Jana repeated in a dead voice. "From who—?"

"And your mother's here. Oh, and the Water Board called to reschedule lunch."

Nothing like everything happening at once. Jana frowned at her watch. "A half hour before we're supposed to meet, the Water Board cancels? Sure, pencil them in for lunch after Easter recess. Did they say why they canceled?"

"They said you did."

"Uh, no, I didn't."

As she absorbed what her secretary had said, Jana's expression reflected the uncomfortable feeling in her gut. No one in her office would cancel a lunch meeting without expressly getting her permission. "Have Nona look into it," Jana said.

Vicky backed up and Larisa Porizkova Jasper, arms full of white roses, soared into the office, immediately gilding it with her golden-blond glamour. Jana had inherited her mother's coloring and agility, but not her extraordinary presence and classic beauty. But thanks to her mother's loving encouragement and praise every step of the way through childhood, Jana never felt inadequate in her presence. In fact, the opposite was true. Her mother inspired her.

The scents of real roses and her mother's expensive perfume filled the office. Mom set the bouquet on Jana's desk. "Ah, look! Are they not beautiful?"

"They're gorgeous. Who sent them?"

Her mother dug a card out of layers of velvety petals. "'To help make a rotten day smell a little sweeter. Alex.' Awww."

"Alex Neiman?"

"See? He is a good, sweet boy. Thinking of you in this hard time for our family."

"It was a thoughtful thing for him to do," Jana acknowledged. Then she noticed her mother's eyes. Even a careful application of makeup couldn't hide the puffy lids. "Mom, you've been crying."

She waved her hand airily. "For a few indulgent moments, only. I have decided, no more crying. What good does it do?"

Jana scooted her chair closer to the desk. "What happened? What are they saying now?"

"My relatives in Moscow have connections to the Russian Mafia."

"What?"

"Yes, it is true."

"It is? We have family in the Russian Mafia?"

Her eyes sparked blue fire. *"Nyet*, Janushka! But they have mentioned this in the news. Grandpa saw it. It was on CNN."

Jana slapped her hands on the desk. Papers scattered. *"Yenflarg."*

"What is that?

"It means shit in alien. Or something." Jana sagged back in her chair. "Dad's campaign finances, Jared's company, now your family. It's such an obvious witch hunt, how can anyone believe it?"

Her mother clutched her hands in her lap. Her three-carat diamond wedding ring sparkled in the overhead light. "Grandpa's in the hospital."

Unexpected tears stung Jana's eyes. "When?"

"An hour ago. You're the first to know. He's not in immediate danger, but his pressure was too high. He was so angry, so worried that you are next in line to be attacked. I was afraid to leave him alone. The nurse at home is too afraid of him."

"He is a force to reckon with."

"He has a private room. They're running tests."

"It's the smart thing to do." Poor Grandpa.

"But we will do no crying. Here—I want you to have this." Her mother opened her pale green, quilted leather Chanel purse and pulled out a lump wrapped in perfumed tissue paper. "A gift for you."

"What is it?"

"Go. Open it and see."

Jana pulled apart the paper and revealed a small, exquisitely painted matryoshka doll. "This was a gift from Dad to you. I can't keep this."

"Yes, you must. You of all my children have treasured my matryoshkas since you were small. I remember how you'd gather them and read all the notes, replacing them so carefully."

Jana guarded the precious bundle in her hands. "But why are you giving me this now?"

"If in the coming weeks, it is hard for you—"

"I'm going to be fine, Mom. Please, don't worry." What her mother didn't know was that Jana was already battling the biggest possible threat to her reputation: it was six foot one and hiding in Evie's house.

Correction—he was on Evie's roof.

Jana squeezed her eyes closed briefly and listened to her mother say, "Life is sometimes easy, and sometimes hard, but love is the only constant. No matter how far you rise, or how hard you fall, a good love will always be there for you. I want you to keep the matryoshka to remind you of this."

Jana opened her eyes and came around the desk to embrace her mother. Their hug was long and emotional. Then her mother kissed the top of her head as she used to when Jana was a child. "Thank you for being a good girl," Mom said. "For doing as Grandpa asked. He asks a lot of you, but he knows, as we all do, that you are strong enough to rise to the occasion."

Good? She'd been anything but. Jana's smile felt so forced that she wouldn't be surprised if it came out looking like a grimace.

Mom patted her on the hands. "Now let's pay Viktor a visit. Perhaps it will be a much-needed distraction."

But as Jana reached for her suit jacket, she couldn't help inhaling a whiff of roses. Two dozen white roses. Alex Neiman was exactly the kind of distraction she didn't need.

CHAPTER TEN

COUSIN VIKTOR FILLED five shot glasses with ice-cold Stolichnaya vodka. "Za vashe zdorov'yeh!" Everyone chorused the toast. Jana tossed back the shot and slammed the glass down. The numbing effect of the vodka was welcome. Probably it would be too forward of her to ask for the rest of the bottle, a straw and some privacy.

An expansive wall of photos of celebrities was the first thing anyone saw walking into Ice: Sacramento Kings players, Governor Schwarzkopf, the mayor, Hollywood movie stars and even Jana, all of them posed with a one, two, or three combination of Alex, Viktor, or Brace Bowie, the three investors in the venture. Brace's involvement was solely financial. Viktor ran the kitchen, and Alex handled the business side of things. There was even a photo of Janna and Brace taken before his big tantrum, before he hung billboards across the city criticizing her political motives and promising he was going to take her down. Jana's eyes narrowed at the picture. Her former fiancé's absence at lunch was about the only good thing that had happened today. Viktor might not be the master of tact, but at least he knew better than to ask the jerkwad to join them.

Sometimes, when she was feeling magnanimous, she'd explain away Brace's behavior as acute, financial-related stress. He'd sunk a lot of money into Ice. Just looking around at the place made her hear the *ca-ching* of cash registers. Ice lived up to its name: everything was built of either steel, glacial glass or quartz. The cool, blue tones soothed Jana's underlying hysteria. Or maybe it was the subzero shot of Stoli that had temporarily deadened the scream that seemed to bubble constantly just beneath her faux-calm exterior.

"Sit, eat!" Viktor waved to his best table. The restaurant was noisy and crowded. If Viktor's goal was to introduce upscale Sacramento diners to the art of zakuski, it was working. According to the explanation on the menus, zakuski meant "a few bites" but growing up half-Russian, Jana knew it really meant "a few bites to go with vodka." A good zakuski selection was supposed to cover the table, and Viktor's certainly did: salads, cold chicken and potatoes in sour cream, pickled herring and smoked whitefish, pickled garlic, pickled beets, and everything else Russians loved to pickle, along with thick hunks of black bread. A frosty bowl of caviar was being handed around the table to be spooned onto blini and other treats.

"Eat! Eat!" Viktor called out and took a seat next to Jared. Alex settled next to Jana, of course. She caught a whiff of his aftershave mixed with starch from the Korean cleaners down the street. His pale lavender shirt was pressed so crisply that the creases could give someone a paper cut. In contrast, his tie, decorated with loud yellow daffodils, all but shouted spring, an outfit that somehow worked. Jana had always admired his unique sense of style, but when she compared him to Cavin's spare, functional, all-black military simplicity, Alex through no fault of his own looked like an overwrought butterfly.

"Thanks for the flowers, Alex. It was sweet. Very thoughtful."

His dark brown eyes sparkled. He was boyish and cute with an underlying intensity she found attractive. But she knew there'd be no magic in his kiss. She missed Cavin, she realized with a pang. Really missed him, missed the man who saved her from an alien assassin's killing shot, who could sent her into orgasmic bliss with words alone…Cavin, who last she'd heard was prowling on Evie's roof.

Her heartsick pang changed to the kind you might have dangling over a pit of hungry alligators. She had to get back to Evie's, but she was stuck here for at least another hour. Downing another shot might be helpful, but she'd already had plenty.

Alex spooned a dollop of caviar onto a stuffed egg. "I'm glad you liked them. I couldn't help thinking of you with all this going on."

"Let's not talk about that."

"No, let's not. Let's talk about what time I'm going to pick you up, later."

Later? The Kings game. "Oh, crap. Alex, I forgot all about it." She'd agreed to the basketball game date before anything had happened. That was five days ago but it might as well have been five years ago it seemed so far away. He'd been after her for so long to go out. She'd finally said yes, and now she couldn't go.

"So you forgot. You're a busy girl. But now you remember. Do you want to eat before or after?"

"I can't go, Alex."

"Don't work late. You work too much."

"I'm not working. I…I have plans. It was very last-minute." *Like last night in the supermarket.* She tipped her chin down and tried to look as apologetic as she sounded. "Rain check?"

Something darker flickered in his eyes. "Sure."

"If you really want to put our Alex in a bad mood, tell us how much higher caviar prices will go, Senator," Viktor scolded Jana in a teasing tone she suspected was meant to mask a more serious one.

"Viktor," Alex warned.

"You're in a better position to tell me that, Viktor," Jana said, licking sour cream off her spoon.

"Not so. Last October, this country banned imports of Russian caviar. You know this, because your father was behind it."

"My father and the rest of the U.S. Congress," she pointed out.

"What is left of the Caspian Sea stock is several thousand dollars a kilo. So, we are now totally dependent on domestic supply. In Russia, the caviar industry is controlled by the Mafia, but in California, it is controlled with your iron fist. In certain circles in the Russian community, you are known as the czarina. Your Fish and Game thugs have become as feared in the community as the Soviet KGB. Here in America."

Jana put down her spoon. "I don't know where you get your facts, Viktor."

"I get my facts from my wallet. That's where I get them. Caviar prices have gone through the roof."

"Sturgeon were fished to near extinction. There's a

fact for you. For a while the population in the wild came back, but suddenly it's falling again. There's another fact for you. Fishermen are calling Fish and Game because they've noticed the decline. And they've noticed several men asking around, seeing who'd be willing to catch them a sturgeon, which as you know is against the law. My so-called thugs are hardworking men and women trying to stop the hemorrhage. My special ops wardens are on the case."

Viktor's dark eyes slid to the side. His near arrest during the last big bust-up of a poaching ring had left him sensitive to the subject.

"We're creating farms to bring the population back. But it's a long-lived, slow-maturing species. It won't happen overnight."

"My businesses may not be here overnight."

Viktor had his main business in San Francisco. It was vast and sprawling, and she knew the new ban on exports from Russia had given him headaches. Many in the Russian community saw U.S. caviar as inferior, an image Jana was working hard to change. Because of her position, Viktor was careful what he said around her, but it wouldn't surprise her to learn his hands were dirtied occasionally by black market caviar. But until today, she'd never talked shop and neither had he. It was an unspoken promise of family get-togethers that he'd now broken. She'd get up and walk out if it wasn't so important to her mother that they share this "family" lunch.

"You limit me to fish farms, Jana, yet you keep the prices high. How am I supposed to make a profit?"

Jana passed the bowl to her mother and exchanged an annoyed glance with Jared. "If I don't limit it to the farms, sturgeon will disappear—here and all over the world. Then you'll be paying five hundred an ounce or more for your precious caviar, *wholesale,* if you can even find any. Or you'll learn to like catfish eggs."

"*Nyet,*" her mother said softly. "May it never be."

"With your father, my own uncle, cutting off my Russian supply, and you cutting off my California supply, I have no choice but to descend into ruin."

Jana fumed. "I'm not cutting off anyone's supply. I am trying hard to keep a species from extinction."

"It seems you care more about a fish than a businessman trying to feed his family."

"Shut up, Viktor," Jared snapped. "Just shut up." His eyes had narrowed and his shoulders were tight. A muscle twitched in his jaw. "And what family, Viktor? Last I checked, you don't have one."

"Enough!" Mom slammed her hand on the table, rattling the cutlery and silencing everyone. Her soft, sky-blue eyes had turned to ice. Her stare was so frosty and focused on Viktor that Jana half expected him to turn into a snowman. Siberian winter had arrived at the table.

Suddenly, cousin Viktor didn't look so brave.

Mom's voice was low and cold. "I brought your father to this country, Viktor. I brought him here and I will send him back."

He stuttered. "Aunt Larisa, he's dead."

"So? Everyone dies. If I want him to go home, he will go. I will send him back to Russia in his box."

Jana had no doubt her mother would do it, too.

Viktor downed a shot of Stoli and dragged the back of his thick hand across his face and nodded. "I have been rude. Please accept my apologies."

Mom gave him the epitome of a Russian shrug. Jana had never seen another ethnic group who could shrug like the Russians could.

Alex sighed. "I apologize for my partner's passion. It hasn't been easy. We all feel the pressure lately."

Then why didn't you stop him, Alex? What kind of man lets the girl he's interested in get pulverized by his business partner? Not the kind of man she'd ever be interested in. Cavin never would have let that happen. In that moment, Jana crossed Alex off her list for good. Their eyes met, and he seemed to sense it. Anger heated his gaze, not disappointment, or regret, and that unbalanced her even more.

Alex Neiman doesn't like you.

But if he didn't like her, why send the flowers, why ask her out?

"I was out of place," Viktor grumbled. "Mixing business with what should be only pleasure. Jana, I'm sorry." He dipped in a small bow. "You will forgive me, yes?"

"This time," she muttered. "Next time I beat the shit out of you."

"Jana!" Mom gasped as Jared fell back, laughing.

Viktor appeared stunned. "What happened to the sweet, mild-mannered girl?"

"She's on leave. Maybe permanently." Jana reached for the bottle of Stoli sitting deep in a melting hunk of ice. Time for another glacial, brain-deadening, and very necessary shot.

"Wait," Alex said, stopping her hand short of the bottle. "We've got something better. Viktor, go get it." Viktor hesitated. "Go. You owe her big-time, buddy, bringing up things you had no business discussing over a civilized meal. A family meal."

Suddenly Alex was family?

"You mean...*it?*" Viktor asked.

"Yes. It. It's what we've been saving it for, right?"

Still, Viktor hesitated. Alex rolled his eyes and dragged Jana's cousin from the room. There was the sound of a heavy freezer door slamming shut, murmured voices. Then the men returned to the table. The bottle Viktor carried was triple the size of a normal liquor bottle. Frosted over, it smoked with water vapor.

"This is the vodka Stoli wishes it could be," Viktor declared in triumph and dropped the freezing bottle in Jana's lap.

"Ooph." The bottle was as cold and heavy as a torpedo pulled from the Bering Sea. Inside, subzero vodka sloshed like syrup. She grabbed hold of the bottle to keep it from falling. "Ow, this is really cold, Viktor."

"Jewel of Russia. Ultra-ultra. A three-liter bottle. Hand-painted with traditional Russian designs." Viktor scratched at the frost, clearing some away. "And signed by the artist."

Again, Jana tried to get rid of the cold, heavy bottle, but Viktor kept talking. Her arms were aching, and her hands stung.

Bizarre Medical News Daily: Woman Recovering After Surgical Removal Of Liquor Bottle.

"Only two of these were released to the United States this year," Viktor bragged. "One of them to the Russian ambassador, and one of them to me. I won't tell you what it cost, but you could buy a small car for the price. Me? I'd rather drink the vodka. Jana, please accept this small token of apology."

Suddenly, the frosty bottle was a hot potato. California had very strict disclosure laws for elected officials. Anything over fifty dollars that wasn't from immediate family she had to disclose. Even then, there was the problem of the appearance of accepting perks from those with agendas. It allowed her to keep little of what was given to her all year long.

Viktor should have known that, but he was an idiot. A bumbling well-meaning idiot, but still an idiot. She was glad other diners hadn't noticed the presentation. It would be hard to explain away.

"Thank you," she told the men. "It's a wonderful and generous gift. And beautiful, too." The sunshine from the window cut diamondlike jewels in the vodka, and the ice cut like knives into her wrists, which sort of diluted the loveliness of the light show. "Do you mind if I leave this here with you for now? My staff will pick it up for me. Rules and more rules. You know how it is."

"I will keep it here for you, Jana. Locked in the freezer vault, for you when you come. You come to drink vodka, I will have the best for you." Finally, her cousin lifted the heavy bottle from her frostbitten arms.

Almost regretfully, Jana watched him carry it away. But considering she was at her personal limit with police encounters and near arrests in a twenty-four-hour period, she'd better be sober when it came time to get in her car.

"I WON'T BE BACK in the office today," she told Nona an hour later, driving from the capitol to her apartment a few short blocks away. A doggie bag for Cavin sat on the seat next to her.

"I can't remember you ever taking the afternoon off."

"Not since I was nine," Jana mumbled.

"Sorry?"

"Not important. I have a small emergency going on. Personal stuff."

"What's wrong? Are you okay?"

"Yes, I'm fine, Nona. Everything's fine." *Liar, liar.* "It'll be easily taken care of if I can give the matter a little attention." *Pants on fire.* "Cancel out my afternoon, or go in my place. I'll see you in the morning."

Jana pulled into the Sacramento Sky Towers parking garage, rode the elevator up to the lobby to transfer to the residence elevators.

Malvo, the doorman, greeted her and said, "Hello, Senator."

"Hello, Malvo. What's up?"

"The good news or the bad news first?"

"Why, I'll take the bad news." She always did when someone asked. She hated to ruin the good news. "What is it?"

"The police are waiting for you upstairs in your apartment."

CHAPTER ELEVEN

"THE POLICE ARE HERE?" They'd found out about last night, Jana thought frantically, her eyes shifting back and forth. Where were the exits? Could she run away in time? She'd disappear, drive to Mexico and disappear: Fugitive Senator Flees Over The Border After Drunken Vodka Spree.

Her chin came up. You're not a fugitive. You've done nothing wrong.

Ha! Nothing like a conscience in denial. Besides, she promised Cavin she was coming back. Maybe they could escape to Mexico together. Someplace steamy. Rainy. With trees.

"Security was supposed to call you. Someone saw someone outside your door trying to break in."

"Oh, good," she said, relieved. Malvo gave her a funny glance. *I mean, good that I'm not about to be hauled away to jail.* She dug deep for a more alarmed reaction. "Oh, no. I'd better get up there."

She ran into the elevator and rode it up to her floor. Only when the doors opened did she remember she never asked Malvo for the good news.

A couple of police officers hovered by her apartment. One of them was busy making out a report. The lock was broken, the door ajar. It was creepy, picturing someone stalking around at her place only hours after she'd left it.

She came forward, her arm outstretched. "Good afternoon, gentlemen. I'm Jana Jasper. I understand someone tried to break into my apartment."

"Not tried, did." The officer pushed on the door, opening it. Someone had been inside. Someone out to get her. A malevolent presence hung in the air. She wasn't sure how she sensed it, she just did. Her unease skyrocketed.

"We got an anonymous call from one of your neighbors," the officer continued. "Unfortunately, they couldn't get us a description." He pocketed a pad he'd been writing on. "Well, file a report if anything is missing. We've got another call."

"Wait." Jana's mouth had gone dry. "Can you come inside with me? Make sure no one's there? I'm a little nervous about going in alone."

"We checked for trespassers, ma'am."

Nonalien ones, she thought frantically. She didn't want to encounter the REEF behind her shower curtain. "Please?"

The busy cops shrugged. "For you, Senator, we will."

Jana followed them inside. She blinked in the bright sunshine flooding the living room. It was airy and sparsely furnished in ultramodern decor: glass, maple, granite and steel, with hues of blue, gray and white dominating. All very different from Evie's house. It was supposed to remind her of the sky, but she wondered if it had been an unconscious attempt to distill life down to the essentials of the magic she'd experienced and lost.

And now, found.

As the officers looked around, Jana placed her mother's matryoshka on the shelf above the fireplace. *Love is the only constant.* She changed her mind and slipped the doll into her purse.

"Do you ever cook in here?" one of the officers called from her kitchen as he inspected the gleaming smoke-gray granite counters, pristine stainless steel appliances, her digital espresso machine, the cobalt-blue glass bowls of the blender and mixer that were as new now as they were when she took them out of the box.

"Sometimes." Okay, rarely. Fine, maybe never. "I eat a lot of takeout."

"That was my guess. It's so model-perfect I wasn't sure if you lived here full-time."

Come to think of it, she wasn't sure if she lived here, either. The apartment was a place she slept in when she wasn't at work, nothing more. Maybe that was why she didn't feel as violated by the break-in as she was frightened that someone had come looking for her, namely the REEF. She thought of the naked men found last night, and their description of someone dressed like Cavin. Where the incident occurred was not too far from downtown, an older section, but less than five miles away.

She shuddered, dialed Cavin. No answer. Then she dialed the number Evie had left for her pet sitter, Patti. "All circuits are busy," droned an operator's voice. Busy? How could they be busy? What was going on back at Evie's house? Jana gulped. Probably nothing. It was a new area, lots of construction going on. They were probably doing work on the phone lines or cell towers. Or something.

It was the "or something" that bothered her.

The cops regrouped in the living room. "Senator, no one's here."

"Good," she half whispered.

"Is anything missing?"

"I don't think so." That she wasn't sure and didn't care drove home how little in the apartment actually meant anything. There was her computer, her photos, some art she'd collected, and her favorite clothes and shoes. What few jewels she owned were safe in a vault at the ranch, taken out and worn to the occasional glam function.

Jana walked past her desk and stopped. The file cabinet door was ajar. Her heart turned over. "My files. I'm sure I didn't leave them open." What Jana opened, Jana closed; she was orderly that way. Maybe she'd left it open in her rush to get ready early this morning. Or, maybe she was just being paranoid. She thought of the REEF and shivered. Paranoid was good. Paranoid would keep her alive.

She gave the files a cursory check. "Nothing seems to be missing." What could someone have wanted with what amounted to a bunch of old paperwork, anyway? Probably whoever broke in wanted information, not valuables.

No, they wanted you.

Jana began to sweat despite the chill in the apartment.

"Are you going to be okay, ma'am?"

Funny how many times she'd been asked that today. "As long as I know I've got the place to myself, yes." She escorted the officers to the door and thanked them. Then she launched into action. After calling security to get them to work fixing the lock, she packed a suitcase with a week's worth of clothes and traded her business suit for boots, jeans, a dove-gray cashmere sweater and brought along a vintage brown leather aviator jacket. She couldn't wheel her suitcase out the door fast enough to make it home to Evie's house.

What a difference a day made. This morning she couldn't wait to flee Cavin. Now, she couldn't wait to get back to him.

GRANDPA FINALLY RETURNED Jana's earlier call as she drove up to the gates leading to Evie's subdivision. She hooked up her cell phone earpiece and tried for the brightest voice she could manage. "Grandpa! Are you home now?"

"Hell no. They want to keep me overnight for observation." He spat out "observation" with such contempt that she had to smile. "Said my blood pressure was too high this morning. Said I was overwrought. I'm fine. Your parents should be locked up next for imprisoning an old man."

"Grandpa, you're not old."

"They tell me I am."

"Don't believe it. But I do want you to take care of yourself. Don't worry. Be happy." In her borderline hysteria, she hummed a few bars of the song.

"Are you okay, punkin?"

"Seventeen."

"Seventeen?"

"That's how many times I've been asked that question today. An average of twice an hour. But back to you. How are you doing?"

"I'm angry I'm imprisoned in this hospital. I'm

angry at the rumors and lies directed at my family. I'm goddamn angry at the thought of this affecting your reelection. But don't tell your mother."

She took a shuddering breath, wished she could tell him the truth, that her reelection was going to be affected, only not by rumors and lies. *It's going to be affected by things beyond your worst nightmares, Grandpa, if what Cavin tells me is true.* She wanted to confide everything to him, but couldn't. If lies about her father's ethics and rumors about her mother's ties to the Russian Mafia had sent him to the hospital, news that she was madly in love with an alien who'd brought warnings of an impending invasion after landing a spaceship at the Jasper ranch would likely put Grandpa in an irreversible vegetative coma.

Ahead, the street was blocked by trucks from Pacific Gas and Electric truck and Comcast Cable. A tow truck drove away in the opposite direction, pulling a car behind it. Jana slowed the Jeep. A wisp of unease coiled through her.

A muscle in her cheek twitched as she absorbed the sight of a couple of abandoned passenger cars with their hoods up. She pulled over to the curb and parked. And realized her grandfather was still talking. She hadn't heard a thing he'd said. "I gotta go, Grandpa. Something's come up." She'd become the master of understatement. "I'll call you in the morning."

"Be good," he told her before they said goodbye.

Be good. Such a simple request. One look at the scene in front of Evie's house told her how futile it was.

Jaspers Bring Alien Menace To The Suburbs.

She pulled her keys from the ignition, grabbed her

suitcase, a small bag of groceries she'd picked up and the doggie bag from lunch and ran to her sister's house. Evie's neighbor Cheryl waved at her from her front yard. "Crazy, isn't it?"

Jana stopped, wheezing for air. "What happened?"

"First the cars started dying. The power came back a few hours ago, but no one has phones. Not even cell service." She held out her wrist for Jana to see. "Eight fifty-four this morning. That's when it happened. My watch stopped. Weird, huh?"

Jana cast a wild glance at Evie's house. No one was on the roof. The house looked normal, if nothing else did.

"Did you see that movie *War of the Worlds?*"

Jana swerved a panicked glance back to Cheryl. "Why?"

"You know in the beginning when that lightning came down? It knocked out everything in the town. Even the watches."

There was an EMP pulse, Jana thought with a start. Cheryl was right. The lightning bolts in the *War of the Worlds* movie were an electromagnetic pulse. The attack knocked out car starters, computers, interrupted everything. Then she remembered the security system Cavin had been working on before she left. "It emits a harmless pulse of energy," he'd told her. Harmless, yes. Something no one would notice, no.

Cheryl laughed. "But we don't have aliens here."

Jana shook her head almost violently.

"So I'm blaming it on the cable company. By the way, cute boyfriend you got there. He's a doll."

Jana's knees almost buckled. "You met Cavin?" She winced. She should have said he wasn't her boyfriend.

And why did she say his name? Not only that, what was he doing, talking to the neighbors? A drumbeat started up in Jana's head: not erotic, I-want-to-get-naked-with-you drumbeats, but migraine drumbeats. *I'm going to kill you, Cavin. Slowly and with my bare hands.* But somehow the thought of putting her bare hands on Cavin didn't have the effect she intended.

"We met him this morning," Cheryl replied. "I introduced myself. He was in the driveway with a really cute sad face watching you drive away. Are you okay, Jana?"

Eighteen. "Fine."

"Well, got to get back inside and see what the kids are up to. No TV. No Nintendo. I don't trust their alternative solutions for entertainment." The woman ran up a few steps to her door and disappeared inside.

Yenflarg. Jana squared her shoulders and marched to Evie's front door.

CHAPTER TWELVE

"YARP, YARP!" From the other side of the front door, Sadie barked. Jana hunted for her keys. Before she could unlock the door, Cavin let her in. From her scalp to her toes and everything in between, she reacted to being near him. No one could fill out black long johns and boots the way he could. His short hair looked damp and spiky, and he'd shaved. As if that wasn't delicious enough, he smelled like the buttery vanilla soap Evie kept in all the bathrooms. Worse, he saw her reaction to him—one look at his pleased, almost mischievous smile told her that.

Woman Self-combusts. Raging Sexual Hormones Blamed On Toenail Polish. FDA To Issue Warning.

"Call me shallow and horny, but everything would be so much easier if you weren't so hot." She shoved the groceries and the doggie bag into his arms. "Turn it off."

"Off?" He glanced down at his body with a look of confusion.

"Yes, off! Now. The security system. Your EMP thingies. Before someone finds out it's coming from this house."

She stormed past him into the kitchen, looking for evidence of a security array, fully intending to rip out anything that looked capable of knocking out the power, killing cars, or freezing watches. "If I get my hands on those darn balls—I mean those damn balls, I'm flushing them down the toilet."

Evie's ginger tomcat Pumpkin wisely fled Jana's wrath and disappeared out the pet door.

Cavin put the bags on the counter next to the sink. "I already disabled the security array. I did it this morning after something set it off. One of the cats, I'm sure. Or maybe it was Sadie. The little creature wouldn't confess, even after an extensive interrogation."

"Yarp, yarp!" Sadie pranced around their feet, barking happily. Cavin appeared maddeningly unconcerned, as well.

"This is no joke." Did he have any idea how close the REEF had come to finding her today? Jana threw down her keys. They skittered across the granite countertop and fell into the sink. "You said it was an electromagnetic pulse, I give you that, but for crying out loud, Cavin, it knocked out the phones, the power, everything. We're supposed to be staying undercover, not attracting attention. Be more careful, Cavin. I couldn't bear losing you. I couldn't—"

"Hello." He swept a hand behind her head and pulled her, stumbling, into a kiss, kissing her until she softened like butter and melted into the hard contours of his body. His hand slid around until he cupped her jaw, keeping her face at just the right angle to explore her deeply with his tongue. His hair was like coarse silk under her fingers, and his mouth, so sweet. Familiar and sweet. He tasted like chocolate, she realized. Her tirade was far from over, but his kiss was so intense, so tender, so luscious, that not even her gift of gab could fight back.

He released her, and she swayed on her feet. "That was quite a hello."

"We have many hellos to catch up on, Jana. Twenty-three years' worth." She was unable to resist when he lowered his head to hers one more time. When she slipped her arms around his shoulders and kissed him back, he made a rumble of pleasure in his chest and his fingers splayed on the back of her head to hold her close. It didn't feel as if he had quickie hello-kisses in mind. No, not at all. In fact, if he kept this up, they'd be in the guest bedroom for a different kind of quickie. Did she really want to be good?

No, but she had to. She couldn't afford to delay bringing Cavin her news. Breathless, she broke off the embrace. "We have to talk, Cavin, or there's a good chance our next kiss will be a goodbye kiss. Someone broke into my apartment today."

Cavin went rigid. His focus was laser sharp. Hard eyes. A soldier's stare. "More information," he demanded.

"It happened while I was at work. No one saw who did it. Nothing was taken, but I think someone went through my personal files. It has to be the REEF."

"He wouldn't have searched and left. He would have retreated to a safe location, waited, and then followed you." Cavin adjusted his wrist gauntlet, turning it on briefly to take a look. "He did not follow you here," he said to her relief.

"There's something else you should know. We made the news today. Front page." How calm she sounded when she really wanted to scream at the top of her lungs. She pulled a newspaper from the grocery bag. Cavin picked it up and held it to his eyes. He couldn't read, but the pictures were loud and clear.

"There's more. They found two men last night. Someone dumped them naked and unconscious in a trash bin near a warehouse. Their attacker was dressed like you. How do I know? Because the guy that stripped the men fits the description circulating of you in your armor at the supermarket. It has to be the REEF. He's out there and, worse, Cavin, now he's dressed like an Earthling."

Cavin shook his head. "Not the REEF."

"How can you be sure? We don't know. Do we take the chance?"

"I'm not advocating taking chances, not with my life or yours. I have one goal while here, to save your world, and that includes saving you. My death would complicate things tremendously."

"Ya think?" She pinched the bridge of her nose to stave off a headache. "How can you make a joke about dying?"

"It helps keep me sane," he said, quieter.

Again, it choked her up what a sacrifice and huge risk Cavin had taken in coming here. She'd always considered the men in her family heroes, but Cavin defined the word. His government was suffering a huge loss if their policies alienated a man like him.

"Jana, I assure you, the REEF would have killed the men."

"He almost did. It was cold last night. They almost died of exposure."

"A REEF assassin knows how to kill. If he left them alive, it's because he wanted to, either for tactical reasons, to flaunt his presence and perhaps flush me out of hiding or, as we've discussed before, he may be malfunctioning. I don't know."

There was a lot they didn't know. But for the moment, they were safe. She tried to cling to that. "I'm starving, and I bet you are, too. What did you eat today, besides chocolate?"

"How do you know I ate chocolate?"

"Because in this house it's everywhere, and I tasted it when you kissed me." She turned away to finish unloading the groceries she'd bought to replenish what they might use of Evie's, plus a bottle of pinot grigio and a container of Ben & Jerry's Phish Food. She savored every second of doing something so mundane, so normal, in the midst of the chaos her life had become. "One hour, Cavin, just one hour of peace to eat a sit-down meal like civilized people, that's all I ask. Then we can linger over after-dinner drinks and talk about assassination attempts, government betrayals, alien invasions, doing it against a tree... That's what I love about us. We never seem to run out of things to talk about."

Cavin slid his arms around her from behind and rested his chin on the top of her head. "Now it's you who is joking about dying."

"Yeah." She sighed. "Sanity has suddenly become quite the commodity around here."

She leaned backward as Cavin kissed the sensitive place under her ear. Smiling, she hunched her shoulders and shivered. One big hand slid down her rib cage to the line of bare skin exposed between the hem of her sweater and her jeans. He dragged his fingertips from her spine to her tummy and back again. His other hand was just as busy, smoothing up and down her ribs. It was warmer in the kitchen than before. Uh-oh. Warning sign.

"You keep me sane more than words do, Squee," he whispered in her ear. With each upward caress, his thumb moved closer to the underside of her breast.

Breathe, Jana, breathe. You are a higher life-form than the sturgeon. Or was she? All she knew was that survival and saving the world had dropped to a distant second place in the face of pure, unadulterated lust.

She snatched his wrist and put his hand where she wanted it: inside her sweater. Cavin's fingers disappeared under the cashmere and slid upward until he found her bra. His breath hitched then he took advantage, molding her, caressing her. The sensation was exquisite, and seemed hardwired to the place between her legs that went *boom, boom, boom.*

She flattened her hands on the cold granite countertop and moaned softly, unintentionally thrusting her butt into Cavin. Her jeans were thin enough to feel that he was hard, very hard and aroused. It made her knees go weak.

He moved her hair aside, nipped the back of her neck. His finger slid under the waistband of her jeans and scooted around to her fly. He was about to pop the top button when he froze. "Gods, you make it difficult to behave," he whispered harshly. His hand slid out from under her sweater. The searing memory of his touch lingered like the afterimage of a flashbulb. He scooted his hips back and safely away, but kept his cheek pressed to hers for a moment. "I'm sorry," he said. "I swore to you. My fault. I'm usually more disciplined than this. Something happens to me when I'm around you."

He didn't need to explain. The same thing happened to her also. Laughing, she let her head fall forward, using her elbows as support as she leaned over the counter. Or maybe it was because she'd lost the ability to stand on her own. "You started it, spaceman."

"You facilitated it."

She laughed. Turning, she linked her arms over his neck. "I guess I did." Cavin fixed her rumpled sweater, pulling on the hem to smooth it, a gesture so casually tender she tingled all over with a surge of affection.

Her cell phone vibrated in her jeans pocket, and she jumped a mile. Was it nerves from the assassin lurking about, or guilt about things heating up with Cavin? She pulled out the phone to read the number. "It's my father," she said, her heart leaping. "Hi, Dad."

"Hi, sweetheart. I'm glad I caught up with you."

Knowing how much he was suffering caused her stomach to knot up. "Tell me what I can do to help. Isn't there anything? Just say the word."

"I need you to hold down the fort for me at the ranch. I'm not going to be able to make it home for Easter."

"I understand, Dad." But she didn't understand. Not really. She didn't understand how one person's or a few people's words could bring a man like her father to his knees.

"Your mother's flying to DC Monday. She'll spend the holiday here. Evie will stay at the ranch all week, looking after Grandpa."

"Mrs. Salazar can't make it?"

"You know him. He refuses to have what he calls a babysitter."

Jana laughed. "I'm surprised she was willing to come back. He's an incorrigible old coot when it comes to caregivers."

"Keep an eye on him, Jana. Keep him steady. He listens to you. I'm concerned about the effect on him with these charges against me. Damn it. I'll learn who did this, and who defamed the Porizkova side of the family. The Russian Mafia, can you believe it?" He made a sound of disgust. "On a more positive note, the accountants going over my finance records haven't found a thing. It's been a ray of light in a couple of very dark days. I taped a press conference earlier. Check the news."

Jana found the remote control Evie kept in the kitchen and turned on a small TV mounted under the counter. She gave the remote to Cavin, who peered at it, turning the remote over and over in his hands with curiosity. His first lesson on blending in as an Earth man, she thought.

But he held it upside down. She smiled, spinning her finger until he caught on. She pointed to the down arrow, nodding, and then he was off and running.

The channel changed from a cooking show to ESPN. It was a college basketball game. Here he lingered before flipping through more channels to a SpongeBob cartoon. He squinted, his mouth set in a funny expression. One thing for certain, this man hadn't spent a childhood watching Saturday-morning cartoons. But when he got to the news, Jana tugged on his sleeve to stop him. *That's my father*, she mouthed.

Cavin observed Congressman Jasper with interest as Jana returned her attention to the call.

"I've got to go, Jana," Dad was saying. "You keep doing what you're doing."

"Doing?" Jana gulped. Jana glanced at Cavin and bit her lip. Beleaguered Congressman's Woes Go Galactic.

"Yes, upholding the Jasper name, being a model legislator. I know there's extraordinary pressure on you right now, public and private, but you've risen to the occasion. You make me proud, Jana."

"Thanks, Dad," she said weakly.

After they hung up, she let out a breath and sagged back against the counter. "So far no one's been able to come up with any evidence of wrongdoing on my father's part, which is no surprise. He seemed in good spirits about it." And confident in her ability to stay out of trouble, which was exactly what she wasn't doing.

She busied her hands putting leftovers from lunch in the microwave so she didn't burst into tears.

"You don't appear as happy as I thought you'd be upon hearing this promising news," Cavin observed.

She handed him a plate of cold leftovers to bring to the table. "Because there's a tremendous amount of pressure not to do anything that will put the family under more scrutiny. These people who went after my father, they're hiding like cockroaches, waiting for another chance. I've seen these things happen before, but never to us. Never to the Jaspers. Maybe our days of being untouchable are over. I have to watch my step." She gave a tense shrug and massaged the back of her neck.

Cavin removed her hand from her neck and took over, massaging her neck and shoulders. His thumbs pressed and rotated, working out the kinks in her muscles. She sighed. "It's a heavy weight you carry on your shoulders as a member of your family," he said low in her ear.

"It is, sometimes…" Of all the men she'd been with, Cavin was the first to acknowledge the driving force in her life, yet, he'd made the observation seemingly without effort. He got it. He *got her*.

She squeezed her eyes closed for a moment. So many emotions tumbled through her: the pressure of being under attack, of having someone to open up to about it, the relief of knowing she didn't have to walk alone anymore, that she had someone now, like her father had her mother. "'We Jaspers are public servants first and foremost. Our duty to others comes before our own interests and ambition.' I was born, weaned, and raised on that rule. Back when I was nine, when we met, I almost didn't come outside to see you that last night because my grandfather told me it wasn't responsible to be out after dark and Jaspers needed to be responsible."

"But you came," he said, rubbing her back before releasing her.

"Of course, I did."

"So, you can and do rebel when necessary."

Jana was about to argue but stopped. He was right. No one had ever pointed it out before. She glared at him as she took a seat at the table. "What is this, a job interview for a save-the-world sidekick?"

"I've already made my selection. And not for a sidekick. For an equal partner."

"I'm not the girl you knew, Cavin." The girl who used to giggle and pirouette for no other reason than to taste the joy of it; the girl whose love of life was so contagious it infected both a small boy from a faraway planet who hadn't yet spread his wings and an old man who'd lived five lifetimes in the space of one. Jana had spent the past twenty-three years eradicating that girl from her personality. *I don't want to be trouble. I don't want to be different.* "I've changed."

"I don't know about that." Cavin seemed to be holding back a smile as he sat across from her, the feast between them. Hungrily, he heaped food on his plate. "I've seen that girl surface several times already."

"Look, I'm not a rebel. I've spent more of my life conforming than rebelling."

"Like me, you choose your battles. What's important for you to fight, you do."

As long as it was the right fight, the socially acceptable fight. When was the last time you took a great personal risk for something you believed in? Her last true act of defiance with potential negative consequences was the night she slipped out her bedroom to meet Cavin despite her grandfather's orders to stay inside. At the time she'd believed it was the right thing to do, and that was all that mattered. But that was decades ago. Since then, she could be proud of her accomplishments, but every single one of them was achieved with acute awareness of her public image, how others saw her. With a rush of insight, Jana saw what she'd become. And wasn't sure she liked it.

They ate their meal with the television. "Is it spring fever?" asked a local news anchor. "Strange happenings continue to occur in the Roseville, Granite Bay area."

Jana dropped her fork. She picked up the remote and upped the volume.

"Last night, an SUV torn in half. Now today, what appears to have been an electromagnetic pulse disrupted a Roseville subdivision. Residents of Granite Canyon Drive remain puzzled by the unexplained phenomenon—and so do local utility companies."

Great going, Jana. Her grandfather's metaphorically smelly kitchen hadn't gotten the barest chance to air out before she'd managed to stink it up all over again.

REEF DECIDED to pass the night in the comfortable shelter of an inn. Cold warehouses were hard on his healing body. Perhaps a real bed would speed the maddeningly slow process. The room was dark except for the illumination given off by the entertainment box. All day, he'd watched the news, relentlessly viewing the summaries to find hints as to what happened to his target. With his internal systems damaged and his armor intermittent, he'd resorted to more conventional means of gathering information, his only option until the nanobots in his physical body finished repairs.

But, his biological components were warm, rested and sated, thanks to the ease with which he could help himself to local paper currency via the boxes called ATMs. Several meals' worth of empty take-out boxes covered the bedside table. He'd developed a taste for the cuisine called Italian. He'd never tasted anything like it in the galaxy. The rat still chilled in his armored freezer pocket, but Reef was glad to see that it was unlikely he'd have to consume it to keep up his strength.

"Is it spring fever?" the newsreader asked. "Strange happenings continue to occur in the Roseville, Granite Bay area. Last night, an SUV torn in half. And today, what appears to have been an electromagnetic pulse disrupted a Roseville subdivision."

Reef sharpened his focus. What was this?

"Residents of Granite Canyon Drive remain puzzled by the unexplained phenomenon, and so do local utility companies."

An electromagnetic pulse. "Greetings, Far Star," he murmured, sitting up. He'd found his target. Based on Earth data collected thus far, an electromagnetic pulse equaled a 98.3 percent probability Far Star was nearby. The man had created a security array for self-protection, apparently, but he'd caught someone or something else in his net, not Reef, and the mistake could very well be his last.

Reef smiled a true smile for the first time since arriving on this gods-forsaken world. He swung his feet off the bed and pulled up a sleeve of the thick shirt he'd obtained from one of the men. The necklaces around his neck tinkled as he accessed his wrist computer. First he tried to call up the target's gauntlet computer, but the man remained off-line. No matter; now Reef knew where he was.

Next, Reef accessed data on the location mentioned in the news: *Roseville: 35.62 square miles. Location: eastern edge of the Sacramento Valley at the base of the Sierra Nevada foothills. Elevation: 165 feet above sea level. Population: 103,783.*

He powered up his internal map and zoomed in on the area. Granite Canyon Drive. He saved the data and prepared to leave the inn.

Working quickly, he stripped, donned his body armor, and dressed all over again in his new clothing as a disguise. Since his invisibility was intermittent, the Earth clothing would make him invisible in a different but just as effective way.

With his assassin's special armor set to the smallest thickness, making it virtually undetectable under his clothing, he readied his weapons and explosives and stored them in various places around his body. With his tongue, he checked for the proper position of the self-destruct cap fitted in a recessed compartment hidden behind his rear left molar in case he was apprehended by Earth authorities and could not escape. An unlikely possibility, but he had orders not to let Coalition technology get into Earthling hands. Should that happen, one brief flash of plasma, and there'd be nothing left of him to pick through.

Ignoring a sudden and unexplained chill, Reef slipped out the door and into the anonymity of the night.

CHAPTER THIRTEEN

CAVIN PUSHED BACK from the table. "Jana, pack your things. We're leaving."

"Now?" Jana looked positively frazzled. He'd hoped to give her a night to recover, but it was not to be. "What's wrong with staying here in Evie's house until the morning?"

"The moment the REEF arrives, a lot will be wrong."

Jana's chair moved back with a sharp scrape. "I'll start packing if you start explaining."

"The security array I fashioned set off an electromagnetic pulse. It was nothing I ever dreamed would be of public mention. The EMP was a terrible inconvenience for the locals, I admit, but a danger only to a bioengineered combatant like the assassin hunting me. And now it's news, our location announced for all to hear. Compromising our security!" Irritably, he shoved a hand through his hair. "Don't you have any privacy on this planet?"

"No." She shoved belongings in her suitcase. "Don't even get me started on that subject."

"The REEF could very well have been watching the same program. That's why we must leave this dwelling and find new shelter before he comes in search of me."

"Got it. We're out of here." She secured what food they hadn't devoured in their hunger in cold storage. Then she donned a hat and pulled it low over her face. It hid her expression. She was afraid, and he'd caused that fear.

Cavin fisted his hands at his sides, ignored the twinge in his side from his healing wound. Nothing, simply nothing he'd expected upon landing here had gone as planned. Only his love for Jana, and that was not enough to bring this mission to its conclusion. *Act as if you expect the unexpected, and perhaps you'll hold on to the shred of trust she's given you.* A fragile string he hoped not to snap.

Jana pulled a small container from the freezer. "I'm bringing this. The Phish Food."

"But we have no fish. Do we?" With all the creatures living in this dwelling, he would not be surprised if one of them came along.

"*Phish* Food. P-h-i-s-h. It's an ice-cream flavor. It's what I was hunting for last night when you found me in Safeway, and didn't get to eat due to circumstances beyond my control. By God, I won't go another night without it." She clutched the container to her breasts, her expression intense, defiant, radiating everything about her that he loved, everything he'd come back to Earth to find. Jana Jasper was alive, vividly so. When he was with her, he felt as if he were alive, too, once again the boy who loved mischief, who loved to laugh. The boy who'd become a stranger to him over the years. "If I don't have some soon, I might lose my mind," she said.

"Bring it, then. You're more use to me sane, Earthling."

He walked by her startled face and said low in her ear, "Kidding."

"Alien monster. Creature! Maybe I should demand you take me to *your* leader. How'd you like that?"

That would not, he thought, be a very good idea. He gathered the pieces of his armor to carry with him. Jana stopped him from donning his boots. "No."

"What?"

"Not the Buzz Lightyear shoes."

"I need footwear."

"I made out all right last night without any. It's hard on the soles, but you'll live. Besides, those are slippers. I was practically barefoot in torn stockings."

"Don't make this difficult, Jana. I may need to run."

"And I may need to keep you alive. I don't want my people finding out about you before we're ready for them to find out about you. We Earthlings sometimes have a shoot-the-messenger mentality—especially when it comes to aliens arriving with invasion warnings. Trust me on this."

"Fine." He knew how to choose his battles, as well. He took her hand and pulled her out to the garage.

"Yarp, Yarp!"

Jana tugged back. "Sadie."

The little dog had followed them out and waited expectantly at the car door. "Ah, Sadie." Cavin crouched down and lifted her little body off the ground. Skinny black-clawed feet dangled from his hands. Her rib cage was so small, but her heartbeats were ferocious and strong. "You can't come. You must stay here and guard this dwelling. As for me, I have to take care of Jana. Granted, my methods could use some improvement, but protecting her, keeping her safe was my only reason for coming here. But to do that, I have to take her away from here. We'll be back. I promise you."

He carried the dog to the door and deposited her inside the house. When he turned, Jana was watching him with moist eyes. Tears, he realized with a start. But quickly she turned away to hide her emotion and threw her suitcase in the other vehicle parked in the garage. It was small and blue, and sported a few sizable dents. The peeling paint revealed another color underneath. Brown, perhaps, it was hard to tell. He couldn't see into the interior, but guessed comfort wouldn't be part of the accommodations. "I thought we'd switch cars," she said. "In case the REEF knows what I drive. This is Evie's spare car. She almost never uses it. She's saving it for the kids."

He loaded his gear in the rear cargo compartment. There was no room left over, and it took a few tries to close the hatch. He slid into the passenger seat as she dug in her purse. "I had the keys somewhere…"

He thrust his arm at the ignition. The automobile started. "You don't need your keys."

"It's tough keeping track of all your special features. Do you have a user's manual?"

"No. I'd prefer to instruct you, hands-on and in person."

He loved the way her cheeks flushed with the sexual heat simmering between them. "Cavin," she warned. "That's not helping—"

"You to resist me, I know." He folded his arms over his chest. "It is not helping me, either. I will behave."

"Snow, snow, snow," she muttered and backed the automobile out of the garage. "Where to?"

"Not your apartment. I doubt that the REEF was the one to break in, but your dwelling was compromised nonetheless. Too risky."

"We can stay at a motel. We'll have no problem finding a room. But first we're getting you new clothes."

"Secure shelter for the night first."

"No arguments, soldier. This is a deal breaker. I'm taking you shopping before the stores close. We're getting you out of that black suit before the men wearing a different kind of black suit figure out what you are."

Cavin folded his arms over his chest and frowned at the road ahead. In the past day, Jana had warned him about her fellow Earthlings so frequently that he'd begun to wonder if they would ultimately pose more of a threat to him and his mission than the REEF.

PROTECT CAVIN, CHECK. Protect her family, check. Preserve her reputation, check—well, sort of. Save the world, status pending.

A short hour later, loaded down with shopping bags, Jana brought Cavin to the registration desk of the motel. A baseball cap covered her hair and eyes, the best disguise she could muster on short notice. Checking into a motel with a man late at night, she was desperate for anonymity. With the family still under fire, she didn't dare risk generating gossip that could be twisted into further tarnishing the Jasper name.

But the female desk clerk didn't spare Jana a glance; she was too busy giving Cavin an admiring once-over. More like a twice-over. Jana relaxed a fraction as relief filtered through her. She hadn't been willing to leave the store until Cavin, dressed in hiking boots and outdoorsy gear, looked no different than any other good-looking, thirtyish, Northern California male. No one would guess his jacket hid a futuristic wrist computer that covered half his forearm or a gun deadly enough to have sent Darth Vader into a fit of envy—and she didn't plan on anyone finding out.

"Do you have a reservation?" the clerk asked Cavin, her fingers poised over the keyboard.

Jana answered for him. "No. We need a room, please."

The woman shifted her attention to her. "How many nights?"

"One."

"Name?"

"Mr. and Mrs. Snow," Jana said, just as she'd rehearsed mentally on the drive over.

Cavin's hand brushed over her back. "So we are mates?" His voice was low and hot in her ear.

She whispered back, "Only for tonight," and studiously avoided meeting his eyes.

"One night will not be enough. You will want more."

"How would you like to pay for that?" the clerk asked.

"P-pay?" For what? Jana's vision cleared and she saw the check-in sheet sitting on the counter. Oh, right, pay for the room. Gosh, she'd actually stuttered. Knowing she was about to spend the night alone with Cavin in close quarters apparently had disengaged her ability to speak. Hoping she wasn't blushing half as hard as she suspected she was, Jana reached for her credit card. At the store, she'd made the transaction while Cavin was busy studying "primitive Earthling camping gear" as if he were on an archaeological dig, because she hadn't wanted him to feel embarrassed about not having money. He'd been so overwhelmed by the whole retail experience she didn't think he realized, even now, that money had changed hands. But this was different; here he saw everything. Before she had a chance to pay, Cavin stopped her and pulled out a fat, fist-size wad of hundreds. Thousands and thousands of dollars. Holy crap.

He thrust the money at her. "Use my currency."

The clerk glanced from Cavin with disbelieving eyes to Jana and raised a brow. Sweetly, Jana smiled up at Cavin. "Honey, can we have a little talk?"

She hooked her arm with his and led him out of earshot of the clerk to a grouping of couches in the center of the small lobby. "Is there not enough money to secure the room?" he asked. "I know where to get more."

"It's enough to secure the best suite at the Waldorf-Astoria. And the only way you're going to get more is if you rob a bank."

The way Cavin seemed to contemplate her suggestion with no moral reservations whatsoever terrified her. "Cavin, where did you get this money?"

"Why, from a bank machine. Same as the Earthlings."

"They issue aliens ATM cards now?"

"I accessed the machine the same way I started the cars."

"Oh." She felt queasy. "It gave you hundreds? Not twenties?"

He shrugged. "I didn't question it."

It made Jana wonder if he'd emptied a Brink's truck by mistake. "I hope you used your photo-blocking technology when you took out the money. ATMs have cameras that record the transaction."

"I did. There is no way of tracing the withdrawal to me."

"Withdrawal? You mean robbery." Car stealing, evading police, forging IDs, reckless driving and now bank robbing. Where would it end? *I don't want to know*. On the other hand, arguing over little things like robbing ATMs when the fate of the entire world hung in the balance was pretty much stupid.

"Okay. Let's forget about where you got it, just don't flash the entire wad. No one carries that much cash. It looks like drug money."

"Drug money?"

"Money gotten through illegal means, like drug trafficking." What was she saying? It *was* money gotten through illegal means. She plucked a single hundred from the roll. "Put the rest away," she hissed under her breath and returned to the front desk.

It was clear from the clerk's expression that she'd watched the entire exchange: Cavin thrusting the entire roll at Jana, and her not wanting to take anything but a hundred bucks. Jana thanked her lucky stars that the clerk didn't recognize her. *A true public servant:* Senator Moonlighting As Discount Call Girl.

The clerk slid the paperwork to functionally illiterate Cavin to sign, holding on to the key cards until he did. Before Jana had a chance to reach for it, to save him the embarrassment, he slid the paper to her. "Here, my wife. I left my glasses at home."

She'd never loved him more than in that moment. Smiling, she slipped on her own glasses and signed for him. Then she took Cavin's arm, pulling him as fast as she could toward the elevator that would bring them to their room on the third floor.

She didn't have the heart to tell him she wasn't as worried about being ambushed by the assassin as she was about Grandpa learning she'd checked into a hotel with a stranger. Virgin Snow? At this point, she was looking more like muddy slush.

CHAPTER FOURTEEN

THE ROOM DOOR SLAMMED closed and Jana bolted it. Cavin set to work inspecting the closet, under the bed, the bathroom, every nook and cranny until he ended up at the window. He stayed there for some time, peering down at the parking lot with a device that resembled mini binoculars but that probably saw in the dark or even through clothing for all she knew.

Jana buried her hands in her bomber jacket pockets and watched him from under the rim of her ball cap. His shirt pulled tight across broad shoulders as he covered his wound with a free hand, a gesture she noticed he affected when tired. He resembled a tall, sexy Napoleon.

When he'd assured himself the coast was clear, he turned around and caught her watching him. He seemed pleased that she was. "Mrs. Snow," he said in a deep and husky voice that made her coral-painted toes curl.

She did an about-face and ducked into the bathroom with her bag of toiletries. She grabbed polish remover, a bag of cotton balls, and propped a foot on the toilet seat. "An ounce of prevention is worth a pound of cure," she muttered, rubbing furiously. Anything to help her resist his charms, because none of the reasons why she shouldn't sleep with him made sense anymore. They were safe for the night, they had privacy, and they were in love.

At first there had been the need to avoid romantic entanglements in order to keep focused on her career and her family, but now there was far more distracting her than making it with a sexy alien. Like impending galactic warfare, rumors flying about her family, psycho cousins, shoot-outs and breaking the law—and that was just off the top of her head.

Then why not be intimate with Cavin now that she could?

Because you're afraid once you make love you won't be able to pretend this is just temporary, and you have no idea how you're going to fit this man in your life.

How many other women secretly harbored the fantasy of a dream lover returning to sweep them off their feet? But what about the reality of it? Would a normal life ever be possible with Cavin? Sharing a bed each night as husband and wife. Making love before going to sleep, only to be woken by alarm clocks in the morning like any other couple. What then? She'd commute into the capitol and Cavin would drop their half-alien kids off at school before…before what? Going to work? Staying home?

You're getting way ahead of yourself, Jana.

Cavin showed up in the doorway. A moment of silence told her he was confused. He wrinkled his nose. "What is that substance, Jana?"

"Polish remover." She threw an acetone-soaked cotton ball in the toilet and took a fresh one from the bag. "See, I'm a frosted-pink kind of girl, every once in a while pale peach, but last week my nail lady told me I was too careful, too unadventurous. A bore, but she didn't quite say that. 'You need new color,' she tells me. 'You need sexy. I pick for you sexy color.' The next thing I knew, my nails were 'A Little Too Hot' coral. Turns out it was way too hot." Jana threw the last dirty cotton ball into the toilet and flushed. "There." She wriggled her toes. "Nun's feet. Now I can resist you."

His grin was downright devilish. "Think so?"

She gently but firmly pushed him backward. His abs were hard with just the right amount of sexy give. "Be right with you," she said and shut the door. On went her flannel pajamas, baby blue with crescent moons. She took off her hat, pulled out her ponytail, brushed her hair and shoved on her glasses. There, she thought. Miss Virgin Snow is ready for bed. The outfit alone was a surefire sex deterrent; not to mention the added glamour of her reading glasses and her hair hanging half over them. She flung open the door.

Cavin was back at the window, his hands clasped behind his back, but when he saw her reflection in the glass, he turned around. He looked her up and down with such hunger that she almost passed out on the spot. Jana clasped a fistful of flannel above her bust as if closing a plunging neckline. "I try to resist you, and I can't. I try to get you to resist me, and I can't do that, either. How are we going to make it through the night without…making it?"

Cavin sighed, mischief twinkling in his eyes. "Ah, such is the question all women ask of me. Any planet. Any star system. When I'm near, they cannot control themselves."

"We should have gotten a suite!" Jana grabbed a pillow and hurled it at him. "Because your ego is too large for this room!"

He advanced on her. "My translator suggests an Earthling phrase in response—size matters."

"That doesn't refer to ego." She grabbed another pillow, backing up.

"If not ego, then what?" The wicked curve to his lips assured her he already knew the answer.

Growling, Jana flung the pillow at him. He tried to catch her. Laughing, she ducked and pirouetted out of his reach. But he caught her hand and pulled her close. She muffled a shriek. They spun like a pair of dancers before falling up against the wall.

Cavin caught both her hands in one of his, pulling them over her head and pressing them to the wall behind her. With her shoulders against the wall, her hips thrust forward making her B-cup breasts jut out and brush his chest. His muscular thighs corralled her legs.

They grinned at each other, laughing, breathless. It was playful and erotic and wild and fun. "You didn't lose that girl, Jana, the girl you were," he said. "She's right here, here with me." Before she'd finished giggling, he'd muffled her laughter with a kiss. And then another, each one hotter than the last. When he finally lifted his head, his expression was so open, so un-guarded, it grabbed at her heart. "*You're* here with me." He kissed her again, lightly, tenderly, playfully, on her lips, her nose, her brows, until he'd made her sigh.

In that moment, it was hard to imagine they'd ever been apart. "I wonder what it would have been like if we hadn't separated as children," she said dreamily.

"We would not have been behaving like this, not in the beginning. But as teenagers…" He kissed his way to her shoulder and gave her a little bite that made her yelp. "All I can say is that we would have married young."

"Very young." She slipped her hands from his and framed his hard jaw, tracing his features with her thumbs, absorbing how the boy's face she remembered had been altered by tiny scars and creases left from years of living, sometimes quite brutally it sounded like. "But then you wouldn't have been able to be a soldier."

"Not necessarily. As a young couple, we would have needed an income. One-third of the Coalition population is either in the military or employed serving the military. But I wouldn't have chosen a combat job, not at the risk of leaving you a widow." He folded her hands and lifted her knuckles to his lips. "I would have searched out a backwater posting, a low-risk location. We would have had a quiet life. A life together…"

As he spoke, she let his descriptions sweep her away. Cavin had a gift. He could paint pictures in her mind with words, from erotic images of jungle sex to sweet and blurry-edged visions of an idyllic existence on a distant world: a cozy home, their children running barefoot in the grass. Her, wearing a pretty cotton sundress. Cavin catching her around the waist and spinning her close for a kiss. Then the realist in her filled in the details. "I'd have missed my family. And I'd have lost the chance to go into politics. All I've ever wanted to do is hold elected office. To make a difference in this world. To give something back."

"Then we'd have stayed on Earth," he said simply. "I'd have sent my father off without me."

Jana imagined herself as a nine-year-old bringing Cavin home. *"Look what I found, Grandpa!"*

"Whatever our decision would have been as children, to stay or to go, we'd have made it together," Cavin said. "And whatever our future decisions are to be, we'll make those together, too."

She slid her arms around his waist. "Your planet, or mine?"

He bent his head to kiss her. The embrace was longer and hotter this time. His warm hand slid over her stomach, just inside the flannel, questioning, not wanting to breach any invisible boundaries.

But she wanted him to touch her. Wanted his lips and hands all over her body. The scent of his skin was an aphrodisiac, and his taste, salty sweet. He made her dizzy. He made her ache for more. He made her so many things that she couldn't begin to catalog them all. With his hands and lips on her, she found it nearly impossible to think. Or to remember why she wasn't supposed to make love with him. She'd had her reasons. Whatever they were.

"Phish Food," she whispered. It was her last line of defense. It'd never failed her before. She ducked out of Cavin's embrace and made a beeline for the minibar fridge where she'd stored the container. The ice cream was more than half melted by now, but she didn't care. She peeled off the lid. The aroma of chocolate and caramel drifted out. She was almost shaking with anticipation as she buried a spoon in the melted ice cream and lifted it to her mouth. "That's it, yes." She closed her eyes and savored the taste. "Yes, yes, yes."

She walked back to Cavin and offered him a spoonful. "Here, you have to try—"

He bent his head and kissed her, exploring her mouth, tasting her, until all traces of chocolate had been erased.

"…a taste," she murmured dazedly when their lips finally parted.

"It's very good, this fish food." His green eyes glinted with mischief. "Oh, look. It's run down your arm." He lifted her arm by the wrist. Chocolate had dribbled all the way to her elbow. "You weren't paying attention, Jana. Was something distracting you?"

Or someone. She grew light-headed as he licked and kissed the ice cream from her skin, scooting her sleeve higher to reach her elbow. Desire flowed through her like warm syrup, thick and sweet. *Boom, boom, boom.* The drumbeat between her thighs was pounding harder and hotter. He kissed his way up her arm to her ear, where he breathed, "The next time you utter 'yes, yes, yes' it will be as I make love to you."

Jana uttered a sound that fell somewhere between a moan, a sigh and a cuss. *Grandpa, I want you to know I didn't go down without a fight. I held out until the bitter end, or at least until the end of my apparently short evolutionary rope. But with Cavin it's different; it always has been. Once my hormones reached critical mass, there wasn't anything I could do.*

Jana found his delicious lips, sipping, teasing, enticing, until she'd drawn him into a full kiss. Blindly, she reached between their bodies to unbutton his pants. Her knuckles brushed over his stomach; his muscles contracted from her touch. The bulge a little farther down told her how aroused he was. One flick of her fingers over the button on his waistband and he'd be hers…

...moving inside her. Flying, the two of them.

She popped the button on his fly and pulled on the zipper, freeing him. He groaned and pinned her to his body. "Jana..." He gasped her name, harshly, desperately, like a drowning man trying to stay afloat. It was a warning: if they continued, he was going under and taking her with him.

"I want to make love. I do," she whispered. "I tried staying away. It doesn't work."

He scooped her into his arms as if she weighed nothing and carried her to the bed. In one smooth motion, he'd lowered her to the mattress.

"Your wound," she cautioned. "Be careful."

"Right now, pain is the last thing on my mind. Trust me on that. The only inconvenience for you due to my injury is that tonight you may have to be on top."

May the rest of my life be filled with such inconveniences. "Top, bottom, left, right, upside down, inside out, up against trees, walls, on tables, I don't care."

The heat in his stare made her shiver. "We'll try all of those, in time."

At that point, self-combustion was a real possibility.

His hands slid under the flannel. She didn't stop him when he caressed her bare breast. She tightened under his hand and between her legs, a double explosion of sensation. He kissed her under her ear which made her giggle, but his hands were busy the whole while. By the time she'd realized what he'd done, her pajama top was unbuttoned.

He parted the fabric, baring her to him for the first time. The air was cool, his hands hot, his tongue even hotter. When he took a nipple into his mouth, they both sighed.

"This only reinforces my opinion that you have the most amazing mouth," she half whispered.

"And this—" he kissed and nibbled and licked his way from her breasts to her throat to her collarbone and back down to her belly button without missing anything in between "—only reinforces that you have the most amazing body."

He knew his way around a woman's body, too. His fingers slid under the elastic waistband of her pajama pants, lowering them. He cupped her bare bottom as he brought his mouth to her ear. "You're so soft, Jana. So sweet. All mine," he breathed and slipped his fingers between her legs.

If Cavin's mouth was amazing, his hands were even more so. Her desire for him went from syrupy thick and sweet to as swift and molten-hot as lava. The drumbeat pounded, harder, louder. "Yes," she whispered. "Yes, yes." Deftly, he explored her. She arched into his hand, greedy for more. Her thighs opened for him. No inhibitions, nothing to hide. His fingers caressed, tortured, dipped inside her. He took her to the edge, holding her there. The sensation was exquisite. Quickly it became almost too much. She gripped his hand and moaned. "Please…"

"Come for me, Jana," he whispered, sliding lower on her body. He touched his mouth to her, to her very center, and her world exploded. She closed one hand in his hair; the other twisted in the bedsheet until her last moans of pleasure whimpered into silence.

When she at last floated down from orbit, Cavin smiled down at her. "Better than fish food?"

"What's Phish Food?" she asked dazedly.

He grinned. "Good answer." He rolled onto his back, pulling her astride him. "I want you, Jana. Gods, how I want you." Before he could pull her close, an ear-shattering explosion boomed from outside.

Cavin rolled again, flipping her beneath him to protect her. A fireball flashed in the gap between the curtains. Thunder rocked the room, and the window shook. A dozen car alarms whooped and beeped as chunks of debris clanged back to earth.

"Stay," Cavin ordered. He was on his feet with his gun in his hand before Jana had a chance to reach for her pajama pants. By the time she yanked them to her waist, he was already peering around the curtains at the window, his gun at the ready. With lips rosy from kissing, his shirt wrinkled and his pants unbuttoned, and a gun dangling from his hand, Cavin looked like a cowboy wrested from the saloon girl's bed. Outside, orange light flickered. Something was on fire. In the distance, police sirens wailed.

"What happened?" Jana's need to scream her head off alternated with an almost overwhelming urge to barf. "What was that?" Or was it overconfident to be asking questions in the past tense?

Cavin turned back to her, his soldier's face taut. "Your sister's car blew up."

CHAPTER FIFTEEN

AFTER THE FIRE TRUCKS LEFT, police festooned the charred remains of Evie's car with a ring of yellow crime-scene ribbon. The few larger pieces of the Honda that had survived were loaded in a truck and hauled away. Everything else was swept into boxes, including the powdery remains of Cavin's armor and boots.

Staring out the window, Jana pressed a fist to her stomach to stifle a wave of fear. "They're going to run tests on everything they find. They'll see the bits of armor. Your gear isn't made of stuff we have on Earth. The men in black will come looking for my sister. She won't be very happy about that, I can tell you." Unless, of course, the agents were male and cute. And available. Evie was, after all, single and looking. Still, it was a situation Jana wanted to avoid at all costs.

Cavin guided her backward to lean against his chest, slinging a protective arm around her. "There is no danger to your sister. The armor has already broken down into benign, commonly found compounds. It's a security precaution to keep our technology from falling into Drakken claws."

"They have claws?" A sinister image filled her mind, something straight out of an old, dubbed Godzilla movie.

He shook his head. "Sorry. It was a figure of speech provided by my translator. Their DNA is no different from your people, or mine." Darkly, he added, "But, somewhere along the way, they seem to have lost their humanity."

"Like the REEF?"

"Yes."

Jana shuddered as she peered down from the room window to the scene below. Only one patrol car was left. A couple of cops were busy filling out paperwork for the hotel guests whose cars had been damaged in the explosion. Explosive Passion! Senator Steals Sister's Car For Secret Rendezvous With Alien Lover.

Jana stopped breathing for a moment. Her imagined headlines were starting to sound awfully close to ones that might actually make it to print. *"No making headlines for anything but the bills you pass."* In her mind, she saw Grandpa wagging a finger at her.

"Yenflarg." Jana ground her fingertips into her temples. "What else can possibly go wrong?"

"I've been asking myself the same question since I arrived here," Cavin replied dryly.

"It feels wrong not to confess it was our car. Dishonest."

"No, Jana. Safe. We can't take the chance of going outside and revealing our connection to the vehicle."

"They'll figure out the connection. I saw at least one license plate that was recognizable."

"They'll call your sister, not you. And as we discussed, she will pretend it was stolen from her dwelling."

More lies, Jana thought gloomily. Why suffer alone when she could drag the rest of the Jasper family down into the deep, dank pit of notoriety with her? And she wasn't looking forward to the call she'd have to give her sister, either. "Wait until Evie finds out an assassin from outer space wrecked Godiva."

"Godiva?"

"The Honda was her college car. She named it Godiva. In those days it was chocolate-brown. Her ex-husband repainted it blue. It was the beginning of the end for them, I think."

"I'm not convinced it was the assassin who destroyed your sister's vehicle. It's not his style."

"This one ever pursue you before?"

"This REEF. Why, no, but—"

"Then you don't know his style. This one may be different. You said yourself he was damaged in the crash."

Cavin rubbed a hand over his face as he pondered that. "Possibly." He didn't look convinced, though.

But who else could it be? Who would do something like this to her on purpose? *Or break into your apartment, stealing nothing but going through your old files?* A chill washed over her. The incidents were related; they had to be, but how would the REEF or anyone else know to attack Evie's car unless they'd followed her from Evie's house to here? And if they had, now they knew about Cavin.

Jana opened her cell phone. "I hope my sister has her cell shut off. I'd rather not have to tell her this in person." She punched in the number and hit Send.

After several rings, Evie answered in a sleepy voice. "Jana. It's one-fifty-three in the morning."

"Fifty-four. Are you sitting down?"

"I'm in bed," Evie croaked. "I was sleeping. Normal

people do that in the middle of the night, you know. Families do that when on vacation—"

"Sorry, I'm so sorry. It's an emergency, or I wouldn't be bothering you. No one's hurt. No one's sick. I wrecked Godiva."

"Jana! Oh, baby. Are you okay?"

"I'm fine. I wasn't even in the car."

"I'm confused."

"It blew up, but—"

"Godiva blew up? How bad is the garage? Are the animals okay?" Evie yelled.

"Yes! Your house is fine. Godiva blew up in the parking lot of the Garden Inn. Evie, please, let me explain—"

"What are you doing in a motel? I thought you were staying at my place." Jana heard noises from the other end, Evie telling the kids: "It's Aunt Jana. Shush, go back to sleep. I don't know. No. I'm sure the man is off the roof by now." More rustling noises and Evie's voice changed to a loud whisper. "I'm in the bathroom now. Tell me what the hell is going on. How did my car explode?"

"I borrowed your car and went to a motel because I thought someone might be following me. It turns out I was probably right. Don't freak out, but he might be trying to kill me."

Evie muffled what sounded like a shriek. "Why would someone want to kill you? You're not exactly controversial."

In other words, even her sister thought she was boring. Well, not for long. That was all about to change. "He's not exactly after me. He wants to kill the man I'm with."

Silence. "The man on my roof?"

"Yeah. That one."

"The, uh, Peter guy."

Jana met Cavin's vivid green eyes. His concerned gaze softened as his fingers brushed down her cheek. "Yes," she said quietly. "Peter."

"But are you alone now, Jana? Is he with you?"

"Yes."

"I think you need to get away from him. He's brainwashed you, baby. He's not the boy from that summer. That boy was imaginary. Made up. I'm coming home, Jana. You need help."

Evie's concern hit a sensitive spot. *I want to be normal. To be like everyone else.* Jana braced against the old insecurities. "Evie, listen to me. I'm safer in his company that I'd be alone. There's a lot more going on than you can even imagine, and, no, I'm not going to discuss it over the phone, especially a cell phone where people can listen in."

"I'm coming home tomorrow. Dad asked me to stay over spring break and look after Grandpa. Meet me at the ranch tomorrow night. I want to talk to you."

How could she refuse Evie after borrowing her house and blowing up her car? "Sure," Jana said, trying hard to infuse enthusiasm into her voice. She had no choice but to bring Cavin with her. A nightmarish image of introducing him to Grandpa plunged through her mind. *Keep an eye on him, Jana*, her father had said. *Keep him steady.* What she intended to tell her grandfather would do anything but keep him calm. But she needed his help. He knew General Mahoney, who knew about Area 51. Deranged Legislator Woos Two Elderly Retirees Into Alien Caper.

Jana squeezed her eyes shut to stave off a headache that badly wanted to happen. "Last thing, Evie. Listen carefully. It's important and may save my life."

"Go ahead," Evie said. Her tone was all at once disapproving, angry and frightened.

"The police will probably call you about the Honda. They have a license plate—it's pretty much all that was left. They'll be able to get your contact information from it. When they call, pretend you never heard from me tonight. You have an alibi—you were on vacation. Someone must have stolen the car, and torched it for kicks. Tell them that."

"No one would steal Godiva, Jana." Evie's voice was dry.

"Steal it, no. Bomb it, yes. It was really ugly, Evie. Especially after Reese painted it."

"It was my Godiva," Evie wailed. "And don't mention that sonofabitch. I've been having a good year."

"I'm truly sorry, Evie. I'll make it up to you. I'll make everything up to you. I promise." Guilt sickened Jana when she thought of all that Evie didn't know. The impending invasion for starters. "Remember, don't connect my name to the Honda when the police call. You were in Disneyland—"

"And some crazy people stole my car. Yeah, yeah, I know the drill." Her voice softened. "I won't do anything to get you killed, baby. I won't."

"Love you, big sister," Jana whispered and hung up.

She sat on the edge of the bed, gnawing her knuckle. "She's been briefed," she told Cavin when she'd gotten a hold of herself. "Now, us. I have to be at work too early for us to get a rental car. Nothing will be open yet." Steve or Nona would give her a ride, but then there was the problem of Cavin. She didn't want to risk calling attention to him too early. "We'll take the light-rail. I voted for the expansion of the system so might as well take a train sometimes." Jana rubbed her eyes. "I'm exhausted. How about we try to get some sleep?"

He glanced at the rumpled bed and back to her. "I will prepare a sleeping place on the floor."

"I'd feel safer with you next to me."

"Temptation," he warned. "Whether it was the REEF or another party who destroyed the vehicle, it means danger. I don't want to lose my ability to protect you if we were to be focused too much on each other and not on what is going on around us. Distraction kills."

"Distraction. Like fooling around."

"Fooling around." His brows drew together. "It is an alternate definition for sexual activity, yes?"

She smiled. "And foreplay. Making out. Making love, it's all included. Any of those are better definitions. Sexual activity makes it sound cold and clinical."

"Trust me, Squee. Nothing I do with you or to you will ever be cold and clinical." He ran his hand over her hair, touching her as if she were something precious to him. It made her chest squeeze tight. And other things…

She knew he was right about fighting their attraction in the face of the serious danger they were in, but how many more times was the REEF going to interrupt before she could have a piece of Cavin? She wanted to yowl like a cat in heat. Apparently Healthy Young Woman Found Dead In Motel Room. Sexual Denial To Blame.

"Then we'll just sleep, which we both need anyway. No fooling around. Come on. We're focused, disciplined adults. Look at all we've achieved in our lives. We can do this." She patted the mattress, wiggled her pristine, nunlike toes.

Cavin pulled the curtains closed. "Not before we talk."

"Sure. What about?"

Did she detect guilt in the sigh he heaved? "Jana, I meant to tell you sooner, I just didn't know how. But it's only fair that you know everything about me before we grow closer. Before we ultimately make love," he added.

"Earth guys usually wait until *after* you do it to drop the big bombshell. I knew there was something about aliens I liked."

Tension visibly tightened his facial muscles. Her stomach suddenly swarmed with butterflies. "Whoa. Is it that bad?"

"I have not been entirely honest with you."

"I knew it. You're married."

"I am not married."

"Engaged."

He rolled his eyes.

"Pregnant? Sterile?" She crossed herself. "*Impotent?*"

Cavin slapped his palm to his forehead. "Jana, no. I'm a Coalition military officer. Not an enlisted man."

"So? That's wonderful."

"A high-ranking officer."

"Um, that's even better, right?" She was trying hard to see why this was a problem.

"Very high, Jana."

At his grave tone, a wriggle of concern sprang to life in her stomach. "How high?"

"To be exact, I am the sixteenth highest ranking officer in the Coalition military of three billion soldiers."

"That's high," she whispered.

"Shortly before coming to Earth I received a promotion to Galactic Prime-major. There are fourteen prime-majors, total. Above us are only the Supreme Commander and the Supreme Second. Above them are the Prime Minister and the Queen. Jana?" he asked when she didn't say anything.

"Keep going." She waved her hand, which seemed to be the only part of her not frozen. "I'm absorbing."

"At heart, my needs are simple. I don't require much, and certainly not power. I would have been happy as a grunt, a ground soldier, but after a few years, I won a slot to the officer academy, and I excelled. As a young officer, I never rested, I rarely took leave. I volunteered for the most difficult assignments, the so-called impossible tasks, and made them work. I soared up through the ranks.

"Why? One reason. A high position was the only way I'd be privy to planetary acquisition plans. I wanted to know the moment Earth advanced to the top of the list, so that when it did, I could take action. It wasn't only to keep you safe. To do that, I could have flown back and taken you and your family back with me, could have rescued only you and your loved ones."

"But you want to save the entire planet."

"Your home is here. I saw your love of it, your attachment to the land. I never had a real home of my own, and I wanted you to be able to keep yours."

His forthright expression spun her back to a summer night, twenty-three years ago: a boy's frank, open face as he returned her pet potbellied pig. *Here.* Then it was a pig. Tonight it was an entire world. Though the stakes were much different, when it came to giving without expecting anything in return, Cavin had changed little since Peter.

How could she be worried about covering her butt when Cavin was risking his for over six billion butts? The entire population of planet Earth! He'd given up his identity, his achievements, his future, everything a man could give, and almost his life, and all she could think of was her personal insecurities, of eliminating any doubts that she belonged to the Jaspers, of wanting to be seen as "normal." A storm of emotions seethed inside her, shame principal amongst them.

"You have so much heart," Grandpa told her when she was small. *"Heart is what'll take you to the top. It's what this country needs. Heart and the smarts to go with it. You're going to go far, Jana Jasper, mind this old man's words. The highest office of this country is not beyond your abilities."*

But in learning to conform, maybe she'd lost the heart Grandpa said set her apart from the rest. Well, she was going to fix that. She was going to find her heart.

"Starting tomorrow," she said. "I'm sticking my neck out so you don't have to stick out yours. You've lost too much already. Your power and position, everything you worked for."

"Pah! I worked for you, Jana. Not for me. The promotion means nothing now that I've found you again. Seeing you, being with you, it confirmed my belief that I'll never be happy unless I have you in my life. But we're wasting time arguing about it. I can't go home now, even if I repaired my ship. Because someone wants me dead. The REEF is proof of that. I've thought about it, Jana. Thought about it all day. If I'm not killed here, it will happen in the halls of parliament, or while I'm asleep in my bed, or it will come disguised as an accident when a ship transporting me happens to crash. The only certainty is that it will happen, Jana, if I return. It's only a matter of when and how."

"But this is what I don't understand. The whole assassin thing. You're brilliant. You're sociable. And a top-notch officer, from what I can tell. Why would anyone want you dead?"

"Because of my politics, Jana. My so-called controversial views—on acquisitioning inhabited planets, for one. There is more. I'll share all of them in time. What you need to know for now is that I was targeted for elimination by someone who doesn't want me to be in a position of influence. Perhaps it will help explain more of what is happening—to me, and to you."

He paced a few steps, his hands clasped behind his back. She could easily imagine Cavin as he must have appeared in his world, glittering epaulets on his broad shoulders, a fitted uniform, dozens and dozens of medals on his chest. "I'm glad you told me, Cavin. The danger you're in makes more sense now."

He let out a tired breath and turned back to her. "There's more."

"More?"

The dismay in her voice must have been obvious, because he appeared almost sheepish. "Last thing, I promise."

"Good, because I'm getting close to my bombshell limit for a twenty-four-hour period. In fact, I've probably exceeded it."

"After this, you certainly will."

She stomped her foot. "Bikini wax it, Cavin!"

He tipped his head. "Say again?"

"Let 'er rip. Make it fast. It's less painful that way."

"There's been talk of me being chosen as consort to the queen."

Jana choked. "The sword queen? The wiener-slicer, ball-dicer chick?"

His lips slid into a wry smile. "That one, yes. Queen Keira. In fact, I suspect it was one reason behind my promotion to Prime-major at only thirty-five of your Earth years. The queen is nearing thirty and in the royal view of things, overdue to produce an heir to the throne. They thought a military man would make a good consort."

"And you were the man. The queen's stud."

"Her proposed stud. I never met her. However, she was said to be…ah, in favor of the idea. The idea of me." Cavin shrugged. He seemed somewhat embarrassed by the whole thing. "Perhaps she'd have changed her mind once we met in person."

"No," Jana said with conviction. "She wouldn't have. Trust me." The queen would want Cavin even more. What woman wouldn't? It was irrational, but Jana felt a flicker of jealousy. How could a lowly state senator compete with the queen of the galaxy? A gorgeous vixen who whacked off offending male parts while she, nerd-to-the-max, got woozy over a paper cut. Jana might have Cavin's heart, but the queen without a doubt had a better wardrobe, a better hairstyle and un-limited facials. And she'd bet her bottom dollar the queen wore jeweled tiaras, not baseball caps. "Would you have considered it? If she asked and you didn't have me?"

"If I didn't have you, Jana, I wouldn't be in the position to be chosen as the queen's consort. I'd be an unknown scientist's son who was quite content being an anonymous, low-ranking soldier. But if I hadn't dis-appeared when I did, and the royal summons was made…" Tiredly he rubbed his face. "I don't know what I would have done, quite frankly. Likely, I wouldn't have had much choice in the matter. Duty would have required me to comply. You don't turn down the queen."

"Especially that queen. Not if you don't want your voice a few octaves higher, that is. At least you vanished before wedding plans began."

"Unfortunately, it means more people looking for me. Fortunately, only a few want to actually kill me. Everyone else simply wants to locate me."

"Oh, well that's heartening."

"Better than having to face a squadron of Drakken Imperial troopers."

"I'll take your word on that."

"Do," he said. "It is my goal in life to make sure you never come within a hundred light-years of a Drakken."

The tension in the room ran high. Not only was the most-feared assassin on Cavin's trail, the entire galaxy was looking for him. Suddenly, the physical distance between them was too much. Unbearable. She needed to hold him. "Come to bed," she said, pulling down the blanket. He'd gotten no sleep the night before and she'd managed only a few hours. They were exhausted. "Come, sleep with me. Just sleep."

He nodded in silence and turned off the room light. He unbuttoned his shirt and pulled it off, draping it over the back of a chair. His broad shoulders and biceps were rounded, well developed, hinting at time spent lifting weights. He unfastened the wrist gauntlet and set it aside. His waist was narrow, his stomach hard with muscle. Other than a shadowing of hair across his chest and the bandage on his stomach, his golden skin gleamed. No scars accounted for a life spent as a soldier. And not because he'd held desk jobs, either. In fact, the opposite was true; he'd been out on the field most of his career. No, the perfection of his skin was due to advanced technology, healing using microscopic computers, what he sorely needed now to heal his injury and didn't have.

Last, he withdrew his gun from his pants and placed it within easy reach under a pillow. She tried not to think of why. He stretched out next to her. She molded the length of her body to his. They fit together without trying, her leg draped over his hip, his knee between her thighs. She ran her hands over his bare back, feeling the ripple of hard muscle under smooth, silken skin. Linking her arms around his waist, she inhaled his scent. "Sorry it didn't work out tonight," she murmured against his warm skin. "You know, in bed." Even though he couldn't see her face, she felt her cheeks warm. "We got only halfway done."

"Halfway? Bah. An eighth, if that. Closer to a six-teenth."

She giggled. "If you'd been my math instructor and

with those kinds of word problems when I was in school, I might have paid more attention."

He pressed his lips to her hair. "We will make love fully, and thoroughly. But for now, you are right. Sleep is more important."

Sleep was important because he'd need all his wits about him. At this very moment, his government was combing the stars, looking for him, and an assassin was in the shadows here on Earth doing the same thing. And now she and Cavin were about to go public with the greatest story in human history, which put him at the mercy of the people of Earth, too. Prime-major Far Star was a wanted man with a capital *W*.

And a hero with a capital *H. Her* hero.

At least now she understood why he'd wanted her to know everything before they grew closer. There was a real risk of losing him, and he needed her to understand that, to be prepared for the worst. "I'm scared," she whispered in the dark, embarrassed by how small her voice sounded. "I'm scared I'll close my eyes and you'll be gone."

He sighed deeply and gathered her close. His arms were strong, his body was solid. "I'll be here when you wake up, Squee. I swear on the gods."

"My God, too." She sensed rather than saw him smile.

"Yes. As always, your god, too. Close your eyes," he whispered in her ear.

"How am I supposed to sleep?"

"Try." He slipped his hand under the strands of hair at the nape of her neck, massaging her there. "You're not alone in this. I'm with you."

"You're not alone in this, either. Or in anything you do for the rest of your life. After what you told me tonight, I never want to be apart from you again."

He crushed her close in a profound embrace. She could tell by the way he paused, his lips pressed to her jaw, his breaths quickening slightly, that he, too, felt the heat simmering between them flare to life. It was also obvious in the reluctance with which he ended the passionate hug that to continue would mean tumbling into more. Only because they were both essentially disciplined people did they somehow back away from the edge.

So, he held her, quiet and still. Despite the worry boiling inside her, exhaustion and the security of Cavin's warm body pulled her under fast. She didn't recall falling asleep, or for how long she was out, but she stirred awake when Cavin eased her to his side. Groggily, she was aware of him pulling the sheets and blanket over them. Then he stretched out alongside her and wrapped her in his arms.

His heart thumped under her ear, reminding her of his courage with every beat. Reminding her of the heart she'd have to find within herself tomorrow when despite the attacks against her and her family, she'd take the first steps to bring Cavin's warning to the rest of Earth.

CHAPTER SIXTEEN

"TWO TRIPLE VENTI vanilla lattes, please," Jana told the barista early the next morning at a Starbucks outside the light-rail station. "And a newspaper." She was impatient to see what, if any news from the explosion last night had made it into the paper. If it had, she hoped there was no mention of the Jasper name. Keeping scandal-free the next couple of days was critical. All she had to do was make it to the end of the week, and she'd be able to disappear with Cavin and try to do what he needed her to do to help rescue Earth. Discreetly, of course. It would be the epitome of Jasper efficiency: saving the world over spring break, averting an alien invasion without missing any time at work.

Cavin looked as exhausted as she felt as he warily scanned the patrons inside the coffee shop, the order-taker, the cars outside. The Starbucks experience seemed to overwhelm him as much as clothes shopping the night before had. The only explanation she had was that it was so far removed from any of his life experiences. It would be like her going back to the thirteenth century and shopping for bread and mead outside the castle walls. Yet, when the assassin was shooting at Cavin, or cars were exploding, he was icy-cool, the epitome of calm. They filled in each other's gaps, complemented each other's weaknesses and strengths, something she had the feeling would come in handy, and sooner than she'd have liked.

"That'll be eight twenty-seven," the order-taker said.

Cavin thrust the rolled wad of hundreds at him. "Cavin, no," she said under her breath.

Too late, judging by the order-taker's rounded eyes. "I can't break a hundred," he said.

Jana rooted through her purse for spare change to add to her last five bucks. She didn't want to give up those lattes. Or the paper. But she needed to come up with two dollars and—she counted change—eighty-six more cents. "Make that seventy-six." She added a dime to the pile of spare change on the counter.

Cavin seemed insulted on her behalf. "Is our money not good enough at this establishment?"

"The problem is that it's too much. He can't make change. They don't have enough."

He huffed. "Paper money. A primitive system."

Jana dug through her purse. There were pockets and zippered compartments she hadn't opened in months. "Ooh, more change. A whole dollar!"

The order-taker heaved an impatient sigh. "Sorry," Jana said, turning. "Sorry!" she called to the people waiting behind her. Then she dumped the last handful of change on the counter. She put the paper under her arm and waited with Cavin for the coffees.

"Primitive?" She made a face at him. "I'll have you know I could have paid with my ATM, electronically, but in light of everything that's happened I want to keep as many transactions as I can anonymous."

"I don't fault your logic, only your monetary system. We will find a place to tear the hundreds so we can use them."

"That's *break* them. And, yes, we will."

They took their coffees and walked to the train. As Cavin wheeled her suitcase for her, his new clothing now packed inside, he took a sip of coffee. He made a gurgling noise, cast a panicked glance around. Then he spat a mouthful of coffee into the bushes. "What is this, Jana?" he demanded.

"A latte. Coffee mixed with steamed milk and some vanilla syrup. You don't like it?"

He wrinkled his nose. "It tastes like swamp water. Sweetened swamp water."

She tasted his coffee. "It tastes fine." She narrowed her eyes. "This isn't one of those Cavin-kidding moments, is it?"

He shuddered. He held up a hand, stopping her from returning the cup to him. "With all due respect to your Earth customs and cuisine, Jana, but I cannot bear to even smell it."

She threw the coffee away. She couldn't believe he'd hated it. "What do you drink in the mornings to wake up?"

"I don't have the words to translate, but it's hot, thick and salty. Made from a root. A little bitter if aged." He made a soft sound. "I have missed it these past few days."

Chinese hot and sour soup only thicker and stronger was the first thing that jumped into her mind. But for breakfast? "Ugh!"

He smiled. "Now you see my problem with your coffee."

He gave one last shudder and led her onto the train. His soldier's eyes did a complete scan of the compartment before he let her take a seat.

As the train pulled out of the station, Jana juggled her attaché case, napkins and her coffee as she unfolded the rolled-up paper. May there be no mention of Evie and her exploding Honda. She held her breath and looked down. The headline blared: California's Fragile Environment: Jasper And Other Key State Legislators, Do Personal Interests Influence Policy? Right under the headline was a huge photo of her in Ice, wearing a nervous smile as she cradled a titanic bottle of vodka.

Jana spewed coffee over the page, over a smaller photo of Viktor, grinning as he gave her the bottle, and the caption: Jasper: Conservationist, Czarina. Policies May Keep Caviar Prices High.

Czarina? Viktor, she thought, growling. Was he responsible for this? Was it revenge for the disastrous lunch yesterday? But the article was massive; it had been some time in the making. This was no overnight exposé.

Frantic, she rubbed off drops of coffee, smearing the ink. Then she jammed on her reading glasses. The photos were grainy and dark, as if snapped in the back room of a shady business when in fact they were probably taken from across the street from Ice with a telephoto lens. The last photo was of her at the sturgeon farm, not making the speech or cutting the ribbon, but waiting for champagne to be poured into her glass, of which she'd had one freaking sip. One!

Jana raced through the article. No one had accused her of anything directly; it merely showed her in ways that *suggested* she took bribes and favors. There was one direct quote, an old one, where when asked if rising caviar prices had boosted Viktor's profits, she'd denied knowledge, stating she was not privy to the details nor involved in any way with her cousin's private business. But in this context, it raised the question of whether her allocation of environmental spending served to pad the pockets of family members.

It's what people think that counts, not what you actually do—or not do. She remembered Grandpa's words well. It mattered not what she'd actually done, that she'd refused the gift of vodka. The mere fact she was seen holding it was a character-assassination bull's-eye.

"Cavin, I'm in fucking deep shit." It wasn't too long ago that swearing would make her blush. Now look at her. Then again, she wasn't exactly living the life of a Girl Scout anymore, was she? Her language had to come down to match her criminal existence. "Look," she whispered so the other riders wouldn't overhear. "The photos make it look like I accept bribes, or maybe thank-you gifts for favors rendered."

Cavin took the paper from her shaking hands. He might not be able to read, but he sure as hell could see the pictures. "If they say you accept enticements and you do not, won't the newspaper be held accountable?"

It was an incredibly shrewd observation for a man from a different culture, let alone a different planet. "Yes. If the *Sun* accused me of something and they were wrong, they'd be looking at a libel suit. An ethical journalist wouldn't publish photos and make a statement regarding them, because photos offer just a glimpse. Nothing they depict is shown in context. But these…" She worked to keep her voice steady and low. "I campaigned on the platform that special interest groups can't sway me. And yet here I appear to be cheerfully accepting gifts and favors. Worse, from family members. That's nepotism."

"Lies," he hissed back. "What was done to your father was done to you."

She knew that, but nothing prepared her for the boom being lowered on her. She thought she'd understood what her father must have felt being accused of campaign funds fraud, but now she knew she hadn't come close to realizing the sickening frustration of this unwarranted, unprovoked attack.

Heart thumping, she glanced around the train, where some of the commuters reading the paper, too, cast discreet and some not-so discreet glances at her. Dressed in a navy-blue suit with baby-blue pinstripes and a killer pair of Coach pumps, her hair swept back in a French twist with Tahitian pearls adorning her ears and neck, she actually looked like Senator Jana Jasper today. There would be no mistaking her identity this time.

Normal face. She used every bit of training from her upbringing to get hold of herself. She smoothed her skirt, crossed her legs at the ankle, tried to act composed.

Her cell phone vibrated in her hand. "Nona," Jana said into the phone, recognizing the office number.

"It's Steve. Did you see the *Sun?*"

"Unfortunately."

"Where are you?"

"On light-rail, heading in. My, um, car broke down," she told him before he could ask the question.

"Everything happens at once," he sympathized.

She glanced at Cavin, aka Mr. *War of the Worlds,* and then the newspaper. "You could say that."

"Rob Nixon from the *Sun* called."

"And what did he have to say for himself?" While he hadn't penned today's article, the journalist had covered most of the Jasper stories over the past decade. Jana considered him a friend. A sense of betrayal stung her realizing he'd known the incriminating pictures were going in, and maybe even who'd given them to the paper.

"He tried to stop the feature," Steve said. "Because the reporter who received the photos of you with the vodka won't reveal his source, which is making it all stickier. Says the source fears for his life."

Jana growled. "And for good reason, too. If I get my hands on his so-called source…" She stopped herself before her fantasies of torture and mutilation hit the cell phone airwaves or the ears of anyone who might be eavesdropping. She wasn't quite ready to add conspiracy to murder to her lengthening list of committed crimes.

"Nixon did say he'd be writing a follow-up of his own, to showcase your record. We're meeting later over lunch."

Jana hoped it wasn't too little, too late. "Excellent." It felt good to have a friend remain a friend during the difficult times. In politics, it was too often not the case. "Thank him for me. Please do that."

"Roger. And I'm working up a press release," he said. "Press conference on the west steps later?"

"Green light, Steve. Meanwhile, get Nona on finding out who supplied those pictures. And the one from the fish farm." A burst of memory illuminated an image of a man in a hat and trench coat, taking photos at the fish farm. "Have her look into the identity of that reporter from the Russian paper yesterday. Let's find out who he really works for."

With her staff busy working on countermeasures, Jana told Cavin, "I'd better warn my mother." She dialed the ranch. On the very last ring before the answering machine would have picked up, her mother answered.

"If I woke you, Mom, I'm sorry. It's early, but it's important."

"I know."

Jana's heartbeat skittered. "You do?"

A dramatic sigh. "Mothers know these things. Janushka, what is it?"

"Today's *Sun* published some photos that suggest I take bribes. Front page. They were shot yesterday at lunch."

"Who shot them?" she asked in a deadly voice.

"I don't know. Not yet. But you have to get to the newspaper before Grandpa does. There's an unfavorable article on State legislators and their ties to special interest. I'm the only one in any photos, though, and they imply that my votes can be bought. Hide the front section, destroy the front page, lie, use it for toilet paper, whatever you can do to keep him from seeing it until I can break it to him. Do it—or he'll get sick again, or worse."

With her mother dispatched on her mission, Jana closed the cell phone. Her crisp blue suit was already growing damp around the collar. Her silk shirt clung to her skin. She had a napkin in one hand, a latte in her other hand, and the *Sacramento Sun* heralding the ruin of her career sitting open in her lap.

She took another slug of coffee. The vanilla tasted cloyingly sweet. Probably straight tequila would have gone down better. Vodka, she'd rather not think about. "What bothers me most is the pain this is going to cause my grandfather. If he gets anywhere near the newspaper this morning, he'll be back in the hospital. He's ninety-two. He can't take this much stress."

Cavin's hand slid along the seat to touch hers, pinkie to pinkie. If only she could press her hand in his as she so desperately wanted. "I will never forget the sound of his voice when he came to chase us from the lake that night," Cavin said. "Your grandfather is fiercely protective of you and, I think, you are just as protective of him."

She stopped, thought about that. "You're right. I've always assumed it was the other way around. I do know I'd do anything for that old man." When she turned back to Cavin, his green eyes were dark and troubled. "What?" Her hand crept over his, but she snatched it back in her lap to avoid further temptation.

He kept his voice in a low, private tone so no one would overhear. "Last night you said you would, in your Earth words, stick your neck out for me. In light of your current troubles, I don't think that's wise."

"What are our options?" she whispered back.

"I go to your leadership. Alone. I don't involve you."

"No." Fear formed an ice-cold ball in her stomach. "Absolutely not. As soon as they find out who and what you are, you're in danger." She swiped a hand over the newspaper. "Even if this blows up into a full-fledged scandal and complicates my getting people to believe you, because everything I say is suspect, the alternative is unthinkable. I will not place you at risk."

His voice gentled. "It seems you are as protective of me as you are your grandfather."

She didn't argue. She loved both men. They'd both shaped her life. She couldn't contemplate living without either one of them.

"Are you so sure your people will harm me, Jana?"

"No, I'm not," she whispered. "But I do know that when people are afraid, they'll do almost anything. Why is the assassin after you, for instance? Because whoever hired him was afraid."

Cavin's expression was dark as he pondered her reply.

The train slowed. "This is our stop." They quickly made plans on how they'd handle the inevitable separation when she went to work and he hunkered down to wait for her. The thought of leaving Cavin alone in Capitol Park for hours made her sick. But the thought of trying to get him through security and X-ray, not to mention a gauntlet of policemen, made her even sicker.

They exited the train and walked toward the capitol. The morning was chilly and damp, but the sky was already blue. It would be a pretty spring day. Jana wished she could enjoy it. But what was the loss of one spring day if it meant the continuation of spring days for humanity for a long time to come? In her mind, there was no argument. "Okay, I go inside, and you hang out in the park." Acres of lush lawn and trees surrounded the gold-domed capitol building. It was a beautiful place to be this time of year. "Act like a tourist."

"How does one do this?"

"Just be yourself. Take in the sights. Relax on a bench. Think about what you're going to say to the president of the United States when you meet her. And do not, I repeat, do not take out that roll of money." She veered over to an ATM machine. She stopped him with her hand when he tried to come with her. "No. Stay out of camera range."

Cavin sighed through his nose but cooperated. The protector did not like being protected. Jana withdrew a hundred dollars worth of twenties, giving four of them to Cavin. "Lunch money. The park has vendors that sell hot food—just look for the umbrellas, pictures of food. I hope you like hot dogs better than lattes— skinny red sausages, not dog dogs," she clarified when he recoiled. Sadie had Cavin so wrapped around her little paw that he was ready to come to the defense of all dogs, everywhere, including hot dogs.

"I should be out by three this afternoon. I've got a senate floor session this morning then a caucus luncheon or I'd eat with you. I have to stick to my routine. The more normal I appear, the more boring, the faster this scandal will get swept under the rug." She believed it with all her heart. Her father would get out from under the attack, and so would she. And now it was more important than ever to hold on to her stellar reputation as a legislator. The fate of the world was riding on it.

The awful sensation of being swept out to sea in advance of a killer wave intensified and the tsunami finally rushed in. In one jarring, composure-ripping, soul-crushing moment, she was in over her head. She sucked in a breath as if drowning. "This thing feels so much bigger than me."

"I rue the day I brought so much trouble to your life, Jana. I truly do."

"No, you're not taking the blame. This is my issue. You're a hero. I…I don't know if I am."

Cavin's hand brushed lightly down her rigid back. "I've found one truism when under heavy attack. And that is, worry is wasted energy. It will tear you down when you most need your strength and wits."

"It's hard not to worry."

"You must try."

She gave him a sideways smile. "Now who's being protective over whom?"

"I'll always be that way with you." His voice deepened. "I suggest you get used to it."

With reluctance, they parted ways on the sidewalk bordering the park. The goodbye was no easier than the day before, no less wrenching. She lived for the day she could be openly in love with him. Would that day ever come? Holding her attaché bag and the handle of her rolling suitcase in one hand, she pointed to a towering redwood. "At 3:00 p.m., meet me at that tree. Not in the tree, okay? Under it."

His mouth gave the barest of amused twitches. "Understood. I will be waiting under the tree."

She walked away as fast as she could toward the gold-domed California State Capitol, her high heels clicking on the sidewalk. The plan was simple. Go to the office, meet with her staff, plot her rebuttal to the outrageous insinuations in the paper, work up the courage to ask for a meeting with Governor Schwarzkopf regarding the alien invasion, and figure out what she was going to say to her grandfather when she brought Cavin home for dinner.

CHAPTER SEVENTEEN

NORMAL FACE, Jana reminded herself as she strode into the staff-only elevator. It was packed. Jana wedged her body inside. Instead of one desk chair with an operator, there were two, one on each side of the tiny elevator. She saw the looks on the other staffers' faces: a *training session* for an automatic elevator? The new-hire was young, skinny, and slouched on a padded swivel chair, looking bored to tears as Joseph coached him. Joseph had been around for years. And he didn't call her sweet pea like Lucky did.

"Three, please," Jana said.

"Push the three," Joseph directed the new guy.

One of the riders snickered and received two dirty looks. "Try not to think of this when you spend your morning in meetings listening to whining over budget cuts and lack of funding for social service programs," the assemblyman muttered.

Jana tried to act anonymous, but she caught a few glares and a couple of curious stares. Even the elevator operator trainee studied her with dark, calculating eyes, making her feel as if she sported a huge scarlet *B* on her forehead. *Bribe taker!* Other legislators simply waited for their floor. The glaring and curious folks had seen the newspaper, she knew. The uninterested were those with unread newspapers tucked under their arms. By lunchtime, everyone would have read it and she'd be dirt. Nothing was more disgusting to honest lawmakers than someone profiting from their power. And the accusations of nepotism? It was simply the icing on the shit cake.

Steve and Nona were waiting when she arrived at the office. They shut and locked the doors and hunkered down around Jana's desk. Jana grabbed an iced Krispy Kreme doughnut and bit into it. The sugar was like a shot of morphine. Quickly, she took another bite.

"More bad news," Nona said.

"More?" Jana mumbled, her mouth full of doughnut.

"Brace Bowie's going to be on KBFK this afternoon. *The Tom Kennedy Show.*"

Jana went rigid. Nona hovered close, poised to smack her on the back should she start choking. But somehow Jana steered the bite of doughnut down the right pipe. Maybe she was getting used to the carnival of shocks her life had become. By next week she bet people would be able to say anything to her and she wouldn't even twitch. "Why is Brace going on a talk show?" But even as she asked the question, the answer lodged in her brain like a poison arrow. "Kick me while I'm down, why doesn't he? I'd like to get my hands on the queen's plasma sword and lop off his male organs."

It was suddenly silent in the office. She glanced up to see two confused and worried faces. "It's a figure of speech," she said. Everyone went back to eating and drinking.

"Obviously, he's piggybacking on the attack to pull

you down with him," Nona said. "It's not impossible that he was behind getting those photos to the *Sun*. The restaurant is, of course, an investment of his."

And Brace was, after all, curiously missing from the lunch. She'd assumed it was because his presence would have made things awkward, but maybe there had been another, darker reason for his absence. Like picture taking during the perfect setup.

Jana couldn't imagine Brace hating her so much. Or hating her family. At one time, they'd had something good, she and Brace. He'd never made her blood run hot, but he wasn't a coldhearted man, either. Since their breakup, Brace had been a pain in the butt with his attempts to regain his reputation at the expense of hers but she'd attributed it to his need to have someone to blame after being humiliated, not on deliberate cruelty. Maybe she'd been too lenient.

Jana stuffed the rest of the doughnut into her mouth.

Steve pushed the box toward her. "I brought extra today."

"Good man," she mumbled.

"I'll try to get you on the talk show tomorrow," Nona said. "I'm talking to the station as we speak."

"Excellent. If Brace is going to kick me while I'm down, I'm kicking back." She wasn't going to let it go unchallenged when he accused her of padding the Natural Resources budget. Because if the public turned against her, the budget would surely be cut the next round, and she'd lose the money she needed to maintain enough Fish and Game wardens—her "thugs" as Viktor had dubbed them—to fight the growing poaching threat.

All her efforts since taking office to preserve endangered wildlife would be lost in the current fervor for government spending cutbacks. It wasn't that she didn't believe in fiscal responsibility, but some things you just didn't get back after losing them—like entire species of animals. When it came to extinction, there were no second chances.

Like Earthling extinction. Her stomach rolled as the reality of impending doom returned and tumbled over her. Shouldn't she be doing something about that? Or was she still living in denial? The looming invasion was where her focus ought to be, not on her detractors' attempts to turn the state into a poacher's playground, because if Cavin's plan failed and the Coalition "acquired" Earth, there'd be nothing left to poach.

REEF STALKED down the street where the news reports had claimed the EMP had originated. His computer detected faint traces of energy that could only be from Coalition equipment. His target was near. But where? He stopped periodically to take measurements. His idea of acquiring Earth clothing had served him well. Not only did the local Earthlings ignore him, they avoided him altogether, crossing to the other side of the street and casting him nervous glances. He was only a few inches over six foot tall and in perfect physical condition, but with no scars to speak of or fearsome weapons that were visible, he didn't understand why they were so afraid. He was dressed like them, was he not?

A large boxy vehicle drove up to one of the dwellings. UPS, it read. A man dressed in a brown uniform hopped out. Energetically, he carried a box to the door.

When no one answered, he left the parcel, took a few steps toward his truck and noticed Reef. He slowed, eyes narrowing.

No, Reef thought. There was something wrong with the way he'd dressed. His attire may have been appropriate where he'd spent the night, but not here.

After the man in brown climbed into his vehicle and departed, Reef removed the necklaces from around his neck. Not a single individual he'd spied on this street had sported such a cluster of necklaces. He crushed them in his fist and, with a burst of energy, powdered them.

Immediately, dizziness made his head swirl. His vision dimmed, and a piercing whine filled his ears. He took a staggering step forward to gain his balance. Were his energy reserves so low that a simple act such as destroying the necklaces drained him? Or was he still malfunctioning?

He shook it off, set his jaw and pressed on, looking for the source for the energy pulse. *There*. He stopped in front of a large brown dwelling. Readings confirmed that his target was here—or had been here.

An odd sound caught his attention. Reef increased the volume of his auditory implants. "*Yarp, yarp, yarp.*" He could not identify the sound. It emanated from the front window. Reef narrowed his eyes. Through partially open window coverings, he saw something darting back and forth across what appeared to be the top of a piece of furniture—a couch.

"Yarp, yarp. Yarp!"

He zoomed in on the strange sight. It was a creature of some sort. And frenzied, apparently. Moisture fogged the window, obscuring flashes of white teeth.

Frowning, Reef accessed his computer: *Species: Canine, Earth. Breed: Chihuahua. Purpose: Humanoid pet. Weight: 4 pounds, 7 ounces.*

Reef dismissed the creature as a potential danger. Nothing of that infinitesimal size would be of any threat to him.

He opened a side gate and walked into the backyard to look for further hints and perhaps a way inside the dwelling. There was an azure, rectangular pool for swimming, an area of lawn and dozens of potted planets. Out of the corner of his eye, he saw what resembled a small, golden missile shoot through an opening in the rear door of the dwelling. It was the Chihuahua.

"Yarp, yarp. Yarp!" The little beast came at him, brown eyes wide, blazing with fury. And wholly oblivious to the danger into which it had hurtled.

AFTER AN ABBREVIATED, pre-Easter break floor session, a spate of meetings, phone calls to and from her family, worried constituents, and newspaper reporters, and frantic peeks out the window futilely looking for signs of Cavin, Jana waited for the elevator to take her up to the luncheon. The floor session with the other senators had been somewhat chilly. On the other hand, no one had wanted to waste time with chitchat. Most were anxious to hurry out of the capitol and back to their districts for spring break. Jana expected more reaction at the caucus lunch with only senators in her party in attendance. They would have seen the damaging photos and, she hoped, would sympathize. They knew her, knew her character and record. That is, if things like character and record still mattered.

The elevator doors opened. The car was crammed with legislators. Jana walked in, stuffing last-minute paperwork into her attaché. All at once, the elevator emptied. She felt like a salmon swimming upstream as staffers and legislators flowed past, jostling her, until the only people left were her and Lucky.

Everyone else who'd been on the elevator formed up to wait for the next one. She stared forlornly after them as the doors closed. No doubt about it, it was a deliberate snub.

It was like going back in time; she was the kid in the school yard no one wanted to play with, all over again. *I'm normal, I really am. I can talk, I can, just give me a chance.* The pain of embarrassment was a familiar knife twisting in old wounds. *I don't take bribes. My family is honest, I tell you. Come back! Don't ostracize me. I don't have an alien waiting outside in the park for me, really I don't!*

"Hi, sweet pea," Lucky said. "You're having a bad day."

"A bad week." Jana tried her darnedest not to pout. "Three, please."

"Three." Lucky went back to knitting a pale green baby-size sweater as the elevator ascended.

"Well, Lucky, this is just the beginning. Soon no one's going to return my calls. Meetings will be called and I won't be told. And until my name's cleared, even though I'm innocent, I'll be riding the staff elevators alone. Just me and you, Lucky."

"That's how things work around here, sweet pea. See, you're like a freshly painted fence post right now. Don't matter what the wood's like underneath—clean and sanded or worm-eaten—no one wants to brush up against wet paint."

"I feel like wet paint." Jana felt like a lot of things, crying her guts out, followed up by a primal scream, included.

In the moment before the doors opened, Lucky took Jana's hand in her strong, roughened one. "You gotta hold your head high. That's what I tell my girls. Keep up the fight. You know what you have to do."

"I know," Jana said in a thick voice and squeezed the woman's hand. "I do."

The doors opened. The people waiting to ride gave her a wide berth as she exited.

She walked swiftly down the hall. Her chin weighed about a thousand pounds, but she managed to keep it high. Bruce Keene, the party leader, stopped her before she could enter the room where the weekly caucus luncheon took place. "Bad luck with the photos," he said.

"I'm not taking this lying down. I have a press conference scheduled this afternoon, the radio tomorrow. No one buys me, Bruce. My ethics are beyond reproach. I represent the people and I came to office to accomplish what they elected me to do. Special interest groups have no hold over me."

Her words emboldened her, and she actually felt up to lunch, discussing the situation with the more experienced members of her party, but Bruce shook his head and took her by the arm, leading her a few yards away from the door. From inside came the delicious aroma of a catered lunch and the din of voices. "You're not invited."

The heat of mortification flamed in her face. "Bruce, you're not allowing me inside?"

"Look, we've got the press lined up downstairs. My phone's been ringing off the hook. I don't want this kind of attention on the party, not with so many elections hanging in the balance this fall. I'm sorry, Jana. Get things cleaned up on your end, and you can come back." With an apologetic look, he stepped backward and closed the door. Closing her off from her colleagues.

Jana fell against the wall. She was shaking from her head to her toes. If she'd had any doubts about it before, they were gone now: she was officially *persona non grata*.

It was a wake-up call.

Despite her promises to Cavin that she'd stick her neck out, she hadn't done it. All day she'd naively maintained the status quo, going about her routine, as if her world wasn't crumbling around her. And all because she hadn't broken free of her lifelong fear of being seen as different, as something less than everyone else. Something to be pitied. Well, if there was any pitying to be going on, it should be her feeling sorry for herself!

How could she still be so worried about how others saw her when she was in hot water for something she didn't do? How could she be so concerned about her reputation when with one word, someone could trash her public image in the space of a few hours? Sure, she needed to keep her nose clean while her father and brother were under investigation, but her efforts were futile with someone so determined to take her down. Being good did no good. Hadn't she learned that by now? It was time to do what was right no matter how she might look coming out the other side.

But the idea of doing so made her knees wobbly. She wasn't wired like Cavin. Heroics weren't her strong suit. Dependability was. Loyalty. Hard work. Not this, not what she was being asked to do—convincing, at the likelihood of her own ruin, those in positions of power to give an extraterrestrial access to a spacecraft everyone denied existed. What made her so sure they'd believe her story? What if General Mahoney insisted that no alien craft had ever existed? Why would the president of the United States bother listening to a lowly state legislator whose family was under investigation for everything from fraud to involvement in syndicated crime? Hadn't she already lost this race before she got out of the starting gate?

Never be afraid of going for it, even when someone tells you your chances of succeeding are one in a million.

Jana caught her breath. The words echoed inside her mind. Her father had told her that countless times, but she'd never had to test herself until now. "Okay, Dad," she whispered. "You asked for it. You created a monster and for better or for worse, it's just been unleashed."

She opened her cell phone and dialed the governor's office. The secretary answered. "Governor Schwarzkopf's office."

"Hi, Willa. It's Senator Jana Jasper." After the usual brief pleasantries were exchanged, Jana got to business. "Would you please see what the governor's schedule looks like for a private meeting today or tomorrow?" *And I bet it's one he remembers all year.*

"He's completely booked. It'll have to wait until after recess. I can fit you in the second week after the holiday."

Two weeks. Too late. "Tell him I understand it may be difficult to work me in, but that I must see him as soon as possible. It's urgent," she said, her heart in her mouth because it wasn't the vodka and caviar scandal she'd be bringing up, but a subject of far more consequence. "It affects the entire state." *Actually, it affects the entire world, Willa, but maybe we should feed this to the governor a little at a time.*

Jana hung up after the secretary promised to do what she could. The ball was now in motion.

The day hurtled onward with no more catastrophes. It was like being in the eye of a hurricane: a false impression of calm before the storm. Because it *was* the calm before the storm. After today, nothing would be the same.

THE ENRAGED CHIHUAHUA lunged at Reef and sank its teeth into his pants leg. He didn't feel a thing through his armor, only incessant tugging at his ankle as he stalked up to the rear doors of the dwelling. He unlocked the door and stepped inside.

He was struck by the immediate and almost overwhelming sense of calm that stole over him. He could not recall ever experiencing such a sensation simply from entering a dwelling anywhere in the galaxy. He could not recall experiencing such a sensation period, for that matter.

The dwelling was rich in deep hues that reminded him of gourmet delights, the earthy color of ebbe bark, the furry underside of icquit leaves, the latter a surprisingly vivid impression left from what were only snatches of very faint memories of the few years spent as a normal youngster on his home world before he'd been taken away to become a bioengineered combat-ant. The scents he couldn't identify, but the spicy sweet-ness was extraordinarily pleasing. He breathed deep. Then caught himself. It was not his place to feel such things. Not in the middle of a hunt.

"Yarp! Yarp!" The annoying pet danced around his boots, alternately tearing at his pants and nearly tripping him as he paused to study a grouping of two-dimensional images enclosed in wood frames. A woman with a glowing smile and thick, shining dark brown hair stood alone in one, her head tossed to the side, her luxuriant hair spilling over one shoulder. Her body was as lush as her hair. The creamy tops of her breasts were tantalizingly visible above the neckline of her shirt, and she seemed to be laughing, teasing him, luring him into her private world of warmth and happiness. A man could lose himself in a woman like that...

A man. Not a REEF. He shook thoughts of the woman from his mind. Was this the female Far Star had escaped with? If so, Reef could see why the soldier had taken her.

"Yarp, yarp. Yarp!" Irritably, Reef used his foot to shove the irksome beast away. The Chihuahua slid across the wood floor and spun into the wall. In an instant, it was back on its feet, claws scrabbling for purchase as it launched its heaving, scrawny body at him. Reef considered snapping the little creature's neck, but it would leave a sign Far Star might interpret as him having visited here. Reef's best chance at killing cleanly and efficiently came from an element of surprise. He'd lost that surprise when he lost his target in the Earth market. Now he had to try to get it back. Once he did, Far Star was his.

Reef heard his pants rip. The Chihuahua tore off a

piece of the fabric, shaking it, and returned for another mouthful. "Enough." He aimed his gauntlet at the pet. In a whirl of blue-white energy, it lifted off the floor. He floated it up toward the ceiling. The little dog pedaled its legs, as determined as ever to attack him. Its mouth dripped with foam. "Stay there."

A wave of dizziness overtook him once more. This time his vision took longer to recover. After the whine in his ears subsided, a faint whistle remained. He didn't like this, not in the least. A simple act such as floating the dog had taxed his systems. No matter. He had his weapons. He didn't need his biotech to operate those.

He turned on his gauntlet and did another search. Nothing. No sign of the man. Unfamiliar frustration sparked inside him. The thrill of a difficult hunt was one thing, but taking this long to locate his prey was entirely another. This, he didn't like.

Reef turned in a circle. Where had Far Star disappeared to? Energy traces confirmed he'd been inside the dwelling. As recently as last night. But Reef was too late in coming here. Once again, his prey had slipped out of his hands.

This mission must not fail. For one, failure was personally abhorrent. It would be even more so to those who'd hired him. And with Reef's ship too damaged to fly, at the completion of his mission he'd have called for a covert pickup. But who would come retrieve an assassin who could not kill? Without confidence in his abilities to carry out a termination assignment, there would be no more reason for anyone to employ his services. If he failed here, he failed utterly: his trip to Earth became one-way, and his life became meaningless.

Failure, it appeared, was no more an option than it ever was, but Reef felt a sweat break over him realizing how much more hung in the balance than the mere completion of a kill.

He must find Far Star.

He reviewed his options. *The code*. Yes, there was that, but he hadn't considered it because it was personally repulsive to him. Those who'd paid for this mission had supplied the code to him, but he had dismissed its use, because of pride, but perhaps its use could stand as a last resort, should Reef get to that point.

All Coalition military personnel had access codes built in to their bioimplants, though few, if any, knew it was the case. Reef certainly had not been aware until he'd been told. The code allowed a foreign computer to deliver a signal to the internal bioimplants found in all Coalition soldiers. It was how the Coalition kept ultimate control of their resources, Reef surmised; without a doubt there was a code for him as well. If used maliciously, the technique ultimately degraded the host body by destroying the bioimplants. As far as Reef knew, no other assassin had ever been given such a code. Probably because no other REEF had been hired by such a highly positioned government official.

If used maliciously…

Reef had no qualms about malicious behavior. If he hacked into Far Star's body, he'd be able to wreak all sorts of havoc. He found it distastefully unprofessional to play overly much with his prey before killing it. But in light of the circumstances, perhaps it wouldn't be so bad to slow Far Star down enough to allow Reef to catch up to him. Then the fight would be on. He'd even let Far Star run and get a head start.

Reef loaded the code into his computer and transmitted.

Nothing happened.

Now that was decidedly unsatisfying, he thought. He neither saw nor felt what the access had done to Far Star, if anything at all.

He would try again later.

Reef cast a sharp gaze around the room. A stack of rolled packets of grayish-white papers littered the dining table. Earth news, he realized. In printed form. He'd had luck gleaning the information he needed from visual news; perhaps news in print would yield similar results. His visual scanner-translator for Earth text was slow, but he had a few moments to spare. He sat in one of the chairs. The wood table gleamed. He saw in its polished, fragranced surface a hard face. A cold face. It told him that he didn't belong in this inviting, comfortable dwelling. As it should be. The REEF-O1A was not designed for domestic use.

He opened all the newspapers and ordered them by date. He chose the most recent, from that very morning, and tried to make sense of the odd, blocky letters. The front page contained only several gray-toned images of a pretty, slender, crisply dressed woman. He saw no text about the EM pulse, no hints regarding his target. As he lifted the corner of the page to turn to the next, the sight of the woman's shoes stopped him. They were familiar. But why?

"Yarp, yarp!" The dog protested its flight. But Reef's attention remained on the shoes on the woman's

feet. She stood there, tipping a drink into her mouth. He zoomed in on the shoes and recorded the image. Then he accessed his archives, looking for a match. In point-eight seconds, he had it.

The shoe was identical in every way to the one found abandoned in the street the night Reef had pursued and had failed to catch his target. All the television news shows had carried the image, because they, like Reef, believed Far Star had taken a hostage that night. Now Reef knew who she was.

Senator Jana Jasper.

Finally, a break. Where the woman was, Far Star was. This, Reef knew in his gut, that human part of him that often gave information with as much accuracy if not more than his bio-computers.

He returned the paper to its precise, original condition and turned to leave.

"Yarp, yarp. Yarp!" The creature's barking changed in tone. From where it floated, the snarling snapping humanoid pet tried like mad to reach the front entrance. Reef saw why. Two heat signatures appeared at the door: *Humanoid, male. Quantity: 1. Weight: 202. Humanoid, female. Quantity 1. Weight: 146.*

They carried weapons. Their uniforms indicated they were paramilitary personnel, perhaps law enforcement wardens.

Reef drew his weapon and stood. As the door flew open, he invoked invisibility. To his relief, his balky systems cooperated. The wardens had not seen him. Reef wasn't certain how long he'd remain invisible, or how long he could stave off the inevitable dizziness, and he moved away quickly.

He ducked out the rear exit, but not before he glimpsed the amusing sight of the Chihuahua dropping from the ceiling, foaming and furious, onto a startled warden's head. They would, he suspected, be talking about this incident for a long time to come.

He strode out of the backyard and to the vehicle that had carried him here. As he did, he brought up the profile on Jana Jasper stored on his computer. As was the case with all Earth leaders, every fact was in the databank, at his fingertips. Fingertips itching to pull the trigger that would terminate Prime-major Far Star and free the both of them, albeit in different ways, from this gods-forsaken world. *Jana Tatiana Jasper, I very much look forward to meeting you.*

CHAPTER EIGHTEEN

CLUTCHING HIS LEFT ARM to his stomach, Cavin kept moving, walking endless circuits around the park. The sharp pain he'd felt some time ago in the area of his left forearm had subsided to a dull throbbing ache. Disturbingly, it came from the area of the bioimplant that interfaced with his gauntlet computer. Was it another injury he'd suffered in the crash? If so, why hadn't it bothered him until now? It would have to heal slowly, like his abdominal wound had done, now nearly healed. The level of nano-meds in his body was low, but given time, they would heal him internally. It just might take days, maybe even weeks, instead of hours.

Cavin continued his patrol. He felt useless, uneasy. Jana's long absence bothered him due to his inability to protect her should something go wrong. His only consolation was that the building maintained a reasonable level of security, for Earth.

After another trip around the park, keeping watch on the building within which Jana labored, a male voice called out to him. "You gotta put it down, man."

Cavin turned toward the man sitting on a bench. Despite the pleasant temperature, he was swaddled in a thick green jacket. A ragged, soiled jacket. His belongings sat in bags on the grass. He sported a baseball cap like Jana had worn, but his read: Proud Vietnam Vet.

The man patted the bench. "You gotta put it down. They're watching you."

Cavin's pulse kicked into a higher speed as he scanned the park, looking for threats. "Who is?"

"The capitol cops. There, on the steps."

Cavin peered at two men in civilian clothes that looked to be loitering on the steps of Jana's building.

"Plainclothes security," the older man explained. "Anti-terrorist. They've made at least two phone calls about you. Next time past, they might stop you, ask you questions. Maybe pull you in if they don't like your answers."

Cavin sat on the opposite side of the bench. He could ill afford being "taken in" anywhere, by anyone. Not at the risk of delaying or even ending his mission. "They won't like my answers," he muttered.

The man coughed out a wheezy laugh. He squeezed the stub of a cigarette pinched between two fingers. A slight palsy made his hand quiver. "Don't matter how many times you walk the park, you ain't gonna look like you're from around here."

Cavin glanced at him, startled. "I'm a tourist."

The man seemed smug as he threw the cigarette stub to the ground and crushed it with battered boots. He coughed, one that came from deep within his lungs. "I guess you can say I'm a tourist, too. I never hang around for long. I'm a rolling stone." He chuckled then coughed some more. It made his eyes water. "Been that way since the war, you know." He pointed to his dirty cap. "'Nam."

"This 'Nam, it was a war?"

"You got it right, man. They never admitted it, did they? I fought, I saw buddies killed over there. But, no, they said, it wasn't a war." He convulsed in another spasm of coughing and spat on the grass. "You look like a military man yourself."

Cavin grunted. Said nothing.

"If you tell me, you have to kill me, right?" The older man nodded with respect. "I don't need no help doing that. You ever in combat?"

"Many times."

"Enlisted man or officer?"

"Started off as a grunt. Ended up as an officer."

"Then you're still okay. Still okay." He gave another wheezy laugh.

This tattered man was a stranger, and yet he was familiar. Cavin had known many men like this one, soldiers who'd experienced things in combat that made it nearly impossible to blend back in with society. Without the anchor of family, and often even with that anchor, they were buffeted by nightmares and ultimately lost at sea. In particular, Cavin had seen what happened to soldiers after the Drakken got hold of them, and it was ugly. The Coalition may not be perfect, and he might disagree with them on many things, but they were all that stood between the galaxy and the Drakken horde.

"You got a smoke?"

"A smoke? Ah, no. Sorry."

The man dug in his coat pocket for a pack of "smokes." He lit one and sucked on it, long and hard. Then, in between bouts of coughing, he told Cavin about the war and his role in it.

For a long time afterward, they watched the sun reach its zenith and then track down the other side. Sunshine spilled over the grass. They sat in silence, enjoying the odd camaraderie veterans had. It transcended culture, race and apparently planets, as well.

After a while, Cavin went in search of food and brought back dogs and cans of drink for them to consume.

"Ten hot dogs?" the man asked in obvious surprise.

"I'm hungry." Cavin was starving, actually.

"I am, too, but...ten?"

Cavin shrugged. Jana never seemed to require much food, but that was not the case with him. "What we don't eat, you can keep." He bit into one of the bread-wrapped dogs. "Tasty," Cavin murmured in appreciation. "Better than lattes."

"Where's home?" the man asked.

The answer, for Cavin, was an easy one. "I don't have a home. I never did, not really."

"You got a woman?

Jana's scent, her face, the sweet feel of her, it filled his mind, and a familiar ache of missing her followed. "Yes, I do."

"Home is where your woman is, man. Ain't no home without her. I don't have mine no more, so, I ain't got no home.

Home is where your woman is. Cavin nodded. He knew without a doubt that it was true. With one simple sentence, the old soldier had summed up the entire reason he was here.

The soldier lifted his cigarette, pointed. "That's her."

Sure enough, Jana had arrived under the tree that

was their meeting place. Cavin rose and lifted a hand to catch her attention. Jana grinned at him but held her wave to a discreet flutter of her hand. "Yes, it is her," he said. "You could tell?"

"It's all over your face, man. And I see why. She ain't bad to look at. Ain't bad at all."

"I must go. But, first…" To Cavin's surprise and the soldier's, he grasped the man's wrist and pressed his gauntlet to the man's thin arm in a modified Coalition handshake, and handshake of soldiers, but this one would be so much more.

The man's eyes rounded. "You got a weapon under there. I can feel it."

"Not a weapon. A…computer." The man tried to wriggle from his grip. Cavin held on. For a split second, he turned on the gauntlet. A split second more, and he'd deposited a stream of nano-meds into the man's bloodstream.

The man jerked away. "What you do?"

"Thanked you for your help." Cavin secured the gauntlet. The risk of the REEF detecting what he'd done was small. Especially now that Jana had arrived, they wouldn't be sticking around for the assassin to find them.

"What help? I didn't do nothing." The man rubbed his arm.

"You kept me from arrest. And then you shared your afternoon with me. Consider our handshake my thanks to you." Cavin backed up and gave the soldier what he knew from his studies of Earth culture was a salute. Then he strode to Jana's side.

Her face lit up. Seeing the look in her eyes, a look

reserved only for him, made his heart leap. Nothing had changed in twenty-three years. She still made him come alive inside. She made him feel as if anything were possible. "Squee," he greeted her in a quiet voice.

"Boy, am I glad to see you," she said back.

It was a struggle for both of them not to fall into an embrace. The struggle worsened when he breathed in the scent of her skin. But he fisted his hands, clenched his abs, anything to keep from pulling her close and crushing her to him. The intimacy they'd shared the night before hadn't come close to taking the edge off his desire to have her, to make her his, fully. He'd managed to stay alive through years of combat, but now that he'd arrived on Earth, he lived in doubt of surviving another moment without making love to Jana.

"Why were you shaking that man's hand?"

It occurred to him that she'd asked a question. Maybe twice. "Ah, yes, the man. Like a fool, I was patrolling the grounds, waiting for you, and he alerted me to the fact that I'd gained the suspicions of the local police force."

"He deserves more than thanks. He deserves a medal."

"I gave him something better than a medal. I put nano-meds in his bloodstream—microscopic computers programmed for medical purposes. A short burst, a few million or so. I couldn't risk keeping my gauntlet turned on for longer. But over time, perhaps in weeks and months, the meds will erase the cancer from his lungs." He rubbed his forearm, near where he wore his gauntlet. "My own supply is low, but I have enough for my basic health needs."

She gazed up at him, her eyes luminous, almost

glowing. "You give so much, Cavin. To me, to others. To this entire planet. What's in it for you? What do you get in return?"

"I get you. Or, I hope I do."

"You hope?" Laughing softly, she shook her head. "Baby, you had me from greetings, Earthling."

He pulled her close. Lights flashed. At first he thought the gods in the heavens were cheering their love for one another. Then Jana jerked away. "Tabloid photographers. Come on. Let's get out of here."

"No privacy on this planet," he growled.

"See why I'm so protective of you? Now bored people on supermarket checkout lines everywhere will be able to see us together. Only they won't know who you are, or what our relationship is, and I intend to keep it that way. Oh, but they'll speculate." She made a face and rolled her eyes. "But I'm bringing you home tonight. That'll end any speculation on my grandfather's part, at least."

He slowed his steps. She tugged on his arm. "Hurry. I have to get out of this place. I had the day from hell. And I just got done with the press conference from hell."

"Press conference?" His translator offered no solution.

"A press conference is where journalists ask you questions and no matter what answer you give, they don't like it. Then they print their own version in the newspaper. Or at least that's how it went today. On the plus side, they're finally talking about more than my social life." She paused, winced, casting a pained backward glare at the photographers they'd encountered. "Maybe not."

She pulled him across the street to where they would obtain a vehicle for hire. "Rewind, Jana. The part about bringing me home. Do you mean your family home?"

"Yes. The ranch. It's time to tell my grandfather what you've told me. He knows a man who might be able to facilitate getting you to Area 51. My father won't be home, but everyone else will be."

Gods. He was going to meet her kin. He didn't know what worried him more, convincing Earth that they were in danger, or convincing Jana's family he was good for her.

SPEEDING ALONG the highway in a rented white Ford Expedition, Jana gnawed on her knuckle until it stung.

"It will bleed, Squee." Cavin lifted her sore knuckle to his lips and kissed it. Then he kept her hand pressed to his hard thigh, protectively. Possessively. She liked that he took pains to take care of her. Since childhood, she'd sought independence with fervor. After being so doted upon, so worried about, she never wanted to be anyone's problem again. But Cavin's care was different. It was equal parts affection and respect. Nonetheless, it was there, his wanting to keep her safe, and their argument over it had been going on nonstop for a half hour while they waited for Brace Bowie's appearance on *The Tom Kennedy Show* to begin.

She turned off the radio.

"Jana…"

"No. I don't want to listen to it. My nerves are shot. It's just going to make me upset."

"He may reveal information you don't have." Cavin

turned the radio on. "Moreover, how can you be so certain the man is going to say negative words about you?"

She looked down her nose at him. "Is the grass green? The sky blue?"

"Not on all worlds, no."

"You are so literal sometimes." Jana smacked the heels of her palms to her forehead.

"Keep your hands on the wheel. Your vehicles are not designed for hands-free use."

"You drive then."

"I can't. It's not the driving itself that holds me back—I have an aptitude for vehicles of all kinds. But I can't read your numbers." He pointed to the dashboard. "Not the primitive dials that you use to crosscheck your speed, nor road signs. They're gibberish to me."

"I didn't see a single road sign the other night driving in the fog, but somehow I still drove. 'Go right, go left. Slow down, speed up…'" Revenge will be sweet, she thought. Then she remembered the terrifying sight of the assassin bearing down on them as she raced through the streets. "How does the REEF do it if he can't read?"

"He's equipped with visual scanners that allow him to translate written language. My equipment is inferior to his."

"Trust me, baby. There's nothing wrong with your equipment."

They exchanged a heated glance. "You're distracting me, Jana," he warned.

"That's because I don't want to listen to this creep call me a dishonest, self-serving nepotistic bribe-taker." She shut off the radio.

Cavin turned it back on. "To be able to fight your enemy, you must understand him."

"I do understand him. He's a mean, vindictive whiner. I'd say asshole, too, but I think you've learned enough bad Earthling language for the time being."

"I have every swearword in every major language loaded in my translator. As well as most jokes, insults and colloquial phrases."

"You're thoroughly corrupted is what you're saying."

A flash of sexy mischief glinted in his eyes. It told her he had in mind a very different kind of corruption when it came to her. Little good her nun's toes did her.

"The mere fact that you once agreed to marry this man proves he cannot be as horrible as you claim."

She snorted and turned off the radio. "I can't believe you're defending him."

"I'm not defending him so much as I'm complimenting your judgment. I agree that your former fiancé was wrong to say the things he did. He should have gotten more facts before blaming you for his arrest on poaching charges."

"Instead of accusing me of strong-arm techniques to uphold my so-called Fish and Game empire. My cousin told me the Russian community thinks I run a gang of thugs. Thugs! Well, those so-called thugs are about to crack a major poaching ring. The investigation's been going on for the better part of two years. Any day now and they'll move in and make their busts. Everything up until now has been small stuff. This one's going to be big." And it would be a major victory for her, for the state. It would punctuate her resolve to defend the environment with more than rhetoric. No way would she let anyone intimidate her into backing down. And especially not Brace Bowie. She swerved off the highway to cut across town.

"We're taking a slight detour," she said. "A detour to the radio station. It's about two miles from here. If Brace has something to say to me, he can say it to my face." Her hands squeezed the steering wheel until her fingers throbbed. Brace would be dealing with a different Jana this time around. A new and improved, tough-chick Jana. *Being good does no good.* "If today taught me anything, Cavin, it's that taking the high road doesn't always work." Maybe the only way to get her enemies to shut up was to get down in the mud with them and fight.

CHAPTER NINETEEN

"ARE YOU SURE YOU NEVER served in the Coalition officer corps?" Cavin's tone was a loaded mix of surprise, admiration and amusement at her decision to show up at the station.

"No," she said, scowling at the sound of the host encouraging callers to phone in their questions. Brace was coming on after the next news break.

"See, this is self-preservation on his part," Jana tried to explain to help Cavin understand. "If I look bad, he looks good, and voilà, his reputation is restored."

"I'll give you that. But why go after your family when he could have focused on only you?"

"I don't know…" It was a very good question. She'd suspected Brace may have been behind the attacks on her family because he'd gone after her. But what if that wasn't true? "Still, why grab an appearance on a talk show the day a scandal hits if not to pull me down further? He got those pictures in the paper, and now he's going to capitalize on his coup."

"Don't assume Brace gave those photos to the newspaper. To recognize your true enemies, you must be able to see through their deceptions and diversions."

"If it wasn't Brace, then who…?" She frowned at the

road ahead. Viktor, maybe? Then she remembered Alex's face, the frightening look of hatred. "Yesterday, Brace's partners came after me pretty hard… Maybe it's all three of them with Brace as ringleader."

"Or, it's not Brace at all."

"You want me to match you two up? Clearly, you love this guy." She offered him her cell phone. "Or here, call the show and tell him what a great human being he is."

Cavin ignored her. "You said yourself he was a financial backer of the restaurant but had no day-to-day interest in it. You said, too, that he'd done it as a favor to your cousin while you were engaged to be married. Perhaps he wanted to leave the venture once it became apparent you would not marry."

"It would be devastating to their business if Brace pulled his capital. They're struggling. They told me so yesterday."

"So your cousin and his partner looked to illegal means to bolster their profits—and encouraged chaos between you and Brace to distract you from their activities. It makes sense, does it not? You and Brace are the two main threats to criminal activity. Defuse the threat and they can operate as they please."

"Are you serious?" One look at his expression answered the question. "Alex and Viktor masterminding a feud between me and Brace to deflect attention from their illegal activity? That is so convoluted, so farfetched." And not entirely impossible. "Good Lord, Cavin, how do you think of this stuff? How can your mind work this way?"

"Survival. Compared to the Coalition officer politics, this is child's play. A puzzle. I enjoy figuring it out."

"Glad you're having fun," she said sarcastically, squeezing the life out of the steering wheel. If it were true, what Cavin suggested, what would Alex and Viktor be trying to hide?

Caviar smuggling, for instance, or poaching. The answers came to her disturbingly fast, because the suspicions already lurked in the back of her mind. Knowing that a Fish and Game special operations team was closing in on possibly their biggest smuggling and poaching bust ever, Jana wondered if when they pulled in their net, her cousin would be caught in it.

Fish were known to struggle desperately when pulled from the water. They fought for survival. Were Alex and Viktor fighting for survival in an environment increasingly unfavorable to smuggling and poaching? It was entirely plausible. But pit Brace against her for the purposes of distracting him from his investments, while making her look bad so she couldn't get her strict policies approved—or so she'd lose her seat entirely? Well, it was too diabolical to contemplate.

But still plausible.

A sick feeling lay coldly in the pit of her stomach as she careened into the parking lot of KBFK. The moment of truth had arrived.

She shut off the motor and shoved open the door. "Come inside with me, Cavin." Her voice softened. "For moral support."

His hand lifted to her cheek. His eyes told her everything she needed to know.

"If anyone asks, you're my security detail," she said. "If they ask you anything about your identity, make up something."

They got out of the car. She was shaking. That she was doing this at all underscored how averse to risk she'd been through the years. But everything had changed. *She'd* changed. If she was going to live up to what destiny was asking of her, she had to start somewhere. She had to start now.

She walked up to the doors, and her courage wavered. She girded herself against it, forced her feet forward. At the very minimum, she was going to make sure the public heard both sides of the story. And on a grander scale, she'd shore up her reputation, which was her single greatest asset in convincing the world to listen when she announced an alien invasion was on the way, and that all she needed to do to stop it was allow an alien to hot-wire a spacecraft that didn't exist at a place no one was allowed to visit. Suddenly, what she was about to do seemed a hell of a lot easier.

Jana threw open the door and strode inside. A receptionist sat behind a desk. Understandably, Cavin drew her attention first, but when she saw Jana, her eyes lit up. "Jana Jasper. Senator Jana Jasper."

Jana thrust out her hand. "So nice to meet you."

The woman shook her hand, beaming.

Cavin had taken up a strategic spot by the door with a view of the studio room. Behind the soundproof glass sat Tom and Brace, whose back was to the glass. The On Air light wasn't illuminated yet. Jana's stomach churned.

"What can I do for you, Senator?"

"Let Tom know I'm here if he has any questions regarding Mr. Bowie's statements." She tried to utter Brace's name without spitting it.

"I'll tell Tom you're here." The woman spoke into

her headset. The host made eye contact with Jana and nodded, his eyes going round with surprise. To Jana's delight, he didn't say anything to Brace. Heh, heh. The element of surprise was a beautiful thing. Let Brace see what it felt like to have your guts pulled out without warning. Let him know what she'd felt like this morning when she saw the photos in the newspaper.

The On Air illuminated. Jana's heart kicked her ribs. The receptionist flipped a switch that allowed her to hear the voices inside the studio. Jana had sat in that chair many times, interviewed by Tom and others. Now she was on the outside looking in, which seemed dismally apropos considering the day she'd experienced. *No, don't feel sorry for yourself. Stand up for yourself.*

When the intro music faded, Tom began the show. "With us today is Brace Bowie, local land developer, charitable benefactor and businessman."

"Grrr," Jana said.

The men exchanged the usual pleasantries then Tom got right to the point. "Brace, your name is behind many of the big commercial development projects here in the city, including the eagerly anticipated River Tower high-rise. But let's be honest, it was your romance and the very public breakup with Senator Jana Jasper that catapulted you into the public eye."

"Of course it was, Tom. I was a benefactor for some of the larger causes in the city, and always an avid political supporter of the Jaspers and other fine politicians."

Fine? He'd actually complimented her and her family?

"But, hey, I know my relationship with Jana was what interested most people, and made them remember my name. That's why I'm on your show today. To talk about Jana. She's one special woman. An admirable woman."

"Get to it already," she muttered.

"Unfortunately, Jana's under fire right now. I'm here as a civic-minded ordinary citizen to say that the accusations against her are undeserved. I stake my reputation, such as it is, on her innocence in this vicious scandal. I knew her for a year and a half. I know we've had our differences, but Jana Jasper is the most up-front, honest and loyal woman, the most up-front, honest and loyal *politician*, I've ever met."

Jana rubbed her ear, sure she'd misunderstood.

"There was quite a lot of mudslinging last fall," Tom asked. "What changed?"

"I was out of line. I regret the billboards. I had what was in fact a very public tantrum following our breakup. If Jana's listening, I bet she's smiling hearing me say that, because she used that term to describe my behavior. Jana, I'm sorry."

Jana would have been smiling if she wasn't so frozen in shock.

"I've grown from the experience. I have nothing but the utmost of respect for her. And I wish her all the best."

Brace went on to extol her record and then to chat about some of the charitable programs his organization was involved with.

Incredulous, Jana turned to look at Cavin, who didn't appear smug, or have an I-told-you-so expression on his face; he appeared desperately, infinitely relieved.

Butterflies swirled in her stomach when she thought of why. He needed her full focus on what loomed ahead of them. He wanted her help, yes, but not at the expense of her ruin. With Brace's change of heart, her ruin was, well, a little less imminent.

On the commercial break, Tom opened the sound-proof door and waved her in. Brace turned, saw her, and went absolutely white. In the next instant, pink rushed into his cheeks as he shot an accusing look at Tom. "He didn't set you up, Brace," Jana said. "He didn't know I was going to show up. And I didn't know you were going to say what you did." Her eyes threatened to fill. But senators didn't bawl in front of former fiancés in radio stations, or she would have. "Thank you. It was a wonderful show of support. I came here because I thought the public deserved both sides of the story. And you gave it to them."

"I meant it, Jana. Every word."

"I hated knowing we were enemies," she said, softer.

"Me, too."

"I'm not sure who's making trouble for you, but I wanted it on public record it wasn't me."

If not Brace, then who? The question haunted her.

"Senator, would you like to stay for a while as a guest on the show?" Tom asked. "We can take some calls."

"I would be delighted." She sent Cavin a glance that told him she'd be entering the soundproof area. He nodded and took a place by the door. He folded his arms and leaned a hip against the wall next to the front door. His mouth tightened momentarily in pain. He rubbed his arm where he wore the gauntlet as he did whenever he thought she wasn't looking. He didn't want her to know he was in pain. Lately his arm was bothering him more than the wound in his stomach ever did. It seemed to be getting worse, too, sudden flashes of pain. Anxiety clutched at her stomach. If he got to the point of needing medical help, who would she take him to see? Who could keep a secret?

The music that kicked off the show played, dragging her attention back inside the glass. Before Jana turned away from the lobby, she saw the receptionist coaxing Cavin to sit down and relax. Only Prime-major Far Star would never do that while on official guard duty. He maintained a deceptively casual alert stance throughout the next hour, while Tom and a dozen callers gave Jana the opportunity to use her gift of gab to promote and, for the first time, defend her legislation. She was as serious and hard-line about poachers and smugglers as the FBI was on drug traffickers. It might not make her popular, but it didn't make her a crooked politician, either. By the end of the show she hoped more people understood that.

"New man in your life?" Brace asked at the end of the show.

She shook her head. "New bodyguard."

"Right."

"What?"

"Had you looked at me like you look at him, maybe I'd have stood half a chance."

"Brace, he's a bodyguard." But he'd already pushed through the glass door to meet Cavin.

Familiar panic washed over her. But when the men shook hands, Cavin gave his name as "John Smith."

She fought a smile. He was learning fast.

If only she could hide Cavin behind an alias when

it came time to introduce him to her grandfather. Former California Governor Has Close Encounter With Alien!

Yes, very close. Every molecule in Jana's body screamed at her to avoid going to the ranch. But she didn't listen. No one would ever call Jana Jasper a sissy again. Or, at least that was the plan.

CHAPTER TWENTY

JANA'S HEART THUMPED hard as she climbed down from the rented white Ford Expedition parked in the expansive circular driveway at the front of the ranch house. It was already dark. The lights were on inside. Floodlights illuminated the driveway and lawn. Only two days ago she'd been here eating breakfast with her grandfather. Two days. It felt like a lifetime.

She turned to Cavin. "Are you ready for this?"

Looking as tense as he'd been the night news of the EMP was broadcast on TV, he brought his hand to her cheek, a calming touch. "We're in this together," he reminded her.

"You may not feel that way once he starts the interrogation. When I was in high school, it was tough getting dates because Grandpa would want to meet all of them, and his interrogation skills were legendary. Only the brave risked it to have a date with me. And there weren't a lot of brave boys in high school. As for you, there's nothing to worry about." Since when had she become such a liar? "I'm going to introduce you as just a friend." Then she'd just sort of ease into the rest of it.

Two border collies and an Australian shepherd

bounded around the side of the house. Jana called out to them. "Hey, girls!" Barking delightedly, they ran rings around them. While curious about Cavin, they gave him a wide berth.

"My bioimplant emits a frequency that dogs can detect. Except, apparently, for Sadie."

"It just proves she's one of a kind."

One of the border collies sported a bandage across her muzzle and another below her ear. "My goodness, Tala. Were you in a car accident? Poor thing. What happened, girl?"

"Your mother thinks she was out chasing rabbits, didn't look where she was going and ran into a tree," Grandpa called from the front door as he wheeled out onto the patio.

"Hi, Grandpa."

"Hi, punkin." As they unloaded the car, Grandpa observed Cavin with suspicion. With each passing month, he became more fragile, but there was plenty of life in him yet, a point driven home by how dapper he looked in a dark blue velvet robe over crisp linen pajama pants and his favorite suede slippers. "But I don't know about that dog running into a tree," he continued. "Metal made those cuts, not wood. I'd say she ran into an old wreck. But we don't have any old wrecks on the property."

It felt as though Jana's heart plunged to her toes. "The ship," she said under her breath to Cavin. It was in the fields, invisible. She hadn't thought of the dangers of the invisible hulk of a spacecraft until now, but it could have hurt more than a dog. It could have killed someone. If her mother had been out riding and…

"I will make it visible again." Cavin appeared as guilty as she felt.

"And risk someone seeing it? No way. We leave it as is for now. Soon enough, they'll know where it is and they can keep the dogs away from it."

"Who's that you're whispering to, Jana? Bring him here." Grandpa beckoned irritably.

Jana took Cavin by the elbow and propelled him up the steps. The wheels of the suitcase rattled along the flagstones. Their *one* suitcase. Grandpa noticed that, too. His white brows came over his eyes, which unfortunately hid his inner thoughts from Jana. She willed the nervousness from her body and her voice. This first meeting had to go well. It had to. Everything else to come hinged on it. "Cavin, this is my grandfather, Jake Jasper. Grandpa, I'd like you to meet my friend Cavin Far Star."

"Kevin Foster, eh."

"Cavin...Far...Star," Jana said, slower.

"What kind of name is that—Far Star?" Grandpa's sharp eyes didn't miss a detail of Cavin's appearance.

"It's a name from the north," Cavin explained as they'd rehearsed.

Jana waved somewhere in the vicinity of the North Star. "Pretty far up."

Grandpa grunted. "A Canadian, eh?"

Jana elbowed Cavin so he wouldn't correct her grandfather.

"I am honored to meet you, sir." Cavin shook the older man's hand.

Despite mild palsy, Grandpa's grip remained as powerful as his intense blue eyes. He held on to Cavin's hand a moment or two longer than necessary. It was a test, she thought, designed to unbalance Cavin; she'd seen it do exactly that to too many men over the years. But Cavin was polite and composed, his expression pleasant. He'd met worse than Jake Jasper during his time serving the Coalition.

"So, what do you do, Far Star?" The frown came back. "You're not an actor, are you?"

"An actor? No, sir. I'm an officer in the military."

"Ah. Very good." The military was a profession highly respected in the Jasper family. But just wait until Grandpa found out what kind of officer Cavin was—and that it wasn't in the Canadian Armed Forces. "How long have you known my granddaughter, Foster? She had breakfast with me on Tuesday and didn't say a thing about you."

"Grandpa, Cavin is just a friend. He—"

"How long?"

"I have known Jana for almost twenty-three years, sir. For most of that time, we lived apart, but we never forgot each other."

Jana bit her lip.

"Twenty-three years?" It seemed to take a moment for him to absorb the news. "Are you sleeping with my granddaughter, boy?"

Cavin snapped to attention. "No, sir."

Grandpa looked him over with a mix of pleasure and surprise. He started wheeling inside then stopped. "Do you *want* to sleep with my granddaughter?"

Jana made a choking sound. "Grandpa!"

Had Cavin actually blushed? "Uh, yes, sir. I do."

"Hmmph. Honesty. I like that in a man."

But Cavin wasn't being as honest as Grandpa thought. If not for Evie's Honda blowing up, they would have slept together. One look at Cavin, and she knew he was thinking the same thing. They'd been close, so close, and it had been incredible, what little they'd done. Who knew when they'd next have another chance to be together like that? Certainly not staying at the ranch under Grandpa's eagle eye and the rest of her curious family's scrutiny.

Grandpa didn't miss the loaded glance they exchanged. The hungry look. His fluffy white brows descended over his eyes. "Stay for dinner," he told Cavin. Jana suspected it was more to have the opportunity to question Cavin further than genuine hospitality.

He turned the wheelchair with a whir of an electrical motor. Jana and Cavin followed him and the aroma of steaks barbecuing through the foyer and down the hallway. The kitchen opened to the back patio, where Jared and Evie stood, talking, around a barbecue stacked with sizzling steaks and teriyaki-glazed chicken breasts.

Jared wore a gray Yale hooded sweatshirt and jeans. Evie looked perky and comfortable in a bouncy ponytail and pumpkin-colored terry sweats. Beyond them, cast in light from the floods shining down from the roof, was the yard with its pens for animals, where Minnie, Jana's long-ago pet potbellied pig, had lived. Jana remembered sprinting through the yard in her pink flip-flops and tripping in her haste to find Cavin before he left. She remembered the scrape he'd healed with just a touch. And how she'd shouted after him when he'd turned to go. Shouted, because he'd healed so much more than her knee.

She caught Cavin gazing at the yard and the barn with a sweet, sort of faraway expression and wondered if he was caught up in the memories, too.

Jana's mother turned as they came in. Tears streamed down her wan face. "Oh, Mom," Jana said, walking into her outstretched arms. "You're crying."

"This time, it is onions." She dabbed her eyes with the back of her hand. Jana saw the cutting board and made a sound of relief. Jaspers never ate a steak without crispy fried onions on top.

"Ah! And who is this man?" Suddenly her mother was all aglow.

"He's Jana's *friend*," Grandpa said with no small amount of sarcasm placed on that last word. "A Canadian she's known for twenty years whom we've somehow heard nothing about."

"It is an honor and pleasure to meet you, Mrs. Jasper," Cavin said.

Mom focused the full force of her glamorous warmth on Cavin, beaming as he clasped her hand. "What is his name?" she asked Jana as if he weren't standing there.

"Cavin Far Star."

"Far Star. An unusual name, yes?"

"Not in the far north, apparently," Grandpa said. He pulled a couple of beers out of the refrigerator, popped the tops on both, and handed them to Jana and Cavin. Jana took a long, grateful swig.

Mom dropped onions into sizzling oil. Soon the aroma of fried onions filled the kitchen. "Tonight we will forget our troubles," she proclaimed. "We will be happy in our company and delicious food. There is time to be sad tomorrow, but not tonight."

"Then let's clear the air right now," Grandpa said. "I don't like being coddled. Since when do you think you can insulate me from the news?" he demanded.

Jana wanted to sink into the wood floor. "You found out."

"Of course, I did. That newspaper has come to this house without fail for decades. I knew that if it was missing, someone made it so. Plus, your mother is a terrible liar. I called the *Sun,* and they delivered a copy. Easy as that."

"I didn't want you to see the photos. Not until I could break it to you. I…didn't want you to get sick."

"You worry about your health, not mine. I won't let a bunch of lying cowards ruin your chance at reelection this fall. I'm doing what you and your father can't do because of your positions and all the eyes on you looking for conflicts of interest—I've put an army of hard-assed attorneys and private investigators on the case. We'll get to the bottom of this. I heard *The Tom Kennedy Show,* by the way. You handled yourself quite nicely, I might add, taking that loose cannon Brace Bowie and defusing him."

"Jake, you promised!" her mother scolded him. "No talk of these attacks on our family. Tonight we enjoy each other. We enjoy Cavin Far Star, too, yes? From Canada!"

Just then Evie carried a platter of barbecued chicken breasts through the sliding-glass doors. She saw Cavin and stopped. Jana took another, even longer swallow of beer. "Hi, Evie," she said, her eyes watering from the stinging bubbles.

Evie's voice sounded curiously flat. "Is this your friend Peter?"

"Shush," Mom warned. "No talk of past friends. This is a new friend of Jana's. Cavin Far Star. From Canada."

"Cavin, meet my sister, Evie," Jana said.

"It is my pleasure to meet you," he told her. "Jana's told me much about you."

"She's told me a lot about you, too. I'm still not sure what to believe." Evie put down the platter and shook Cavin's offered hand. "We'll talk about the car later."

"Car?" Mom lifted a brow.

Jana's knees felt dangerously weak. She locked them and pasted a pleasant expression on her face. "Nothing important, Mom. We borrowed Evie's Honda. We have some details to work out."

"A few," Evie said dryly.

"That old thing? What details can there be? It is a wonder it has not blown up yet."

Cavin, Jana and Evie coughed simultaneously. Grandpa narrowed his eyes. Unlike Mom, he knew something was going on. From the counter, Evie ran an admiring gaze over Cavin's muscular frame and gave Jana a conspiratorial "he's hot" wink that reminded her more of the sister she knew.

"Yarp! Yarp!"

Suddenly the din of barking and the scrabble of claws on hardwood filled the kitchen. Sadie bolted through the door, preceding Jana's niece and nephew inside. Seeing Cavin, the little dog skidded sideways, slid into a kitchen cabinet before regaining her footing and lunging at Cavin. Her tail wagged so hard that her entire tiny frame wiggled. Cavin bent over and scooped her up. Sadie wriggled, squirming in delight, covering Cavin's face with kisses. Cavin laughed, juggling the ecstatic dog in his muscular arms. The family watched, stunned.

"Omigod, Mom, she loves him," Jana's niece Ellen said. "Sadie hates strangers."

"They had a chance to meet the night before last," Jana explained. "They slept together."

"Slept together, huh? He gets around."

"Evie," Jana growled warningly.

Grandpa was silent, absorbing it all.

Jana turned to her niece and nephew. "Hey, you two. How was Disneyland?"

"Aunt Jana!" Ellen and John joined Jana in a group hug. Away from their friends, it was okay to be uncool and do things like let your aunt hug and kiss you. They didn't stare at Cavin as they gushed about their trip, or even after Jana introduced them, which told her they hadn't made the connection between Cavin and the man on the roof.

Finally Jared came inside, his hands filled with a heavy platter of steaks. The sight of Cavin brought him up short. "Hey, Jana," he said and put the platter on the counter. "How's the nun life these days?"

Jana shot him a frown and a mimed "shush." The men shook hands.

Cavin had so many qualities in common with Jared. For one, they were both military officers. Would fate allow them to someday be friends? Here on Earth, she hoped. Not pitching tents on Mars because they'd been evicted from the planet.

As conversation swirled around him, Cavin quietly absorbed it all with an adorably hungry expression. It was almost poignant, to Jana, the way he seemed to enjoy the chaos of her family. She was reminded once again how little exposure he'd had to a family environment. *You can give him this. A gift.*

That was, if her family still saw Cavin in a favorable light after they found out who—and what—he really was.

Everyone took seats at the table. Mom asked Cavin, "How long are you going to be in town?"

"It will be, perhaps, a long visit," he answered evasively.

"Mom, Grandpa, do you mind if Cavin and I stay the night? We don't feel comfortable going to a hotel."

Evie made a noise.

Jana narrowed her eyes at her. "My apartment was broken into. Nothing was stolen," she said to everyone's sounds of dismay. "It looked like someone went through my files."

Evie looked worried now. "Funny you should say that. The police told me there was a prowler in my house today. The neighbors saw some guy dressed in ghetto chic. With lots of bling."

Jana and Cavin froze.

"Nothing was taken, either," Evie went on. "But someone went through my newspapers, and when I came in, Sadie was hiding under the bed, trembling more than usual. I never saw her so distraught. We're staying here, too. I don't feel safe at home right now."

Icy fear filled Jana's chest. Was it the REEF? While Cavin didn't believe it was the assassin who'd broken into her apartment, it was pretty damn likely the killer had come looking for Cavin after hearing of the EMP. And missed him. Narrowly.

While Jared, Mom and Grandpa argued over what lines political detractors and journalists should never cross, namely breaking and entering to look for dirt, Cavin glanced covertly at his gauntlet, checking for the REEF's proximity. He met her eyes and shook his head.

Relief trembled through her. The REEF was not omniscient. He wasn't a mind reader. He'd found his way to Evie's house only because of the news. Now all she had to hope was that he'd found nothing in the newspapers that could lead him here.

What kind of danger had she brought to her family? *They'll be in greater danger if you do nothing at all.*

Mom wore her matriarch face, but Jana knew she was frightened. "Of course, you may stay. And for as long as you need to be here, my children. I fear for your safety."

"Your worst nightmare, Mom," Jared said. "All of us moving back home."

"I'll hire security for each of you come morning," Grandpa said. "And for you, too, Larisa. Four security agents."

But the last thing Jana and Cavin needed was someone trailing them, even if it were for their protection. "Make that three," she said. "I've got Cavin. He's acting as my bodyguard."

"Are you armed?" Grandpa challenged him.

"Yes, sir. I am."

"Hmm." Grandpa liked that, apparently. He went back to eating, his hand slow, shaky.

When the end of the meal came around and Evie's teens had excused themselves for computer games in one of the upstairs bedrooms, Jana folded her hands on the dining table. "I...actually we—me and Cavin—we have something to tell you." Everyone's attention shifted to her, growing worried when they read the tension in her face. *You have an expressive face,* Cavin had told her.

"You went to Reno, got married," Jared guessed.

"No!"

"You're engaged," her mother said.

"Listen to me. It's nothing like that."

Grandpa glared at Cavin. "He got you pregnant."

Jana slapped her palm to her forehead. "No, no and no."

Cavin's mouth gave an amused twist. "This conversation is quite familiar."

"It's not about me. It's bigger than that." She swallowed. "It's bigger than all of us."

Evie patted her bottom. "My butt."

"Not only does this affect my election, it will affect my presidential election. And all the elections to come, here and around the world."

Grandpa sighed. "Punkin, I haven't seen you exaggerate this much since you were a child. What an imagination you had then. Remember the glowing boy?" His irritation melted with affection and the pleasure of old memories.

She pointed to Cavin. "*He's* the glowing boy! He's Peter. Cavin is. He isn't any more imaginary than you are."

Cavin nodded, his face solemn. The silence at the table went from deep to bottomless.

"Take my advice and grab a drink, a strong one, before I tell you the rest. It may make it go down easier."

She felt Cavin's hand land on her thigh, as reassuring as it was guilty. He regretted putting her in a tight spot. But when did doing the right thing come with a guarantee it'd be easy? Probably never. If the moment Bruce Keene told her she wasn't invited to the caucus luncheon had been her wake-up call to take action, then equally defining was this moment of revealing the alien threat and her role in it to her family. It would begin the fight of her life, the true test of her character.

And the end of life as she knew it.

CHAPTER TWENTY-ONE

NO ONE GOT UP TO GET DRINKS. Fine. Have it their way. They'd regret it soon enough. Family Members Found Dead Around Dinner Table. Food Poisoning Ruled Out.

Jana grabbed hold of Cavin's hand under the table. He squeezed hers back, fingers twined together. Her heart was pounding so loudly it was hard to hear her voice. "About Tala's nose," she began. "She didn't hit a tree. She did, as you suspected, Grandpa, injure her muzzle running into a wreck."

It was silent for a few more seconds. Then Grandpa scoffed, "We Jaspers are no hillbillies. We don't have cars on blocks on our property."

"I'm not talking about a beat-up car. I'm talking about a beat-up spaceship."

"Get the vodka, Evie," Mom said. Her voice was even. Calm. "And the single malt for Jared and your grandfather. Six glasses."

Everyone sat stiffly until Evie returned. No one said a thing until the shot glasses were full.

Without preliminaries, everyone except Cavin tossed back the drink. Grandpa set down the glass with a loud clink. "You were the boy she ran out to see?" But he turned to Jana before Cavin had a chance to reply. "You told me he was magic," he accused. "You told me he was imaginary."

"That's what I thought. But he wasn't, Grandpa. Cavin is an extraterrestrial."

In the corner of her eye, she saw her mother reach for the bottle of vodka.

"He was here with his father on a scientific expedition. I thought his advanced technology was magic. He went away when his father had to leave—"

"In a spaceship, I presume?" Grandpa asked.

"Yes. And he returned two nights ago. After we had our family powwow about Dad, I stopped at the Safeway on Douglas Boulevard to pick up some ice cream. Cavin tracked me down and found me. We've been on the run ever since."

By the time she finished the story—with pictures, if she counted the newspaper articles, and visual aids, Cavin's gauntlet computer and Darth Vader gun—Grandpa's cheeks were flushed. Fortunately, he'd turned more of a pink, white and blue than a true red, white and blue that would have showed his blood pressure spiking. He was either getting used to shocking news, as she was, or they'd put him on some really good medicine yesterday. "The queen's consort-to-be, eh, Far Star?" he said, looking Cavin over with a fresh eye that was both discerning and, Jana had to admit, admiring.

"This Keira chick sounds like a real ballbuster," Jared added with sympathy.

Cavin took the ribbing politely, but Jana couldn't believe they were making a joke out of it. "There are deep problems in Cavin's government if someone is willing to assassinate a potential royal consort. It doesn't say a whole lot about that someone's respect for the queen, either. The only good thing I see in all this is that Coalition turmoil in any form is a weakness that we, Earth, can exploit, if it ever came to that. If Cavin's plan fails and we were fighting for our lives to the last desperate hour. And by God we'll exploit everything we can."

She started to get up, thought better of it and stayed seated. This wasn't a campaign stop; it was the family dinner table. "There will be some who won't believe us. Some will say wait and see. I know. I did. When Cavin first told me what I just told you, I denied it all. I covered my ears. But then I saw all he risked coming here and it inspired me. Winston Churchill said, 'One ought never to turn one's back on a threatened danger and try to run away from it. If you do that, you will double the danger. But if you meet it promptly and without flinching, you will reduce the danger by half.'"

Her impromptu, unexpectedly impassioned speech faded into silence. Deep silence. Then, after a shocked moment had passed, Jared said, "Okay, I'm in. Where do I sign up?"

Evie simply applauded, while Mom's eyes were tear-filled and full of admiration.

Cavin gave her hand a firm squeeze. "Spoken like the world leader you will be someday."

Grandpa shared a look with Cavin. "Far Star, boy, I have the feeling we're going to get along just fine."

Cavin nodded. In that moment, the men became allies: allies in their big dreams for her. But were those dreams more than what she was capable of achieving?

"Winston Churchill also told us that the price of

greatness is responsibility," her grandfather said thoughtfully. "That means it's up to we Jaspers to save the world, even while under attack. Our duty to others comes before our own interests and ambition. But there is no greater calling than to serve our fellow men and women. I've asked you, my family, never to forget that. Never to forget you're a Jasper." His veined fist landed on the table. "Now the world will see what this family is made of."

Jared let out a fighter-pilot whoop. "We'll show 'em." He stood, leaning over the table, and gripped Cavin's hand in a hearty handshake.

Jana pressed a hand to her mouth to keep the tears of relief from starting. She'd done it. She'd gotten her family on her side. But bigger obstacles loomed ahead, like talking their way onto Area 51, for one, without getting her or Cavin shot in the process.

LATER, JANA LAY AWAKE in bed in her girlhood room. Everyone had stayed over and they were now fast asleep. Cavin's room was at the opposite end of the sprawling house. No accident there; she was positive Grandpa had influenced the arrangements.

Before they retired for the night, they'd set Grandpa on the task of contacting his old friend General Mahoney. When Jana had worriedly asked if the man were still alive, Grandpa had answered, "Not only is he alive, he lives in Las Vegas with a fourth wife half his age. I suppose what doesn't kill you makes you stronger."

Jana had almost made a crack about the rejuvenating effects of sex, only she hadn't had enough herself lately to qualify as an expert. *You agreed to this nun's life.*

Yeah, and now she wanted contract negotiations reopened. She closed her eyes and thought of the hotel room, of getting almost naked with Cavin, and how deliciously close they'd come to making love. If not for Evie's Honda, they would have, too. He'd be her real lover now, not some imaginary guy she'd pined after for two decades.

Jana let out a disappointed sigh. A sexually frustrated, hungry-as-hell sigh. She ached for Cavin, body and soul, and there was nothing she could do about it. Here at home surrounded by family she'd never be able to get him alone. If there had been any coral nail polish in the house, she might have painted it on her toes and prayed for some action. Sort of like a rain dance, but for sex.

"Squee..."

Jana smiled in the darkness. She was so hungry for Cavin that she could actually hear his sexy whisper. It was as if he were there with her.

Something pinged against the window. A pebble.

She shot up in bed and pushed aside the blinds. Cavin was outside her window in the big oak tree, the same tree that had trapped him when they first met as children. Now, he sat on a thick, horizontal branch, swinging his legs. She coughed out a laugh of delight and disbelief. *You're crazy,* she mouthed to him.

His lopsided grin said, *Aren't you going to let me in?* as she had twenty-three years before. "Shush, shush," she cautioned, giggling as Cavin climbed through the window. He seemed huge landing on the narrow bed in her girlhood bedroom. Bits of bark scattered on the sheets and on the floor. He smelled like the outdoors, and his clothing was cold. "You're half-frozen," she whispered.

"I was hoping you'd warm me up."

She bounded to her door and locked it. In a flash, she'd returned to bed. He tossed her beneath him, muffling her laughter with a playful kiss that turned so hot so fast she almost self-combusted. Her narrow bed creaked under the strain of their combined weights as he kissed his way from her mouth to her neck and lower, burying his face between her breasts. She could feel the heat of his lips through the cotton of her pajamas. "I can't believe you're here," she said. "And *there*..." She sighed when his mouth found what it was searching for. "I say we finish what we started in the hotel."

"Barring any car bombs, I plan to do exactly that."

Their clothes went everywhere. When they'd stripped bare, they came together, skin to hot skin. Finally, after all this time, they were going to be lovers. She was almost frantic for him, no time to waste. Nothing would stop them now, she thought in bliss as Cavin leaned over her, his hand slipping under her hips, lifting her—

"Ah, gods, no." He went rigid, poised over her as if caught in freeze-frame.

"Is it your wound? Did I hurt you?" She hadn't meant to be so rough.

He shook his head. For some odd reason, he wouldn't meet her eyes. "Jana...I'm not like other men."

She took a frantic inventory of the parts he'd need to complete the act. They all seemed to be rock-hard and in working order. "Sure you are," she said.

"But, to make love to you, I have to assume my true, alien form."

For a second or two, the silence in the bedroom roared.

His true *alien* form? What did he mean? Was he green…with pointy ears? Tentacles? *Antennae!* Her mind spun with possibilities, most of them awful. She didn't know what to think, or, to say.

"I understand if you no longer want me."

"You know me better than that." She lifted her chin and tried to be brave. She was less sure about the sex, though. Depending what he looked like, it might be something she'd have to work into. Probably not tonight. "Cavin of Far Star, look at me. I've loved you since the day I first saw you. I'll love you no matter what you looked like."

There was a breathless pause. Then Cavin's mischief-filled eyes lifted to hers. He was Peter, all over again. "Kidding," he said, his face glowing with held-in laughter.

A sound came out of her that fell somewhere between a laugh, a curse and a sob of relief. "You… you…" She shoved him, but he was too solid to move. "Alien monster. Beast," she hissed. Trying hard to be fierce, she pushed at him as he tried to appease her, slapping his hands away. How could he laugh so hard and manage to appear apologetic at the same time?

Finally, he overpowered her with brute strength and size. Holding her arms over her head, he pressed their hands into the pillow as he gazed down at her. At first, laughter lingered in his face. Then, for a long, intense moment, he soaked in the sight of her, his expression open, vulnerable. "Gods, Jana. I love you. With all my heart, I do. I may do my share of kidding, but never about my feelings for you."

"I know," she whispered. The intensity of Cavin's expression touched her, the way the moment seemed to almost overwhelm him: this seasoned soldier, this galactic warrior, this man who was at his very core a sweet and hopeful boy named Peter.

He pressed his lips to her shoulder, kissing her there, his hot hand sliding down to cup her breast, his thumb gently moving back and forth over her nipple until it had hardened, sending a whirlwind of sensation through her. He was clearly savoring her. But she didn't want savoring, not yet. The last time she savored, Evie's car blew up and spoiled it all. "If you make me wait any longer to *have you,* I'll need to be hospitalized."

"Intensive care?" he asked.

She nodded. "With little hope for survival. So, am I going to have to call an ambulance, or are you going to—?"

He splayed his hand behind her head and forced her back down to the pillow with a crushing kiss. His knee moved her thighs apart. He was heavy, his body solid, and she craved it, craved his strength. An erotic drumbeat pounded between her legs and in her ears, drowning out her ragged breaths. No one could make her respond as Cavin did. Never had. *Never will.* From the very first time they shared an innocent, childhood kiss, he'd spoiled her for anyone else.

Then he pushed inside her, filling her, filling her senses, making her drunk on magic.

Magic...

He gripped her hands, whispering to her, his voice rough, raw. But not English words, she realized. His words. Love words. He found her lips again and took her soft cries into his mouth as she swallowed his groans of pleasure. The fierceness of their lovemaking startled her: the sharp intimacy, the poignancy of their reunion, the sense of *homecoming*. And the fear, it was always there beneath the surface, the fear of losing him. They made love as if every moment counted, because as they'd learned in the past, you never knew how many were left. But the heat of their passion made it easy to forget what was outside the cozy bedroom, hunting them. Relentlessly hunting them.

Jana hugged him closer to block out the dark thoughts, the fears, everything she didn't want intruding here in bed with them. As he brought her higher and higher, his muscles coiled with building tension. She clung to him, taking him inside her soul, giving him everything she had, holding nothing back, until everything that was hers was his, too.

In that moment, a clear, pure surge of joy took her. Arching against him, she came apart, and Cavin crushed her to him, his body shuddering, a physical upheaval that rocked her to the core and plunged them both into stunned exhaustion.

Still joined, they sagged to the mattress, twined together, their bodies writhing against each other until the last aftershocks of pleasure finally subsided.

After a while, Cavin folded her in his arms and rolled them onto their sides, holding her until their breathing had slowed. He nuzzled the place between her neck and shoulder, inhaling her scent as his hand stroked up and down her thigh. "Now that was worth the wait, my sweet Earthling," he said.

She laughed softly. "It was good for me, too. Actually, it was better than good. It was phenomenal."

"Not only the sex, Jana. All of it." He gazed down at her, suddenly serious. "You. This world. It's where I belong. Here, with you. I never really had a home, and I never missed having one. But for the first time in my life, I do."

"You have a home here." She took his sincere face in her hands. "We'll never be apart again. Never."

They kissed on the promise as if their love could seal it.

If only it could.

"I had better go," he said after a while, "though I don't want to."

"I don't want you to leave, either."

"Your grandfather will give me a whipping if he finds me in bed with you in the morning."

"True. Forget about his wanting to see your space-ship. He'll be too busy running you off the property."

"It wouldn't be the first time. I had to leave the dock pretty quickly that night he came looking for you." He pushed off the bed, lifting his arms over his head to stretch before going off in search of his scattered clothes. He was gloriously, unselfconsciously naked. Nothing beat watching him pull on his clothes. Well, except watching him take them off.

When he'd dressed, he took a few steps backward, grinning at her as he put a hand on the door handle. "Until the morning, then."

"Wait." She hopped out of bed, naked, and he held her close. He kissed her damp hair, his hand circling protectively over her back.

"This was the first time," he promised her. "It won't be the last."

He kissed her again before padding silently back to his bedroom, holding his shoes in his hands.

Jana shut the door and leaned her forehead against the cool wood. After all this time, they were finally lovers. But it had barely whetted her appetite for him. She'd wanted him for too long, whether consciously or unconsciously, for this one short tryst to satisfy. "Gods," she murmured. And her God, too. She could barely stand. Her thighs trembled. She still throbbed deep inside from little aftershocks of pleasure. She'd be sore in the morning, no doubt about it. The sex, for lack of a better word, had been mind-blowing. Coral polish or no.

THE NEXT MORNING, everyone gathered for breakfast around the big kitchen table. Sunshine streamed through the windows.

"Jana, you look unusually refreshed this morning," Jared noted, stirring sugar into a mug of coffee.

"I feel refreshed." Jana smiled and pressed her thigh against Cavin's.

Evie cast a knowing glance in their direction before smearing cream cheese on a bagel. "Nothing like a good night to perk a girl up."

Thankfully, Jana's mother appeared oblivious as she made her morning tea.

Grandpa wheeled up to the table with the *Sacramento Sun* in his lap and a cup of coffee. "When I went outside to get the paper, the alarm was off."

Jana's face burned. Cavin. He'd gone outside to climb the tree, but he'd left via the hallway. *Yenflarg.*

"I distinctly remember turning it on before I went to bed," he said. "But this morning, it was off." He opened the paper with a loud snap. "How do you suppose that happened?"

Under the smirking scrutiny of her siblings, Jana shared a bursting look with Cavin before turning her eyes to her cereal. As always, silence was the best defense in this family.

"You weren't sneaking out to meet a girl, were you, Jared?"

Jared laughed, reminded as they all were of the conversations that had taken place on so many long-ago mornings when Grandpa was tasked with babysitting.

"And you, Evie? Is there a boy?"

"If only," she said on a sigh.

Jana sneaked a peek at Grandpa. He lifted a brow at her. "Jana?"

"Actually, this time it wasn't me."

"Hmm. And you, Larisa?"

Amused by the whole thing, her mother delicately sipped black tea and shook her head.

All eyes went to Cavin, who was hungrily devouring the ham and eggs Jared had prepared for them.

"Cavin? Did you sneak out last night?"

Pale, Cavin swallowed. He looked so endearingly nervous that Jana almost hugged him. "Yes, sir. It was me, sir."

"Really." Grandpa rubbed his chin. "Now, what would coax you from a warm bed in the middle of the night?"

Jana spoke up before honest-to-a-fault Cavin did. "Can we change the subject, please? There are children present."

That induced loud protests from Ellen and John: "We're teenagers, not kids."

"Sorry, we're keeping it a PG-13 level, everyone." It was bad enough knowing everyone except her niece and nephew could tell by looking at her face what happened last night; she didn't need it rehashed for the entertainment of her family.

Grandpa went back to his coffee and paper. "If I see any damage in the oak tree, I'll know it wasn't a bear."

Everyone laughed.

Cavin stood and excused himself. Jana gave her family a withering glare. Then she threw down her napkin and followed Cavin out of the kitchen and into the backyard.

He sat on one of the patio benches. Sadie jumped in his lap. "Hey, everyone was just teasing about the alarm," Jana said. "Believe me, they wouldn't do it if they didn't like you so much."

But as he turned, she glimpsed his pale face and the way he sat, slightly hunched over.

"Oh, no. You're feeling sick again."

"It's been this way for days, Jana. One minute I'm fine, the next, the pain is almost incapacitating."

She sat down next to him. "Where?"

He gripped his arm above his wrist. "My arm."

"Maybe the gauntlet's too tight."

"No, the pain comes from underneath, where the biocomputer implant interfaces with the gauntlet. Under the gauntlet, embedded in my forearm, is the command center for all my biocomputers."

Jana pictured a bloody piece of machinery buried in his arm and fought a wave of queasiness.

He rubbed the side of his head. "But this is new—now when my arm aches, my head does, too."

"More bioimplants?" she asked, fighting panic.

"Yes. For my translator and other functions. I also have corneal implants for enhanced night vision, but so far, my eyes are fine."

"So far?" Something was very wrong. His internal medicines should have healed him by now. He shouldn't be breaking down. They'd both known he wasn't operating at a hundred percent, but she wasn't aware it was this bad. And his eyes could be affected next. The thought that he could go blind freaked her out.

He took her hand and studied her fingers clasped with his. "Before we arrive at Area 51, I'll brief you on my plan—how to accomplish it, every detail, so you'll know what to do in case I can't complete the mission."

"You're going to be fine."

"And if I am not, Jana? What then?"

Mute, she shook her head. As a senator, she juggled life-or-death decisions with infinite composure, yet when it came to Cavin, the idea of losing him all but paralyzed her.

"Then everything I've come here to do is ended? Everything I risked to save you and your world is for nothing?"

"No," she whispered. But she'd thought they were in this together. Going it alone was not in the plan. It hit her that she'd become awfully brave the past few days, except not where it concerned Cavin. But she forced herself to reassure him if only because he seemed to need her cooperation so desperately. "I'll learn what you want me to know. I'll do it."

"Is everything okay out here?"

Jana turned to see her family clustered by the door. "Cavin's just told me a few things I wasn't aware of." She twined her fingers with his. "If we're going to band together to save the world, we may have less time than we think. We'd better get on out there and see that ship."

CHAPTER TWENTY-TWO

CAVIN HAD JARED drive Jana, Jana's grandfather and her sister out to the wreckage of the ship. Jana's mother stayed behind to make sure Evie's children didn't come along.

Cavin was disturbed to see his condition had worsened overnight. He controlled his outward reaction to the aches in his arm and his head, which went without warning from nearly no pain at all to searing, teeth-crushing jolts. And this morning, when he woke, his vision had dimmed briefly. He couldn't explain what was happening to his body, but it always began in the gauntlet interface embedded in his forearm and spread from there. If he had to, he'd rid himself of the implant like a snurrefox gnawed off its leg to escape a trap. Nothing would keep him from completing his mission. Not even death, for Jana was now briefed on the procedure to use in the scout ship. She wouldn't be prepared for all contingencies, however. He'd simply have to hope there were none.

"Here," he told her brother when they reached the crash site. Scars gouged the muddy fields. Several trees were snapped in half. Branches were scattered over the ground. He'd left the area in worse shape than he remembered. Then again, he had been a bit dazed at the time, his only thought to reach Jana as soon as possible.

Jared wheeled his grandfather over the uneven ground. "I don't know how you didn't hear this, Grandpa."

"The crash happened a good mile from the house," Jana's grandfather answered. "We probably did hear it, and attributed it to something else."

"It looks like it was a spectacular landing," Evie remarked, looking around at the uprooted undergrowth.

"Not so spectacular." Cavin winced.

Jared grinned. "Hey, pal, any landing you walk away from is a good landing."

Cavin chuckled and rested his fingers on Jana's back as they trekked to the ship. He longed to hold her close, but with her family surrounding them, knew he must content himself with casual touches for now. "Stop here," he said when they reached the site. The Jaspers clustered around him. "Don't you see it?" he asked them.

Everyone squinted into the field. "No," Jana said. "It's really here?"

"Stretch out your arms, like this. He extended his arm and carefully walked forward. With a muted thump, his hand hit the fuselage. That was a crowd pleaser, he thought, watching the wonder in their faces and especially in Jana's. They joined him and flattened their hands on the outer walls of the invisible ship.

"Now step back and I will make it appear."

The transport vessel shimmered to life to a chorus of *oohs* and *ahs*.

As the family walked around the ship, exploring it,

Jared snapped photos on a digital camera, capturing it from every angle. He stood back and admired the craft. "I'd give my right testicle to fly this puppy."

"Save your testicle for something better," Cavin said.

"Haven't found her yet. But this…call me in love." Jared swept his hand over the fuselage in clear wonder.

"What I mean is that this transport is considered an ugly craft by Coalition standards. But not so the craft that followed me here." A beauty, the REEF's ship still sat, invisible, at the end of a deep gouge in the fields not too far from the transport. "Now that might have been worth sacrificing a testicle for—had it not crashed."

Evie said out the corner of her mouth to Jana, "I can't decide if it's comforting or oddly disturbing that even men from other worlds pepper their conversations with references to their male parts."

Cavin smiled. He wasn't sure Evie was convinced of his intentions for her sister—she didn't seem to be too enamored of the male species in general after being hurt by her divorce, according to what Jana said—but he and Jana's pilot brother had gotten along from the start.

"Let's go see that other crashed ship," Jared proposed to Cavin in a private tone while the family explored the outside of the transport.

"Not while its pilot is missing. I won't risk disturbing the craft and setting off a security warning he might detect."

"Understood."

"How about a tour of my cockpit?"

Jared's eyes sparked with delight. "I'm there. Let's go."

"Wait." Cavin lowered his voice so neither Jana or

her family could overhear the conversation. He'd tell her soon enough, but he didn't want to distress her in front of her family. "Later, we'll return to the ship, alone. I will show you how to power it up. Not for sport, but because I need your help in this mission."

Jared had turned serious. "You got it."

"When I leave with Jana for the base, I want you to stand guard in my spaceship—inside in the pilot's seat. You'll be on alert possibly for several days."

Jared answered with a curt nod. "Whatever you need, bro."

"You're my backup if we don't make it to the Roswell ship. On my command or, in the event I am no longer alive, Jana's, you're to power up my ship. It will create a signal that Coalition sensors will pick up, giving them pause. They'll be less eager to invade a planet they think might have space-capable weapons." He knew that Jared's one lonely signal wouldn't seem like much to the fleet, but if all else was lost, the last-ditch effort would buy Earth a little more time, whether it be another day or a month. Who knew what miracle might be performed in that time?

"Why not use your ship in the first place?" Jana asked.

The men jumped. Jana had been listening all along and so quietly that he hadn't noticed her presence. It seemed he'd underestimated her ability to plan calmly. It was only when it came to his health that she grew more emotional. He couldn't say anyone had ever cared that much for him, not even his father. Gods, he loved her.

"I kind of like the idea of working from home," she continued.

"My transport can only produce a single signal, not

the battle force of false signals I need to deter the fleet. The same goes for the REEF's crashed ship. Both are modern craft, built with codes to prevent hacking, but the Roswell ship is much older and has no such firewalls."

He glanced at the sun. It was growing late. Another day almost gone and he was no closer to saving this world. Did things always move so slowly here? And he'd thought the Coalition Parliament was a bureaucratic nightmare.

He lifted his arm toward the ship. "Stand back. I am about to return the ship to its state of invisibility."

"All he needs is a rabbit and a beautiful assistant," Evie said, "and David Copperfield will be out of business."

Cavin looked to Jana for a translation. "Copperfield is a magician," she explained. "He creates illusions for entertainment. Magic, it's commonly called."

Jana watched her family take their last looks at the ship before he returned it to invisibility. "When I was in school, I had a teacher. Her name was Miss Richards. She told me there was no such thing as magic. She said it was just how people explained what they didn't understand." Jana came up on her toes, her hand curving around his cheek, and kissed him lightly on the lips. "She was wrong. Magic is so much more. You taught me that." She moved close to whisper in his ear, "And last night proved it."

He closed his eyes with the feel of her warm breath against his skin. His fingers drifted up her back, settling in the curve of her spine. It was easy to remember how it felt making love to her. He inhaled her scent, trembling with the effort of keeping control, of his body, of his emotions. Then he realized where he was, and who he was with, and jumped away from Jana.

As he feared, her family was watching: her brother and sister smiling, her grandfather glowering fiercely. "Far Star, I'll have no more of that."

Cavin snapped to attention. "Sorry, sir."

"I mean, no more being afraid to touch her. My granddaughter's finally chosen a worthy man, and a man worthy of her. I'll not have you starving for each other's affection out of fear of angering an old man." With a grunt of exasperation, he turned back to the ship to run a veined, trembling hand over the gleaming luranium hull before the transport disappeared in a glittering shower of light.

Cavin was struck by the symbolism of the sight. The ship's advanced construction, the elderly man's hand: it encapsulated his past and his future, a future that might never be unless the Earthlings got him to where he needed to go before his body gave out on them.

THE PHONE in the library rang. The private line. Grandpa wheeled across the room and answered the call. "About time you called me back." *Mahoney,* he mouthed, giving them a thumbs-up, then putting the call on speakerphone so everyone could hear.

Jana, Cavin and Jared leaned forward in their chairs. The general sounded jovial. "Jake, long time no hear!"

The two elderly men exchanged the usual pleasantries about families and the weather then Grandpa got right to point: "All those years you told me there was no alien spacecraft at Groom Lake you were mighty convincing. Hell, I even believed you. Now I know you're a goddamn liar."

Jana threw her face in her hands.

But Mahoney laughed heartily. "Let me guess—an alien landed in your backyard."

"As a matter of fact, he did!"

"And he told you he came back to pick up the ship he left behind in 1947."

"That's where you're wrong. It's ours to keep, a scout ship, he says, a throwaway, but he needs to use it first to deter a massive alien invasion force on the way to Earth as we speak."

Silence. "You been drinking, Jake?"

"No, I haven't been drinking. I'm not playing a practical joke, either. Listen to me, Chet. As hard as it is to believe, space invaders are on the way. But our extraterrestrial visitor, a damn hero if you ask me, knows how to rig that ship you're hiding there at Dreamland to send them away. He has a plan. We don't have much time. You need to get with the current leadership and get him clearance inside. Right away. A Colonel Thomas Connick, right? Tell him our boy's got a job to do."

"There is no alien ship at Area 51, Jake. There never was. I didn't lie to you about that."

"They didn't call you Baloney Mahoney for nothing. Chet, your own people gave you the name. Your fellow soldiers."

Cavin sat hunched over with his hands laced together and his index fingers pressed to his lips. His expression was dark, worried.

"I have proof. Once you see the photos, you'll believe me."

"Jake, proof or not, there's no alien ship parked at Area 51."

"Bullshit." Grandpa's face was increasingly pink and in danger of turning red.

"Your pressure," Mom warned.

It took some effort, but he tried to calm down. "I know you're wondering how it is that this extraterrestrial came to me out of all the men in the world. See, he's in love with my granddaughter. At great personal risk he came here to warn her—to warn all of us—that his people plan to invade Earth."

"Jake, who is he? A stranger. A con artist. He's taking advantage of an old man—a man who was always too much of an idealist for his own good."

Jana stood, unable to take any more of the back-and-forth. Unable to bear any more of Cavin's building frustration over the general's skepticism. "Give me the phone, Grandpa."

"Idealist? Not this time, Mahoney. Not this time."

"Grandpa, please." She thrust her hand at him.

Admittedly, he looked a little worried surrendering the phone. *I won't yell,* she mouthed. "Hi, General. This is Jana Jasper. Let's dispense with the pleasantries, in light of this national emergency." It was a worldwide emergency, but the general was a very patriotic man. The U.S.A. was a good place to start. "We need to talk. Better yet, I need you to listen. There is no con artist. No one trying to fool my grandfather—or me. This alien is for real. I've seen his spaceship. I've seen his weapons and computers."

"You've seen a spacecraft—an *alien* spacecraft?"

"Yes, sir. I've touched it."

Silence. Then a "hmmph."

"I have digital photos. I'm going to send them to you

now, sir. I understand you receive e-mail photos of your grandchildren all the time, so you'll know what to do." She wouldn't reveal Cavin's identity, but there was nothing wrong with photos of the crashed ship. Grandpa had slipped up and said where it was parked, but the few digital pictures they'd taken that morning of the ship showed no identifying landmarks linking them to the ranch. "Do it," she whispered to Jared.

By the time he hit Send on the laptop, Jana was almost giddy with nerves. Another irreversible step: the photos were on their way. "They should be arriving in your in-box any minute now, sir. I'd like you to look at them and then tell me there's no spacecraft at Area 51."

"This is no spacecraft there, Jana. I'm sorry to say. That's an urban legend. One we never could kill."

She sighed. *Baloney.* "You're the founding father of the place. The original commander. If anyone knows what's there, and what's still there, it's you, sir. If you say there's no spaceship, I have no choice but to believe you. However, if you know where we might find such a ship, I sure would appreciate you telling me. Blind-fold us and bring us there, for all we care. We need access to that craft—and fast. Please help me in this."

Jana put everything she had into her plea, her whole heart. "All I've ever wanted is a political career. Public service, doing good, it's all I've wanted my whole life. I'm willing to sacrifice everything for this, General. I'm staking my reputation on it." Or what was left of her reputation. "If it means the end of my career, so be it. That's how strongly I feel about the accuracy of this information. Earth is in terrible danger. Along with a very special extraterrestrial hero, I'm going to save our planet. To do that, I need your help, your unique insider knowledge. A chance like this comes along once in history. Once. Are you with us?"

Grandpa snatched the phone from her, midspeech, just when her gift of gab was warming up, when instinct told her she might be getting through to the crusty old general. "Call me when you open your e-mail, Chet. It might jog your worthless memory about that goddamn ship." He returned the phone to its cradle with a crash.

Amusement played around Jared's mouth. "That kind of diplomacy work much for you in office, Grandpa?"

The old man simply growled and wheeled out of the room.

THE REST OF THE AFTERNOON was excruciating, spent waiting for General Mahoney to call back with his impression of the photos from Cavin's crashed ship. Jana had informed her staff she'd be working from the ranch. If she was going to work from home, this was the day to do it. It was the Friday before Easter recess. By afternoon, most capitol staffers would have left to spend time with family. In the past she'd always put in a full day. But that was before she had a world to help save.

Tapping an ebony Montblanc pen against her lips, Jana paced in front of Cavin in her father's office at the ranch. "Why isn't Mahoney calling back? He has to have seen the photos by now."

"It's good news, I think. If he has any real experience with Coalition vessels, he'll immediately see the authenticity of my ship. He's contemplating what to do now, what steps to take next."

As in what cage in the secret lab will best accommodate Cavin. Jana bit the pen so hard she almost cracked a tooth. "And if he doesn't call back, or he refuses to help, which we have to admit is a very likely possibility, we need a Plan B."

Cavin grabbed her hand and pulled her close. She stood between his legs, her hands on his broad shoulders as she looked down at his handsome, upturned face. Despite everything going on, her body reacted to him. It remembered last night. Hell, it would remember last night for the rest of her life. "Plan B is your father's phone call with the president," he said.

"That's if he gets his phone call. It's Easter recess. The president's vacationing at home in Fort Myers with her family." Jana thought of the conversation she'd just completed with her father. He'd sounded so hopeful, so determined. She'd never loved him more than in that moment. In order to get anywhere near the president's ear over vacation, he had to be making a huge stink, and a huge stink was the last thing her father needed in the wake of the insinuations about his campaign financing. "And if the president refuses to help or delays unnecessarily, we need a Plan C."

"That's simple. I go there myself. I locate the ship using my gauntlet, and activate it."

No, you won't, she wanted to say, *you won't sacrifice yourself for this,* but her brain wouldn't disengage from its horror long enough to form the words. She gave her head a hard shake. "Uh-uh." His lids fell halfway over his eyes, and he set his jaw in a stubborn angle she saw rarely but that she was sure those who'd served with Prime-major Far Star over the years had glimpsed often.

The phone rang and cut off their impending argument. She saw her high hopes echoed in Cavin's eyes. But it wasn't the secure line. It was Nona from work. Hopes dashed, Jana fell into the desk chair and answered.

"Stop moping," Nona said. "It's good news."

"Good news? There's actually good news for once?"

"Yes. Willa sent a memo. The governor granted your request for a private meeting."

Jana made a fist and kissed it. Then she closed her eyes as relief flooded her. Maybe her luck and Cavin's was finally beginning to turn. The governor wasn't the key to the operation, but having him throw his support behind them would help their credibility tremendously. "I was sure he was going to put me off until after the break."

"He just about did. He doesn't want you until ten tonight."

"Whoa. Late." What was Schwarzkopf doing hanging around that long, and before a holiday? Getting last-minute business done, she guessed, like the rest of them. But this was one time she was glad to be included in the governor's last-minute agenda.

She hung up. Her hands shook. Her pulse had turned to a roar in her ears. She swiveled her chair to face Cavin. "You said you needed a leader?" she said. "One California State Governor, coming up."

REEF RODE A SERVICE elevator up to the dwelling that Jana Jasper listed as her primary residence. He disarmed the lock by using first his see-through vision and then his gauntlet to manipulate the lock components. It was routine procedure he'd done countless times, but when he slipped inside and shut the door behind him, the nearly constant whine in his ears surged to a screech. He felt the wall hitting his back, wondered stupidly how it could be. When he opened his eyes, he realized it wasn't the wall that had hit his back, but his back hitting the floor when he blacked out.

He climbed to his knees, stayed there until he stabilized physically. His head hung low. Shame filtered through him, at himself, his vulnerability, and out of the fear that someone had seen his display of weakness. The latter was even more repulsive to him than the former and drove him to his feet.

What was happening to him? A simple act of opening a lock had knocked him out cold. Had he been engaged in battle, he would have been defeated. No one had ever defeated him.

What was happening to his systems? If the malfunctions were due to the crash, he would have been healed by now, or nearly so. Instead, he was getting worse. He'd sorted through the possibilities for his breakdowns. Two topped the list. *Injuries caused by the crash: probability 88.2%. External initiation: 67.6%.* External initiation? Impossible. It meant someone outside his body was manipulating his systems. It could not be. *But did you not do the same to Far Star?* What if someone, perhaps even Far Star, was attempting to disable his systems?

But the Prime-major didn't know Reef's exact identity, only what he was—a REEF-O1A assassin— not who he was. *Those who hired you know who you are*. Reef's pulse accelerated. His head began to ache with a rise in blood pressure. Reef controlled his human body's physiological reaction and probed deeper, but slammed up against a brick wall when he tried to find out more information.

Focus on your task, assassin.

Weapons drawn, he turned in a slow circle. The noise in his ears had subsided some, making it easier to hear. The woman's dwelling was cold, still. He tasted the air, listened, observed, using both his faltering robotic senses and the human ones upon which he'd grown increasingly more dependent over the past few days. One thing was certain: no one had been in this place for some time.

After finding no hints of Far Star's presence, he departed. But he'd locate Jana Jasper. Yes, he would. Now he knew where she worked, where he was certain he'd find a wealth of information on her habits and schedule. And where she was, Far Star would be, or close enough. Then he'd be able to complete this frustrating mission and be on his way off this wretched rock.

"MY BRAIN IS KILLING ME," Jana groaned to Cavin as they stopped at a traffic light one block from the legislators-only parking garage at the capitol. Her hands were damp as she gripped the steering wheel. Her head throbbed from all the facts and figures she'd crammed in after hours of meeting with Cavin and her family, including her father on the secure house line to and from Washington, in preparation for her meeting with the governor. "I think I've memorized enough Winston Churchill quotes to write a book."

"Simply tell him what you told your family yesterday after dinner and you'll have no problem convincing the governor to support us in this."

And that's all they needed, really, a leader's support, a vote of confidence that came from outside the immediate family. If they got one high-profile leader to sign on, others would follow. A multipronged assault was how Cavin had put it; it's what they needed to convince the government to allow him access to the long-ago-crashed scout ship.

As they waited in anxious silence for the traffic light to change, Cavin kept a protective hand on the attaché case sitting between them. Inside were photos of the spaceship and Cavin's gauntlet, but not of Cavin himself. There was also a legal pad filled with the results of an afternoon and evening brainstorming alternate plans to get access to Dreamland in case Mahoney fell through, none of which Jana liked, because all of them involved an uncomfortable level of public exposure for Cavin.

"I'm too impatient for this tonight." He aimed his gauntlet at the lazy traffic light. It changed from red to green.

She rolled through the intersection. "You liked doing that, didn't you?"

His smile was quietly smug. Then he rubbed the side of his head when he thought she wasn't watching.

She touched his arm. "Hurting again?"

"I'll recharge momentarily."

Jana bit her lip. It was getting to the point where he couldn't use his alien superpowers at all without making himself sick.

At the garage security booth, Jana showed her ID to the two CHP officers on duty. Cavin played his little card trick with Jared's driver's license that he'd borrowed for the night, substituting his image for Jared's. It passed a cursory check from one guard while the other man checked the undercarriage of the car for bombs using a mirror on a long handle. "Mr. Jasper won't be allowed upstairs, Senator," one of the officers told her, referring to Cavin.

"I know. After hours, I don't like coming in alone, so he's going to wait for me. I have to run upstairs to the governor's office for a few minutes."

"I thought the gov went home already."

"He may have, but he's here now. We have a meeting."

She and Cavin stood outside the car while the interior was inspected. When they got the okay, they parked. "Explain the layout of this place," Cavin said, scanning the area with his soldier's eyes.

"We're in the basement of the building you saw the other day in the park. There are three elevator banks, and they go to all floors. The one over there on the south side is for senators only. There's another on the north side for the assembly members. But everyone usually uses these central elevators because of convenience. The governor's office is on the first floor. That's where I'll be after I grab some paperwork from my office on the third floor."

Cavin nodded. His miss-nothing gaze took in the dozens of security cameras keeping watch. There were more upstairs in the hallways. She sat next to him in the car and clutched her attaché case. "This is it, baby. Are you going to wish me luck?"

He pulled her close for a kiss. It was hotter than she'd expected, and she melted into a sizzling pile of limp bones in his arms. "Wow," she murmured against his jaw when they finally separated. "If that doesn't bring me luck, I don't know what will."

"Your grandfather says luck is when preparation and opportunity come together."

"Yep. That's a favorite of his." She smiled, shaking her head as she gazed into Cavin's open, earnest face. "He really likes you. You're the first guy of all the ones I've dated he's more than tolerated. I should have brought home an alien a long time ago."

"Only if it were me." He pressed a hand to his chest. "This is the only alien for you."

She smiled. "Damn right."

"And I'm relieved to hear he likes me." He skimmed a hand over her hair, not wanting to mess her carefully styled chignon. "Because when this is all over, when we are safe again, you're going to be my mate, Squee."

"On Earth the man usually asks the woman to marry him. Not tells her."

His eyes turned a deeper shade of green. "Oh, I will ask. When the time and place suit."

She hugged him close, breathing in his scent to take with her for good luck. Then she closed her eyes and planted a hard kiss on his lips before she stepped out of the warm, protective circle of his arms and then the car. "I won't be long. Schwarzkopf's either with us, or he's not." She gave Cavin one last lingering gaze then walked briskly through the doors to the building to catch an elevator.

Only one elevator was working. The others sported

"out of service" signs. The doors slid open and she walked inside. The sight of a bored-looking young man sitting on a desk chair brought her up short: Joseph's elevator-operator trainee from yesterday, now all checked out apparently. Startled, she took a spot opposite him in the small car. She tried to get her heartbeat slowed back down. But the elevator operator unnerved her. His eyes were mean, and his black leather gloves made him look more like a thug than an elevator operator. A silly thought. The meeting with Schwarzkopf had made her too jumpy. "I didn't know you guys worked this late."

"They pay me, I work," he said in a thick Russian accent.

A recent immigrant, she thought and greeted him in his language. *"Dobryy vecher. Kak Vy pozhivaete?"*

He answered her friendly "Good evening. How are you?" with little more than a mumble. "Three, please," she said with a mental shrug. He hit the three. The doors closed. Just as the elevator started its hideously slow ascent, he lunged at her.

His gloved hand slammed over her face, cutting off her scream. His fingers dug into her face. It hurt like hell. His palm pressed over her mouth and nose. Hard to breathe. Fear blotted out much of the pain.

She struggled, but he jerked her roughly against a wiry body as if she was a beanbag doll, floppy and compliant. "Time to die, bitch."

She made a sound in her throat that sounded like a whimper. She wasn't a fighter, a tough chick. She was a geeky little intellectual, cerebral, not physical.

Then think your way out of this one, Jana.

But she didn't know what to do, how to save her life. Her mind was scattered, couldn't focus. Too afraid.

He was suffocating her. Her vision was going gray. Blood rang in her ears.

"They told me to be fast, not to make noise. You will die quietly, yes, little czarina?"

Czarina? Viktor had called her that at the restaurant. Her mind spun with the implications, whirled in a panic-accelerated kaleidoscope of crazy cousins, daffodil neckties and illegal caviar.

The man was getting something out of his pocket now. What? A gun? A knife? He was going to kill her. *What about Cavin? What about Earth?* It hit her, then, hit hard, the realization of all she had to lose.

No! It would not end this way, her fairy tale. She drove her stiletto heel into her assailant's instep so hard that it jarred her entire body. He shrieked in pain. Some women lifted cars off their kids, driven to superhuman strength in an emergency. Her? She twisted around, wrenching free of him while screaming like a martial arts star, and kicked him in the balls.

The man bent over. Something clattered to the ground. The knife in his hand? No, a cell phone. He cursed her out in fluent Russian. Naughty words, the ones her mother told her never to say, but that Jared had taught her anyway.

As the elevator doors opened, the man came at her again. She got a crazy, desperate idea that she'd kick the knife out of his hand, and she would have, too, if someone hadn't grabbed her by the collar from behind, pulling her from the elevator—and right out of one of her shoes.

Hobbling, she fought for balance. The hand on her

collar was strong and held her upright. Call her Cinderella, she thought, wild with terror. Only it was a three-hundred-dollar "glass slipper" she'd just left in the elevator with her would-be murderer. Not as expensive as the yellow shoes she'd lost the night Cavin showed up, but still a loss. *Note to self: for all future knife fights and high-speed chases, choose pumps from Payless.*

Something white and hot zinged past her ear. There was a *crack,* like the sound of a bug zapper, amplified. Her attacker's scream was cut short as the inside of the elevator car erupted in a green-white flash. The Russian slumped into a heap. Jana's eyes burned from the acrid stench. Where had she smelled that distinctive odor before?

The parking lot at Safeway.

Oh, God, no. Not him. Whoever gripped her by the collar let her go. She spun around, unbalanced, standing on one shoe, and came face-to-face with the REEF.

CHAPTER TWENTY-THREE

JANA KNEW RIGHT AWAY it was him. The REEF. He'd
disguised himself with a hooded sweatshirt with the
sleeves hiked up and baggy pants, but he had that lean,
mean, musculature common to prisoners serving life
sentences. He was taller, larger than she expected,
eerily handsome with intense blue eyes as frigid and
clear as an arctic night. Yet, he looked...well, ill. It was
the only way she could describe it. His skin was pale,
practically greenish, and covered with a film of perspiration. Cold sweats? His aim seemed true enough,
though, with two futuristic rifles pointed at her forehead. "Jana Jasper?" he asked in a flat voice.

She swallowed. Okay, in the movies, only the stupid
people said yes. She was not going to say yes. She might
be a nerd, but she was a nerd with a learning curve.

Heart pumping, dizzy with panic, sucking in great
gasps of air, she hunted for an escape with her eyes.
There was the stairwell. Or the elevator, the way she'd
come up. Both seemed equally impossible at the moment. But if she ran to Cavin, wouldn't that lead the
REEF right to him?

"Where is he? Where is Far Star?"

"I don't know what you mean."

He grabbed her shoulder and shoved her up against the wall. Her head snapped with whiplash. Now she finally knew what people meant when they said they saw stars. Something smacked against her shins. Her attaché case, she realized. Leave it to a Jasper not to lose important paperwork—especially when it related to alien spacecraft parked in the backyard

The assassin looked so mean he sent chills spinning down her spine. This man was an interstellar assassin. He killed for pay. He'd taken lives. Many times. One more wouldn't bother him. Soldiers, at least, had a code of honor. Mercenaries like the REEF were in it for the profit. "Are you going to kill me?"

"Extraneous kills dilute the pleasure of the real thing," he said, his voice level.

Somehow, she knew he'd say something like that.

"Where is he, Jana Jasper? Where is Prime-major Far Star?"

"He's hiding. He didn't tell me where." Not only was her voice quivering, she was the worst liar in the world. Plus, the REEF was no stupid *Terminator* robot. One look at his exhausted face, his short black hair dampened with sweat, and the tension lines around his mouth told her there was more human in him than machine, something on which she hoped she could capitalize. After all, he'd spared the men he threw in the Dumpster.

Remind him of his mercy. Her attacker was lying in the elevator in a smoking heap. Unlike the men in the Dumpster, this one wasn't getting up again. The REEF had saved her life.

A selfish act. He needed her to bring him to Cavin.

He needed her alive. He needed a hostage. *Remind him anyway.*

"Thank you," she gasped.

His brow went up.

"If you didn't help me when you did, I'd be dead. You saved my life." To her shock, genuine gratitude leaked from her heart to her voice.

He gave her an angry, impatient shake. "Stop babbling and bring me to him."

So much for the mercy idea. Again, she cast a desperate glance around, looking for escape ideas. Where were the security guys? There were cameras everywhere. They should have been here already. The only explanation she had was that the REEF had disabled the surveillance cameras. She had to get downstairs herself. She had to warn Cavin before he sensed something and came up looking for her. But how?

Cavin gave you the gift of gab. Use it!

"You were hired by mistake," she blurted out. "Hired by mistake because he's never coming back—ever. He's staying here with me. You don't have to kill him."

"I don't care what his plans are." His tone dripped with disdain.

"He called home today," she lied. "He told them he was staying here. With me. They know. He resigned his commission. He's done. Over. He's an Earthling now. The people who hired you, they won't pay you such a huge sum for nothing when they realize he's gone anyway, that their mission is already accomplished— without you in the mix." Since when was she an expert in interstellar intrigue? She didn't know where she was coming up with this stuff; she was making it up as she went along, drawing on what Cavin had said and expanding using her gift of gab. "You're going through all this trouble to kill him and when you show up expecting to get paid they'll pretend they never knew you, never hired you."

As frigid as his eyes were, almost inhuman, in them she saw uncertainty flicker. She'd hit on something. A weakness. A doubt. "They're powerful individuals, probably the most powerful in your government, and to them you're just a lowly administrative worker. Persist, and they'll terminate you."

His forehead was shiny with sweat. He was in pain, physical pain, and hiding it.

"Look at you. You're breaking down as we speak. And if you lose your computers, you'll be useless. Obsolete. Nothing."

Mistake. A tic started up in his cheek. She'd hit a sore point. He lifted the rifle. For an instant she thought he'd blow a hole in her head. Not only was the REEF sick, he seemed crazy. Or desperate. Did it matter? Neither was a good place for a man with guns to be.

"Freeze!"

A CHP officer stalked down the hallway, his gun aimed at the REEF. The REEF sighed and swung a gauntlet similar to Cavin's in the man's direction. The officer lifted off the floor.

"What the hell?" he said simultaneously with Jana as he floated up to the ceiling. Then he swore and dropped his gun. It clattered to the floor, red-hot. It fired off a couple of rounds that ricocheted off the walls. Jana screamed.

The REEF winced. "Please don't do that. The gunfire is loud enough."

Jana exchanged a petrified glance with the guard, who clutched his burned hand by the wrist. So much for keeping the presence of aliens on Earth secret, she thought.

The REEF's facial muscles clenched with the effort he expended to keep the guard in the air. He took a step backward as if thrown off balance. His eyes had glazed over. He holstered one rifle, but the other, the one aimed at her head, wobbled. He looked as if he was about to pass out. In fact, he looked a lot like Cavin did when his bioimplants were acting up. Whatever he'd done to float the guard had taken a terrible toll.

"Are you okay?" she blurted out. *"Jana, you have so much heart."* She'd heard that many times from Grandpa and others. But she couldn't shut off her heart, even for this assassin. This human had been raised from a very young age to be a machine, according to Cavin. He killed because he'd had no other choice. She felt sorry for him. It must have come through on some level because he brought his gaze back around to hers. He seemed almost hungry for kindness. There, that was the weakness. Using her gift of gab, she'd found it. "What's happening to you?"

I don't know, his eyes said. Growing paler still, he brought his hand to his eyes and grimaced.

"You're ill. Look at you. You're sick." Sick like Cavin was. Sicker, instinct told her, than what could be attributed to the crash itself. "What if your own people are doing this to you? Did you ever consider that? That they may be trying to kill you long-distance." She was grabbing at straws now, using the imagination that had gotten her into so much trouble as a child.

For a heartbeat, she thought she saw shock and real fear in the REEF's stare but his eyes turned so glacial, so fast, she was sure she was wrong. "Like this?" he hissed. His gaze turned distant for a moment or two, as if he were reaching inside himself. He let out a grunt. Then his eyes came back to her, and he smiled. What had he done? Had he hurt Cavin somehow? "I can kill him this way, too, Earthling. But it's slower, more painful. It's your choice, really. Bring me to him and I make it quick, or run and I make him die from the inside out."

A SHARP PAIN exploded inside Cavin's forearm, beneath where he wore his gauntlet. He braced himself for what he knew would happen next. But it was worse this time. Much worse. Searing agony exploded in his head. It nearly brought him to his knees. A groan escaped him before he could stop it.

He let his head dip to the dashboard while he fought to take control of the pain. He'd been wounded in combat before; he could handle this. Gods, but it was so much worse than anything he'd experienced before. It was as if he was coming apart from the inside out.

Finally, his vision cleared, but grayness flickered at the edges, distorting his peripheral vision. He was sweating, but cold, sickly cold. He shoved open the car door and swung his legs out. He drove his fingers through his hair and let his head fall into his hands. Dread gnawed at him and made him doubt his fitness for the coming challenges, and for his ability to protect Jana. He and

Jana had their biggest battles yet to come, and here he was, falling apart. He couldn't fall victim to his own body. He could not. Whatever was happening to him, he had to fight on. Surrender was not an option.

"Would you like a newspaper, sir?" one of the law enforcement men called to him from where they relaxed at a table in the garage.

Cavin pushed off the car seat with an effort. His first steps were unsteady, but he gained balance as he walked to the men.

"You okay?" one of the guards asked.

"I've been under the weather," he said, drawing from his database of colloquial phrases. "I'm getting better. It's taking time."

"Flu?"

"Mmm." He looked over the papers scattered across the table. He couldn't read a word of Jana's language, or any Earth language, but he did his best to act like an Earthling, to blend in. Now more than ever, in his weakness, it was important not to attract the wrong kind of attention.

Not all the papers were current. He recognized one from the morning after he found Jana in the market. There was the image of her shoe that she'd found so distressing, and there, in the most recent copy, were images that had distressed her even more. He frowned as he studied the pictures, and became so angered by those who sought to damage her reputation and that of her family that he was able to block some of the piercing throbbing in his head and arm.

He picked up the paper and held it closer to his face, studying the image of Jana sipping a drink at the fish farm. His eyes soaked in the sight of her sweet, slender body, slipping down her long legs to her pointy-toed shoes. He swerved his focus to the older newspaper. To the close-up image of…the *very same* shoes. Adrenaline surged. *Yenflarg*. The shoes connected Jana to the "hostage" supposedly taken from the market, which then linked her to him, something of little value to anyone else but the REEF.

Cavin threw down the paper. He was a fool, a blind, careless fool, not noticing it until now. And here he'd let her out of his sight when the possibility was strong the REEF knew who she was—and where she worked. His mistake could very well cost Jana her life.

He strode away, limping toward the elevators. "Sir," the guards called. "Sir!"

"The senator's in danger," he barked and pressed the button to call down the elevator. No sound indicated that the machine was working. He hit the button hard, impatiently. He felt like putting his fist through the primitive control panel.

"You are not authorized, sir."

Again he punched the call button. He looked around for an alternative route upstairs.

One of the guards called over his radio. "Mark, you got anything on your security cameras?"

No one answered.

"Mark? Mark! You there? Hey," he called to his partner. "Levy's not at his station."

Cavin paced until he was ready to come out of his skin.

"The elevator's dead," the guard muttered. "It's stuck up on the third floor."

Cavin's blood turned to ice. His focus tunneled to one thing and one thing only—getting upstairs to Jana. He tried the door to the stairs. It wouldn't open.

"Sir, you can't—"

Like hell he couldn't. Cavin used his gauntlet to open the security lock. He flung open the door and a guard grabbed him. Cavin shoved the man—too hard—and sent him flying into his partner. Both men sprawled on the cement floor. The guards took out their guns as they got up.

Cavin kicked the door closed with his boot, used his gauntlet to alter the key code. To what, he didn't know, but their cards would not work. Jana would be angry with him for doing so, most likely, but she could scold him all she wanted once he was assured she was safe. He wasn't going to take the risk of the guards keeping him from reaching her. To the sounds of pounding fists on the door, he took the stairs two at a time up to the third floor.

THE REEF HAD HURT Cavin somehow, without touching him.

But the toll it took was tremendous on the assassin. His breaths were harsh and uneven. He was barely able to hold up the rifle. Any color had left his skin. But his eyes were pure evil. Malice shone in them. "Go to Far Star and tell him the choice you made for him. Days, Jana Jasper—you'll be back looking for me in mere days. Begging me to put Far Star to death, because this way will be so much worse."

His words sank like cold stones in her belly. Her ears rang. Her stomach threatened to unload its contents all over the REEF's basketball shoes. What had she just done? What had she encouraged the REEF to do to Cavin?

In the corner of her eye, she saw Cavin sneak out of the stairwell door and flatten his body against the wall. He was almost invisible in the shadows. His pistol glimmered darkly.

Her heart exploded with relief that he was here. He was hunched slightly, his mouth set in a grimace. Sweat ran down his cheeks and jaw. He was hurting, badly, yet he'd made his way upstairs to find her. Her chest contracted in terror. Nowhere near top form, Cavin was about to walk into the jaws of his killer.

She cast her panicked stare to the CHP officer bobbing near the ceiling like a bizarre party balloon. She knew with one look in his eyes that he wouldn't say anything about Cavin. She turned her focus back to the REEF. Would her fear for Cavin show in her face? The only thing going for her was that she was expected to appear terrified.

The REEF poked his rifle at her. "I am giving you a head start, woman. But you're still here. Are you going to leave, or will I have to give Far Star an extra little something to get you moving?"

The last thing she wanted was for Cavin to be debilitated at the moment of facing his mortal enemy. She looped the strap of her attaché over her head and shoulder and kicked off her remaining shoe as she moved away, slowly at first, making sure to hold the assassin's slightly amused gaze. She couldn't escape to the stairwell, because it would swing the REEF's attention directly to Cavin. Her only option was to run in the opposite direction. But it would bring her to a dead end. She winced. Bad choice of words.

Dead end or not, she wasn't leading the REEF to his target. She had to trust that Cavin, an experienced soldier, knew what to do.

One...two...three. She dived into a full run. The floor was like ice under her panty hose. Her back crawled as she imagined the REEF's rifle aimed between her shoulder blades. If he wanted her, he had her.

In fact, when the firing started, she was sure the shots were meant for her. But somehow, she was still on her feet.

The blasts deafened her. Bursts of white-green light lit up the entire area. It was loud, painfully so, cracks of thunder like when lightning hit too close during a storm.

She skidded to a stop and spun around in time to catch Cavin pumping one shot after another into the REEF. The man wore armor under his street clothes— clothing that was shredding before her eyes under the barrage from Cavin's gun.

CHAPTER TWENTY-FOUR

BOOM, BOOM, BOOM. Cavin fired nonstop. The REEF's armor sparked and sizzled. Without having fired a shot, the assassin slid to the floor and landed in a sitting position with his long legs sprawled out in front of him. The rifles fell from his hands, clattered to the floor. His chin sagged to his chest.

Cavin turned to Jana, took a step toward her as if he meant to run to her, but his body jerked backward, a hand going to his head. His neck corded. He grimaced and fell to his knees, hunched over and convulsing. He dropped his pistol. It bubbled and melted into a foul-smelling metallic puddle.

"Cavin!" she cried.

The assassin gave Cavin another mental push. Cavin's body went rigid, his back arching, as if he'd been shot through with a bolt of electricity.

The half-conscious REEF wasn't even touching him, but he was doing something to Cavin, to his internal computers, destroying him from the inside as he'd promised.

Nausea and utter terror rose like bile in her throat. She swung her head around, searching for a weapon. She needed to kill the REEF before he killed Cavin. A discarded rifle sat near the wall. She dived for it, grabbed it with one hand. The REEF turned slitted eyes to her and clamped his hand around her wrist so she couldn't aim. His body sputtered in and out of view, like a picture on an old TV. And then he was gone.

She felt his hand release her, felt his fingers slip away. "Where did he go? Where did he go?" She danced in a circle, searching high and low. The body was gone, but, luckily, his weapons remained behind.

The guard fell down from the ceiling. He hit hard, rolled onto his side. "Are you okay?" Jana yelled.

"Yeah. Fine." He got up stiffly.

Jana fell to Cavin's side. He was still conscious, but barely. The arm with his gauntlet seemed to be paralyzed as it hung at his side. She helped him to a kneeling position.

He looked terrible, pale and in pain. Yet, he ran questioning blunt fingers over her bruised jaw. She winced at that gentlest of touches, and murder flashed in his eyes. As debilitated as he was, he looked as though he wanted to hunt down the REEF and finish the fight.

"No, Cavin. He's gone. Let him go." She grabbed the material at his collar and forced him to look at her. "Listen to me. He did something to you—to your internal computers. It's what's making you sick. He said he can kill you without even touching you, but that he'd rather do it in person. If you go looking for him, he'll finish it. He'll finish you." She squeezed her eyes shut. Swallowed a lump in her throat. "He can make it worse, he said. He can make it so bad that you'll beg him to kill you."

"The only one begging for death will be him if I ever

find his neck in my hands," Cavin growled. He tried to struggle to his feet, but she stopped him.

"You have bigger things to conquer than him. You came here to save the world, not to fight that monster. Do you hear me? Save the world. Save me!" She gave him a hard kiss so full of desperation and passion that in seconds she'd dragged his focus from the assassin back to her.

They separated, panting, crouching there, forehead to forehead. She heard the CHP officer calling for reinforcements. "Are you going to be able to walk?"

"I don't know," Cavin said. "I'll try. My balance, it's not the best. And I've lost vision in my left eye."

She steadied his head with her hands pressed to the sides of his cool, damp face. "We're in this together, remember? Stick with me, and I'll get you out of here. You have some world-saving to do."

"Damn right," he said. Jana tugged on his good arm with every ounce of strength that she had and helped him stand. When they were sure he'd stay upright, she snatched her attaché off the floor and held on to his arm to guide him. The police officer supported his other arm. Cavin seemed all at once embarrassed by the need for help and frustrated by his failing body.

They clambered down the stairs. The thundering of boots from below warned of guards on the way up. "Got a DOA in the elevator, and a perp…hell, the perp's gone. Six-two. Caucasian, black, blue."

"Gun run?"

"No, man. He, ah, disappeared. I mean, literally. And he…" He struggled to come up with words to explain what the REEF had done to him and gave up. "Weird shit going on."

Two of the police ran the rest of the way up the stairs. The third stopped at the sight of Cavin, who was in obvious physical pain. "He needs a doctor."

"I'm bringing him to one," Jana lied. No doctor could fix what Cavin had. The only place she was bringing him was out of this building.

Back in the parking garage, she told the officer who'd helped her get Cavin into the car, "The guy in the elevator attacked me before you got upstairs." If her heart pounded any harder, it was going to register on the Richter scale. "But he tried to kill me. This was an attack I believe is related to an ongoing investigation into a huge smuggling and poaching ring. If they came after me, likely they'll launch similar attacks on the other officials involved. Have someone call Katherine Garner, chief of Fish and Game special ops. Right now. We need to make sure every warden on the team is checked in and safe. Hell, make sure Katherine is checked in and safe."

He answered with a curt nod. "After you get him some medical help, go down to the station, Senator. File a report."

Mess around with paperwork at a time like this? Not in this lifetime, she thought.

The officer brought his radio to his mouth to pass along Jana's warning.

She started the Jeep, the old-fashioned way. Jamming her bare foot on the accelerator, Jana jerked the wheel around. Skidding, she fishtailed out of the parking garage and roared up the dark street.

"What is this about another attack on you, Jana?"

"Someone tried to stab me in the elevator."

"Not the REEF?"

"No. In fact, he probably saved my life. I was set up. There never was going to be a meeting with the governor. Someone posing as his secretary sent a memo to my staff to lure me here, alone. I never questioned it. I got careless, because I was expecting the meeting." She'd made the phone call to Willa in a very public place. Anyone could have overheard—and passed along the information to whoever wanted her dead.

Who had ordered her execution? She started to shake, post-traumatic stress, as she mentally reviewed the week's disastrous events: the Russian photographer at the fish farm who she'd now bet had supplied photos to the *Sun;* the canceled meeting so she'd have to have lunch at Ice and be set up with more photos; the attempted ruin of her father to make her family look bad; and finally the break-in at her apartment and Evie's car blowing up, both of which she'd blamed on Cavin's would-be killer when it was now obvious she had an assassin of her very own. His-and-her executioners—she and Cavin were truly the couple with everything.

Within minutes, she was on the highway. "How did the REEF figure out who I was, Cavin? I thought we were careful."

"We were. However, the newspapers weren't. The guards offered me a paper to read. I saw an old issue side by side with the most recent. I saw your shoes, Jana."

"My shoes?"

"One photo shows your shoes as evidence where we abandoned the first car that night. Another photo shows you making the speech at the fish farm…wearing those very shoes. To a careful observer, the pictures connect you to me. The REEF is a careful observer. I knew then it would only be a matter of time before he found you."

"He sure didn't waste any—time, that is. But he let me live. He'd already let me go when you got there."

"For the sport of the hunt."

She pressed a fist to her stomach so she didn't get sick.

More police cars zoomed past. Before long, the entire Sacramento Police Department would be at the capitol. But she and Cavin would be long gone by then. They were about to disappear. And they weren't surfacing until they'd saved the world.

ONCE IN NEVADA, Jana merged onto Highway 95 and headed south. "We're five hours from Las Vegas. We'll be there by midday. General 'Baloney' Mahoney might not want to return our phone calls, but it's going to be harder turning away an alien at his doorstep."

They stopped once, at a truck stop as the sun rose over the bleak landscape of the high desert. Cavin looped an arm protectively over her shoulders. He was in his socks, having given his boots to her. Jana shivered in her thin business suit. The day would be warm, but for now, the air hung on to the chill of the night. "It's not the middle of nowhere, but you can see it from here. That's what Grandpa would say if he were with us."

That won her a smile from Cavin, and she thanked the heavens for it. He was getting worse, not better. His face was pale, and he was sweating. His suffering tore her apart. She tried not to think of what the REEF had told her. *Days, Jana Jasper…you'll be back looking for me in mere days…*

For Cavin, they bought a large foam container of

chicken noodle soup and a quart of milk. For her, a quilted camouflage hunting jacket and lined boots, an extra large coffee and a box of doughnuts. There were newspapers from five major cities to choose from and they brought them all back to the Jeep.

Slugging down some coffee, she chanced a peek at the first newspaper. "Star Wars In Sacramento. Elevator Operator Left For Dead. Capitol In Disarray After Playgirl Senator Flees Crime Scene With Alien Lover." She drank more coffee, wishing it were tequila. Reading the headlines felt surreal. She couldn't have made up with better ones if she'd tried. "'Damage Estimates To California Capitol Soar, Governor Says, After Police Wage Late-Night Gun Battle With Aliens. Jaspers Mum As Officials Find Strange Vessel Covered By Tarp In Backyard Midnight Raid.' And check out this one— Healed By Alien. Homeless Vet Claims Miracle."

She put the papers on the seat between them. "So now you're a religious figure."

Cavin made a sound of disbelief. "Better a religious figure than a monster."

True. Thanks to the REEF floating the police officer like a party balloon, at least they didn't have to worry about convincing the world of the existence of aliens. If only it was as easy convincing the government to give them access to the ship at Area 51. "The men in black are going to be all over this, Cavin."

"If that's what it takes to get us into Dreamland, we'll take it."

"As long as the men in black don't take you." She started up the Jeep and rolled back onto the highway. Gauntlet engine starts were too taxing for Cavin now, and she refused to let him do it. His voice was hoarser, his accent stronger. He had sight in only one eye, and the full use of only one arm. He was deteriorating before her eyes. What if he didn't make it to the ship? "Maybe we should find a doctor, Cavin."

"I'm fine."

"You're not fine."

He answered with a stubborn glare. But as he turned his focus back to the road ahead, he said, "There is an option, should my condition worsen."

"What kind of option are we talking about? I'm not putting you down like a sick dog, so forget it."

"Do you remember our discussion about my gauntlet?"

"That it's the command center for the rest of your biocomputer systems—yes."

"I believe the REEF's interference is targeting the gauntlet. The bad signals start there and spread from there. But if I take out the implant, no more problems."

"You mean, like…cut it out?"

He turned his arm over and made a slicing motion with his index finger. "I'd cut along the seam, here, peel back the flap of skin and lift it out."

"Ugh." Jana fought to hold down the contents of her stomach. She blew air into her cheeks and held it there until her stomach settled. She couldn't argue his logic. It was the method she couldn't handle. She wasn't anything like that tough chick Sarah Connor in the *Terminator* movie, praised by the hero for her natural ability for patching gunshot wounds with a homemade field dressing. No, Jana was perfectly capable of fainting at the sight of a box of unopened Band-Aids.

Her cell phone rang. She'd never been so grateful for a cell phone call changing the topic of conversation.

Jared was on the phone. "How are you holding up in that transport?" she asked him. "Bored out of your skull yet?"

"If the adrenaline stops pumping, which I doubt, I've got caffeine as a backup. And my iPod and cell if it comes to that. But trust me, Jana, at this point the adrenaline rush is more than adequate to keep my eyes open—that and Evie's cooking. She just brought out breakfast. And I've got an update for you, so listen up."

Jana put the cell phone on speaker. "Go ahead. We can both hear now."

"No word from the general yet, but I thought you'd rest easier knowing that your wannabe killers are in jail. They busted up that smuggling ring last night. They made the decision to move in after you were attacked."

Katherine, Jana thought. Fish and Game's chief of special ops had acted fast.

"They rounded up over twenty men and women. And Alex. He gave a whopper of a confession, too, after they found messages from him to your almost-killer on the guy's cell phone."

"Alex," she hissed.

"Apparently his smuggling ring brought in a majority of the illegally obtained caviar from Russia. But you kept foiling his plans to boost dependence on illegal importation, because everything you did increased the local domestic sturgeon population. And all those fish farms opening up, it was going to ruin him. So he put a contract out on you."

With a shudder, she thought of Evie's car and wondered if the bomb had detonated too early or too late. "There's big money where the Mafia's involved. It can change people. Turn them into killers." How else could she rationalize that she'd almost dated the man?

"For what it's worth, Alex tried *not* to kill you. He meant to get rid of you by ruining you."

Or by sleeping with her, thinking he could neutralize her through a relationship. It was all making sense now. "So he went after you and Dad, our entire family. He wanted to make the Jaspers look bad so he could make me look bad." She suspected the charges against her father and brother would be dropped Monday. *If* the world was still around Monday. She chanced an apprehensive glance at the sky.

"He poisoned your friends, the ones he could influence, like Brace, who was actually a legitimate businessman, not a Mafioso, and good cover for Alex. And he broke into your apartment looking for dirt. Except there wasn't any dirt, Girl Scout that you are, so he had to make some."

"What about Viktor?"

"Viktor is an idiot."

"Tell me something I don't know," she muttered.

"He had no idea Alex was using the restaurant for money laundering. The profits from the Russian smuggling had to go somewhere."

"I don't understand why Alex confessed to all this, though. And so fast. Okay, so there was the cell phone, but why not have his day in court?"

"He made some sort of plea deal."

"How come I don't get to deal with him?" Alex would be singing soprano by the time she was done with him. Where was a plasma sword when you needed one?

"Apparently he pointed fingers at all his Mafia buddies. Dumb, huh? I wouldn't feel too sorry for the guy. With the Russian Mafia after him, he's going to be a lot safer in jail than he'll be out of it."

Something dragged Jana's attention to the rearview mirror. A black sedan with tinted windows followed them on the deserted highway. "Jared...I gotta go. Talk later." She hung up and focused on the car. If she sped up, it did, too. She slowed, and so did the sedan. Her first thought was the Russian Mafia. Her second was the men in black. "Cavin," she said with dread. "We have company."

CHAPTER TWENTY-FIVE

"STOP THE CAR, JANA. This is our chance to talk to them."

"What if they want to hurt you?"

"Continuing to drive won't change that. This is our chance, our chance to convince them to give us access to the ship through legal means, so we don't have to go to Plan C."

"No. No Plan C." She pulled over to the shoulder. The sedan drove up behind them with an ominous popping of gravel under its tires. And then it was quiet, very quiet. For miles around them stretched empty desert. In the distance were the snowy peaks of the White Mountains. The area was riddled with tiny towns and mines. Somewhere to the east was Nellis Air Force Base.

They weren't far from Area 51. These men might be their ticket onto that base—if she could convince them to take them there. But what would she say to them?

Feeling helpless, she scraped a hand over her face. Up until now, she'd let her family do the talking for her: the initial contact with Mahoney and President Ramos. It was as if she were once again the mute little girl who let everyone speak for her. What kind of politician, what kind of *leader* was she if she couldn't speak for herself?

You feel this way because you were never supposed to talk. The gift of gab was something you wished for, but you weren't born with it. You're a phony. Did you really think you could keep fooling everyone forever?

She dropped her hand. "I can't do this. I'm not qualified to do this—to talk, to convince the world to get behind us. To keep these men from killing you."

Cavin pressed his thumb to her chin and turned her to face him. "You have the only qualifications needed—heart and your ability for public speaking."

"Only because you gave it to me, Cavin—the gift of gab. I wouldn't have had it otherwise."

He shook his head, confused. Didn't he remember?

"I grew up not being able to talk. I was mute. I had to leave school to be educated at home. I had no friends except for my family. I was a freak. You—" her voice caught "—you were the first friend I had who didn't care that I couldn't speak. I didn't have to with you. We didn't need to talk. You liked me the way I was. And then, the night you left, you gave me the most wonderful gift of all. You healed me. That homeless vet might call what you do a miracle, but to me it was magic. Magic, Cavin."

Cavin concentrated, clearly thinking back to that starry summer night. "I healed your knee. Is that what you mean?"

"No. I thought you were like a genie, and that when I freed you, you'd grant me three wishes. I wished for a first kiss, which you gave me. I wished that I'd see you again," she blushed, "well, that I'd marry you, actually. And I wished that I could talk. You touched my knee and healed it. Then you kissed me, and from then on, I was able to talk. You changed my life forever, Cavin. I went on to do everything I'd dreamed of doing." She glanced at the black sedan. "One problem. I'm a fake. I've achieved a lot, but it wasn't because of me. It was because of you."

"All these years, you believed this?" he asked, incredulous.

"Well, yeah. Why wouldn't I?"

"Ah, Squee…" He heaved a sigh and moved her hair back from where it had fallen over her cheek, gazing at her with deep green eyes so full of love it made her throat ache. "I didn't give you your gift of gab. You were born with it. I healed your knee using simple bioregeneration. I never did anything to your voice."

"But you—"

"I kissed you. That's all.'

"But, Cavin, I—"

"Jana, I didn't know you couldn't speak! You were silent, yes, but so was I. I thought it was because we didn't know each other's languages. I healed your knee, but I didn't give you the ability to speak. That gift is yours, and yours alone."

She sat still, frozen in shock. Everything she'd ever assumed about herself had been knocked on its head. Then she gave Cavin a hard stare. "You're not kidding, right? You're telling the truth."

"I swear to you. Your beginning to speak at that time was coincidence. From the sheer novelty of our meeting, perhaps, or new confidence."

Doctors would agree with Cavin. They'd say she was a delayed speaker because something hadn't been working quite right in her brain. They'd explain away her sudden chattiness as a result of the excitement from meeting Cavin and her desire to tell Evie about the experience. But Jana shook her head. "No, Cavin. It was magic." She touched his incredible mouth with shaking fingers and whispered, "Magic may be how we explain what we don't understand, but it's magic all the same."

His good hand curved behind her head to pull her close for a kiss. A poignantly tender kiss.

The cell phone rang. Her eyes tracked to the phone number. "It's the general!" She made sure the headset was fitted firmly in her ear and said, "Jana Jasper here."

"Hold on, Jana. I have Colonel Connick on the line…"

"Senator, this is Tom Connick. I'm the commander of the base that contains the hangar known as Area 51. I wanted you to hear it from me. There's no ship hidden there."

"Yes, there is. I know there is."

"No, there's not."

They sounded like petulant four-year-olds fighting over a teddy bear rather than adults debating the fate of the world.

She steadied herself. *The gift of gab is yours. Yours!* "We're about to be invaded by an army intent on evicting all six-plus billion of us from this planet, and you can't cough up the truth? No ship at Area 51? Bullshit. Even in our darkest hour, you and your associates insist on perpetuating the lie, Colonel. How shameful is that? We're going to be invaded. If this isn't an example of a threat to national security, I don't know what is. Maybe we Earthlings deserve to lose our home. We certainly aren't fighting very hard to keep it!" Shaking, she hung up.

Cavin gaped at her. "What did you just do, Jana?"

"I used Grandpa's brand of diplomacy." She frowned at the sedan in the mirror. It just sat there, doors closed. What were the goons doing—waiting for Connick's kill order? "Men like Connick, the ones who won't bend the rules, they're going to allow the invasion. I can't wrap my mind around the unimaginable horror of that. I know you told me that Coalition policy discourages civilian casualties when acquiring populated worlds, but death and destruction are inevitable. Inevitable when it doesn't have to be. Inevitable because no one has the backbone to make a fucking decision!"

The phone rang again. Jana's mouth curved into a smile. Oh, yeah. The boys are eating out of my hand.

Astonishment and respect lit up Cavin's eyes. "You sure you never served in the Coalition Army?"

Jana snorted and took the call. Connick said, "Perhaps we can talk about this."

"Where? We don't have a lot of time, Colonel."

"We're, uh, closer than you think."

The sedan honked. Jana jumped and glanced in the rearview mirror. "Omigod. It's them, Cavin. They're in the car, the general and the colonel."

The sedan pulled up beside them. The window slid down. Behind the wheel was a handsome, silver-haired air force officer sporting a pair of Oakley sunglasses. In the passenger seat was an elderly man dressed in a pale denim shirt and crisp Dockers. His smile revealed perfect teeth. She remembered that Hollywood smile. "General Mahoney," she said. "Or should I call you Baloney?"

The old man ignored her sarcasm. "Let me introduce you to Colonel Tom Connick."

She shook both men's hands. But it was Cavin they seemed eager to see, staring across the seat at him. "I'll go meet them," he said, taking off his seat belt and opening the door.

"Don't be too trusting," she warned him under her breath. "If they ask if you want to see their puppy, run."

Cavin gave her a funny look.

"Just be careful."

He nodded. The men got out of the car to shake his hand. Despite how ill he was, Cavin greeted them with a proud, military stance. The colonel opened a folder of photos to show him. Cavin beckoned to her. "Jana, you may want to see this."

She climbed down from the Jeep. It was silent outside, no traffic noise. A dry wind stirred what little brush there was eking an existence from the hard-packed dirt. Three military men, one active, two former, and one politician huddled around classified photographs on an isolated stretch of highway. It could be a scene out of a Tom Clancy novel, or a 007 movie, but definitely nothing resembling her former life.

The colonel's folder contained four black-and-white photos: close-ups of machinery, or aircraft parts. "If one of these was a photo taken of an alien ship, which do you think it would be?"

Cavin answered without hesitation. "I see two photos that fit your description, not one."

The slightest movement of the colonel's mouth told her Cavin had chosen the right answer. "Which two?"

Cavin pointed to the lower left image. "That's the ship's identification number." He translated the blocky little hieroglyphics using his fingers. "And its name.

Shakree." He wrinkled his forehead. "It translates roughly to a type of seedpod that is distributed by the wind." Then he pointed to the lower right photo. "And that is part of the forward instrument panel."

"This is an alien ship?" Jana glared at the officers. "You said there was no spacecraft hidden at Area 51."

Connick's expression didn't change. "There isn't. But I'm going to tell you where it is, and how to get there."

ALONE AGAIN, THEY SPED along a road they'd taken from Highway 6 East. There were some ranches, but little else. Someone pulling a horse trailer had been behind them for some time. No one else was on the road. "Scratch what I said about being able to *see* the middle of nowhere from here, Cavin. This *is* the middle of nowhere."

First they were supposed to find a farmhouse. There, they were to meet up with someone Connick called the Gatekeeper, a name that was satisfyingly mysterious. He'd given no other directions except that they had to find exit 17 and take the unmarked road immediately following.

Jana veered into the right lane. The horse trailer followed. If only it would pass them already. She was in no mood for tailgaters.

A small road marker came into view. "There it is," Jana called out, her heart leaping. "Seventeen."

"I confirm that," Cavin said. He'd rolled his window partway open. The wind ruffled his hair and he seemed to welcome the air. His skin was pasty. Likely he was sick to his stomach.

"Tell me if you need to stop," she said.

He shook his head, and the movement seemed to cause him pain. He grimaced, sucking in some air. "Keep going. Not much time."

Not much time for whom? For Cavin or for Earth? Or both? *Gods.* Her stomach hurt.

The turnoff came quicker than she expected. Worse, the horse trailer was right on her butt. Idiot! She didn't want to slam on the brakes and cause an accident, nor did she want to miss the turnoff. Letting off on the gas pedal, she jerked the wheel to the right. Tires skidding, she fought to stay on the road which was hard-baked dirt. The second the tires got traction, she sped up. There was no time to waste.

Cavin's expression didn't change in reaction to her wild driving. It told her how much pain he was in. All his concentration was on survival.

But as soon as she was headed straight again, the sound of scraping and skidding echoed behind them. "I don't believe it. That horse trailer just followed us off the road."

Cavin was instantly alert. He turned in his seat, and his lips compressed. "It's him."

She threw an alarmed glance at the rearview mirror. She couldn't see who was behind the wheel, only the silhouette of a lone man, unmoving as he bore down on them. Her stomach sank with dread. It was the REEF. "But I thought he was gone."

"He's a REEF."

No time to reason it out now. She shoved the gas pedal to the floor, but the assassin pulled up even with the Jeep. Side by side, they were road racing on what was little more than a dirt path.

The REEF rammed into the Jeep's driver's side. Wind whistled through broken glass as Jana fought wildly to keep the Jeep on the road. She ground her foot to the floor, trying to squeeze every last bit of speed from the poor Jeep, and pulled ahead of the heavier vehicle. The horse trailer swung from side to side, causing the truck to fishtail, but he gained on them. This time he hit the Jeep even harder. Her door caved in, shoving her sideways in the seat.

"Faster, Jana."

The damaged Jeep shook, sending vibrations up her arms to rattle her teeth. "I'm giving it all she's got." She couldn't believe she'd said that. It was as if she'd fallen into a cheesy sci-fi thriller.

But everything depended on her being able to evade the REEF. *Everything*: Cavin, the fate of the world, their future.

Perspiration ran into her eyes. Her legs quivered with adrenaline. But her only thoughts were the gas pedal under her foot and the road ahead. If she kept control of both, she kept Cavin alive.

The horse trailer pulled up alongside them. Ready for the next hit, Jana braced herself. Thick seconds clicked past and no crash. She glanced over at the REEF. He pointed something at her. It glinted in his hand as he took wobbly aim. Fear flared in her chest. "Cavin," she yelled. "He's got a gun!"

Cavin grabbed her by the back of the collar and yanked her lower in the seat. Jana spun the wheel, hoping to cause a miss when the assassin shot at them. A sharp bang rang out, followed by a whistling hiss. The Jeep pulled hard to the left. Somehow, she stayed on the road. The stench of burning rubber made her eyes water. She gritted her teeth, squeezed the steering wheel, and kept the gas pedal jammed to the floor. The car was shaking violently now, riding on a bare rim. It sounded as if it were coming apart.

Another shot boomed. A geyser of water gushed out from under the hood and splattered all over the windshield, turning the dust to mud. "We're going to have to ditch this baby!" she yelled. It sounded like something her fighter-pilot brother would say. For a woman who never had any desire to be in the military, she'd seen enough combat in one week to last a lifetime.

While she still had some speed to play with, she rolled the steering wheel to the left. The Jeep hurtled off the road, into a ditch and flipped over. *Yenflarg.* She hadn't planned on the rollover. The screeching was horrific. *Please, I don't want to die this way, not me, not Cavin.* Finally the Jeep spun to a whimpering stop, upside down.

Pebbles and sand rained down on her as she hung in her shoulder and seat belts. The smell of dust and hot rubber burned her nose. "Get out," Cavin shouted hoarsely as he untangled himself from his seat belt. "He'll be back, but we can get a head start."

She grabbed her tattered purse, threw the strap over her shoulder, and they took off running across the desert. Leaning on her heavily, sometimes grunting in obvious agony, Cavin grew worse by the minute. He steered her to where the landscape was rockier. It afforded a few hiding places but it was at least a half mile away. She wasn't sure Cavin could manage that far of a run, but his face reflected such raw determination. He'd die trying, no doubt about it.

Her heart wrenched. She loved him so much. She couldn't bear the thought of losing him.

And Earth couldn't *afford* to lose him.

The horse trailer roared up behind them. Cavin caught her by the hand and almost jerked her off her feet in his rush to get to a dried river bed strewn with boulders. The REEF would not be able to drive between the rocks. She gasped, the dry air burning its way down her throat. Cavin was slowing, grunting as he pushed himself despite his failing body.

But the horse trailer fishtailed to a stop. Smoke billowed out from under the hood. The REEF jumped out—and plunged to his knees before staggering back up. He was in bad shape, too.

"Run," Cavin demanded harshly.

A shot rang out from behind. In front of them, the side of a boulder splintered. Slivers of stone arced in all directions. Shrapnel. Another bullet plowed harmlessly into the sand about six feet away.

The REEF missed because he was sick, she thought, her hopes rising. Then something whizzed by so close that she felt hot wind as the bullet screamed past her right ear. Scratch what she'd thought about his condition; his aim was improving—and he still had one last bullet before he had to stop to reload.

With grudging respect, Jana acknowledged the single-minded, almost superhuman tenacity of their enemy. He'd left all his futuristic weapons behind at the Capitol, but despite being so ill, the ever-resourceful assassin had managed to rearm himself.

The REEF fired again. The last shot made a deafening crack. Cavin stumbled, and she caught his arm. He was so heavy he took her down with him. "Where did he hit you? *Where?*" she screamed, running her hands over his chest and stomach, dreading the sight of blood. *Please, please don't die. Don't die.*

"I stumbled." Cavin's voice was hoarser now. "He missed."

She spun around to see the REEF closing on them. He'd thrown down the empty pistol. As he neared, she expected him to look as he did in the Capitol: a hard face and even harder eyes, blue and laser sharp. But he was sweating and pale, and sported a horrible grimace. Limping along, he resembled Quasimodo with a bad hangover.

Cavin pushed her away and struggled to his knees. "If anything happens to me, you know what to do. You know where to go."

"Nothing is going to happen to you. Stop talking that way."

"Jana." He took her chin between his fingers and forced her to look at him. "You will go back to the road and continue in the same direction. They'll come looking for us eventually. Once you are safe with the Gatekeeper, you'll call your brother. Jared will do as I briefed him, and you will turn on the spaceship here."

"But what if I can't? What if it's been sitting cold for too long? What if—?"

"Then Jared's signal will go out. The fleet will see it. It will give them something to ponder."

"For how long?"

His voice took on an edge. "A day. A month. I don't know. It's all we have, and we have no choice but to take it."

Cavin said "we" with such ease. We as in Earth. He'd truly come over on their side, heart and soul. She twined her fingers with his. She'd met many heroes in her life as a public figure, but none as incredibly selfless as this man.

He lifted their clasped hands to his mouth and pressed a kiss to her knuckles. His eyes were bright with emotion. "I'd rather have half a chance at saving you than none at all."

Then he rose to his feet. After taking a few seconds to gain his balance, he stormed off, or rather limped off, his bad arm hugged to his ribs.

"Wait a second," she screamed. "Where are you going?"

He didn't answer. He was on his way to confront the REEF.

He was crazy. They both were crazy, she decided. As sick as they were, how could they fight?

Seething, the men glared at each other, teeth bared, like two champion gladiators in their final confrontation. Both looked as though they were dead on their feet the way they wobbled, hunched over and in pain. The REEF made the first move. Cavin blocked his kick, sending him sprawling. The assassin climbed to his feet. He hissed in rage, in pain, or maybe plain old frustration, and lunged at him.

Cavin went flying backward. He landed hard, skidding across the dirt. And got back up and dived for the REEF's midsection. With none of their alien equipment functioning, it was an old-fashioned street fight. A barroom brawl. Punches flew. Grunts and muffled cries of pain had Jana fearing neither of them would come out alive. They rolled over the ground, leaving smears of blood.

Ugh! Woozy, Jana almost passed out.

Then, the assassin went down. At first she thought he was kicking to fight off Cavin, but soon saw that his legs jerked and twitched uncontrollably.

"Seizure," Cavin explained when she ran to him. He pulled the killer's head back and wedged a piece of his torn shirt in his mouth so he wouldn't bite his tongue.

When the seizure passed, the REEF opened his eyes. They really were a disconcerting blue, she thought. At first he seemed unable to focus, then he moved his gaze from Jana to Cavin, where it remained.

"If you agree to a peace treaty between us, I'll make sure you get to safety," Cavin told him, removing the tongue guard.

The REEF seemed both shocked and repelled by Cavin's offer. He was weak, in far worse shape than Cavin. Tremors ran through his body, and palsy affected his hands. No wonder his shots had gone wild. "Leave me here."

"You require medical care."

"On this primitive world? I think not."

Jana recoiled. Earth wasn't that primitive…was it?

"I'm dying," the REEF said. "I will do so alone. Go!" Another small seizure silenced him.

"Jana, help me lift him."

"Do not touch me. *Do not*. Obey my wishes." The REEF's blue eyes shone with the determination they'd previously seen only when he had Cavin in his sights. "I rigged your internal computers to self-destruct, just as I suspect someone has done to mine. I cannot do anything about it, but you can." He paused to grimace in pain. "The destruct signal is coming from me. Me, Far Star. And my malfunctioning systems will not allow me to shut it off. As long as I am alive, you will continue to break down. Do you understand? If I die, *you live*." He reached up and grabbed his arm. "Go, don't be a fool. Make a new life now that you have the chance." Then, as if ashamed, he looked away, self-loathing tightening his mouth. "My contract is void. Ended. *I have* ended it. I will not track you anymore. Or anyone…"

The assassin's head sagged back to the dirt. As he gazed up at the sky, his expression turned from ashamed to pensive to, finally, regret. Jana wondered what he was seeing, or thinking. Then his pupils contracted as his eyes rolled back. A shudder ran through him. And then he lay still.

Jana jumped forward to administer CPR. It was crazy, trying to breathe life into Cavin's killer, gasping as she attempted to start his heart, but it seemed wrong somehow to let him die. It would make her no better than him. She wasn't sure how long she fought to save the REEF, but Cavin stopped her.

"He's gone," he said.

The realization brought an odd mix of emotions. The relief was intense, yes, but it was sad, too. What a lonely wasted life.

With her help, Cavin climbed to his feet. "We can't leave him like this." But they couldn't bring him, either. With Cavin's halting help, she pulled the assassin's heavy body closer to the trailer. "But there's no one out here to pick up the body."

"We'll inform the Gatekeeper when we get there."

They stood, casting shadows over the body. In death, the killer seemed somehow at peace. Jana shook her head. "It's like he gave up. That he just decided to stop living. I thought a REEF fought to the end, even after the end."

Cavin's voice was gruff. "Not this one," he said. "Not this one…"

THEY'D WALKED—staggered mostly—across five miles of desert on a narrow paved road with no signs. Even though the REEF was gone, the consequences of his interference with Cavin's bioimplants remained. Cavin leaned on her like a drunk. It took all her strength to keep him upright. The Coalition invasion force was on the way, and the one man who could save them was half-delirious.

"Jana…" Cavin took a faltering step. Then his lips pulled back in agony as his hand flew to the side of his head. His grunt of pain tore at her heart. His boots crisscrossed, and he tripped, taking her down with him. This time he didn't get up.

"Come on, spaceman. We're almost there." She touched trembling fingers to his lips, his eyelids, his bristly jaw. His cheeks were sunken. Black rings under his eyes stood out starkly against his pale skin. He looked like hell. He looked as if he was dying.

He shook his head. "It has to come out," he gasped. "The gauntlet computer."

"Cavin, you're in no condition to do surgery."

"*You* are."

She reared back. "Oh, no. No, no."

"I'm almost blind." He felt along the dirt until he found her hand. "Take out the pocketknife, Squee. Do it now."

"I can't," she whispered.

His hand flew to the side of his head. His mouth opened in a silent curse. He was in agony, and she was the only one who could help him, the only one who could perform the operation.

Outside and without anesthetic.

A surge of nausea overwhelmed her. She ran several feet away from the side of the road and barfed.

When she returned to Cavin, tears streamed down her face. She unzipped her purse and hunted around blindly for her little red Swiss Army knife. As she contemplated the knife in her hand, she said, "I don't know how I can do this. I can't look at blood."

"Think of it as fruit juice."

Her stomach rolled. "Cavin…"

"I have faith in you, Squee." He clasped her shaking hand to reassure her. Or maybe he just wanted to stop the shaking before she cut him.

She removed the gauntlet's outer shell, the cuff he wore like a bracelet. He guided her fingers over the internal computer. The edges were easy to feel. "That's where you will cut. Feel the seam."

She slapped her hand over her mouth as her empty stomach convulsed. Again she ran off to be sick.

She wanted to panic, she thought as she retched. She wanted the self-indulgent pleasure of screaming until her voice gave out. She wanted an irreversible coma.

Be brave. Be everything you're not. Your hero needs you now. He needs you to be strong.

If she let him down, she let the entire planet down.

With that realization, something seemed to change in her, deep down inside her. It was like the day she'd found her voice, only this time she'd found something else: courage. And although she knew Cavin wouldn't take credit for either, she gave him silent thanks for both.

Sweating, she returned to him. Blinking to clear her vision, she dug blindly through her purse for a Handi Wipes cloth to clean the knife and his skin. It was sadly unsanitary. Infection was a real possibility. He was going to need stitches and real medical care after this.

But as she searched for the wipes, her hand closed over a wad of tissue paper. It was the little matryoshka doll her mother had given her. It was like an artifact from another time, another place. She pulled off the wrapping, releasing a whiff of rose scent.

Cavin inhaled the perfume. "Am I hallucinating, or have you brought me flowers?"

"Something better. It's a gift my father gave my mother when they first met. It's a matryoshka, a Russian doll. He gave my mom a series of these over the weeks he courted her." Jana lifted the lid off the doll, revealing the smaller one inside. "In each doll you find another one hidden. They get tinier and tinier. My father tucked love notes inside the littlest doll in the center. I treasured these as a child." She closed her eyes briefly, reciting: "'Life is sometimes easy and some-times hard, but love is the only constant. No matter how far you rise, or how hard you fall, a good love will always be there for you.' Last week my mother gave me this matryoshka to remind me of that."

Jana placed the wooden egg-shaped figure in Cavin's good hand, closing his fingers around the doll. "Now I'm giving it to you, so you can be reminded, too." She tried to keep her voice steady, for him, for her, but it was getting difficult.

She hefted the knife. Nearly weightless in her hand, it glinted in the sunshine. "God, Cavin. I wish I had a leather strap for you to bite, or a bottle of whiskey for you to slug down, but all I have is this doll."

His expression softened with a mix of tenderness and confidence—confidence in her. "This is better than any strap or whiskey."

Jana brought the knife to his skin. Cavin's hand tightened around the matryoshka doll, clamping down as she pushed the blade into his flesh and made the first cut.

CHAPTER TWENTY-SIX

WITH HIS FOREARM wrapped tightly in the remains of Jana's silk suit jacket, Cavin stood, feet spread wide for balance, gratefully leaning on her as they started to walk again. They didn't know yet if the operation had worked, but at least Cavin was no longer in excruciating pain. What discomfort that came from the unstitched wound in his arm didn't come close to what he'd felt before she'd cut him.

Although he'd lost all of his computer-assisted abilities, he hadn't reverted back to his native language with the failure of the translator. His English was more accented and a little less smooth, but still there. Likely the translator had facilitated his human brain's natural transition to fluency.

Somewhere over the next hill was the farmhouse Connick had described. And the Gatekeeper. "Damn them," she muttered. "Where are they? Why haven't they come looking for us?" A *Men In Black* taxi service would be just the ticket. When this was over, she was putting in a suggestion so the next people who had to save the world wouldn't have to go through this much trouble.

They'd covered maybe another quarter mile when a distant roar broke the silence. A cloud of dust rose on the horizon ahead. The dust cloud coalesced into a car. Her stomach dropped and a chill washed over her. What if it was the REEF? What if he'd come back to life to finish the job for the third time, *Terminator*-style. She should have known he wouldn't have let them go, no matter how damaged he was, no matter how changed he seemed to be.

No matter that he'd died and she felt his heart stop.

Pebbles and grit popped under truck tires as the vehicle pulled alongside them. Inside was an old man with skin that looked like leather. He wore mirrored aviator Ray-Bans, which seemed somehow perfect on his seamed face. When he smiled, his lips were so thin they were nonexistent. "You took so long to get here that she sent me out to find you. Not supposed to pick anyone up, usually. Under the circumstances, thought we'd make an exception.

"You must be the Gatekeeper," Jana said.

"No. I'm the Handyman."

Who was next? The Hairdresser? The UPS guy? "No one told us about a Handyman."

He shrugged. "Isn't much to tell. The Gatekeeper is who you need to see. She's waiting for you."

So the Gatekeeper was a woman. A female guarding the grand prize in a male-dominated world of secrecy. There was a sort of poetic justice in that.

Cavin seemed more alert as they helped him into the roomy cab of the truck. He pulled his seat belt around Jana first and then himself. It was a typically protective Cavin gesture, and the best sign yet that he was returning to normal.

She took Cavin's hand in hers, holding it on her lap

as the truck bumped along the pitted road. "They don't keep up with the maintenance around here, do they?" she remarked.

"No one's complained in forty years. But then no one's been up this road in forty years, either."

"How do you get your food and supplies? What do you eat?"

He made that lipless grin again. "Can't give away all the secrets, Senator."

"No." Jana guessed he couldn't.

A farm appeared. There was a tumbledown barn and a small house. It was probably once white but harsh weather had turned it gray. No crops, no animals, only sand. It put the *D* in desolation. "Do you live here year round?"

Another grin. Sans lips. "Sorry, can't give away all—"

"—the secrets," Jana finished for him. He and the Gatekeeper must be on the government payroll. She hoped they got a generous salary, vacation and benefits, too, because no one should have to live like this.

The Handyman parked and helped Cavin down from the truck. They walked to the farmhouse. There was nothing that indicated that the original, recovered crashed spacecraft from Roswell, New Mexico was hidden here.

The screen door opened with a squeak of old hinges. A short woman with a shining smile greeted them. Improbably, she wore an apron. Crinkly, graying orange hair was pulled back from her face in a bun. Freckles speckled her pale skin, and her brown eyes shone. She looked to be in her fifties—too young to have been alive for the original crash landing, but maybe her age was as much a ruse as the rest of this place. "I'm the Gate-keeper."

"I'm Jana Jasper. This is Cavin of Far Star."

"I baked cookies."

Um, okay. "Thanks. Probably we should save Earth first, though. Then have a cookie break."

The woman chuckled. "All right." She gave Cavin a long, admiring stare. "So, here you are at last. He who can unlock the gate. The Key."

"We have little time," he said, also apparently feeling the need, as Jana did, to coax her into action. Everyone on this farm seemed to move in slow motion.

The woman squinted at the sky. "I know. They're coming, aren't they? Follow me now."

She walked around the side of the house where an ancient-looking pair of doors led to a root cellar. The Handyman hoisted them open. The doors fell to the ground and dust poofed up in a cloud. The Handyman shone a flashlight into the darkness. Dust motes swirled. Spiderwebs laced across the opening. Whatever was down here had not been looked at in a very long time.

Cavin supported his weight on the handrails. They creaked under the strain. Beneath the house it smelled musty and like dirt. Jana couldn't believe there was a spacecraft hidden there. She looked around for a large lump covered by a dusty old tarp like you'd find over a treasured antique car in someone's garage.

"It's downstairs," the Gatekeeper said. "Step here, next to me. Now, hold on tight." She pulled on a thick rope dangling from the low ceiling, and the floor fell away.

Jana yelped as they plummeted down with it, feeling suddenly light on their feet. The sensation was unnerving. The walls raced past and then the walls were gone. They were in near total darkness.

The square piece of floor on which they stood was an elevator. The Gatekeeper was with them. The Handyman was not. "He has to look after things on top," the woman called out above the noise of wind. "In case someone comes calling."

If the road hadn't been used in forty years, it wasn't likely too many people came calling. Maybe the real story was that the Handyman didn't have the security clearance the angelic redheaded Gatekeeper did.

The president didn't even know where this place was, according to General Mahoney. Neither did the Joint Chiefs of Staff. Only a select few, slightly crazy people. Fanatics, perhaps, were the best keepers of secrets.

Jana's stomach and the wind whipping her hair told her they were still falling, but the area was so vast it was easy to lose the sensation of speed. Her ears popped. There was a impression of deepness. At last, the elevator slowed, stopping smoothly.

"Turn around," the Gatekeeper said.

And there it was. The famous spaceship. The Roswell saucer. The shape was oval and the wings were so stubby that she could understand how the flying saucer legend had started. Only it wasn't a legend.

The dark, smooth metal hull gleamed dully as they stepped closer. There were no lights, no sounds. No signs that it worked, or that it ever had worked, flown here from another world. Jana hoped it was dormant and not dead.

A row of blocky symbols decorated one side. *Seedpod,* she thought: the little ship's name. A film of some kind coated the windows, preventing her from seeing inside.

Cavin approached the ship confidently and walked up the open ramp. The trim around the hatch was mangled, bearing the scars of tools. Earthling tools. It had been pried open.

The cockpit was small and dark. Cavin slid into the pilot seat as if he owned it. As Jana waited with the Gatekeeper at the root of the ramp, he uttered a sound that sounded suspiciously like a growl. *"Yenflarg,"* he snapped.

The Gatekeeper's eyebrows lifted. *"Yenflarg?"*

"It translates roughly to 'shit,'" Jana said.

Cavin slapped his hands down on the armrests and turned around. His eyes blazed with anger at the Gatekeeper. "It's damaged. Badly. Computers are missing. Vital panels! Your tinkering has destroyed this craft."

Jana had never seen Cavin lose his temper like that. Everything he'd risked, the fate of the world, it was all in jeopardy because of Earth's clumsy curiosity and years of tinkering. Maybe they *were* as primitive as the REEF had suggested.

The Gatekeeper scurried to an ancient-looking cardboard carton with Orange Crush Soda printed on the side. "They saved all the parts—right here. We never threw anything away." She delivered the box to the cockpit. The contents rattled as she set it on the floor. Cavin pulled something out and fitted it to the instrument panel. Soft chimes heralded the awakening of long-slumbering equipment. Illumination came on in the cockpit, spilling light onto the smooth concrete floor below where Jana and the Gatekeeper waited.

Jana whooped. "You did it, Cavin!"

The Gatekeeper showed her first true signs of emotion as she wrung her hands in her apron. "I lived to see the day. I lived to see it."

More lights came on up and down and all around the sides of the ship. Then the windshield erupted in a swirl of colors that faded into a serene backdrop of stars.

Jana took a closer look. "How come some stars are moving?"

"They're not stars," Cavin said. "They're ships."

Jana felt faint. "It's the fleet."

"Yes," he said, continuing to work. "They're almost here."

Almost? What did that mean? "How long?" Call her sick, but she had to know how narrow the margin had been with them getting here.

"A week, more or less. No…it's less." He squinted at scrolling, three-dimensional text in his native language. "I'll get an exact reading in a moment. Hold on—"

There was a loud snap. Jana smelled something burning. Then all the lights in the ship went out. The little saucer was completely dead.

Silence, then Cavin's swearing and the thud of his fist hitting the dashboard. Looking weak, the Gatekeeper took a seat. Jana formed words somehow. "What happened?"

"I tried a shortcut," Cavin said. "It didn't work. I'll have to find the rest of the power panels." He spun around in the chair and went in search for more parts in the Orange Crush carton. Every once in a while, he'd attach something. But the ship remained dead.

Hours passed. Jana alternated sitting with Cavin for moral support and pacing. She couldn't stay still. Somewhere out there an invasion force approached, while Cavin fought to get their best defense up and running...with a hammer and screwdriver! Talk about working against the clock.

Cavin held the handle of a screwdriver clamped in his mouth while he fiddled with a cylindrical crystalline object that stubbornly wouldn't go where it was supposed to fit. Blood was seeping through the makeshift bandage where his gauntlet had been. He needed stitches, a doctor's care. Jana swallowed and forced her eyes away from the incision. He'd already refused painkillers and wouldn't submit to a bandage change until he was done. But they were supposed to have been done by now.

"Jana, I need you to hold this down for me."

She climbed into the cockpit. He pressed her hand over a warped metal panel. "Hold pressure—there—and I'm going to try to apply power."

"Okay." Cavin's fingers danced over a perfectly flat keyboard of some kind. Nothing happened.

She pressed harder. He tried again. And again. Nothing.

"I'm going to have to try it manually. I'll either melt what's left of the systems, or we'll get this crate powered up." He fell to his knees and fiddled with the underside of the pilot station. Sweat glistened on his forehead. "All right. Here we go." His eyes closed, and he concentrated. Or prayed. It was hard to tell the difference. Even the Gatekeeper held her breath.

Nothing.

Jana could almost taste the bitter disappointment in the air as Cavin fell wearily back into the seat. "It's up to Jared now," he said.

For the first time, Jana acknowledged the possibility that Cavin might not be able to accomplish what he'd set out to do. That it meant the destruction of all that she knew and loved.

"Damn it," she snapped. "We need some magic!" She slammed a fist on the console. Something within the little ship clicked and whirred to life. "We're back—we're back. Cavin, send out the signal."

But he was already in action, his hands flying over the panels as he hacked into the system. "I've got to do this fast. If it dies again, we may not have a second chance."

Each second that ticked by was tenser than the last. Jana tried to remember to breathe.

"Here we go," Cavin said.

There was a flicker, and nothing more. "What happened?" Jana blurted out.

"Wait." Cavin held up his hand. "Watch."

Nobody breathed. Then, like fireflies fanning out over a starry sky, dozens and dozens of tiny lights appeared on the lower portion of the screen and rose toward the fleet.

"Earth's fleet." Cavin sat back in the pilot chair. Folding his arms over his chest, he looked a lot like his old smug self.

He looked a lot like Peter, she thought. "But did it work? Did they see it?"

He shrugged and turned around in the chair. "Probably."

"Probably?" the two women chorused.

A familiar telltale glimmer of mischief appeared in his eyes. Jana gaped at him in disbelief. "Tell me you didn't just make one of your kidding jokes."

"Something tells me this is a damned if you do, damned if you do situation," he said.

"I'm going to kill you," Jana whispered.

Cavin pulled her onto his lap and kissed her soundly. "Yes, Squee, it worked. It worked." Emotion had made his voice thick. "We multiplied the *Shakree* by the hundreds. To the Coalition, it will look like Earth has advanced tech and a massive space-faring fleet."

The Gatekeeper peered at the little lights on the windshield, each representing a huge spaceship. "But they are still coming in our direction."

"The Coalition fleet is like an enormous lumbering elephant. It will take some time to turn it around. I assure you, they will. But again, as I told the president, it's not a permanent fix. They'll be back, eventually, if not to invade, then to form a treaty because they will be fearful of us. Earth has much to do before that day comes. We have a very big secret and not a lot of time to figure out how to keep them from finding it out."

"We'll be ready," Jana said. This time, diplomacy would be a genuine possibility with Earth negotiating from a position of strength—or at least from a position of *perceived* strength. As a senator, that particular path to peace was far more palatable than a war they might not be able to win.

A senator who needed to appear a little more professional, she reminded herself and climbed out of Cavin's lap.

"Well, then." The Gatekeeper wiped her hands on her apron. "It's time to go upstairs for milk and cookies. And then I would like for you to tell the president everything you have just told me."

THE HANDYMAN DROPPED Jana and Cavin off at the highway. "See you next time," he called from the truck before driving away to retrieve the REEF's body.

"That's just weird," she said. "The whole thing was weird. The farm, the vast underground basement. The ship that doesn't exist."

"People will know it exists now."

"But not where it is." She doubted that would ever be discovered.

The helicopter sent to pick them up descended. The rotor blades kicked up a tornado of dust and pebbles. She and Cavin ran to it and boarded. "Home, James," Jana quipped, still giddy from their hard-won victory.

The pilot turned around. It was Connick. He tipped his sunglasses up. "I can't take you home yet."

Her blood turned cold. "Why not?"

"I'm afraid I have some bad news. Your grandfather had a stroke."

As the helicopter took off for Mercy Hospital in Sacramento, Cavin drew her close. "We're in this together, Squee. From now on, we're together." Under the smells of sweat and dust, he smelled like Cavin. She breathed in, holding his essence deep inside her, feeling her blood carry it throughout her body until he was in every pore. And even then, she didn't let go.

CHAPTER TWENTY-SEVEN

JANA AND CAVIN RAN down the hospital corridor toward Grandpa's private room. A pair of nurses flashed them disapproving looks, saw who they were and nodded sympathetically. An honor of state troopers stood guard at the hospital room door. Grandpa had been much-loved by California's law enforcement back in the day when he'd served as governor. To have the officers volunteer to be here when he was at his most vulnerable was touching, and fitting.

From inside the room, a heart monitor beeped, slowly. The murmur of hushed voices filtered out, but no boisterous laughter, no growled swearwords. Inside that room, Grandpa was dying. She couldn't imagine losing him. *He had a full life, the most amazing life. He lived hard and long, and now it's time for him to go*. Logically she knew it was true, but it didn't make it any easier to accept.

Jana stopped in the hallway, unable to go any farther. Her throat almost closed, and the tears she'd tried holding back spilled over. Cavin squeezed her hands. "You're like ice."

Because she felt so cold inside. "Do you know what the most painful thing is for me? He wanted to see me elected president of the United States. The latter is so crazy, Cavin, a long shot. But he never relented. He always believed."

"He will see you as president," Cavin interrupted. He dabbed at her tears, ignoring her confusion. "Now dry your eyes and let's go see him."

Her father and mother sat by the bed. Her father's eyes were moist. Mom and Evie were openly crying. The children had been there earlier, but had been taken home. Jared sat hunched in the corner, smiling briefly as they walked in. Having come here straight from sitting alert in Cavin's ship, he probably hadn't slept in days.

"He's slipping away," Dad informed them. He and her mother gave up their chairs so Jana and Cavin could move closer.

Grandpa was very white and still. His eyes were closed. The lids were bluish, almost transparent. His white hair seemed wispier, more inconsequential. It was as if he'd become as ghostly as his hold on life. The monitors displaying his vital signs seemed to make a lot of noise.

Jana crouched by the bed and took his cold hand. If hers were ice, his must be… She tried not to think about it. "Hi Grandpa, it's me, Jana."

Maybe it was her imagination, but she could swear the beeping of the heart monitor increased in frequency. Maybe it was her imagination, too, that his hand seemed to tighten over hers. "I'm sorry it took so long for me to get here. All that saving the world paperwork, you know."

She squeezed his hand. She wanted to say so many things, but how did you encapsulate a lifetime's worth of gratitude into a few words? "I love you, Grandpa. I love you for so many reasons. You taught me it was wonderful and right to see the magic in everyday things, and I will always be grateful for that. And you taught Dad never to be afraid of going for it, even when someone tells you your chances of succeeding are one in a million. He passed that philosophy on to me, and I remind myself of it constantly. I want you to know, I won't give up on the presidency."

There was another hiccup on the heart monitor.

Cavin crouched next to her. Quietly, he said, "Jana is going to be elected overwhelmingly to a second term serving on the state level."

Jana gave him a startled look. But his nod willed her into silence. "She'll continue her political ascent, first as the head of Earth-Space Security, an organization she'll help create from the ground up, and one that brings Earth into the future with a bright hope for peace. But politics is her first love, as we know, and after serving five years in this capacity, she'll run for California's U.S. senate seat, winning handily."

Jana's family listened intently, enchanted by Cavin's story. From descriptions of making love in the jungle to an imagined presidential campaign, Cavin's word pictures were as vivid as ever.

"Still, Jana resists calls to run for president until the end of her second term. We Jaspers finish what we start, she tells them. And so she does. Eight years later, when she's accumulated the experience to match her desire, she finally enters the presidential race."

The heart monitor stumbled, and so did Jana's heart. Could Grandpa hear Cavin? If so, was it too much?

"Jana Jasper wins in a landslide, riding an over-whelming wave of support that began when she saved the world. All because she believed that with heart and a little bit of magic, anything was possible—something she learned from her grandfather. A few months later, on the clearest, sunniest winter day in memory, Jana Jasper is inaugurated as president of the United States of America. She takes the oath with her family surrounding her—her brother, her sister, and their families, and her proud parents. Holding the family Bible is her husband, Cavin of Far Star."

Love swelled inside Jana, warm and sweet.

"And gazing up with smiles of pride at their mother are their five children."

Five? Jana mouthed in terror.

"The Jasper's go home that day to celebrate as they always do over a delicious meal, only this time, for the first time, dinner is eaten in the White House. And so begins a new era in the Jasper political dynasty."

The only sound other than the hospital monitors was Jana's mother's soft sniffles. Grandpa lay perfectly still. Jana brought her lips to his cold, rough knuckles and kissed him.

To her shock, a sound whispered past his lips.

"I can't hear you, Grandpa."

Everyone gathered close to listen.

"All hail the chief," he whispered. Then, with a soft, happy smile, he let go of Jana's hand and slipped away.

EPILOGUE

IT TOOK TIME for the family to adjust to Jake Jasper's passing. Some weeks later, Cavin had the chance to take Jana away for a vacation and time alone together. He'd been kept busy flying back and forth to Washington, many times in Jana's father's company. He had been given a position as advisor to the president for all alien affairs, tasked with preparing Earth for the next time an interstellar army came knocking at the door.

He was a hero on Earth, the Jaspers told him. That was fine and good, but that was not what drove him. He'd always been a simple man with simple needs. He could think of no better life than that of Jana Jasper's husband. He loved her, and he'd saved her. In doing so, he'd saved her world. Call it a delightful consequence.

"Speaking of delightful…" He whirled on Jana, who held on to his hand as he led her up a narrow path past a waterfall in the middle of a jungle. When he returned home, he would have to thank her brother for recommending Costa Rica as a vacation spot.

Cavin scooped Jana up and carried her the rest of the way up the path. The sound of her giggles always made him smile. She kicked her feet. Bright nail polish sparkled in the sun. Coral, she called it.

He set her down near where the river spilled into the gorge. Jana threw her arms wide and spun a graceful pirouette. "Look at it, Cavin. It's gorgeous up here."

Steam rose. By now her hair was wet and her skin glistened with the spray. He pulled her close to kiss her. Her kiss was hot and wet and full of feeling. Gods, she could kiss like no other.

He kept tasting and nibbling and suckling her lips as he moved her backward. Her eyes opened wide when her back bumped gently against a tall *Jocote* in bloom. She laughed as she lifted her gaze to a canopy of leaves and clusters of small purple flowers. Then she turned her attention to him and grinned. "A tree," she said, her voice huskier. "Ever since your jungle tale, I've had fantasies of us…"

He lowered his head to kiss the side of her throat. "In jungles?"

"Namely jungles with big, thick, smooth-trunked trees." Her breath hitched as he took her breast into his hand, cupping her, feeling the heat of her flesh burning through her bikini. He kissed and caressed her until she moaned his name. He ached for her, as he always did, but first…

He slid down to one knee before gathering her hands in his. He was supposed to have waited until after they arrived home, but the moment just seemed right.

She smiled down at him, half amused, half baffled, her eyes dark with desire. "Jana, my sweet Earth-ling," he began.

Her mouth tipped in a smirk. "Yes, Cavin, my sweet spaceman."

"Would you do me the honor of being my mate—

er..." Nerves had almost made him forget the proper Earth words. "I mean *my wife*. Would you do me the honor of being my wife?"

He saw her love for him shining bright, and he thanked the gods he'd had the common sense and good fortune to make the decision to return to her. *Life is sometimes easy, and sometimes hard, but love is the only constant. No matter how far you rise, or how hard you fall, a good love will always be there for you.* "Yes," she said. "I'll be your wife, your mate, you name it."

"My love slave?"

"Oooh, and especially that."

Laughing, he grabbed her and spun her around. Their swimsuits went every which way in the thick foliage. With his mouth pressed to hers, he hoisted Jana, warm and naked, off her feet and pressed her against the tree. She wrapped her soft thighs high around his hips. "Don't make me wait another second," she breathed in his ear. "It's been four hours since the last time, and I miss you already."

They never could stand time apart, he thought.

Grinning, he gripped her bottom and with a blinding surge of pleasure he found his way home, again, and again.

JANA AND HER NEW HUSBAND emerged from the wedding reception in a shower of birdseed and flower petals. Reporters and paparazzi mingled with onlookers and her family members. Cameras flashed. Jana waved and smiled at them as she and Cavin ran to their getaway car: a brand-new Jeep.

Cavin opened the passenger door for her before

jumping into the driver's seat. He reached across the car and took her hand. His happy gaze went from their sparkling wedding rings to her smiling face. "I loved you at first sight," he said.

"Me, too."

Time stood still as they regarded each other, more passing between them in those silent seconds than words could ever convey. Cavin gave her hand a squeeze and turned the key, starting up the car. "Ready?"

She slipped on her sunglasses. "Ready." And she was ready, ready for everything to come. The future might not be assured, or even safe, but the power of magic would keep hope alive.

As they drove away from the cheering wedding guests, she imagined what the headline would say: Third Wish Is A Charm: Woman Gets Happily Ever After Ending.

HQN™

We *are* romance™

**From the *New York Times* bestselling
queen-of-the-beach-read**

CARLY
PHILLIPS

Security specialist Zoe Costas isn't fooled by the charm of rich,
upright—and uptight—Ryan Baldwin who's in town looking for
his niece Sam. But someone else has already tracked Sam down—
someone who never wanted the child to be found. And Ryan is
determined to protect her, and Zoe "Whatever-It-Takes" Costas
is just the woman to help him do it....

SUMMER LOVIN'

**Don't miss this summer's romance phenomenon!
In stores this August.**

www.HQNBooks.com

PHCP110

HQN™

We *are* romance™

**National Reader's Choice
Award-winning author**

RITA HERRON

Someone wants to bid Ivy a final farewell...

Fearful yet determined, Ivy Stanton returns to the small Appalachian town she left fifteen years ago...the night her parents were murdered. But in coming home, she discovers she is not alone in her search for the truth: Matt Malone, the man who saved her life, who haunts her dreams, who was wrongfully accused of the crime, is also looking for answers—and upon meeting Ivy, learns to fight for more than vengeance....

LAST KISS GOODBYE

Available in bookstores this August.

www.HQNBooks.com

PHRH102

If you enjoyed what you just read,
then we've got an offer you can't resist!

Take 2 novels FREE!
Plus get a FREE surprise gift!

Clip this page and mail it to The Reader Service

IN U.S.A.
3010 Walden Ave.
P.O. Box 1867
Buffalo, N.Y. 14240-1867

IN CANADA
P.O. Box 609
Fort Erie, Ontario
L2A 5X3

YES! Please send me 2 free novels from the Romance/Suspense Collection and my free surprise gift. After receiving them, if I don't wish to receive any more, I can return the shipping statement marked "cancel". If I don't cancel, I will receive 4 brand-new novels every month, before they're available in stores! In the U.S.A., bill me at the bargain price of $5.24 plus 25¢ shipping and handling per book and applicable sales tax, if any*. In Canada, bill me at the bargain price of $5.74 plus 25¢ shipping and handling per book and applicable taxes**. That's the complete price and a savings of over 10% off the cover prices—what a great deal! I understand that accepting the 2 free books and gift places me under no obligation ever to buy any books. I can always return a shipment and cancel at any time. Even if I never buy another book, the 2 free books and gift are mine to keep forever.

185 MDN EFVD
385 MDN EFVP

Name	(PLEASE PRINT)	
Address	Apt.#	
City	State/Prov.	Zip/Postal Code

*Not valid to current subscribers of the Romance Collection,
the Suspense Collection or the Romance/Suspense Collection.*

*Want to try two free books from another series?
Call 1-800-873-8635 or visit www.morefreebooks.com.*

* Terms and prices subject to change without notice. Sales tax applicable in N.Y.
** Canadian residents will be charged applicable provincial taxes and GST.

All orders subject to approval. Offer limited to one per household. Credit or debit balances in a customer's account(s) may be offset by any other outstanding balance owed by or to the customer. Please allow 4 to 6 weeks for delivery.
® and ™ are trademarks owned and used by the trademark owner and/or its licensee.

BOB06R

© 2004 Harlequin Enterprises Limited

HQN™

We *are* romance™

"Sexy, funny and a little outrageous,
Leslie Kelly is a must-read!"
—*New York Times* bestselling author Carly Phillips

Leslie Kelly

Joining the mile-high club with a playboy
pilot was not on her to-do list!

Former air force pilot Max Taylor
is swearing off women—at least
until the rumors die down. As
the subject of a tell-all novel
by the wealthy widow of a late
congressman, he seeks refuge in the
tiny town of Trouble, Pennsylvania.
But swearing off women becomes
a challenge when he meets sultry
heiress Sabrina—and she's got a
secret. One that could destroy him.
The attraction between them is
white-hot, but is it worth the
trouble?

HERE COMES TROUBLE

In bookstores this August.

www.HQNBooks.com

PHLK133

**New from *New York Times*
bestselling author**

CARLY PHILLIPS

Lacey Kinkaid likes life shaken, not stirred,
but can she handle sexy lawyer Hunter?

Another sexy, fun read
from bestselling author Carly Phillips!

We *are* romance™

On sale
August 2006.

Visit your
local bookseller.

www.HQNBooks.com

HQN126